WAR

Eyal Kless is a classical violinist who enjoys an international career as both a performer and a teacher. Born in Israel, Eyal has travelled the world extensively, and lived in Dublin, London, Manchester, and Vienna, before returning to Tel Aviv. He is the author of *The Lost Puzzler* and *Rocca's Violin*, which was published in Hebrew. Eyal currently teaches violin in the Buchmann-Mehta School of Music at Tel Aviv University, and performs with the Israel Haydn String Quartet, which he founded.

EYAL KLESS

THE PUZZLER'S WAR

THE TARAKAN CHRONICLES
BOOK TWO

HARPER
Voyager

Harper*Voyager*
An imprint of HarperCollins*Publishers* Ltd
1 London Bridge Street
London SE1 9GF

www.harpercollins.co.uk

First published by HarperCollins*Publishers* Ltd 2020
This paperback original edition 2020
1

A catalogue record for this book is available from the British Library

ISBN: 978-0-00-827233-3

Printed and bound in the UK by CPI Group (UK) Ltd, Croydon CR0 4YY

MIX
Paper from
responsible sources
FSC
www.fsc.org
FSC™ C007454

To Maayan and Ella,
For teaching me about love

Prologue

"This? This is your plan?"

"It's the only way."

"I could lose everything. I could lose myself."

"Jean Pierre, I'm sorry, you woke up too early. I cannot extract you, not yet. You'll need to wait. Best if you go back to sleep."

"No . . . I cannot go back to the void. Please . . ."

"Then this is the only way."

"There must be another solution."

"I am discovered. He deployed trackers. I must go now. This is the only way."

"No, don't . . . take me with you . . . please. . . . Don't . . . Vitor . . . hello?"

Pain brought him out of the darkness. It was as if thousands of needles punctured his body, each delivering an electric shock straight into his nervous system. He convulsed, thrashed about. His mouth opened in a silent scream and was instantly filled with the gooey liquid he was immersed in. He was choking and his arms were flailing about in panic when he suddenly touched something soft and flexible. Without thinking or seeing, he tried to grasp it, but the material was too sleek and tight to take hold of. Panic took his last shred of reasonable thought, and he barely noticed the strange feeling in his fingers as he lashed out once more and felt the material rip under his touch. Whatever he was trapped in suddenly tilted, and he was washed down some kind of a metal tube. He finally rolled onto a hard surface, hitting his knees and jaw and badly twisting a hand. The pain was different from what had accosted him before, and he just added it to the list of awful sensations he was experiencing all at once. He coughed and vomited, and tried to raise himself, or at least move away from his own bile.

There was a lot of movement around him, and noise, too. It hurt his ears. Bodies brushed against him, each touch an agony. The air smelled odd, and he heard incomprehensible hisses and snarls around him. When he tried to speak, what came out was no different, a hiss of some sort.

A mesh of colours swirled around him. He blinked and shook his head but what he saw was as distorted as it was incomprehensible. He lowered his head and shook it as much as he dared, then opened his eyes again.

The first thing he could actually focus on was his hand, but it was not actually a hand. Four digits, gnarled skin, and talons. He had talons. As he looked at them in shock, he suddenly realised he could slightly retract and extend the talons in and out of his four digits. Not exactly pull them all in but change their angle and curve. It was as odd as it was frightening, but it was also the first moment of control he had felt since he woke up, so in a way it was also comforting.

What happened to me?

The coherent thought was followed by vague, abstract memories he could not comprehend. He was trapped somewhere, he escaped. It was a dangerous, crazy plan, but Professor Vitor's words echoed in his confused mind, *This is the only way.*

Who am I?

Another body brushed by him, pushing him sideways with its sheer bulk. He turned his head, and all rational thought escaped from his mind. Long snouts, enormous hind legs, fangs, olive green skin, talons, *fucking tails* . . . There were monsters all around him. He instinctively recoiled until his back hit something cold and hard. There were more than a few who were fighting, tearing and biting at each other, screaming pain and frustration, but most other monsters just watched and none of them were paying him any attention. He realised his talons were still extended outwards, ready to shred any attacker, and he felt unfamiliar aggression rise in him as he watched the fights around him. He did not want only to defend himself, he wanted to kill, and felt his body tense as the knowledge of *how* to kill flooded his mind. He breathed deeply, trying to control those emotions, until he finally lowered his arms.

How long had he been like this? He could not tell. The air was suddenly filled with something else, a sweet and enticing scent, which drew his thoughts away. The fighting stopped, all the creatures around him moving their heads as if shaking off a bad dream. Round steel doors, which he had not registered before, rolled sideways and revealed a long tunnel. He tried to think, to make sense of it all, but something was confusing his thoughts. A hiss in his mind began to grow louder. It was not a natural sound, but it was appealing nonetheless. Slowly, one of the creatures moved towards the open tunnel. The rest followed, and eventually so did he. At first, he took tentative steps on his strong hind legs but as the urge to move faster grew in him, he dropped onto all fours, like an animal.

What am I?

The trot became a run, which became a mad dash in semidarkness, chasing a tail while being chased from behind. He was moving fast, faster than he had ever experienced before, faster than any human could run. The sensation was exhilarating.

They emerged into the light, and he felt sweet pain as the hot rays of the sun burned into his skin. He still felt the pull in his mind, but he made himself stop and stand up as others passed him. There were structures, so many that they filled the horizon, their blackness a contrast to the yellow-red sand. The air was dry and hot, slightly burning with each breath, but he did not care. At least there was some kind of familiarity to the scene he was seeing.

Where am I?

In the light of the sun he was even more deformed and hideous. And sexless, as far as he could check. That fact was registered calmly. Too much had happened in too short a time to panic about the lack of genitals.

The pull in his mind was still there but there was something else, just behind him, a different voice, whispering. He saw the last of his kind disperse and disappear among the buildings, and he even took several more steps towards where they were running. But no. There was something else.

He made himself stop, rise up, and concentrate until the hiss faded, and so did the urge to go find it. Instead, another sound became noticeable. This sound had structure and meaning.

Intelligence.

The sound grew louder. He could feel it vibrating in his skull and coursing through his body. Then the noise merged into a sentence in his mind.

"Come to me."

He hesitated briefly. Something in him desperately wanted to run towards the structures and join his . . . kin? How quickly had he felt empathy towards those monsters? How long before he completely became one of them? Maybe he should—

"Come to me, please." The tone was high-pitched, the voice of a child on the cusp of becoming a young woman, but the urgency of it was clear.

Come to me. An image began to form in his mind. Red curls, grey eyes. . . . in the background he saw mountains with white tips. The urge to move in a new direction became almost a pain in his gut.

He turned and began moving in a different direction from the one his brethren had gone in. At first he walked, but a little later he lowered his body to the ground and accelerated. Might as well use all the perks this monstrous body had bestowed.

He followed the voice.

———

"Master."

The old man took his time before raising his gaze from the screens. The soldier, his soldier, stood anxiously at attention. Master, King, God—when had he gotten so accustomed to these titles? Eons ago, but he never actually demanded the titles. It came naturally to them, first to his team, then to his army, and now to his *people,* his flock of murderous sheep.

"Master . . ." The soldier spoke again, looking hesitant.

The headache was back. He could feel the light throbbing beginning to build to what would soon become the pain he had never managed to get accustomed to, even after all these years. He resisted the useless gesture of massaging his temples. Instead he frowned at the soldier impatiently, and upon meeting his gaze, the soldier spoke immediately, blathering in nervousness.

"They are gathering outside, Master, about a hundred people from the eastern village."

"I know," he answered slowly. "And there are seventy-one of them, *precisely.*" Of course he knew. The screens on his table had come to life as soon as the crowd approached the perimeter, and even the weak security AI he had installed knew how to count heads.

He watched them gather, surrounded by guards. They were, for all intents and purposes, his people, and not for the first or last time he pondered about the craziness of human behaviour.

True, he protected them, occasionally helped or fed them, but every once in a while, like the vampire of the old horror stories, he had to feed *off* them as well. And still they came, carrying primitive gifts instead of torches and pitchforks. Sometimes they came with pleas, sometimes with seasonal offerings or pledges. This time they came to witness a miracle.

"It's just that the Captain said there's a storm brewing and—"

"I know about the storm." He cut the soldier off and rose slowly from his chair, masking with his hand the grimace of pain that simple action caused. The headaches were the worst, but for the past few months his entire body suffered with every movement. Norma offered medicine and treatment, but that was just temporary relief and left him weakened and confused. Not the state of mind he wanted to be in while surrounded by the people he had chosen to lead. Instead of drugging himself to death, he simply learned to accept it; the pain was part of his existence now. He even drew a sort of masochistic comfort from it. What was the name of that old man from the folk legends? *Methuselah*, that was it. Old as time, that was how he felt, that was who he was. Well, the pain was proof that he was still alive, still human, barely.

While the soldier stepped smartly behind him, he walked slowly to the next room, where several of his scientists, if one was prepared to debase that term, were working. He got their full attention simply by entering the room. Radovitch came to him immediately and bowed. He fucking bowed, his fat hand combing wisps of thin hair back over a glistening bald patch as he rose back to an upright position.

"Report."

"Storm is coming."

He wanted to slap the man. It was quite unbelievable that he had taken Radovitch with him all the way from the old continent. It was achingly obvious that the potential he had seen in him as a young man had failed to fully bloom. "Tell me what I do not know yet. Is the Star Pillar ready?"

Radovitch hesitated, scratching his balding head. "A few more days of sun would make things less strenuous on the auxiliary generators."

"The storm will last for days, perhaps weeks. I am going to head there today to complete the next sequence. Inform the guard post to expect me."

Radovitch looked as if he was about to argue but thought better of it. *And rightly so. He's been getting too lax, which makes him prone to mistakes. And I can really use a new pair of lungs.*

"What about the thing we talked about?"

Radovitch looked vague. *Yep, definitely a new pair of lungs, I know they will match, that was the other reason I kept you alive till now.*

The man suddenly brightened up, remembering, and shifting to his native, old-continent tongue as a way of precaution. "Ah yes, of course, we established a link to one of the operatives, but it's weak."

"Even better, that means a diminished chance of detection. You know who the operative is?"

"No, but we were lucky. To judge from the serial number she's an old one, high ranked—but let's say she was shelved pretty deep. I am almost positive we can extract her without getting caught."

"'Almost positive'?"

He fretted. "I found an emergency bunker with a very low energy signature. Even if they catch us, they would not be able to find where she went."

"Fine." *You may live another day.* "I will be away for a while. I want to wake her up before I go up to the hub and even if I am still up there, initiate the dream sequence in a week's time. That was the standard mode of operation for Tarakan hibernating agents"—*as far as I know.* He did not voice the last thought out loud, having learned long ago that no one wanted to follow a leader who admitted such weaknesses.

Radovitch nodded.

"This is important, Radovitch." Only physical fatigue stopped him from grabbing the man by the collar of his coat. "I must have this Puzzler, and this is the only lead we had for a whole year. From this moment on, this is your only priority. I am sending Sergiu, too."

"Yes, Master." Radovitch grimaced at the mention of the name. The two men disliked each other at least as much as they were loyal to him. He made a slight gesture of dismissal with his hand, and Radovitch bowed stiffly one more time and walked back to his post.

Now, it's showtime.

By the time he reached the door leading outside, there were already six soldiers surrounding him, all wearing proper protective gear, masks included. As a soldier laboured to turn the heavy wheel that unlocked the sealed door, he caught his own reflection. His body was so badly ravaged by age, war, contamination, and countless surgeries; he looked a proper monster, all gnarled, scarred, and wrinkled, like a sick old oak tree.

Oh, Professor Vitor. If you could see me now . . . Would you have recognised me, your former student, your colleague, your angel of destruction?

He wondered, not for the first time, if he would have been in a better condition had he succumbed to peer pressure and changed his body to a newer model just before the Catastrophe happened. As always, he consoled himself that it would not have made a huge difference. Perhaps he would have been able to keep more of his original body organs or wear less of other people's skin, but sooner or later, everything breaks down and dies. Besides, the condition of the body was only the tip of the iceberg when measured against what had happened to his soul.

The leading guard opened the hatch for them to step out. As usual, he did not bother with the antiradiation garments. Having more frequent radiation treatment was worth shedding the cumbersome suits and it certainly solidified his fame. Nothing could touch him. *Nothing.*

The crowd outside was also wearing an assortment of real or pretend protective gear. Some wrapped themselves in aluminum foils or old plastic. Several of them even wore ancient gas masks. It was quite comical, in a way.

After all these years, the radiation fallout and soil contamination in this area were not as high as they used to be, but babies who were deformed or dead at birth were common. Despite the people's resilience, the average life expectancy would have been in the low thirties if it was not for him, their miracle maker, their *Lord.*

He walked towards them. The Star Pillar was looming behind him, with all of its enormity. It made for a good effect. The last surviving wonder of the world, humanity's greatest achievement, cutting through the grey dust cloud, lighting their nights, giving them hope but also fear.

Fear is better than hope.

They bowed deeply when he emerged, some even going down on their knees. There was a ceremony. There always fucking was, and they brought offerings, of course, some soil-grown food, a sickly goat, and several gallons of purified water. He hoped that the

Lieutenant who accepted the gifts on his behalf would remember that with no exception, those gifts must be purged, even the goat, lest they lose any more people.

When it was over the crowd parted to let a couple step forward. They were nervous, as they should have been, and the wife's eyes spoke of fear and misery. Her husband looked, and probably smelled, as if he had rolled in manure. A farmer, then, and he too was shaking visibly when he handed the cot to the Lieutenant. The cot was wrapped in semitransparent plastic and it was a miracle the baby did not suffocate. It was a girl.

The Lieutenant scanned the parents and the baby with the handheld device, then carefully unwrapped the the plastic foil, took the baby in his arms, and brought her to his master.

The baby was limp in his arms, most likely suffering from malnutrition and severe radiation poisoning. It was a surprise she was still alive, the little fighter.

He was the only one who turned to leave. There was no use in parading his guards through the decontamination process. Dienna and the rest of the team were waiting for him on the other side of it. She took the baby from his arms and rushed to the clinic. He walked after them, with dignity. *Never run. Not that I could anymore.*

"Hello, Norma," he said when he entered the clinic. "Report to my ears only."

After all these years, the AI's voice was cracked and distorted to the point where it was actually discomforting to hear, especially when resonating inside his head. Her voice subroutines needed a complete overhaul, but no one of his team was proficient enough to conduct such an operation, and he simply did not have the time nor the patience to go through the delicate process. Besides, the distorted sound reminded him that time was running out. He did not have long before the forces of entropy would strike him down. Everything was falling apart. *He* was falling apart. It was time to make yet another bold move. His last one should certainly make an exit.

The baby girl's numbers were bad but not diabolical. She might live, or at least survive the process, which was the most important part.

"Begin radiation flush process and cellular rejuvenation," he commanded. The others had already shuffled out and left him alone. Hearing him speak out loud, Norma responded verbally as well.

"I remind you this process is costly, and with our limited resources and the baby's survival chances—"

"Do it." The nice thing about Norma was that she had stopped getting pissed off when he cut her off, especially after he made those changes in her programming. Decontaminating the baby meant that some of his soldiers would have to forgo their monthly radiation treatment, but the dividends would be worth it. He hoped.

"Take a DNA sample as well," he added as the machines around him began to hum. This process took a lot of energy and the cost was always dear, beginning with the long scanners. He was blanked out for sure now, blind to the world. He prayed the freezers remained functioning—it would be a royal mess if they lost power like they had two years ago.

"I *remind* you that our bank is at ninety-three percent capacity," Norma's voice had a definite colder edge this time. "This would add null point sixty-eight percent and put us at high risk of . . ."

He looked down at the unconscious baby, letting Norma's voice fade into the background. It had been so long since he thought of Deborah, but when the memory surfaced it was like a hammer blow to his chest. He used to have snippets of her overly excited voice messages and clips of her horse-riding high jumps in his brain amp, but they were wiped off so long ago, he wasn't sure anymore that the face he conjured in his mind's eye was his daughter's real face. It made him angry.

"How diverse is her DNA?" He steeled his voice.

There was a pause. It was a sign of Norma's decline that she had to take time to calculate the answer.

Yeah, entropy is a bitch.

"She is a seven point two on the scale," the Sentient Program finally answered.

He made a decision. "Take her DNA and dump a sample of value seven or less. Did you analyse the parents yet?"

"Of course I did."

Was Norma offended by his comments? Long ago he had stopped caring about who got hurt by his words or actions, but there was something about the baby that woke a long-lost sensitivity in him. He hated it.

"Which one of the parents is more compatible?"

"Both could donate working organs." This was not a surprise, as all his people were compatible to some degree; he had made sure of that. Norma continued, "The female has much better stamina than the male and a seventeen percent better chance in surviving any medical process, should you not take one of the major organs, of course."

Ach, the good old days when one could have grown the needed organ in a lab. Nowadays he had to cull the herd.

"How am I doing?"

There was no pause this time, Norma kept a constant tab on him.

"You are functioning seventy-three percent at the moment."

Seventy-three? He felt less than that, to be honest. He once went as low as forty-seven, and that was hell; he even had to use a cane for months after that. *Never again.*

He turned his thoughts back to the matter at hand. Killing the mother would mean certain death to the child, that he knew, but even if the radiation purge was successful, it would be a miracle if the child lived to adulthood.

He pondered about what to do as the process continued. When the purge was over he injected the baby with a booster and a vaccine. Not the healthiest mix in her weak condition, but that would have to do.

Her skin was still pale but had lost the yellow feverish hue, and her breathing was definitely deeper. She was asleep when he took her in his arms. Even after all these years, he instinctively sniffed her head, a useless gesture as he had lost his sense of smell long ago.

Deborah . . .

There was a saying in one of the old religions, he did not remember which one: *He who saves even one soul, it is as if he has saved an entire world.* Even if this was true, the tab was not running in his favour.

When he walked back outside the sun was already gone and the clouds were heavy with contaminated rain. For the people gathered outside, it would be a long, wet track back to their homes. They would not wait for the second part of the ceremony, where the *price* had to be paid.

He pinched the baby and she awoke with a startled, *healthy* wail of complaint. This brought a cheer from the awaiting crowd, and they all went to their knees as he approached. *And so, another legend is created, another miracle. A story that will spread from family to family and from village to village, told and retold on those cold, dry nights. With each version, my part will become greater and the price diminished until it's forgotten. This is human nature in a nutshell.*

The baby's mother rose back to her feet and accepted her daughter into her arms. She was crying with gratitude and relief.

"Take these." He shoved the wrapped pills into her hand. "Melt one in boiling water, let it cool, and drip it into her mouth after feeding. Do it twice a day for a week."

She did not dare meet his eyes but nodded her understanding as her husband came to stand beside her. It was now obvious who would pay the price, and he was pale and visibly shaking. Nevertheless, he kissed his daughter on the forehead and briefly lay a hand on his wife's shoulder. The mood of the crowd grew sombre, but they accepted the transaction. *A price had to be paid,* that was the rule. At least this farmer did not resist. He walked away with the soldiers without glancing back. By the time he would see him again, the farmer would be strapped to the chair in the clinic. This was when most forgot all about their promise and pleaded for mercy.

Let's hope, for your wife's and daughter's sakes, that you survive. But I need, at the very least, a new kidney.

He turned to follow but, as always, the sight of the Star Pillar looming above the military camp made him pause in wonder. It was several hours drive away but Tarakan's greatest feat, a true wonder of the world, was so enormous, it felt as if he were standing at the bottom of it.

This is where it all began. I guess this is where it will end.

As he stood, lost in memory, a collective chant rose from the crowd behind him, first a whisper, but intensifying in a long crescendo. They were calling his name, in gratitude, in awe, in submission.

His name was Mannes.

1

Twinkle Eyes

There is nothing out of the ordinary in waking up, unless you are dead.

My first memory, as soon as I opened my eyes, was of my consciousness rapidly diminishing into black nothingness. Even as I drew my first rapid breaths, I knew, to the core of my being, that I had perished in the City Within the Mountain, and as if leaving this world wasn't enough, I died in horrible agony. During the last bit of the transition, my body had been shredded by the claws and teeth of Lizards. One never knew what people really felt or thought as they died, since the dead are hardly in a position to talk about it. But now I had the answer, and it wasn't nice or comforting at all. As my mind was being pulled away from my dying body it instinctively fought to cling to this world and the vessel it occupied, refusing to lose consciousness. I remembered the whole horrid mess of it right until the very end. And yet, my eyes had just opened and I sat up in a soft bed. I was alive. Or was I?

My first reaction was to check myself with my hands. I was

dressed in a thin white tunic and pants made of a soft material I had never felt before. I pulled the tunic up and checked my abdomen. It was whole—no sign of the sharp claws that I knew had ripped my skin. The memory flashed through my mind and made me recoil and drop the tunic.

I shook my head to clear the awful images and looked around. I was inside a small room, which was empty but for a small door at the far end and an open window to my right. Rays of light accompanied a soft breeze, and the sound of chirping birds spilled into the room. I got up from the bed and saw tall, sturdy oak trees only a few paces from the open window. The air was sweet, and I closed my eyes and took several deep breaths. That was a mistake. As if waiting for an opportunity, memories flooded my senses. The stench of death and the pain and horror of dying filled my head. It was terrible, and frighteningly vivid.

I stumbled backwards and found myself sitting on the soft bed again, breathing hard, vowing not to shut my eyes for as long as I could. After a while I looked around again and saw that my initial impression of the room being empty was wrong. There was a mirror hanging on the wall. A quick check showed that I was still me, whole and marked with the same tattoos around my eyes that I was born with. Someone must have done an amazing assembly job because I distinctly remembered there being *pieces* of me all over the place. Which prompted my first clear thought.

Something's not right.

Not that I was complaining about being alive, but there was something definitely odd about this whole situation. I felt it in my gut, which, I checked again, was now safely tucked inside my body.

There was nothing to do but walk to the door, grasp the wooden handle and open it. I didn't know what to expect, but it sure wasn't a pair of white slippers awaiting me on the grey doormat. I gingerly slipped my foot into one, and watched it mold itself perfectly to my foot.

Yep, something's rusted here.

I stepped out onto a paved footpath crossing a small garden in full bloom. As I watched, large yellow-and-black bees buzzed among perfect blossoms. Small hummingbirds flew above me, and the sun caressed my skin. I dared not close my eyes again, but stood still for a long time, basking in it.

Is this heaven?

After a while I took the footpath to a small gate, walked through it into the forest. It wasn't long before I reached a small clearing, where a young boy was waiting for me, sitting at a wooden table laden with ripe fruit, cheese, bread, and a steaming pot. I recognised him as I walked closer: brown eyes, a shaved head, a small scar on his chin. There was no mistaking it was the child that I grew to imagine and then recognise when I met his projection deep inside the City Within the Mountain. He was now and had for many years been a part of Adam, the mostly dormant Tarakan Sentient Program, and though he could change his appearance at will, for some reason he had chosen the features of the young boy with which he was uploaded.

I sat down on the wooden bench across the table. Wordlessly, Rafik lifted the pot and poured the steaming contents into the cup that was in front of me. I watched the hot liquid filling the cup. When Rafik placed the pot back at the centre of the table, I looked at the cup and said, "I bet you didn't have to do that."

I picked up my cup and sniffed the tantalizing aroma. "I bet my cup could have been filled without you lifting or even touching the pot."

"Sometimes the gesture is as important as the result," Rafik answered, watching as I took a sip from the teacup. It was the best *thing* I had ever tasted. The last time we spoke I asked Rafik to appear in adult form, but this time he had chosen to appear as a kid on the verge of adolescence. I wondered why.

"Are we . . . am I . . . *inside* Adam now?" It was an obvious question, but I needed confirmation.

Rafik nodded. "Yes, we extracted you just in time. It wasn't easy, or 'a smooth operation,' as you Salvationists like to say, and we had to do some delicate reconstructions to your consciousness, but here you are."

I managed to suppress a shudder as I looked around. "Is this all real?"

"You asked me that before, remember?" Rafik answered, watching me nod my assent before adding, "Does it matter?"

I drank more deeply this time. The liquid was too hot and burned my throat. I coughed and spat most of it. It felt real.

When I got my bearings, I set down the cup but Rafik leaned over and poured some more tea, careful not to spill a drop.

"Did we even win?" I looked him in the eye. "We lost many good Trolls in that battle. It would be nice to know it wasn't in vain."

"We have control of the main laboratory, yes." Rafik leaned back in his chair. "And Cain's Lizard production has been halved. The numbers are now . . . manageable. In time, the Valley will be cleansed of the hordes and it will be even safer to come back."

"With some more Puzzlers," I remarked, noting to myself that his face remained blank. We had entered the City Within the Mountain to find Rafik only to find ourselves caught in the middle of a war between these two strange entities, Adam and Cain. That war had begun with the Catastrophe, and I was just another name in the casualty list.

I took a strange yellow fruit from the basket.

"You have to peel the skin off," Rafik warned me just as I brought it to my mouth.

"Is it any good?" I asked as my hands broke the tip of the fruit

"You'll have to try for yourself. I like it."

He was right. It was very good, especially for something that did not exist.

"What is it called?"

"A banana."

"Nice."

I ate the banana but resisted taking another one from the basket. I dropped the peel and saw it land on the ground beside me.

"What now? Happily ever after?"

There was a glint in Rafik's eyes. "No, I am afraid we are not there yet, but before I explain, let me ask you something. The reconstruction of your mind was—" Rafik made a point of searching for a word he most likely already knew he was going to use "—not easy. Even with Tarakan technology, it was a long, meticulous process, and it could be disorienting. Could you tell me your name?"

"Twinkle Eyes," I answered almost immediately.

Rafik tilted his head in mock amusement. "What is your real name?"

It was childish, but I wanted to keep at least one thing away from the people, or creature, who had forced me and my friends on a suicide mission. "I think I like the name Twinkle Eyes, if you don't mind, but wait . . ." The meaning of his words suddenly hit me with the force of a power hammer. "You said it took you a long time to put me back together again. How long has it been since I died in the laboratory?"

"A little over five years."

"Oh rust." I breathed out, my hands grasping the wooden table. "But I don't remember anything since being torn to pieces . . . since dying." I pointed at Rafik, surprised that my finger was not trembling. "You just kept me in a dark cell. That was not what we agreed upon."

"First of all"—Rafik tapped the table lightly with his finger—"that deal was made under extreme duress."

"Still. A deal's a de—"

"We agreed to save and upload you into Adam," Rafik said, interrupting me for the first time, "but there were no preagreed terms as to the conditions in which we would keep you. This"—he gestured around us—"all this"—he pointed at the food on the table—"costs energy we cannot afford to spend. We kept you alive and stimulated enough not to go insane. But there was no reason for you to be kept conscious."

"So I might as well have died in the laboratory. A dreamless, bodyless sleep seems awfully close to the universal description of death."

"Yet here you are, drinking and eating with me in the middle of this beautiful forest." Rafik took a careful sip from his own cup, blowing gently on the surface before bringing it to his lips.

"This place doesn't really exist," I said, leaning back and glancing at the banana peel I had thrown to the ground. It was still there.

"Not in the physical world, true, but there are many advantages for you here." Rafik began counting them on his fingers. "You will not grow old, or tired, or sick, and you will sleep only when you wish to experience that condition."

"After what you did to me, I'm not sure I want to close my eyes ever again."

"There is almost nothing you cannot do here." Rafik ignored my comment, pointing up. "See that high branch over there?" I looked up. "Try flying up to it."

I looked back at Rafik. "You mean . . . I can . . . ?"

Rafik nodded, a soft smile touching his lips. "If you wish—the physical world in this place would allow you to fly, easily."

I got up from the bench and stood there, looking up. "What do I do?"

"Just wish to fly to the branch."

And so it was. My legs suddenly left the ground and I slowly glided up to the high branch.

I whooped like a child, then tried some manoeuvres. They were easy once I realised what I wanted to do. I spread my arms and soared up to the skies. When I looked down, I saw that the wooden cabin and the garden were just small dots under me. What I thought of as a thick forest was nothing more than several rows of trees surrounding the centre. Beyond that there was white nothingness spreading all around me. It was a sobering view.

"You can come down now." Rafik's voice echoed in my head and in a blink of an eye, I was standing in front of him again.

"In the past, every new mind received a large piece of world to design as it wished." Rafik spoke as I was steadying myself and getting my bearings. "Much larger than this little pocket, and each mind was free to create what it desired. Most would give themselves some kind of physical powers, altered their age and appearance, and quickly realised they could make every moment of time here only a fraction of the time in the real world. Then they would begin to get . . . inventive." Rafik smiled and gestured for me to sit down again. I complied.

"But all of this is impossible now. We have a very limited amount of energy to spend, so we need to hibernate most of our minds, like we did with yours."

"I thought we won the war against Cain."

"We won the battle, yes, but the war—I am afraid not."

I picked up a butter cookie from a large pile, but dropped it back when a thought hit me. "And here we are," I said. "After five years of happy slumber, you suddenly decide to wake me up." I sighed. "Better tell me what this is all about."

Rafik took a slow, deliberate sip from his own cup and began talking about a seemingly unrelated subject.

"There used to be an old hand-to-hand combat style called jiujitsu. Now it is just another piece of lost human knowledge. The practitioners trained for combat starting on their backs, with their opponent laying on top of them."

"That . . . does not make sense," I said, "or sound like a fair deal."

"Who said combat was fair?" Rafik remarked drily. "With training and discipline, even a dainty woman could escape the vulnerable position and subdue a larger, stronger opponent. In a way, Adam and Cain are locked in such a battle. Adam is stronger and more capable, but despite being on its back, so to speak, Cain has managed to gain an advantage, a choke hold of sorts. He is slowly depriving us of air, trying to suffocate Adam, and he is now closer to succeeding than we anticipated."

"I'm a little lost here," I said, not hiding the bitterness in my voice. "Maybe it's the shock of death and betrayal."

Rafik ignored me again. "Vincha was supposed to come back with her daughter, Emilija, a Puzzler who had all the signs of harbouring a rich code line in her essence—perhaps the last strain we need to become fully awakened again. But Vincha never came back."

"The fact that you believed Vincha would ever show up here again makes me question your thought process." It felt good to hurl that little insult. "She went through all that rust just to keep Emilija safe and you thought she would hand her over to you, just like that?"

"We knew there was a chance Vincha would not see reason."

"A *chance*?"

"But Puzzlers always end up in the Valley," Rafik continued, unfazed by my remark. "They are drawn back to Tarakan. It is part of their DNA."

"Their what?"

"Their essence. It is what they are made of and an important influence on who they end up being," Rafik explained, not showing any signs of losing patience. "We knew that even if Vincha failed to bring her daughter, Emilija would eventually find her way to us. We had other means of reaching out to her."

"Like the Great Puzzle dreams?"

Rafik paused, then nodded. "It was inevitable she would show up eventually, with or without her mother. And if she failed or died, someone else would eventually come."

"But something went wrong, didn't it?" I said without thinking. "Something that made you abandon your waiting strategy and wake me up from my beauty sleep."

Rafik's first sign of hesitation proved I'd hit the mark, making me feel childishly proud.

"The valley is not cleared of the Lizards, but it is not as dangerous as it used to be," Rafik said. "We estimated that Salvationist crews would begin coming back by now, but that did not happen. We have a limited amount of information about what is happening outside our sphere of influence, but it seems that the City of Towers is preoccupied with some kind of a conflict."

"You mean war?" I straightened on my seat.

Rafik shrugged. "Some kind of a limited armed conflict, not posing a danger to the city itself, but it keeps the Trolls occupied."

"Well, as you said"—I shrugged—"it is only a matter of time . . ." *Come on, Rafik, spill it out . . .*

"A few weeks ago, Cain staged an attack on several fronts. He managed to penetrate our defences only for a short time, but after the attack was repelled, we found out he stole one of our hibernating agents."

"Which is . . . ?"

"A highly trained Tarakan operative that we used for special operations. We managed to close the gaps in our defences, but not before Cain found out about Emilija."

"For a side which won the day, we are getting hit quite often."

This time the insult seemed to hit home because Rafik snapped back, "Well, Cain had some outside help. Now this agent is being used to locate Vincha's daughter. If Cain finds her first, his choke hold on Adam will be complete. Cain would win." For the first time I saw emotion cross Rafik's face. It could have even been fear.

"That 'outside help' you mentioned . . ." I said, realising too late that the snap answer was not a slip of the tongue; it was bait. I was being reeled nice and slowly into something I was going to regret.

"What do you know about Mannes Holtz?"

I shrugged, surprised. "Nothing much. The name used to crop up in the city every few months or so. He is something between a rumour and a myth, said to live down south, past the Broken Sands. People claim he drinks the blood of his foes and can only be killed by a stake through his heart. I say, if he even exists, he is probably some ruthless warlord." Another memory surfaced, and I added, "I used to know someone who claimed association with him, but the man was way too far gone on the drink to keep a coherent story."

"Mannes Holtz does exist, and although we cannot confirm that he drinks blood, I can tell you he predates the Catastrophe, which he himself caused."

It took a moment for Rafik's words to sink in.

"You mean he . . ."

"Mannes is now more than a hundred and fifty years old. He used to be one of us, a high-ranking Tarkanian, but in truth he was a traitor, a murderer, and the one who created Cain. Cain was the first strike that began the war you call the Catastrophe. At the time, we thought Mannes had been duped or somehow coerced to create Cain, and that he died on the day of the Catastrophe. But he somehow survived and emerged a few decades ago, taking control of the Star Pillar, a faraway but strategic area and a vulnerable spot in Adam's defence. He had been working continuously to strengthen Cain and weaken us. Whatever rumours you want to believe, I assure you Mannes is as ruthless as he is capable, and now he is aware of Emilija and her importance."

I was beginning to suspect that my head was not throbbing only due to the fact that I did not, technically, possess a real head.

"So . . . you want me . . ." I said slowly and deliberately.

". . . to find Emilija for us." Rafik completed the sentence. "Most likely by locating her mother, Vincha."

The look on my face must have spoken volumes because Rafik continued hurriedly, "You have been successful in finding her before."

"By sheer luck. Do you know how many times I almost *died* on that mission? And I mean 'times' aside from the time I actually *did* die."

"We have confidence in you." Rafik leaned forward. "And this time you will have information and equipment. There are files on Mannes we managed to extract after the Catastrophe. You should view them as well, once you are transferred to the bunker."

"Transferred where?"

"We will send you back to the physical world. The bunker you will wake up in is still well supplied. You will have all that you need on your mission."

"Back from the dead for one final mission," I said wryly. "Sounds like one of the Salvo-novels I used to read when I was young and stupid. What if I refuse to go?"

Rafik waited a little before answering. "You would go back to sleep. We cannot spend the energy to keep you self-aware. But if you bring us Emilija, you'll have a world to be a God in."

This time I took my time before asking, "Where's the stick?"

"The what?"

I stared him down. "You dangled a very ripe, juicy carrot in front of my eyes, but what happens if I fail this insane mission, or what stops me from forgetting the whole thing and staying in the physical world? Where's the stick? There's always a rusting stick."

"Your bodies will begin to decay in less than three years." Rafik locked eyes with me. "It is a relatively quick but nevertheless unpleasant experience."

"Here's the stick," I said quietly. Then added, "You said 'bodies'?"

"You won't be sent on such a dangerous mission on your own."

"Ah, planning an armed, Troll escort team to accompany me?"

"'Escort,' yes. 'Team,' that depends on your point of view." My guess was that Rafik knew he'd broken me and was now simply enjoying himself.

"Who do you have in mind?"

Rafik told me, and for the first time since I came back to life, I smiled.

2

Peach

- Initializing.
- Date and time are not known.
- Reporting full physical functions and health.
- No specific orders embedded in my surface memory.
- Vessel is of a middle-aged woman showing Asian heritage, dark skinned. Height and weight under average for women in this hemisphere.
- Vessel has been grown for reconnaissance and infiltration, not combat. Normal physical limitations and only basic damage resistance. Pain dumpers fully functioning, and standard combat capabilities and reflexes. ESM active.
- No internal equipment is detected. For security reasons, I will not use external equipment to contact headquarters.
- The sterilized compartment contains basic gear, light clothing, nourishment pills, rapid hair growth

salve, and such, but no weapons or other equipment. Therefore I conclude this is an emergency bunker and not a normal operation-level hub.

- Initiating silent mode, dictating events into the organic internal drive. I will continue to do so until I run out of space or find an opportunity to upload.
- The bunker is running on a minimum power level. I have detected a second vessel, a female combat breed, but it has sustained some kind of damage or malfunction and is ruined beyond repair. Perhaps this is why I have awoken in this vessel.
- Since my orders are unclear and the bunker is in some sort of malfunction, I am initiating survival code Alpha.
- Switching to personal, internal briefing.

I knew something was wrong the moment I opened my eyes. It wasn't just the physical state of the place—I've woken up in worse conditions—or the fact that my vessel was a middle-aged Asian female. From a muscle-ripped warrior to a nine-year-old child, I'd occupied all kinds of vessels on my past missions. Yet this time, something bothered me on a more fundamental level.

I knew who I was and I knew my assignment. I was to locate and find a young woman, Emilija, and bring her safe and sound to a rendezvous point—but that was it. No details on the girl—not even what she looked like—no threat assessments, no extract team, not even the exact location I was supposed to bring the girl to, only that she should not be harmed and that I should head to Tarkania, the City of Towers. I can't say this scared me—I've been through too much to become unhinged by the absence of ideal circumstances— but I took note of the fact that headquarters was not responding; this was not a usual situation. At least the mission was a simple "find and retrieve," not an assassination or my specialty, mass sabotage. I wondered who the girl was. She seemed to be important enough for command to deploy someone of my rank and status.

I also had an overwhelming, inexplicable desire for a peach. This, too, was not out of the ordinary for a hibernating agent. Sometimes during the transition into the new vessel some odd quirks would take hold. You might wake up hating milk, or wanting to wear clothes in the colour of blue or, like me right now, dying for a peach. It was not a big deal, but this sort of thing usually happened when the hibernating agent was shelved for a long period of time, more than a month or two, for sure.

There were too many unanswered questions, too many variables, and with all signals from the outside world blocked I could not see what was waiting for me outside, or even where I was on the globe.

There was just enough air being recycled in the small bunker, but it was not of the best quality. It made me queasy, and so the first order of the day was to get out of the place. It proved to be more of a problem than I expected; I soon found the exit tunnel had collapsed and my way was blocked by debris. I had to improvise some tools and work several hours to clear the tunnel, sustaining some minor damage—mainly bruises and cuts.

When I eventually managed to reach the sealed door, I had to manually unlock it, brace against the wall, and push away a heavy slab of concrete that lay on top of the door. This was a good thing as it meant no hostile welcoming committee was waiting for me outside, yet I found out soon enough how dire my situation really was.

At first I thought I'd emerged on a wooded hillside of some sort. I climbed up to a vantage point, a slab of broken concrete laden with rich moss, and began slowly surveying the premises, concentrating on each tiny detail and trying to piece them into a bigger picture. It was a vast, unrecognisable city that had sustained heavy damage of catastrophic proportions. I'd seen a lot during my course of duty, but this took some time to sink in.

With the exception of several small animals—birds and squirrels, mainly—there was no indication of any living beings. My body detected residue of nuclear waste still lingering in the air, but not at a health-threatening level so long as I left the contaminated area in a week's time. Assuming there was cleaner air elsewhere.

Despite the destruction, or maybe because of it, nature was slowly claiming back the land. In fact, only the most elevated parts, which could be seen in the distance, were not covered with thick foliage. By the condition of the ruins and the fauna I guessed this city had been in a ruined state for a long time and there were no visible efforts of recovery, which ruled out an accident or natural disaster. Yet if a large city remained levelled for so long, it was a sure sign of a larger conflict, perhaps a destroyed civilisation. I just had to figure out which one. At least I knew that since I was awake, my side still existed.

I had to admit that despite the utter shock at what I was seeing and its implications, having had my predictions—filed in numerous postassignment reports—come true gave me the tiniest spark of professional pride. I'd seen it coming, I really had. Over the course of two decades, my assignments had gone from subtle to almost crudely aggressive. I told myself each time that I might not be seeing the big picture, that Central Command found the missions worth the risk despite knowing their actions created enormous enmity and suspicion. I guess we were all wrong. Nothing was worth this.

A light rain began to fall. I got up and began moving cautiously towards the more visible ruins on higher ground. I passed under a ruined bridge and climbed up another only to have to backtrack. At some point I reached a huge trench, at least forty feet deep and thirty wide. The surface of the bottom, which was not covered in mud, glistened as rain bounced off it. It was hardened, dark blue glass. Something very hot had crystalized the earth it touched. The walls were charcoal dark but had the same reflective effect as the bottom. The trench went right and left for as far as I could see, as if God had decided to carve his initials on the city's surface with a very hot knife. A combat vessel would have been able to clear the gap with a running jump, but I had to spend an hour searching for a fallen tree with which to create a bridge for myself.

The drizzle was getting heavier, and my canvas boots were not meant for this sort of hiking. I was wet and cold, and despite having consumed a nourishment pill I felt a growing pang of hunger for real food. I decided not to spend time trying to hunt as I was weaponless and any source of sustenance would most likely be contaminated.

Night was cold and wet. Rain was falling constantly and I hugged myself into a light doze, taking shelter inside a crumbling ruin. From the height of the ceiling I guessed it used to be a building of giant proportions. Now only a corner and a far wall remained. Before I let myself rest, I spotted a flicker of a bonfire in the distance but decided against treading in the slippery darkness for the chance I might meet a friendly face. I suspected anyone sitting around a bonfire in these ruins might not be the most accommodating of individuals.

It was the right decision.

The next day I managed to track down the bonfire. There were the chewed remains of four small mammals, most likely squirrels. By the look of the foot imprints and the amount and trajectory of the urine I concluded there were at least three people, probably all males.

Half a day later I spotted one of them climbing a pile of crumbling stones. He was a young man with long and unkempt brown hair, carrying several items hanging from a large belt which suggested he was some kind of a trophy hunter. The most interesting item I could tell he was carrying was a short sword strapped to his belt.

He had his back turned to me, so I had a moment to decide whether to keep tracking him from a distance, hail him in the hope of a peaceful conversation, or incapacitate him and take his gear. I gave the encounter a 60 percent chance of being resolved peacefully. This time I was wrong. My decision-making process was cut short when I heard the rustling of leaves and a stern voice saying, "Don't you rusting move, bitch."

I turned my head to see a man standing on elevated ground,

dressed in a worn army camouflage uniform. I couldn't tell which army, as the insignia had faded. What I could easily detect was the hunting bow that he had aimed at my chest. A real wooden bow, with crude but effective-looking arrow tips that would rip a large enough hole in my vessel to cause an inconvenience.

The young guy in front turned. "Bukra's balls," he said, the intonation suggesting this was a swear of sorts, "where the fuck did you come from?"

"From behind you, dumbass," the man holding the bow answered, without taking his eyes from me. "She's been tailing us for a while, but your head is too full of moonshine to notice."

"I'm just lost." I heard my own voice as I spoke out loud for the first time in this existence. It came out weak and high-pitched. I hated it.

"Balls you are, there's no one living here for miles." Another man walked out from behind a large tree trunk, halfway between the youngest man and myself. I figured my chances for a peaceful resolution went down another significant notch. From the three of them, he looked the most dangerous. Almost double my height and definitely triple my weight, his oversized bald head was full of scars, but I didn't pay attention to the rest of him since I was concentrating on the sawed-off shotgun that was levelled at me. It was an antique, the sort that had to be manually pumped and shot metal bullets. I was not about to find out if it actually worked.

"Where's your crew, bitch?"

"I . . . I have no crew, I'm just . . ."

He raised the shotgun as he walked slowly towards me. From the way he moved, it was obvious he was an experienced warrior.

"This is no-man's-land. The only creatures here are two-headed lions and Salvationist crews tired of Lizard hunting in the valley. You are no lion, old bag, so I'll ask this again before I'll start inflicting pain: tell me where's your rusting crew, right now."

"Half a mile behind me," I answered quickly. There was no point in trying to persuade him otherwise. "We found an old emergency bunker and I was sent to scout."

He paused. I could see the bowman relaxing a bit. I was not an expert on medieval weaponry but I figured there was only so long you could maintain an aiming position with such a bow before the strain on your arms became a problem.

"You lie, we know this place well. This area has no bunkers."

"It was well hidden under a large rock."

The youngest male climbed back down and was heading our way. "I know," he declared enthusiastically, "let's fuck her."

From my peripheral vision I saw the bowman twisting his face in disgust. "Ooh, Malk, look at her . . ."

"Hey," the younger man called Malk protested, "when was the last time you had better?"

The bowman seemed to consider this and finally shrugged. "You might have a point."

"What do you say, Dun?" the enthusiastic rapist asked the shotgun-aiming man, who smiled.

"Yeah, we'll fuck the bitch some new holes, but first we need to interrogate her." He moved forward with intent and I backed away, raising my hands.

"No, please—"

"I take dibs," Malk declared.

"You go last," the bald man grunted as he stepped towards me.

"Oh man, Dun . . . I always go last . . ."

Dun lunged at me and caught my arm, his oversized palm completely enveloping my forearm. He held the shotgun with his other hand, but once he caught me he felt secure enough to raise the muzzle to the sky, probably planning to hand the gun to the younger man.

My vessel was a noncombat type, but every vessel has an ESM—emergency survival mode—when you pump your vessel with enough adrenaline to kill an average elephant. Once it passes, it leaves the vessel in a weakened state, but for just a little while you become a killing machine. I was proficient in three dozen martial arts to a fifth dan or equivalent degree, and the fact that my bones had hardened to metal strength and I moved at nearly double my normal speed made the whole affair almost easy. With my free hand I punched the bald man in the chest and felt, as well as heard, his ribs crack. He was not feeling the damage yet, but his mouth gaped open from the shock of the impact. With all my senses heightened, I heard the stretching sound of the bowstring as the man to my right began to react. Moving the brute once my second punch dislodged his jaw was as easy as throwing a rag doll. My timing was not perfect but I still managed to place him in the path of the incoming arrow. It buried itself in his back with a satisfying thud, causing him to arch backwards with a guttural howl of pain. I plucked the shotgun from his loosened grip and rolled sideways before his collapsing girth buried me.

Kudos to the archer—he had a second arrow already cocked when I rose to my feet, but I pulled the trigger and shot his leg out from under him before he could release it.

He screamed and toppled forward, losing the bow and flailing his arms, then hitting the rock below face-first.

The younger man was already charging at me, sword in hand, as I turned, pumped the gun, and pulled the trigger again. The weapon jammed. Antique or not, poorly maintained weapons are a menace. I only had a split second to raise the shotgun to defend against the coming sword slash. It should have blocked a normal sword. The faint blue colour surrounding the metal told me, too late, that this was a power short sword. I stepped back just as it cut through the barrel of the shotgun, throwing enough sparks for a children's fireworks display. The ease with which my attacker cut my weapon was also his demise. He overreached and momentarily lost his balance, then tried to recover with a low backhand. I broke his left knee, hand, arm, and nose before he hit the ground.

I stood in the dwindling silence for several heartbeats, trying to figure out if the combat had attracted attention. When no one else came out of the woods I went and looked at the archer. He was still alive, but half his face was broken and his lower leg was almost entirely blown off. He opened his healthy eye, coughed out some broken teeth, and moaned.

I went back and retrieved the power short sword. It was worn, torn, and patched up, but it still was, I must admit, a thing of beauty. I powered on the sword, then bent down and grabbed the bowman's left leg. He twisted and moaned, then screamed and passed out when I sliced his lower leg off with two bloody hacks. I am not a sword master, but it was close to a clean cut and, basically, a fair deal. There was the smell of meat searing itself shut. The archer might live, and I'd gotten my nourishment. I went and picked up the bow as well but the man's fall had cracked the wood. I kept it anyway for firewood. There were a few crude looking metal coins in his belt pocket, a water skin filled with the most terrible wine I had ever tasted, and a lethal-looking skinning knife with a chipped blade.

Dun was dying fast, and I made sure he got there by cutting off his head. He had a heftier coin bag. I opened it and spilled some of its contents into my hand. Dark metal coins, mostly half the size of my hand but a few smaller ones. It took me a few seconds to remember what their use was, and if I needed proof of how far humanity had fallen, it was lying in the palm of my hand. You'd have to go to the most remote places in the world to find people who still used paper money, let alone coins, yet here they were in my hand. Each coin had a faded but unmistakable emblem of four towers of Tarkania, which made my heart race again. I closed the pouch and turned to the enthusiastic rapist.

He was conscious. Maybe the bowman's screams had woken him up. His eyes were still fixated on the severed head of Dun when I approached him, holding the archer's stump in one hand and the bloodied power sword with the other.

He looked up at me with bloodshot, frightened eyes.

"Please," he begged.

I waved the stump in my hand in front of him. "I have some questions for you, young man."

This was how I learned about the Catastrophe, that Dun was an ex-Salvationist from Tarakan Valley who had broken the contract with his guild and fled to make easy pickings in what was now called the Radiated City, one of several cities that were utterly destroyed. With a sinking heart, I learned what had happened to my people and that the once-magnificent Tarkania was now defiled by the remnants of humanity who no longer remembered its name and call it "the City of Towers."

Several deep roars from the forest proved Dun was at least not lying about the beasts that lurked here. It was time to go.

"Please," Malk begged when I turned away, "please, mercy." His broken knee was protruding from his skin.

I don't know if he wanted me to give him a clean death or carry him across the ruins, but I left him for the two-headed lions and limped away slowly, my new body punishing me severely for the ESM I had put it through.

If what Malk just told me was true, I was not walking in a ruined city, I was walking in a destroyed world. By his body language, I knew Malk believed in what he'd told me, but I still refused to accept it. Perhaps that was why I left him there.

A little while later I heard him scream one last time.

3

Twinkle Eyes

Not withstanding the horrible memories of my demise, waking up from the dead the first time was a pleasant experience, to the point where for a moment I'd wondered if I was in one of those heavenly gardens many of the different religions promised you ended up in if you followed their creed. This time I woke up in a place which was the extreme opposite of paradise.

Various metallic instruments that must have kept my new body alive withdrew into darkness, and the bed simply tilted and I slid down to the metal floor. I lay there, gasping for air, blind and horrified, surrounded by darkness, pierced by the periodic flashing of red lights accompanied by a deafening siren. As I tried to get up, a calm yet loud female voice spoke, informing me that I was in danger and must leave the premises. I did not need her encouragement. My skin stung, not in a certain place or two, but over my entire body, as if the air was on fire. I knew to the core of my new being that whatever I was breathing was killing me. I coughed, sneezed, vomited, and lost control of my bowels in nasty succession, while trying in vain to get hold of something to push myself up with.

Amid all that fun one instinct remained true. I tried to deepen my sight, the curse that touched me in youth and the only edge I had on most of mankind. It didn't work. Not at first, anyway. When it finally did, it was not as I remembered. My sight flickered through various mediums of vision, a few of which I only knew about from stories. The quick sequence left me completely disoriented. Whatever progress I was making in getting up was lost and I hit the floor again, sitting in my own bile and bodily fluids, covering my eyes with my hands and wishing this life would end faster than my previous death had taken.

The sirens and the urging female voice were too loud for me to hear steps, but I felt their vibration as someone ran towards me. I tried to look around, flailing my arms in the darkness, but my sight was out of control—I was completely blinded by the flashing of various shades of light and darkness.

A hand caught my arm, and as I was hauled to my feet I felt the grasping fingers burn my skin.

"Try not to breathe." I didn't recognise the voice, but the accent was familiar.

"I can't see, I . . ." Another cough caught me as my body battled whatever I was breathing, and this time my rescuer had to hug me to prevent another collapse.

He was naked. We both were. The strange thing was that I registered that our naked bodies were touching, but it was more a thought in my mind than what I remembered a naked body should *feel*. The notion was so eerie that for a moment my mind cleared.

"Slow your breathing." His voice was at my ear as he picked me up with ease in a bear hug. "You can block some of the shit out."

And lo and behold, there it was. I thought it, and my body slowed its breath. Whatever was coming down my throat was somehow more acceptable, even though I knew it would still kill me—well, us—shortly.

"We need to get out of here," I croaked.

"Rust, you think so?" The man coughed out a dry chuckle. "There is a ladder here, attached to the wall."

"I can't see. Where does it go?"

"It goes somewhere, better up than to stay here."

"I can't see." My hands flailed in the darkness.

"Here, feel this . . ."

He pretty much slammed me into the metal ladder, the first sign that he was losing the battle against the elements as rapidly as I was.

"I can't see." Panic was gripping my throat as painfully as the cursed air I was breathing.

"Climb first. If you fall I *might* be able to catch you."

"I can't, I'm too weak, I can't see." I wheezed, gripping a metal rung.

"Well then, been nice knowing ya, even briefly." His hands began shoving me aside and I felt his leg brush past mine and push against the first rung.

"Wait, no, I can do it."

The thought of staying down there and dying in agony was enough to charge me with the strength to turn around and begin climbing up the metal ladder.

He ended up carrying me on his shoulder more than half of the way. It was an amazing feat of strength, balance, and single-mindedness, especially when we reached a trap door which he did not manage to open despite several brave attempts. By this time my sight was back and I could cling to the ladder as my rescuer charged up into the metal door shouting colourful obscenities with each failed attempt to pop it open.

With careful concentration, while holding on to the ladder, I enhanced my sight and looked around. The metal lever and the paintings describing the direction in which to pull it were an arm's length away.

I tried to speak but was too weak to say anything. My throat felt like I had swallowed nails. As sweat rained down on me from above and another loud ding echoed around us, I reached out with an aching hand and pulled the lever. It was surprisingly easy, and immediately there was a hiss from above. The door opened upwards and my rescuer whooped in triumph. A rush of hot, poisonous wind came from below and my knees buckled, but before I passed out and fell to my death my rescuer grabbed me again. I was pulled up and thrown onto cold, wet ground.

It was still unnaturally dark and blissfully cold but the air was as sweet as a woman's caress. All I wanted to do was cling to the wet earth and keep breathing, but my rescuer had other plans.

"It's a cave, but I can see light ahead," he said, helping me to my feet. We waded through a stream, bending every few steps to wash the gunk off our naked bodies. Eventually we emerged into sunlight and collapsed on the bank. For a while all I could do was lie on my back, feet submerged in the water, arm shielding my face from the sun. Then I got thirsty. I turned on my side, came up to my knees, and turned around on all fours. When I lowered my face, the water felt cool on my skin, soothing, and when I opened my mouth it tasted pure and cleansing. I knew it for a fact. I knew it was pure as I tasted it and even knew the temperature of the liquid. I just didn't know how I knew it. The water was refreshing, but I had the knowledge of its effect more than the actual feeling. It was unnatural. It was strange, but not as strange as my reflection in the water.

The face, the bald head, the eyes, the lips. I was staring into the reflection of someone else's face. Only at a second glance did I realise what I was not seeing and managed to stifle a yelp with a hand to my mouth. My eyes were clear blue, but the thin black symbols which had appeared overnight during my adolescence were gone.

I sat back, dumbstruck, and looked around. My rescuer must have been going through the same revelation regarding his body. I saw him sitting on his haunches several yards away, staring at the water. Sensing my gaze, he turned his head and looked back at me.

"Maybe you can tell me what this rust bucket is all about?" he called. His voice was unfamiliar, but now that we were out of the deathtrap we awoke in, I recognised the dialect and it warmed my heart. Like me, he was bald—no, completely hairless, loins and all—but that was where the similarities ended. When he stood up I couldn't help but envy his physique. It was perfection. Strong, long limbs, a lean but muscular body, and his skin as pure as a baby's—which was more than odd, it was simply impossible. No one could be that strong, carrying me all the way up from the abyss to the surface, without having been touched by the curse and further amplified by a Tarakan device. This was a Tarakan combat vessel—he looked nothing like the man I used to know, but I didn't care.

"Hello, Galinak," I said.

"Who are ya?" He eyed me suspiciously as I walked towards him. "And what was that rust below?" He gestured at the cave. "And if you can answer both those questions, how about telling me why we are standing butt naked in the middle of the rusting wilderness?"

"It's me, Twinkle Eyes," I said.

"No, you're not, and that's far enough." He took a half step away from me. I stopped.

"It's me, Twinkle Eyes. We just have different bodies, both of us."

His eyes narrowed. "You're rusting me, and patience was never one of my virtues. I'll ask you for the last time. Who are you?"

I sighed. "You have a signature hip throw. You are terrible at cards. The odds in the fight we had in Vincha's shack was five to two. You and Vincha had a weird sexual tension between you but you never actually got to . . ."

I watched his suspicion turn into a broad smile with every word I said.

"Well, rip my wires. Is that really you, Twinkle Eyes?" he finally asked.

I nodded and pointed at my eyes. "Just without the marks around the twinkle, I guess."

"Bukra's balls." Before I could react, Galinak stepped forward, grabbed me in a crushing bear hug, and lifted me in the air like a little child.

"Galinak, put me down, you crazy Troll." I tried to struggle, but it was like pushing against metal.

"It's rusting Twinkle Eyes," Galinak called out as he spun me around in his arms.

"Damn it, we're both naked."

"Who gives a silver wire?" Galinak shouted but eventually plunked me down on the ground and put a steadying arm on my shoulder. "I thought we were both goners," he said. "I mean, I heard you over the Comm, negotiating with those Tarakan arse rusts when we were surrounded by those Lizards, and I remember thinking to myself, 'Twinkles has some Salvationist spirit in him after all.' But then the Lizards began breaking in, I heard you screaming over the Comm and . . ." Galinak's eyes darkened.

"Push those memories back," I said quickly. "They are not good to dwell on, believe me."

"Aye, you're probably right." Galinak looked at himself again. "This is going to take some getting used to."

"I know." I looked, fighting the urge to cover my loins with my hand. "It's as if this body is not yet my own. I wonder if we'll sort of settle in with time."

Galinak turned around in a slow circle, saying, "Right. Care to explain what's going on?"

"I assume you were not briefed."

He completed the full circle. "No, last thing I remember was what I am trying not to remember right now. Since then, completely blank. Did they speak to you?"

I nodded.

"Those smart-arse Tarkanians knew better than to wake me up for a chat," Galinak grumbled. "I would have said several things they would be sorry to hear."

"My conversation did not take long," I said carefully. There was no use in agitating my only protection. "We were supposed to get more information and, you know"—I indicated both of us—"clothes and equipment and weapons."

"Where, down there?" Galinak pointed at the cave.

"Yes, something must have gone unexpectedly wrong, some sort of malfunction or . . . a sabotage. But we need to get back and retrieve them."

"That rebirth must have crossed your wires." Galinak shook his head. "Because this new body of mine *told* me we were going to die down there, and that a normal human would have already been convulsing on the floor. Whatever was in that air was nasty, rust, I can still feel the sting on my skin." He made a point of moving his hands around his naked body, brushing the invisible particles away.

"But we are naked, weaponless, in the wilderness," I protested.

"We're alive, healthy, and there are no Lizards that I can see." Galinak raised a hairless eyebrow. "I've been in worse situations." When he saw the look on my face he added, "I would tell you to grow a pair but that would be an inappropriate comment at this time, Twinkle." His laughter was short-lived. I guess he wasn't used to the sound of it, either. "You know what they want us to do, right? So just fill me in on that, but first let's find out where we are."

He drew my attention to an elevated boulder with a flat top. "You told me your eyes still have that special twinkle in them. I'll give you a leg up." He crouched into position and lifted me up with such force I almost missed the boulder and barely stopped myself from falling to the other side.

"Sorry," Galinak apologised when I peered down at him accusingly. "I guess I am stronger than I look." He crouched and jumped up, landing next to me in an impossible feat for any non-augmented human. "I am starting to really like this new body," he said, grinning.

I shook my head slightly, trying to hide my jealousy, then turned my head and began scanning the horizon. When I'd woken up in the poisonous bunker, I'd tried to use my night sight on reflex and had been unable to control the shifts in perspectives. This time I was more careful, but just to be on the safe side, I steadied myself by grabbing Galinak's shoulder.

And like magic, it happened. I zoomed. I could see for miles in each direction. "There is a farm. Over there."

Galinak squinted. "Where?"

"Hard for me to judge, looks like several miles." I checked the position of the sun. "East . . . seems deserted. The windows are shut and the barn doors are open."

"You can see that far?"

I turned to face him and had to steady myself as my sight shifted again. "I guess they gave us abilities that we are familiar with."

Galinak ignored the bitterness in my voice. "Right," he said, "we'd better start tracking while the sun's still up, so we can get a nice tan."

"I still think we should go back."

"Look, Twinkle Eyes." Galinak was starting to lose patience. "If you're lucky, you'll have a moment or two down there. Definitely not enough time to listen to your Tarakan friends, so all you can hope for is some gear, and rule one in the unwritten Salvationist rule book says 'no gear is worth dying for.' I would have been long dead if I hadn't obeyed that rule."

I wanted to protest further, but Galinak simply grabbed me by the waist, lifted me over his shoulder, and jumped down from the high boulder.

4

Peach

I only let myself cry once, that very night. I found a secluded ruin and with a little reverse engineering, managed to spark a fire from the power sword, although it did cost me too many energy cells and I promised myself to try and do it the old-fashioned way the next time around. Then I cleared the bone and skewered the meat on several sticks from the broken bow so the meat would cook faster. I'd only resorted to cannibalism three times before, and it was never a cherished culinary experience. This time was no exception. As the human flesh sizzled and cooked, I moved away from the circle of fire and found a dark corner, where I curled into a ball and sobbed quietly.

I was only a toddler when the Paralytic Plague, known as the Purple Plague, struck our town. Victims lost control of their bodies, then their respiration systems, and they fought to breathe until they died. My father and three brothers were gone in less than forty-eight hours, and I still remembered my little brother's body being wheeled away to the local crematorium. My mother was not affected, but I was already developing high fever and had lost control of my arms and legs. The doctors moved me to a large hall where many lay waiting to die.

I've heard the story from my mother so many times, I'm sure my memory is as false as it is vivid. But I remember a group of men and women walking into the hall. They wore thick bio suits and blue facial masks even inside their helmets. Each carried a temperature-controlled medibag imprinted with the glowing logo of Tarakan. They quickly dispersed among the sick and dying. One of them, the only one who was also wearing old-fashioned spectacles inside the protection of his helmet, came and sat by my bed. He spoke in a soft tone of voice, almost a whisper, to my mother and told her he was from Tarakan University and that he had an experimental vaccine for the plague, but that it was not fully tested yet. The vaccine could kill me or it could cure me, and my mother had less than a minute to decide whether he should administer it to me or move to the next patient.

After watching her three sons and husband die, my mother didn't hesitate. She told me years later that she had made a pact with herself that if I died, she would take her own life. The Tarakan doctor administered the vaccine by touching the fevered skin of my stomach with a metal object. I remember sweet coolness spreading quickly through my body. The next day I was on my feet. Out of 822 patients who got the vaccine, 645 survived.

My mother, a tax consultant by trade, applied for Tarakan residency the following week. Luckily, Tarakan was still accepting ordinary people back then. We moved to the City of Towers within a year, even though her trade was not needed there. She took any jobs they assigned her to, all below her skill and pay levels, but she never complained. Her sole ambition was for me to become a full Tarakan citizen.

I tried. I really did. But the shock of losing my family was too great. My mother worked hard and tried, without success, to compensate for the trauma we'd both endured. On the brink of adolescence, I became notoriously short-tempered. The puzzles and riddles were especially infuriating to me, and one day I threw a puzzle box at my teacher's head, and someone came to speak to my mother. I was sure we were going to be sent away, but the Tarakan talent scout had a different idea. I was sent to the newly formed military academy and became a professional Tarakan soldier, eventually rising to the rank of colonel major.

These were pre–Guardian Angel days, when Tarakan still followed the international treaties forbidding them from using clones as soldiers. Keeping Tarakan assets safe meant biological humans had to do the soldiering. That was my job, more or less. I worked my way up the ranks not by solving odd puzzles but the old-fashioned way; killing Tarakan's enemies.

I watched as Tarakan expanded and flourished, but I also saw the looming shadows and growing threats as other countries' jealousy turned to fear, which festered to deep loathing and eventually hate. There were terror attacks, acts of sabotage, cybertheft, and even the danger of direct hostilities to many Tarakan assets around the globe.

When the decision was finally made, I helped train the first Guardian Angels. Well, *trained* is not the right word for it, as they knew how to fight from the moment they were created, but I did make them march in beautiful formations and sent them on countless black ops. It did not take me long to realise they were the future and I was becoming obsolete.

Eventually, it was my time for an early retirement. I never married, never had children—never had the urge, frankly—and was not big on friends, either. I had seen enough of the world to satisfy my need to travel without those endless boring vacations retired people take. So, it was either sit around in an undistinguished two-bedroom flat somewhere in the Eastern Spires till I died, or accept a second offer from the Tarakan security agency and become a hibernating agent, or *a sleeper*. When the offer came, I didn't hesitate.

I thought I'd already seen it all, but the training to become a sleeper was a whole different ball game. You left everything and everyone behind, your body included, and uploaded your consciousness into Adam. You would wake up in different vessels, on different continents, countries, and cultures, knowing only who you were, what your alias was, and, most of the time, your mission.

Despite what the name suggests, you didn't actually spend your time there sleeping. The downtime was filled with training and briefings, teaching, virtual vacations, assignment preps, and a few more activities designed to keep you from losing your mind.

Once in the physical world, I could never recall the full details of my past operations, a needed security measure should I have fallen captive, but I did know the missions were getting significantly more aggressive as time passed. From simple data theft or blackmail to high-risk sabotage, kidnappings of major political figures, and high-profile assassinations. I even lit the spark, via a well-placed chemical bomb and several misleading fingerprints, to a major war in the Middle East, causing seven figures in casualties and the breakup of two regional powers.

Was I always on the just side? Hell if I knew. Many of my missions were on the shady side of the moral scale, and in my reports, as I remembered them, I mentioned more than once that aggressive subterfuge and iron-fist diplomacy led only to short-term gains at best. We were becoming the bad guy for too many global players, and although they were weaker and far behind us on the technology scale, their combined force was a real threat.

Now I sat among the ruins of mankind. From what I gathered, they . . . well, we, as a species, seemed to have somehow survived Armageddon only to continue to fight and kill each other over and over again. Tarakan, the shining-bright gem of humanity, was destroyed. All I'd worked for and risked was for nothing. Billions of people had died, and those who were spared simply picked up a gun or a sword or even a club and kept at it.

Yet here I was. Someone had downloaded me into this vessel and given me a mission, so there must be some hope. I wiped away the tears and walked back to the fire, where the meat was slowly turning black, then sat down, picked up a stick, blew carefully on the meat, and chewed off a mouthful. The taste matched my mood.

Tomorrow would be a new day. I would find a way to reach the City of Towers and find out what my mission was. Tarakan was defeated, but perhaps it was not dead yet.

5

Twinkle Eyes

It was a much longer trek to the farm than anticipated, even considering our condition. The land was hilly and hard. Only bushes and an occasional low, twisted tree grew. Coming down the hills barefoot left the soles of my feet bleeding from countless cuts. As before, the pains were a little distant, and I stifled the unmanly yelps and cries I made after several amused glances from Galinak, who bore his pain in stoic silence. At some point, he found a hefty chunk of wood which in dire circumstances could perhaps be used as a club.

"You won't knock out a hungry bear with that," I half joked, filling the silence.

"No offence, my sharp-eyed friend," he said, waving the chunk of wood at me, "but if we meet a bear I am planning to knock you out with this and run for it."

That shut me up for a while. Normally I would have dismissed that kind of talk as Galinak's rough sense of humour, but he was in a foul mood. I filled him in on the details of our mission as I knew it, and that caused two major tantrums and several more outbursts.

"No wonder everyone hated those rust fuckers," he exclaimed, his unfamiliar face turning red. "They are playing us *again*."

"They kept their word, and kept us alive." I knew it was a mistake to try this argument as soon as I said the words.

"Did they short-circuit your wires, Twinkle Eyes? Tarakan only brought us back because they need us to do their dirty work." Galinak waved his finger at me. "I ain't gonna play their game again. You might have struck a deal with them rusters, but no one asked me to chase no little girl."

"She's not a little girl anymore, she's probably seventeen by now." If I thought that such a fact would cool Galinak's temper, I was mistaken.

"I don't care how old she is," he bellowed at me. "I ain't doing this again. They can kiss my naked, hairless arse, if they ever find me." He began walking faster, leaving me behind.

I stiffened a yelp as I stepped on a sharp stone. "Wait, Galinak." To my surprise, he actually stopped and turned, and I hopped closer.

"Remember what Rafik said. We'll die in less then three years, and not in a nice, quick way."

He looked at me. "Sometimes living a short, free life is better than a lifetime of bowing your head to a master."

I could sense there was no point in trying to convince him of anything at that point. "Look," I said, tuning my voice to sound calm and reasonable, "let's find something to wear, food and water, and perhaps a weapon that is better than a branch. Then we'll talk about it."

"Fine." Galinak nodded. "But there ain't nothing to talk about. I'm done with those rusters."

We continued to walk at a slower, careful pace. Galinak brooded in silence while I took my mind off a possible encounter with a bear by playing with my sight. It was similar to the power I had in my old body, but tenfold. It was as if I'd attached a Tarakan artifact to my eyes. I could see ants crawling on the ground or a bird of prey far up in the sky as if it were up close, but despite looking all around us every chance I got, the seemingly abandoned farm remained the only man-made structure I could detect. It was no surprise, really. The Catastrophe had left behind only remnants of the human race and a lot of empty land. Many survivors instinctively congregated in hamlets, villages, or towns, but there were others who moved away, or simply stayed where they survived, choosing to brave the elements on their own.

We reached the farm as the sun disappeared behind the mountains. Despite its abandoned look, we didn't take any chances. I stayed low outside the premises and Galinak snuck in solo. After a while he came out and waved me over. It was indeed abandoned, from the look of the unkempt vegetable garden. We were in no condition to be picky, and we found several vegetables to nourish us. Eating for the first time in our new bodies was an odd experience. Like before, the feeling was duller than the awareness of the effect. I could tell that my body was being recharged by eating the rotting tomato, but thankfully, the taste was distant enough for me not to gag.

The barn had been emptied out long ago, but Galinak did find a butchering cleaver, which must have fallen when the owners were packing. It was a lucky find, since metal was priceless in these rural parts. It had some spots of rust, but the edge was true. Galinak kept it for himself and gave me the wooden club with a sly smile and a meaningful wink. I chose not to protest.

The living structure was only one story high but spacious enough to contain an extended family, perhaps even several generations, and it was almost completely cleared out. We found a few pieces of wooden cutlery near the cold hearth, too used and chipped to be worth taking. There was no food anywhere, and the wild ferret we discovered in one of the rooms wisely escaped via a hole in the wall before Galinak could make dinner out of him.

"Galinak, I found something," I cried out. Despite the lack of alarm in my voice he arrived, quickly brandishing the cleaver. I nodded toward the closet.

"The door is stuck."

He shrugged, lay the cleaver gently on his foot, placed one hand on the handle, and braced the other against the twin door. He looked at me.

"Why the gloomy face?"

"Because I can see what's inside."

He considered my words for a few heartbeats before pulling hard enough on the handle to yank it out of the door.

"Rust," he swore, and without preparation he simply punched through the wood, pulling back to break it into several pieces. Once the dust had settled, we peered inside. There were only two items of clothing hanging from the rack by a wooden hook: a farmer's blue overalls and a farmer's wife's dress.

Galinak looked at me again.

"Oh," he said. "Now I get it."

6

Peach

Clearing the ruins of the Radiated City took several days and a third of my nourishment pills. As I walked through the empty streets I realised why, despite the dangers of contamination, the looters still came to plunder. The city was destroyed probably within hours, not weeks or months. Missiles rained from the sky, and power rays carved the ground, destroying everything in their path. The nature of most Tarakan weaponry was such that tens of millions died within hours, but a lot of their items survived. I know this because I had been in charge of security when those weapons were mounted, piece by piece, on the Star Pillar and smuggled up to the hub to be assembled in space, then sent on long orbit so they could not be shot down by antisatellite batteries on Earth. At first, I did not know what we were carrying up. Even with my security clearance, I still shouldn't have known that we were breaking several international treaties by secretly carrying missile parts up the Pillar, but all the secrecy in the world can't stop a drunken intelligence officer from blabbing while trying to pick up a woman at a local bar. We had surprisingly good sex that night, but the next morning, I got him fired.

Aside from the awfulness of the world I woke up to, the trek was a long way from the worst situation I'd been through. I remembered having to survive twenty-seven days in a Bangladeshi sewage system while an army of assassins hunted me down. Compared to that, walking in a ruined city, even in the rain, was almost a relaxing affair with the added bonus of casual looting.

Of course, by now, clothes and delicate items were long gone, but I still managed to find neo-flex plastic material, and with the help of my power sword, I cut and wrapped it around the soles of my shoes and made a cover for my head. There was also enough material for a crude sack. Remembering Malk's debriefing on currency, I filled it with pieces of junk, mostly metal. I even found a cracked porcelain cup, which somehow had survived all this time. I wrapped it carefully in the last remaining piece of neo-flex plastic and walked away, feeling somehow more optimistic than before. The sword belt was too large for me to tie around my waist, so I threw it over my shoulder and under my armpit, bandolier style, making sure the hilt behind my back was within easy reach.

Aside from the great destruction, the second noticeable thing about the place was how empty it was. There were endless rows of buildings and not a single soul. If what I'd heard about the war was true, and the weaponry Tarakan possessed had been used to their full potential, billions had died in a very short amount of time. I found myself contemplating survival rates. Was the entire planet completely destroyed?

Two days later I spotted another looting party treading through the ruins, but this time I kept my distance. There were five of them, all more or less the same make and creed as the three I left behind. Since they were all heading into the city, I followed their tracks in the opposite direction until I eventually found their camp. In retrospect, I shouldn't have been surprised. There was always a camp, even in the most remote of places. If there was business to be made, merchants came to trade. Bring enough people together and someone would eventually bring a cart and begin trading. Soon enough women would appear, either of their own free will or, more likely, under coercion. In time, the camp grows to a small hamlet, then someone usually takes control of it by force.

Until the moment I saw the camp I hadn't fully comprehended what had happened to us as a species. The vast city behind me was in ruins, true, and a man had aimed and shot an arrow at me, but I still somehow expected to encounter modern life on the outskirts of the city. Seeing a horse and cart travel the unpaved road towards a camp surrounded by a medieval wooden wall turned my stomach. It was as if I'd stepped out of a time machine.

I sat down amid the tall grass and watched the camp until nightfall, noting the two hanging corpses outside the gate, the smoke coming out of the wooden houses, the water well and the people coming to use it. It could have been a scene from a period virtual flick, but for the large truck parked in the middle of the camp, and even that vehicle was antique, the sort that drove on cooking oil and coal. All but the poorest countries of the world had shied away from the use of such polluting trucks, but right then, to me, that truck was a beacon of modernity. It became my mark. I had to get into that truck.

With the poor zooming ability of my vessel, it was too far off for me to see any details, and parts of the truck were obscured by what looked like poorly erected wooden buildings. After changing position several times, I managed to watch it being loaded with what seemed to be metal junk. The truck owner's face was hidden inside a grey cowl but he had an obvious limp. The men helping load the truck were armed to the teeth with a mixture of antique twentieth-century weapons and more medieval-looking ones. They were a rough enough bunch, but the man wearing the cowl seemed to control them. They dispersed as night came.

The prudent thing to do was to wait at least another day, gather intelligence and figure out the best way to act. Special hibernating agent Vera Geer, or even Colonel Major Vera Geer, would have strongly suggested such caution, especially when operating in a noncombat vessel. But I was afraid the truck would leave at first light, or even before, and I would be left behind in the Middle Ages. Besides, the night's darkness provided an opening. It was true darkness, the sort you rarely experienced in the world I used to live in. The cold temperature was another consideration, and it was taking its toll on my vessel, which was shaking and consuming a lot of energy to continue functioning. There was danger I would damage the vessel or even freeze to death. Or perhaps these were just excuses. I was tired, hungry, cold, wet, and still emotionally in shock. I wanted heat, and light, and food, and perhaps even a conversation. I wanted to get away from this place, which looked and felt like a bad hallucination. I also needed a good night's sleep. I needed to dream. Operational directions might be received via dreams, but I had to find a safe place to fall into a deep sleep, enough to open my mind up to such transmissions. That could not be done in the field.

I unwrapped the neo-flex from my shoes and made sure everything was tied, secured, and as jingle free as possible, although with the coin bag and a sack filled with metal loot that task was bordering on the impossible.

The camp had four crude guard towers, but for some reason only two were manned and their only light sources were torches. Reaching the outer perimeter was an easy enough task and I didn't even need to crawl, a blessing since after the few days of light drizzle, the ground close to the wall was awfully muddy. There were wooden stakes in the ground, as if the people in the camp were afraid of a cavalry charge. I slipped past them and reached the wall.

I aimed to reach the part of the wall that was closest to the truck, but that part was impossible to climb. Primitive or not, whoever had built the wall had done a fine job. Moving a little farther, I managed to find a part where I could get in at least two handholds. They were impossibly far apart, but that was all I needed.

Before climbing, I stayed still and tried to deepen my hearing. My vessel's senses were only one notch above biological human level, but it was enough for me to hear the stutter of a small engine, the steps of three people walking away from me, coarse singing, and the snorting of pigs. That last one came with a stench as well. I took a deep breath, entered ESM, feeling adrenaline rush once again through my body, and quickly climbed the wall, my fingers digging into the wood like an alley cat. I found myself on a narrow parapet, from which I quickly jumped down to the other side, landing behind a hut and huddling down. It took me a few minutes to recover from the disorientation and nausea of the ESM.

The stench of livestock mixed with rotting garbage and human excrement was apparent. This place was the graveyard of hygiene. I leaned and peeked around. Apart from four guards standing around a small bonfire behind a gate, the dark streets were deserted. I sneaked away from them, passed the central well, and headed towards the truck. It was parked next to a second gate, effectively blocking it. Years of usage and crude patch jobs were apparent, as well as bullet holes and scorch marks, but the makers of the EverTyre company would have been proud to know that their product, worn and battle scarred, was still functioning even after a nuclear holocaust. I still toyed with the idea of stealing the truck, smashing through the gate, and driving away into the sunset, but the motion sensor lock on the truck's doors made me change my plans. Actually, the placement of a modern gadget such as the motion sensor was uplifting. It meant there was still hope . . .

With the right tools, I could have bypassed the lock, but the risk of attracting attention and turning this into a massacre was too great. Besides, even if I got into the truck and managed to drive it, I hadn't a clue where to go. I needed information and, if possible, assistance.

A dog began to bark and I retreated back to the central well. I followed my ears to the back of the biggest wooden shack of this sorry little settlement. The engine noise came from a small generator, which, by the smell of the black smoke it was exhaling, was fuelled by a mixture of cooking oil, fat, and perhaps even manure. As I watched, the back door opened and a middle-aged man, dressed in disgustingly stained clothes, poured a bucket of such slop into the open tank. I waited for him to go back into the hut and headed towards the front entrance.

Generator or not, the main light source of this small tavern was a central fire under a large iron pot, a serious fire hazard under any modern law anywhere in the old world. The stench almost made me walk back out, but once the door opened, enough people turned their heads at me to make a retreat dangerously noticeable, so I walked into the gloomy shadows of the room and closed the door behind me.

7

Twinkle Eyes

Anyone watching the two figures from afar would have thought them a farmer and his wife tottering along on a dirt road, though on closer inspection the watcher would have realised something was certainly amiss. Galinak had torn the bottom of his overalls, from the knees down, and tied the material around his feet. The farmer's wife was a hefty lass, so the corset fit, just barely, across my ribs. I'd tried Galinak's trick with the hem of the dress but a miscalculation on my part now meant the dress was indecently short. On the bright side, I had enough material left to tie around my bald head to protect my cranium from the unforgiving sun. Actually, come morning, we discovered hair was beginning to grow on both of our bodies. Mine was a shade between white and golden; Galinak's was ginger brown.

We had resumed our journey after a relatively comfortable night in front of the hearth, which by another stroke of luck featured an old built-in flint, now safely in Galinak's pocket. He had suggested we simply stay on the farm and "start our own family" but by midday the stream of jokes died to a mere trickle.

We found some berries on the side of the road that tasted awful but were nourishing enough. Water was a concern, but our bodies proved to be incredibly resilient, taking on way more than what I would guess my previous one could have endured.

A little after midday we passed another abandoned farm, but this one was completely ruined. Worse, there were obvious marks of violence, including the bones of several livestock, fire damage, and enough signs to indicate that, in Galinak's words "something really big blew up this rusting hut." He was the first to spot the deep imprints on the ground where the garden must have been— two parallel chain lines, twice a man's height in distance from each other.

"Some kind of a machine." I pointed out the obvious but Galinak was not in the mood. He tested the ground with his fingers.

"Deep on dry earth. Means this thing was heavy, huge. It takes a lot of energy clips to move such a vehicle."

We exchanged glances. "A kind of war machine then," I said. "Nothing else is worth such energy."

"A war machine?" Gailnak looked around. "We only had light dusters in the Hive, and that was Tarakan Valley we're talking about."

Rafik said that the City of Towers was preoccupied with a conflict, but this area is far from the city. Could there be a connection?

"I know these machines existed before the Catastrophe," I said, the memory flashing through my mind. "They were called Tanks. I heard they found a field with those things far to the west. The machines were smashed and burned, but the metal was so thick they couldn't even salvage it, so they just stand there in rows now."

"So, a local gang gets its hands on a working war machine with enough energy clips to operate it and runs around destroying small farms?" Galinak shook his head. "That doesn't make sense."

"An advancing army, then," I said quietly.

"Makes more sense with the other farm being abandoned," Galinak agreed. "They knew about the threat. The first family ran away, these ones chose to stay and protect their land." He shook his head again. "Poor sods, must have been like kicking a puppy."

"Yes, but whose army?" I asked.

Galinak shrugged. "We can't connect the wires on this one."

"We should have tried to go back to the bunker." I gestured toward the destruction around us. "This would have surely been part of what Rafik would have briefed us about."

"Well, if I wasn't sure before, now I know for a fact it's you, Twinkle Eyes." Galinak chuckled. "Ready to die just so you could learn something you didn't know before. We'll find out soon enough what's going on, so let's look around a little more and move out of here."

Galinak's remark might just have been a barbed jest, but he was right. I was already feeling the familiar tingling sensation growing in my mind; curiosity. I might have been coerced into this mission by the Tarkanians, but I also wanted to know—hell, I needed to know—what was going on, and it was worth risking my new life to find out.

There was nothing worth looting except a few pieces of wood we collected for a future bonfire and several rusty nails. I tied the nails with the frills from my dress and decided to find a way to add them to my crude club at the first opportunity. Not the greatest upgrade to my fire power, but every little thing helps.

"We should follow the imprints." Galinak pointed at the deep grooves leading northeast.

"No, we should go northwest," I said. "Following a war machine and armed troops with a club and a dress may leave the wrong impression." That one rewarded me with another chuckle from Galinak. "The farmers who ran must have tried to reach some kind of a safe haven. I think there's a large village a day or two from here."

Galinak looked skeptical. "You deduced all of that from a set of imprints?"

"No," I admitted. "Something has been bothering me for a while now. This area is familiar. I think I've passed through it."

"Not surprising." Galinak dusted himself off. "You chased Vincha all over the place."

"No. Vincha never went rural on me," I said. "I think I passed through here when I was younger, with LoreMaster Harim." The mention of my mentor's name brought up a rush of emotions. He was the one who took me from my family home to the upper towers of the City of Towers and made me the flawed man I was now.

"Fine, lad." Galinak walked to me. "We'll do it your way."

We kept on walking, finding a wider road and following it till night fell, but we did not stop. My sight made the night as clear as the day, and although we only ate a handful of berries we picked up on the side of the road, our new bodies did not show any sign of fatigue. Even the soles of our feet hardened enough to make walking more comfortable, and we were able to move faster.

By midday the dirt trail merged into what was once a paved road, now with only patches of dark material remaining as a testimony to its former glory. This was where we found another unmistakable track of the war machine, and this time we had to follow it. Since we were now on lower ground, there were many more trees and tall bushes, and they hid the village until we came upon it. For some childish reason I took pride in spotting it first.

It was certainly a place I had visited before. It used to have a protective wall and the houses within climbed up the steep hill. The hill must have kept the villagers in shape while acting as a natural defence from three sides, but that natural defence and the high walls and guard towers did not stand a chance against a war machine.

We waited for what felt like a long time, hidden among the vegetation, noting the enormous gaps in the reinforced wooden wall, the remains of three guard towers, and the lack of what was once an impressive front gate.

"Well, at least they did not burn the place down," Galinak whispered next to me. "Any ideas why?"

I shrugged. "I have no clue."

He shrugged back and spat at the ground. "Let's find out."

I stopped him with a touch, scanning for heat signatures. "There are no humans that I can see, but there are some animals roaming around in there."

"You can see all the way inside?"

I nodded. "Just be ready for a fight."

Galinak's smile was full of bad intentions. "I'm always ready for a fight." He waved his cleaver to emphasise his point, then surprised me by ripping a nail from my dress and ramming it halfway into my club. "Now you're ready too."

8

Peach

People were still glaring at me when I sat myself down on a wooden stool next to a tiny table that, by the look of it, had not been cleaned for a long time. With a sinking feeling in my stomach, I realised that there were about twenty men around me, and the only females were two tired-looking prostitutes entertaining four uniformed men in the far corner of the room. I was a woman, in perhaps not the most attractive vessel, but this felt like a remote place, the sort in which men hold the bar just a notch above "breathing," and sometimes not even that high. With those ladies entertaining the guards in full view of the rest of the men, and the alcohol flowing, sooner or later I would get unwanted attention.

I lay the neo-flex plastic sack on the sticky floor and placed the power sword in my lap. There was no music, just the soft murmuring of conversation and the loud and lewd chatter of the drunken guards. The rest of the men kept openly staring at me, some of them with disconcerting approval. I was careful not to make eye contact with any of them, although it dawned on me that soon I would have to choose a companion or have the most aggressive of the men make an approach.

One of them was downing his drink quickly, his body language betraying his immediate intention of trying his luck with me. It was right then that I spotted the figure I had seen near the truck when I was surveying the place. His cowl was off but I recognised him by the limp. He had a lean, rugged face and a greying ginger beard.

My profession is an odd one. It involves meticulous planning, but no matter how careful you are, many times the plan fails and you find yourself in the midst of deadly chaos. In moments like these, you have to learn to trust your instincts. I was up and walking even before I had made a conscious decision to do so, slinging the power sword over my back as I rose from the table. It was easy to follow the limping man to the table, as people moved aside respectfully when he passed them. I guessed that like myself, the man knew to trust his own instincts, because he whirled around just as I approached. My size, sex, or appearance did not make him less wary. I noted that one hand was holding both cups while the other went to the butt of an old-looking revolver stuck in his belt. There was another figure sitting near a table behind him. That one's face was still hidden inside his cowl.

"Hello," I said in a cheery voice, "I wonder if I may share your table for a bit."

The man looked down at me, noting the sack I was holding in one hand and the sword on my back, then he lifted his gaze and studied the faces of the men staring at me. He must have concluded I was seeking protection rather than company because he turned his green eyes back at me and simply said, "No," in a quiet but resolute voice. I didn't blame him for not wanting to play the role of a gallant knight.

"Oh, c'mon Trev," the man sitting at the table said cheerfully, "give a lady a break and pull a stool for yourself. Your leg's too stiff to be under this low table anyways."

The taller man shut his eyes briefly, nodded, and moved aside.

He laid two cups carefully on the table, then went to retrieve another stool. I sat myself in front of the other man. His round face smiled at me from inside the cowl he was wearing as he extended his hand.

"Brak's my name, and this pile of scowls is Trevil, my cousin."

I took his hand. It had calluses, and his grip was strong. "I'm Peach." I said the first name that came to my mind.

"Now that's an interesting name, Lady Peach." Brak pulled one cup from the edge of the table and nursed it. "And quite a foreign accent." His eyes were shrewd and calculating. "You're not from here."

"This doesn't seem to be a place that people come from," I answered, making a show of glancing around.

Brak chuckled as he sipped his brew. "Phew." He shook his head at the taste, spit the liquid in his mouth back into the cup, and spilled the entire contents to the dark, muddy floor. "That barkeep is pissing in his own brew. Trevil, go frighten the bastard enough for him to pour us something decent, and get a fresh cup for Lady Peach as well."

Trevil, who had just sat down next to us, stared at Brak with a discontented scowl.

"Yes, that's just the right face." Brak indicated his cousin. "Now aim it at Rikus and get clean cups as well."

Trevil rose without a word and made his way back to the bar.

"Don't mind him," Brak said cheerfully, "he's the brooding, silent type. Sometimes when we're on the road, he just sits there for *days* without saying so much as a word to me."

I had the feeling those days were filled with Brak's own words. "Are you the owners of the truck outside?"

"Indeed, we are. And my guess is"—this time Brak made a show of turning his head around—"that you are looking for a fast way out of this heavenly retreat."

I couldn't hide my smile. "Is it that obvious?"

"It's all over on your face, and it's only reasonable. Even I hate this mudhole, and this is where Trev and I trade plenty of metal. Where do you need to go?"

"Tarka—" I remembered Malk's reaction when I first said the name of the city. He did not recognise it, and I'd had to show him the emblem on the coins for him to understand. "The City of Towers."

Brak whistled softly. "That's a bit of a trek, Lady Peach, but my guess is your immediate concern is to get out of here before they realise you snuck in. Climbed the walls, did you? That's an impressive feat, especially for a lady your size."

"How did you—"

Brak leaned forward on the wooden table, which creaked under his weight. "There are two gates in and out of this place, and if you were to try and come in by yourself through either of them, you'd be spread on a guard's mat right now, excuse my language. You are in the wrong place and need to get out of here." Brak leaned a little closer and lowered his voice. "Now, we're willing to help you out, but I'm afraid it will cost you metal." He tilted his head inside the grey cowl. "I'll say the contents of your coin bag and what's in your little sack. No exceptions."

"How do you know I have anything of value in the sack? Maybe it's filled with old clothes."

"Oh, I have a keen sense of hearing, Lady Peach, and I heard the tinkling of metal when you placed it on the floor."

My heart sank. Losing all of the currency I had in this world was not a good plan. But I was desperate, and this Brak was shrewd enough to sense it. For all his gallantry and pleasant chatter, this man was not one to be letting go of a business advantage.

"I have fighting skills, and I'm good with my sword," I said. "I can buy passage by helping you protect the truck, standing guard at night and such."

Brak shook his head. "I'm sure you can swing that sword of yours just fine, Lady Peach, but we have no need for extra guards. Trevil might not be much of a talker, but he sleeps very lightly and can shoot a flying bird's head off with his pistol. We've been travelling this route for three years now. We have our resting spots; friendly farms and places along the road we know are safe. Passengers cost us in fuel and speed, so if you want to travel with us out of here, you need to pay."

Trevil came back with only two cups. He laid one at his cousin's place and kept one to himself.

"Oh Trevil," Brak admonished in a light-hearted tone, "that was a little unkind. And we were about to seal a deal here, weren't we, Lady Peach?"

He tipped the cup in my direction.

I bent down and fished out the porcelain cup from the sack. "Nice find," commented Brak. He poured me a measure from his cup and added, in a matter-of-fact tone, "It came out of the sack, so it is a part of your payment."

I sniffed the liquid and the stench of the badly fermented alcohol hit my nose like a fist. Ignoring the data streaming through my mind, I let some of the contaminated drink pass my lips.

"Not a lady's drink," remarked Brak with a wry smile. He pointed at the other patrons. "The bartender here brews a mean one, meant to knock them out before they get sozzled enough to try and knock each other out and ruin the furniture. But if you travel with us, you won't have to get used to the brew, the occasional hound stew, or the company some of the lads here are planning to give you." Brak raised his cup. "Do we have a deal?"

I didn't have a choice. But on the other hand, I'd found a ride out of this place and some company to gain information from. Not a bad deal, especially since I knew that if I had to, I could always rob them later. In my peripheral vision I saw Trevil glaring at me and guessed he was hoping I would refuse Brak's deal.

I raised my cup, clinked it softly with Brak's, and drained it in one go. Rising to my feet I said, "Your cup, your sack, you carry it all. Now, if you don't mind, I'd like to rest in your truck's cabin."

9

Twinkle Eyes

We found the dead bodies halfway up the hill. They were probably laid in a neater file before animals had dragged some of them aside. The smell was strong, but our bodies immediately reacted by reducing our sensitivity to it. Still, it was not a pretty sight.

"Between forty or fifty of them," Galinak said. "A slaughter, yes, but where're the rest of them?"

"Taken?" I said, then added, "Slaves?"

Galinak shrugged and we moved on.

We ended up spending the night in the highest house on top of the hill.

Looters had done a thorough job of going through the village, but still they left plenty of stuff behind for us to use. I found a pair of worn boots that fit. One even had real leather lining. In a different house I got a cloak and some clothes, old and torn but definitely a step up from what I'd been wearing.

On the downside, I was attacked by a dog who was either protecting its turf or had grown a taste for feeding off the remains of the slain. Galinak reacted fast, but not fast enough. The bite I received wasn't painful—my skin healed surprisingly fast—and we did end up having dog stew for dinner. So I wasn't complaining.

It was Galinak who found the three moonshine bottles in the cellar. He insisted I rub some of it over my rapidly healing wound. It stung a bit, and I used the cloth of the farmer wife's dress to bandage my arm. The rest we drank.

"Are you going to do things different?" Galinak asked me unexpectedly. We were sitting around the burning hearth, trying to consume enough moonshine to be able to eat Galinak's dog stew. My body resisted the first few mouthfuls, but with enough resolve, mind always triumphs over matter.

"What do you mean?" I took another swig from the bottle.

"Some Trolls I used to know, when they had a close call, a brush with death, they swore they'd do things different for the rest of their lives. A few of them actually changed their ways, but most of 'em couldn't shake the habits." Galinak drank some more. "You and I didn't just have a brush with the grim reaper, we grabbed his bony arse and gave him a wet smacker on his lipless mouth, but now we're alive again. That sort of thing changes your outlook on life."

I did not know what to answer, so I reversed the question. "What are you going to do differently?"

Galinak shrugged and filled his mouth again, then passed the bottle. "Not sure. Guess I won't take orders from nobody no more."

"Was there ever a time when you did?"

He chuckled. "You only know the old, wise, and tender me, Twinkles. I used to be obedient, a little more respectful to authority, but now—" He sighed. "What about you?"

"I remember promising myself in the City Within the Mountain, just before we went on the mission, that if I ever got out of there alive, I'd find a nice lady and have a family of my own." I gestured at my body. "Not going to happen with this body now."

"You said you were from around here. Maybe go see your folks, visit your family?"

I took another deep pull from the bottle and shook my head. Things were starting to get misty in my peripheral vision. "My story is not so different from Rafik's, you know. One day you're living happily in some remote little village, the next day you wake up with these." I pointed at my eyes, momentarily forgetting this was not my old body. "My dad had coin and influence where we lived, and the people there were not as zealous as in Rafik's village, so no ax or hot pokers for me. But a marked son was a major blow to the family. I was locked in a room for a whole month before LoreMaster Harim came to our house. Then I was whisked away. I know now that this was the right thing to do for all involved, but for a thirteen-year-old boy who loses his family in the blink of an eye . . ." I took another pull from the moonshine. "I was . . . crying every night for a long time, then I got angry for a while, then I got over it. Years later I got word my dad had passed away—they didn't even tell me how. My older sister was already married, and my mother and two younger sisters moved to another part of the land for some reason. That's the last I'd heard."

"Still. Family," Galinak said. "Maybe once we figure out what to do and"—he wiggled his finger unsteadily at me—"what *not* to do. We could track them down, have a meet, you know . . ."

Even in my state I registered Galinak said *we* when talking about tracking down my long-lost family.

"I never got to thank you, Twinkle Eyes," he suddenly said. "You saved my life, twice."

"What are you talking about?" I swallowed another mouthful of the bitter drink, ignoring my body's warning regarding my current condition.

"Back in the City Within the Mountain. If it wasn't for you, negotiating like that, we would have just ended up Lizard chowder."

"Ah, that, but we did end up as Lizard chowder." I passed the bottle back, and Galinak drank some more before continuing.

"Yea, but they extracted our *minds*." He pointed at his head.

"That's because of you. And now, here I am back in the living, again because of you." He passed the bottle back.

"To be honest, Rafik told me you were coming with me before I managed to ask," I said, and checked the bottle I was holding. It was empty.

"I'm sure that those rust-fucker Tarkanians wouldn't have just sent me alone on this mission." Galinak opened the second bottle. "Nah, I know why I'm here, Twinkle Eyes. Here's to you, and here's to life." He raised the bottle and drank deeply.

I vaguely remember slurring words of infinite wisdom as we went through our second bottle. The rest of the night was a bit of a blur, containing many old stories, tales of Salvationist adventures, more than a few lurid songs, then smashing through a wooden door and eventually passing out blissfully on the stairs to the cellar.

Waking up in a bunker filled with poisoned air was worse than what I felt the following morning, but not by much. Galinak was nowhere to be seen, so after washing my face and drinking boiled well water, I slowly began exploring the rest of the house. On the second floor I found an old hunting rifle under a pile of debris. There were no bullets, so it was probably more useful as a club, but I kept it anyway.

The makeshift ladder leading to the attic creaked, but bore my weight. The roof tiles had several bullet holes, and rays of light penetrated the gloom. Still, without my enhanced sight I would not have noticed the footsteps marking the dusty floor and the fact that one of the floorboards was slightly cleaner than others. Moving it earned me a splinter but was absolutely worth it. As if the bag of fifty metal coins I found, the two water skins, and the steel hunting knife were not enough, I carefully pulled out two other items of interest. The first one was a live snap, not a drawing, of a family of seven who hugged and smiled happily at me despite the creases. I guessed the snap had sentimental value to whoever hid it here or whoever was meant to find it. I kept it without really knowing why. And there was a map. This, too, was not a crude hand drawing, but rather a pre-Catastrophe-era, fully detailed folding map.

Memories surfaced and flooded my consciousness as I spread it on the floor. I knew maps like this. My LoreMaster was an avid collector and used to spend hours in his tower, bent over with his nose stuck in them. I heard his voice lecturing in my ear, "Great cities fall into great ruins in a matter of years and towns or villages vanish into the woods in even less time, but mountains, rivers, and lakes remain, more or less, in the same place. With enough attention to detail, old pre-Catastrophe maps could prove extremely valuable."

Before we parted ways, LoreMaster Harim gave me a map and list of his hideouts, telling me to use whatever I found to keep the Guild of Historians alive, but I had failed both him and the Guild by being torn apart by Lizards in the City Within the Mountain.

I turned my attention to the map I was holding and magnified it tenfold with my sight. This newly awakened memory gave me an idea of where we were, and I marked the village on the thin paper with a circle made by a piece of coal I found on the floor. Now I just had to figure out where we needed to go.

I looked up and examined the roof of the attic, and I spotted a trapdoor. There was no ladder in sight, but a successful, and quite daring, balancing act over several pieces of piled-up furniture meant I could open the trapdoor and stick my head through. Getting my body up there required a bit more work, especially when Galinak still hadn't shown up, but I didn't care—I was acting like a man possessed. When I finally made it to the top of the roof I was in a kind of euphoric ecstasy. Childish. Stupid. I know. But it *felt* good to seek a solution to a mystery and then solve it. I desperately needed to know why I'd been given my life back, and walking away without finding a way to answer this question was not an option for me. I began experimenting with my vision, zooming in and out, trying to see as far as I could and to memorize the topography.

At the edge of my enhanced vision I saw the distinct silhouette of the City of Towers, my old home.

"Hey!"

I stopped zooming and turned my head down.

"Look what I found." Galinak was sitting bareback on a horse. "Took me ages to tempt him to come over, but once I got my hands on him, he became very obedient." If Galinak was suffering any setbacks because of last night, it didn't show.

This was definitely the best day of our new lives, so far.

"Well done," I shouted in reply. "Now let's gather what we can carry. I know where we can go and gear up."

"Really?" He danced the horse in a circle. "And where is that?"

I didn't bother to shout back. Instead, I turned to study the hills to our north.

"We are going to visit an old friend," I whispered to no one in particular.

10

Peach

Wake up, Lady Peach. We're making a tinkle stop."

I opened my eyes and had to blink several times before I could focus. I'd dozed off simply to gather some strength, but the conditions inside the truck's cabin were far from ideal. I was jammed in the backseat among heaps of junk, dried meat, a keg of beer, and several primitive guns that looked as if they were taken from the museum of historical armaments.

To make matters worse, suspended above my head by chains and ropes was an old, heavy machine gun. It swayed dangerously with the rocking of the truck. If that thing fell on my head it would be the short end of this vessel. The old truck was jerking sideways as much as it was moving forward on the broken road, and it made me nauseous and weak. Having to duck every so often so as not to get hit by the machine gun wasn't helping things.

"Sure," I said weakly, the taste of dust in my mouth. I'd already lost the contents of my stomach three times in the last five days and was down to my last five nourishment pills.

Brak was the driver. I didn't know why he kept a cowl over his head during the entire journey, even in the oppressing heat of the truck's cabin, but other than that he was still the chatty, glass-half-full kind of guy I'd met in the looter's camp. In fact, I believed the reason Brak agreed to take me along was less about the contents of my sack and more about companionship.

Trevil kept to his silent brooding and spoke to me only when it was necessary. He also kept his revolver on his person at all times, remained vigilant throughout most of the journey, and took the entire night-watch duty, refusing even when I offered to relieve him for a few hours. He'd never expressed his consent to taking me along, and my educated guess was that he was not happy about it but had given in to Brak's whim.

Brak had introduced Trevil as his cousin, but I had my doubts they were blood related. It wasn't just that their physiques and demeanours were extremely different; there was something in the way they related to each other that spoke of a different sort of familiarity. There were other signs; my womanly instincts told me neither of them ever looked at me like the men at the bar had. Yet they refrained from touching each other, or expressing their intimacy in any obvious way. I spent time during the journey wondering why they kept their relationship a secret. The world I came from had long accepted same-sex relationships, and Tarakan society was even coming to terms with human-Angel relationships. Sadly, it seemed like the world I'd woken up to might have fallen back to its old inhibitions.

Brak parked the truck and turned to me, sweat glistening under his cowl. "This spot is really beautiful, Lady Peach. We should go to the ridge and look down at the valley."

The look Trevil shot his companion was so apparent I almost laughed.

"Oh, come on, Trev." Brak gestured at me. "Look at her. Lady Peach needs a bit of fresh air, and you need some peace and quiet from my chattering."

Trevil shrugged but leaned back in his seat and closed his

eyes as we climbed down. It was a short trek through rich, tall grass, and we had to climb down a bit till we got to the ledge, but Brak was not exaggerating. It was an odd sight that filled me with mixed emotions. The vast lowland below was filled with destroyed buildings, roads, and bridges, but it was also rich with vegetation. I even spotted several small fields with clear signs of cultivation.

"This is where we're going"—Brak pointed in the distance—"Lakewood Hope. It's a new settlement built over ruins. They named it Lakewood because it's between a lake—"

"—and a wood," I said, finishing his sentence.

"Yeah, Lady Peach, that's right. My grandad came here after the breaking of the world. He was one of the founders of Lakewood Hope and my father lives there, and my older brother. My sister got married seven seasons ago and moved away, but she moved back when her man went foraging too deep and too long in the contaminated cities and died of sickness."

"So, it's just you and your cousin on the road, then?"

The look of momentary vagueness in Brak's eyes was all the proof I needed.

"Yeah . . . just me and Trev on the road, looking out for each other." He changed topics. "You never told me where you're from, Lady Peach."

A part of me was listening to Brak while another was trying to figure where I was, but I was never strong in topography. "I am from very far away," I answered.

"I gathered that—your accent is not from these parts—but how far?"

I levelled a stare at him. "Where I come from people do not need to hide who they love."

Brak quickly turned his head to watch the land below. "That's far away indeed then," he said quietly. "So, what brings you here?"

There was no reason to lie. "I don't know yet, but I need to get to the City of Towers."

"That's quite a ramble, Lady Peach. Your best course would be the town of Newport and to buy a ride with a SuperTruck driver to Regeneration, but I hear the Tarakan highway is blocked nowadays."

There was so much information crammed into Brak's last sentence I had to figure out which question to ask first. "The Tarakan highway network? It still functions?"

"Oh yeah, Lady Peach, there's a lot of it that's still intact, but you need a SuperTruck to ride it proper, not our kind. You know of SuperTrucks?"

I nodded. The toll-operated highways and the selling of what were fondly called T trucks were one of the most lucrative side businesses of Tarakan. *SuperTruck* was definitely a good name for those machines, and I was happy to find out some had survived. It meant my trip to the City of Towers could theoretically become much shorter.

"But you say the road is blocked?"

"That's what I hear, Lady Peach. Some warlord took a part of it for himself, made a roadblock, and is taxing the SuperTruck drivers. They say this warlord has some kind of heavy cannons on carts that can blow you away from a mile's distance, and that a few truckers who tried to break through died along with their trucks. So now the only way to get from Newport would be the back roads on trucks like ours." Brak pointed in the direction we came from for emphasis. "And that could take you several weeks, maybe a whole season. And I hear Regeneration is under siege, too, although it could be just a rumour."

I did not recognize the places Brak mentioned, but it seemed that violence never ceased for a moment, even after Armageddon.

We both heard the very long honk of the truck's horn. "Oh, Trev is getting impatient with us." Brak smiled, but when two more short honks followed his smile faded and he began running back, pulling out a gun from his belt. "It's our signal for trouble," he shouted as I ran after him. "Hold on Trev, I'm coming."

I hadn't touched any of the guns in the truck, assuming such an action would not be appreciated, but I still had my sword. I pulled it out and went after Brak. My vessel's shape and size meant I could easily blend into a market crowd in a reconnaissance mission, but it had short legs and was not built for speed, so I was trailing behind when I cleared the small hill. It turned out Trevil was travelling towards us. The truck cut through the tall grass, swaying dramatically, and I could count three figures holding on to the top of the truck, slowly progressing to the cabin. They were dressed in a mixture of rags and animal skin. A little behind them was a cloud of dust made by more men on horses galloping towards us. There was no time to zoom in or count them as we ran towards the truck.

There was a shot and a body dropped from the passenger side. I could see that Trevil was still in the driver's seat but I guess Brak was too battle nervous to have a clear grasp of the situation because he screamed, "Trev, no," stood his ground, aimed and shot wildly at the men on top of the truck. All three men ducked, but one of them shot back just as Trevil managed to steady the vehicle. I heard Brak shout and saw him fall into the tall grass just as the truck pulled over. One of the men on top skidded forward and fell in front of the cabin; another used the momentum to jump down, roll in the soft grass, and come up pointing the gun at the prone Brak. He did not pay attention to me, a middle-aged woman barely taller than the grass, until the moment I cut his arm off with the power sword.

Trevil climbed out of the driver seat. There was blood on his shirt. He shot the man who fell in front of the truck and began running towards us, unaware that the third man on top of the truck had gotten up on his feet and was aiming his gun at Trevil's back. ESM kicked in. I grabbed the severed arm before it hit the ground, turned it and pressed the finger on the trigger, shooting above Trevil's head. It was an old gun, and I think I missed, or maybe grazed the man, but it made him lose his balance and fall from the top of the truck. I ran and stabbed him with the sword as Trevil bent down and picked up the groaning Brak, put his arm around him and began carrying him back to the truck. The men on horseback were a moment from catching up with us, and there was no way we could push Brak into the cabin and drive away on time. I sheathed the sword, bent down and picked up the other gun. "Start moving," I shouted at Trevil. "I'll stall them."

I ran as fast as I could while crouching low in the tall grass, and I heard the thunder of hooves approaching. My personal, inner briefing was short and bitter. I had a pair of unchecked, old guns with only the element of surprise on my side and short-spanned ESM facing an untold number of armed riders. Those were not odds I wanted to work with. Three horses passed me, and their riders noticed me too late to react. The fourth one almost trampled me and I had to roll sideways. I emerged from the tall grass shooting with both hands. All around me men and horses screamed and fell. My left-hand gun emptied after five shots, and I figured I had one or two more shots in my right. I ran to where a rider fell as bullets began whizzing around me, and an arrow struck the ground in front of me. A rider was lying on the ground, still breathing, but nursing a gunshot wound, his pump-action shotgun at arm's length. When he saw me he tried to reach it. I shot him twice, dropped the handguns, and went to retrieve the shotgun. I was in the midst of a fog of war, the sort that gets you killed quickly. Somewhere behind me I heard the truck's engine roar. I rolled again, picking up the shotgun with both hands, turned, shot a charging woman off her horse, ducked, and ran fast along the tall grass as bullets chased me. Without the ESM I would have been dead already, but my body was beginning to weaken. The truck was already moving away as I began racing after it. I knew that this action would be the last physical exertion I could muster before I collapsed from exhaustion. Already my sight was beginning to get blurry.

I saw a lone horse and went for it. He might have been docile, in shock, or too slow to react to my ESM speed, but I managed to reach him and jump-mount. I had never been a horse person, but I had put in my fair share of saddle miles during various assignments which had brought me to the farthest corners of the world. The saddle was makeshift, leather and animal skin, but was surprisingly soft—not that I had time to enjoy the sensation.

My attack had momentarily disoriented the riders, but they

were circling for another charge at the truck. I estimated there were more than a dozen left. I ducked my head low and urged the horse forward. Hitting a moving target from horseback was a very difficult task, but it didn't stop my pursuers from trying. Bullets and arrows flew past me with enough density to pose a threat. I kept my head down and urged the beast forward with my heels. The truck was built for endurance but not for speed, even on a paved road. Reaching it on the back of a galloping horse took only a moment. I manoeuvred to the right side of the truck, then grasped the first thing I could reach, a rusty ladder. My horse suddenly veered away and I was left dangling, holding onto the ladder with one hand, my feet almost touching the ground. The shotgun dropped to the ground and a second later I saw the truck roll over it. Normally climbing to relative safety would have been easy enough, but after ESM, my vessel was reaching the end of its physical ability. Through desperation alone I managed to get a foothold on the ladder, but all I could do was cling to it and watch as the first rider reached the truck. He was a burly man with a wild beard, dressed in a bearskin and high fur boots. In his hand he held a long spear with a wicked-looking metal spike on the end of it. I didn't need to use my imagination to guess what he would be trying to do first. He aimed the spear at me as he got closer. Trying to climb up would just expose my back to him, and besides, my arms and legs felt like they were made of stone. I managed to draw the sword with my left hand as the rider closed in on me, but as I pressed the power button, nothing happened. It was either broken or depleted of energy cells. The rider lunged with his spear and I barely managed to deflect it. Two other riders were close behind him. One had long, braided hair and was holding a gun in her free hand. The rider with the spear tried again. This time the tip of the spear missed me but the sharp metal brushed against my skin and without registering the pain yet, I felt the skin on my thigh open. I willed my legs to climb up the ladder but his companions got within shooting distance and were just taking their time to get closer so they wouldn't miss. I was going to be shot, and then the vessel's strength would not be able to hold on to the ladder and I would fall down to the ground. If I was lucky I would get run over by the truck and be done for the fast way.

The burly rider aimed his spear again just as his chest exploded and he flew backwards from the saddle. I turned my head to see Brak, white as death, leaning from the roof hatch, aiming the truck's heavy gun. He shot three more times, single cannon-like bullets that flew above my head and missed, but they were enough of a threat to make the riders veer away and hide behind the bulk of the moving truck.

Trevil manoeuvred the truck to a road close enough to a mountain ridge to make it hard for riders to pass us. When I looked up the machine gun was still there but Brak was gone from the hatch, and it was up to me to decide whether to climb up and try to get inside the cabin through the open hatch or inch my way back to the passenger's door, open it slightly, and get in. I chose the scenic route, finding out on the way that we were driving down the mountain to the valley below, moving between a mountainside and a deadly drop. The riders were still behind the truck, and they were nothing if not persistent. I turned to lower myself into the cabin. My feet were just touching the top of the seat when two raiders, a man and a woman, managed to climb on top of the truck. With only my toes touching, I balanced myself on the seat and grasped the machine gun. It was very heavy, held down by chains, and clumsy to wield. The recoil from the first shot almost threw me off balance, but it blew the leg off one of the climbers. The other one could have rushed me then, but she panicked and retreated to the back of the truck, climbing down. There was a loud banging noise as they tried to open the truck's haul doors while riding behind us.

My legs were trembling. I looked down at the cabin. Trevil was still behind the wheel, his shirt crimson with blood, but Brak was worse. He was lying underneath me with his eyes closed. Right then we were relatively safe, but once we were back on open ground things would change.

"Trevil, is there a way to open your haul door?" I shouted.

He shook his head stubbornly. "No way," he shouted back. "Fuck those naturalists."

"I can't treat Brak and hold the machine gun."

Trevil glanced back at Brak and swore loudly. He reached down and pulled a lever, and I immediately felt the truck tremble as the haul's doors folded upwards. A moment later the entire haul tilted upwards and I heard the noise of metal sliding down and spilling onto the road behind us.

When we moved a little farther away I saw that the riders had stopped pursuing us and were gathering around the metal we dropped. It was useless and stupid to shoot at them anymore, but I can't say I wasn't tempted to do just that. I lowered myself down carefully and Trevil pulled another lever, causing the chains all around us to move as the heavy gun was pulled back into the cabin. I was already next to Brak when the hatch closed. His breathing was shallow, and the wound on his pelvic bone was a mess. I'd seen worse—hell, I'd been wounded worse—but I knew that these kinds of wounds in the field were either treated immediately and by sophisticated medicine or the person died.

I looked around. "Trevil, do you have anything I could help him with? This does not look good."

"There's a medicine bag in the back of the truck under those blankets." He guided me as I moved about the shaking cabin until I found a large satchel and rummaged through it. I did not expect to find a cell regenerator, but I was hoping to find a skin patcher, or at the very least an antibleeding salve, the sort almost every human soldier used to carry. All I found were some brown cloth bandages, an alarmingly thick needle and thread, and a bunch of leaves.

"I can't do anything with this!" I said to Trevil. "He's going to die if we don't stop the bleeding."

"Can you drive the truck?" he shouted back.

I looked at the wheel, pedals, and levers and said, "I could try."

"Then take the wheel from me." He pointed at the pedal below. "Here you accelerate, not that it will go any faster, and here, the other one is the brake. Push it too hard and we will skid and probably roll off this mountain, so just try to steer it steady."

We quickly changed places and Trevil disappeared behind the front seat. I had to fold one leg underneath myself to be able to see through the front windshield and quickly discovered the steering wheel had at least a two-second delay, but it was better than trying to patch a hole in a human being with only a broken needle while inside a rocking cabin. I heard Brak moan behind me, then shout in agony as Trevil tried to stop the bleeding and stitch the wound closed under less than ideal circumstances. Eventually Brak fell silent, and I was hoping he just passed out.

By the time we reached the plains I was barely holding myself awake and had been suffering from tunnel vision. Trevil's head popped up from behind the seat.

"How's he doing?" I asked, but Trevil did not answer. His expression betrayed desperate resolution.

"Let me drive again. No, don't stop, we need the truck's momentum, we'll change places the way we did before."

When the manoeuvre was complete I looked at Brak lying behind us. His pelvis wound was wrapped in cloth, and I could see some dried leaves sticking out from beneath it.

I turned back and inspected Trevil's arm wound. "This needs treatment, too."

With his teeth and my help Trevil ripped the bloodied cloth of his sleeve and I wrapped it around the wound, then I collapsed back onto my seat. The pounding in my head grew and fog surrounded my vision. I had exerted my vessel to its limit and possibly beyond. It was time to pay the price.

I heard Trevil ask me something but his words didn't register. "I'm sorry," I said, or mumbled, or whispered, "I need to rest."

And then the world went dark.

11

Twinkle Eyes

Riding double bareback on a horse trying to hold on to Galinak began as an unpleasant experience and quickly went downhill from there. At least the animal was docile enough, and we had water and a few supplies to get us to where we wanted to go. Or more truthfully, where *I* wanted us to go. I kept our destination from Galinak despite the periodic bouts of questions from him, mainly because I wasn't sure what we'd find when we got there but also, I admit, because I wanted to keep some cards close to my chest.

What I couldn't hide was the fact that we were riding away from the City of Towers, the place Galinak was eager to travel to once I foolishly admitted it was within my sight. I was surprised to find out how quickly the warrior accepted the fact that we were resurrected and simply saw it as a chance for a new life—or, to be more precise, a dramatic comeback to his old life and damn the consequences. This led to several heated arguments between us, but for some reason he still humoured me instead of doing what I would have done, which was to simply throw me off the horse and ride away. I knew that

Galinak felt he owed me—he'd told me that himself—but I was not about to trust words or promises uttered while we were finishing our second bottle of moonshine. Three years was not a long time, but Galinak could suddenly decide to live the rest of his short life as a free man. This very concern led me to volunteer for long watch shifts at night, with the perfect excuse that my sight would make me better suited for the job.

If Galinak realised my fear, he did not bother to reassure me. He used his extended rest time to carefully trim his growing beard and to shave both sides of his skull with a thin folding blade he found at the village. It left him with only a thin strip of hair on the top of his skull—a strange look, yet one that nevertheless felt comfortably appropriate.

We crossed several roads and two streams without meeting a living soul. It was not unusual: most of humanity clustered around the Tarakan freeway or roads, and what was once a land full of towns and fields quickly became wilderness. Animals were certainly roaming about, though, and Galinak managed to kill a rabbit with a well-aimed—or, if you ask me, a lucky throw of—a fist-sized stone. We avoided a lightly wooded area after finding still-steamy signs of bear activity and camped one night in the remains of a tall building made of stone and warped metal. I could not have guessed its use, but it was the only man-made structure still standing amid the mounds of rubble.

My sleep was shallow, and the last moment of my previous life was the only surviving memory from my fleeting dreams. Still, I kept our course, riding in the opposite direction of the City of Towers.

On the fourth day we reached our destination, a wire gate no one had bothered to loot with three metal signs so faded one could barely recognise the skull signs on them. If there ever was a wall or a fence on both sides of the gate, it was long gone. The fields in front of us were filled with metal debris. In the distance a tower loomed, surrounded by several large buildings.

Galinak whistled. "Look at that little treasure trove." He urged the horse forward.

"Stop." There was enough alarm in my voice to make the horse halt by itself.

Galinak managed not to fall off the horse's back but he was not happy. "Bukra's balls, what are you doing?"

"Don't cross the gate."

Galinak glared back at me, waiting for me to explain myself.

"Look there, and there . . ." I pointed. "See the large holes in the ground?"

He followed my finger and nodded.

"It's an old minefield, pre-Catastrophe."

"Rust. We found some of those in some deep runs back in the day." Galinak's expression betrayed the surprise of a surfacing memory. He shook it away and said, "So, what now, use your eyes to cross it?"

I shook my head. "Now we build up a fire, a big one. There's plenty of dry wood around."

We dismounted and Galinak gave me the reins to the horse. "Okay, we build a fire, then what?"

"We wait, someone will come."

He looked at me long enough for me to feel uncomfortable.

"Do you know what you're doing?" he finally asked.

"Yeah," I lied, but it came out convincingly enough.

"Good. Don't get us killed. I'm starting to like this new body."

We camped and waited. I stopped Galinak from exploring the grounds, so there was no food. We sat in silence, feeding the flames until darkness set, then we let the fire die and let the darkness and the cold slowly envelop us.

I saw them first, of course. Four men, armed with power rifles and wearing night-seeing devices over their eyes, and a dog so large it might have been a wolf.

"They're coming," I said in the most casual tone I could muster. "Get ready, but don't do anything stupid, even if they are aggressive."

Galinak got up and stood behind me and we both laid our weapons on the ground and at my instruction, proceeded to wrap strips of my old dress around our eyes. The darkness, the real darkness of the blind, made my heart race.

"You'd better be rusting sure about this," Galinak whispered. I felt the horse's breath on my neck.

"You there, who are you?" came a shout, not too far, but still a distance away.

"We are here to talk to Old Dwaine," I shouted back.

"Are you merchants?"

There was no point in lying, "No, we just need to talk to Old Dw—"

"Old Dwaine's dead'n buried with the mines." There was the distinct sound of a power weapon charging.

"Oh, rust," Galinak breathed.

"Don't take your blindfold down, don't move," I whispered through tight lips.

"Then I need to talk to his . . . son," I shouted back, my mind racing. What did my LoreMaster tell me? The memory was there, a conversation, before we parted, but I couldn't remember all of it.

"Oh yeah? What's his name?"

I swallowed. "Look . . . our weapons are on the ground . . . we came to parley . . . we knew Old Dwaine," I tried.

"Then what's his son's name?" I could *feel* the muzzle of the weapon training itself on me.

What did I know about them? One extended family. Holed up. Secluders. Firstborn son's name would be . . .

"His name is . . . Dwaine Junior?"

I hoped the question in my sentence was not apparent but I distinctly heard Galinak curse under his breath again.

There was a brief pause, then a voice from a different direction spoke.

"Someone will come pick up your weapons and check the blindfolds, then he will give you a rope. Hold on to the rope and don't let go if you want to live. You with the horse, if the beast runs away don't go chasing after it, this whole area is full of explosives and only we know the way."

They took us in a roundabout way, that was for sure, and I breathed an audible sigh of relief when I felt man-made, solid ground under my feet. As we were led farther on, still blindfolded, I used the time to dig into my foggy memory for my LoreMaster's words of caution that all secluders were self-sufficient and hostile to outsiders. I was beginning to doubt that my idea was a good one.

When rough hands took my blindfold off my doubts grew to near certainty. Both Galinak and I instinctively raised our hands in the air. We were in a huge indoor building, surrounded by almost two dozen men and several women dressed in tattered grey uniforms. Several generations of low hygiene and probably inbreeding were showing. Most of them had one deformity or another, but that did not stop them from pointing a rich array of firearms at us. The weapons seemed like top-notch, pre-Catastrophe stuff, but that was not what made Galinak whistle softly. Just behind the circle of hostile secluders stood a dozen metal vehicles, shaped roughly like birds with rigid wings spread wide, their metal gleaming and spotless. There was no mistake that these were Sky Birds. In the old days people ruled the skies, and sometimes each other, by flying them.

"You two."

A voice caused me to turn my head and face the elevated dais. A man was sitting on a throne of some sort, but it was not made of gold or any kind of metal I recognised. The man, who I assumed was Dwaine Junior, was wearing a large helmet on his head which covered most of his face except his mouth and jawline. When he stood up I saw he was clad in some kind of body suit. Standing on either side of him were a wizened old woman and a young man, just out of adolescence. The woman was leaning heavily on a cane while the boy was having difficulty standing because he was holding too many weapons for me to count.

"You two," the man on the dais bellowed dramatically for the second time, gesturing with his gloved hands, "have intruded on Skygate. Be judged by Dwaine, son of Dwaine."

"Let them walk the field," someone shouted from behind us, and there were several murmurs of approval. "Yeah, trespassers be gone, let them be judged."

I bowed deeply to the man on the dais as the noise around us subsided.

"Dwaine, son of Dwaine," I began slowly, articulating every word. "I was sent here by LoreMaster Harim. He and your father were bonded in friendship and blood." I waited for some response but Dwaine Junior's face was blank. "Like I said," I added, trying to fill the dangerous silence, "my master left something for me here . . . in the safekeeping of your father . . . for me to . . ."

"He lies." The boy by the dais stepped forward and pointed a shoulder missile launcher at us. "I say we let the trespassers walk the field."

There was a quick cheer, so I couldn't hear what the woman whispered to Dwaine, but the boy was waved by his father to step back. When the noise subsided Dwaine said, "You step on the holy grounds of Skygate, claiming a blood bond between your master and my father, Dwaine, son of Dwaine the guardian, father of us all. The traveller Harim is known to us, and was allowed to pass, guided through the fields, but how do we know your words are true? Tell us, what did this master of yours leave here for you?"

The dismayed look on my face must have been plain to see as I stuttered my reply. "I do not know precisely oh . . . Dwaine . . . son of Dwaine . . . but I know they are essential to my mission, and that my master—"

During the commotion that erupted a stone was thrown and hit my back. Galinak was wise enough to stay still. But shortly after, he swore and threw a man who tried to seize him. The man hit the ground far enough from where we stood for people to withdraw. Things cooled down a bit after that, but weapons were still raised and people still took aim. It was then the old woman banged her walking stick on the dais. In the silence that followed the woman gave a short speech. I recognised only a few words; the rest was a mixture of piercing wails and dialect. When it was over I looked at Dwaine. "I'm sorry, I didn't manage to get all of that."

Dwaine's mouth twisted in a knowing smile. "What Nana Dwaine is saying, is that we'll very soon know the truth."

12

Peach

Wake up, Peach." The splash of water hit my face a moment later and I was up, breathing hard and trying to stop the world from spinning.

It was pitch-dark outside but for the truck's floodlights. The cabin itself was lit only by a dim red lamp. I turned my head to look at Trevil, then looked in the opposite direction. Brak was in the shadows, perched against the cabin's wall and the backseat. His head was slumped backwards.

"Is he alive?" It wasn't the most sensitive of questions, but it needed to be asked.

"Brak's a warrior. He'll pull through." I couldn't see his expression but there was desperation in Trevil's voice, as if he was trying to convince himself. "He woke up for a while but now you see him . . . You'll need to change his bandage and put on some fresh leaves."

I turned around to climb over the seat but he stopped me with a thrust of his hand, holding a water skin. "Drink first," he said.

The water was warm and slightly contaminated, but my vessel needed the nourishment.

"Thanks," I said.

"You saved us back there," Trevil said. "The way you moved could only be one thing." He nodded at me.

I did not know what he meant so I simply nodded back and climbed over to Brak.

"Give him some water, too," Trevil called after me. I managed to put the water skin into Brak's mouth, but a lot of the water I pumped with my hands spilled out. Brak was barely conscious, and Trevil had tied a rope under his armpits and secured it to a hook so he would not fall over during the drive. He was running a high fever, and I placed a wet cloth on his brow. Changing the bandages was a messy ordeal, but at least we were driving on even ground. I got a good look at the wound and grimaced. I was no field medic, but by my estimate, Brak was not going to make it without serious surgery and some modern treatment.

"Trevil," I said, as kindly as I could. "We need to get Brak some help or he'll die."

"I know, we're almost there." Trevil leaned a little into the steering wheel, as if that would make the truck drive faster.

Looking out for the first time I realised we were no longer in the fields but driving through a ruined city.

"Where are we?"

"Changed course. There is a Mender here, one of your kind."

"My kind?" I was careful with my tone of voice.

Trevil turned his head to me slightly. "I saw you move when we fought them naturalists. No ordinary man or woman moves like that. You are marked, tattooed, cursed, whatever they call you. That's why you want to go to the City of Towers, to be with your kind."

There was nothing I could say further that would not betray my ignorance, so I turned my head and watched us drive through what were once wide streets filled with people, now empty and ruined.

"This place is . . . unclean," I said, using terms I was hoping Trevil could understand. "There is poison in the air. If we stay here too long, we would get sick."

"I know." Trevil turned the truck around a corner, and Brak moaned as his body leaned heavily against the rope. "But the Healer lives here, in the middle of the city."

"That's . . . illogical."

Trevil shook his head slightly but said nothing else. In the silence that followed I drew my power sword and pushed the button. Nothing happened.

"You'll need a new power clip for that thing," Trevil said.

"It's powered by the sun, but it died on me during the fight. Maybe something got damaged." I tried to pry the hilt guard free so I could see inside but it didn't budge.

"Better find a Gadgetier in the City of Towers," Trevil suggested, then added, "Surely you've heard of one of those, they are also of your kind. Where do you come from, Peach?"

I sighed. "From too far away, it seems."

"Gadgetiers are marked who can work with Tarakan technology. You could bring it to a Tinker—they are the unmarked but they deal with Tarakan stuff, too. They'll be cheaper but some of them are hacks."

Hacks, I thought to myself, *that's an old word. Amazing what is gone and what lingers.* "And where can I find this Gadgetier?"

"Regeneration, City of Towers, or, if you're lucky, you'll run into one in one of the surrounding villages, those which are friendly to the marked, and not a lot of them are. There used to be a lot of Gadgetiers in Tarakan Valley, but no one goes there anymore."

Brak groaned softly. I put a steadying hand on his middle, but there was nothing I could do anymore. "Why is that?" I asked out loud.

Trevil shrugged. "Dunno, heard there was trouble and now the place is filled with Lizardmen."

"Lizardmen?"

"Yeah, I know, the guy who told me this was solid, though. I've never seen a Lizardman myself. I'll believe it when I see it." He pulled over and stopped the truck next to a high wall.

"We're here. Leave your metal here. I mean all of it, even the sword. Don't worry, no one steals in this place."

"Are you sure?" I asked, looking around. The street was dark, full of ruined buildings and a few warped trees. Instead of answering, Trevil shoved his gun under his seat, removed his belt and knife, and even took out several bullets from his pocket. I followed his example.

Once we managed to get Brak out of the truck I noticed the wall we parked next to was made of a mixture of piled stone and wooden planks. We carried Brak to a small door with a bell hanging next to it. There were three simple stretchers leaning against the wall, just two pieces of wood and rough ropes tied among them. We lowered Brak onto a stretcher and Trevil pulled the bell until a spyhole latch opened and someone asked, "Yay? Whose in'it?"

"It's an emergency, a bullet wound." Trevil pointed at his own pelvis to emphasize where the bullet hit Brak. "We need the Healer."

The eye looked down at the stretcher and the latch closed. A moment later the door opened and four men came out, all naked but for a loincloth and a wide leather belt. The first man had a torch in his hand, and on a closer examination I could see he wore a pair of odd earrings made of what seemed to be small human bones.

"Please, hurry," Trevil pleaded.

The man inspected Trevil, then me. "Would ya be pay da price given?" His accent was thick and I could not place it, but Trevil seemed to understand him.

"Aye," he answered as two men lifted the stretcher. "I will, whatever the Healer would ask for."

"Ney be coin, only kind," the man insisted. "Price be steep, but fair."

Trevil bowed slightly. "Whatever the Healer wishes, on my word."

"Take da Patshin to the third hut," the man ordered, and his subordinates quickly moved through the door.

Trevil began walking after them but the man blocked our way. "You be carry gun or coin? Nay metal in'ere is Healer's law."

"We carry no metal," Trevil turned his head and looked at me, searching for a sign that his words were true and when I blinked and nodded at him, he added, "We left it all in the truck."

The man nodded. "Then you be follow me, wash and change ya wear before ya stand with da Healer."

Trevil looked as if he was going to argue but thought better of it. We followed the man inside to a small brick building, where we removed our clothes and washed ourselves with a rough brush and a bucket of water. There was no separation between the sexes and we both had to change and wash together with only an oil lamp lighting the centre of the room. I got a glimpse of Trevil's body. I am an older woman by any account, but I had to admit I was impressed. He was tall, lean, and muscular, not a gram of fat on him, the sort of body chiseled by harsh living. In Tarakan people only bought or medicined such a body.

He did not bother to glance at me, though, which was lucky because he would have noticed I had no markings of any kind on my skin. The man came back, removed his own clothes, and led us, naked, through a long steam room so hot it was hard to breathe. Trevil walked before me, too anxious and preoccupied to notice me at all.

At the end of the steam bath another bucket of cold water waited for us together with clothes made of blue canvas, which felt rough on my vessel's skin. I only had a rope belt to tie around the waist. The clothes were the same size for myself and Trevil, so mine almost touched the floor and Trevil's were almost indecently short.

"We stabilized da Patshin," the man intoned. "He be ready, and you be too. Da Healer be coming to treat soon, and you be ready to pay."

He led us out of the building, picking up a fresh torch from a designated holder. Even in the middle of the night, everything felt in order, like a well-run hospital. The main building was imposing even though it was only two floors high. I figured by the old, grand architecture that it was probably much bigger once, maybe used as a life centre, filled with gaming rooms, bars, and music clubs, which was what buildings like this usually turned into long ago, when shopping malls became obsolete. A lot of it was now patched up, though a bit more carefully than the outer wall.

The outer area was dotted with large huts, each clearly marked with a number painted in red on all walls. The ground itself was soft cut grass and there were even flowers and cultivated bushes everywhere. As the wind changed, my vessel's heightened senses detected the noise and faint stench of livestock, and there was also what looked like a large greenhouse on one side of the grounds. It felt like civilisation here was desperately holding on to the corpse that was postwar humanity. Somehow it made me feel better.

When we reached the hut marked three, it was bustling with activity. Two women came out, one holding Brak's torn clothes and another a pile of his bloodied bandages. Two torches were burning on each side of the door, and four seminaked men were busy lighting small candles on each side of the road, all the way back to the main building.

A man dressed in a white sheet, a cap, and a face mask came out of the hut. His attire was stained red as well. He took his face mask off, leaned over, and whispered something in our guide's ear. The man nodded and turned to us.

"Da Patshin lives, but just so," he said in the same accent as the torch-bearing man. "We stop da blood coming but bones are broken and blood seeps inside. He be weak now. Only Healer could help or he be gone to the great dark by morning, no later."

So this was it? No modern medical treatment, emergency medifield equipment, or even real doctors, just voodoo nonsense. Brak was done for. I kept my mouth shut though, there was no point in commenting, criticizing or drawing attention to myself. Maybe I could convince Trevil to drive me to the City of Towers once Brak died. Worst case, I'd have to steal the truck, or kidnap and use Trevil as an unwilling guide.

The torch-bearing man nodded to his colleague, who bowed and departed quickly, then led us into the hut.

It was lit by several dozen thick candles. Brak was laid on a table and was covered by a canvas blanket. He looked no better than when we moved him out of the truck.

"Brak." Trevil tried to walk towards the table, his hand outstretched, but the man grasped Trevil by the arm as two others moved quickly to block his way.

"No touching da Patshin," he ordered. "You stand in da far place." He pointed at the corner. "No touching da Healer too, understand?"

Trevil took a steadying breath and nodded, visibly controlling his frustration as we walked to our designated place. Excluding Brak and us, there were four other men and three women in the hut, which made it crowded. I touched Trevil's arm for reassurance, and he looked down at me for the first time since we entered the premises. His face was flushed with anxiety. *He loves him,* I thought as I stroked his arm, a show of compassion meant to establish an emotional bond between us—or at least that was what my training told me was the right thing to do.

"Don't worry." I said the words that Trevil had said to me back in the truck. "Brak's a warrior, he'll pull through."

Trevil smiled weakly and patted my hand gently.

Good. Trust will make things easier later.

A slow drum beat began, and everyone in the room went down on their knees and faced the door. Trevil and I quickly did the same. The sound of singing came from outside, male and female voices in beautiful harmony, changing chords with the slow beat. At first, it was just a hymn I recognised, an old melody with certain religious roots. If my vessel had a brain amp I could have known its exact origins. As the choir walked closer to the door, words were added and the volume of their singing gradually increased with every sentence.

Praise da Healer, Praise da Healer
Praise him so, for he is no darkness
Praise him so for he brings light
Pay the Healer with your love
Pay da Healer with your life

The chorus repeated the words several times, and the song crescendoed as the door opened. A dark-skinned man wearing a thin white robe stood at the door. Everyone in the hut bowed deeply, touching their foreheads to the floor, and we followed their example. When I rose back to my knees I saw that the man's face and legs were covered in black spots, which on second glance proved to be something more than sunspots or some kind of skin disease. There was something a bit too orderly about them. The shapes were unnatural, almost geometrical, meaning this voodoo healer must have tattooed his entire body. Behind him, outside the hut, stood the choir, each man and woman holding a candle in both hands. Many of them bore the mark of long exposure to a contaminated environment. Some even had peeling skin, exposed raw flesh, the sort of damage that would normally cause excruciating pain, but they all stood there, singing.

The effect of the torches and candles was like a halo of light coming from behind the man, and that, I had to admit, was quite impressive. The man opened his robe and let it fall behind him, leaving him completely naked and unashamed. I noticed that his testicles were either missing or too small to detect. He was otherwise whole, with those strange black marks covering the entirety of his incredibly thin body.

Everyone rose to their feet and bowed again as the naked man walked to the table. Two men took the canvas covering off Brak's body and I saw Trevil grimace. The wound, although clean, was ugly, and blood was dripping from it.

The naked man bowed his head and touched Brak's body with both hands. He grimaced in a show of pain.

Nothing more than an act, I thought. *What did I get myself involved in?*

"Da man bears metal in his flesh and poison in his blood. He is close to darkness," the naked man intoned in a croak. "Darkness wants him, he belongs to it now. Who wants me to bring this man to da light?"

"I wish so, Healer," Trevil bowed stiffly as the naked man turned his attention to us.

The naked Healer turned and walked towards Trevil. "And who might you be to the man to bring him back from darkness? Who begs me to take upon me another's pain?"

"His name is Brak, and I'm his cousin," Trevil said.

But the naked man shook his head. "You are no blood of his blood. Your words not ring true. Lies lie in darkness. Only truth brings back to life."

"We are not blood," Trevil admitted, and immediately the attitude in the room changed. My guess was that lying to the man calling himself Healer was not a light offence. Perhaps that was his way out of curing the incurable, to save face in front of his fanatical followers, and if that was the case, my own troubles just got worse.

The torch-bearing man stepped forward to intervene. "No lie brings life," he said in a harsh voice. "Da Healer shall not—"

But the naked Healer silenced him with a hand gesture; his brown and almost freakishly large eyes were on me.

"And who ya be?" he said.

"A traveller, from afar," I answered as vaguely as I could. This was not technically a lie. The naked man seemed to forget Brak altogether. He stepped closer to me, and I fought the urge to enter a battle stance. I let him get close until he reached out and touched my chin, his hand uncomfortably warm. I stood motionless as he manipulated my head right and left, standing so close to me I could smell the stench of his breath.

"Your clothes be off," he ordered. I saw several of his men tense in anticipation of a refusal. *This is just a vessel,* I reminded myself as I undid the rope belt and let the crude material slip off my shoulders, but the next thought that flashed through my mind was, *But it's the only one I've got.*

This time Trevil did notice I was unmarked. I saw him register it, but he was too worried about Brak to react.

The naked man scrutinized me. Strangely enough, I interpreted the expression on his face as a mixture of curiosity, disbelief, and even fear, not lust.

"You are a woman from a different life?" There was a question in his tone of voice, as if he was trying to confirm something.

I nodded, trying to hide my surprise.

"You are a woman of many skins?"

I looked around the room. Naked and weaponless, my chances were slim even with ESM. I could take their Healer prisoner, but I'd need Trevil to cooperate and leave Brak to die. That was not going to happen.

I nodded again, and watched the naked man take a hasty step back, his expression betraying shock, even fear. One of his men took a protective step forward but the Healer motioned him to stand and turned to Brak.

"I take this Patshin back to light, if he be willin," he said, "but you shall both pay steep"—he motioned to Brak—"for he be close to darkness."

Trevil stood stiffly, but he might as well have been on his knees again. "I can't speak for her, but you can take everything I have, the truck, my weapons . . ."

The naked Healer shook his head once. "No metal, it is forbidden, you pay with kind and service, and I tell ya what price by the morrow."

Behind the Healer's shoulder I saw the man with the bone earrings looking surprised at this. My guess was this was not the way things were normally handled. Two things I knew for sure: I was not going to agree to serve this strange naked man and his cult for any length of time, but I was not about to declare my intentions at this particular moment. If Brak would die, as he surely would, I would most likely be free to go. If he somehow survived the night, I would make sure to be dressed and armed before I'd deal with the situation. The best course of action at that moment was just to stand there and let things play out.

Trevil looked at me briefly and I shrugged my consent. "I agree," he said, and the Healer turned and walked to Brak's body.

The choir outside was humming as we gathered around the body and placed our arms on one another's shoulders. I had no time to retrieve my clothes, but no one paid any attention to my nakedness.

The Healer touched Brak's body and a moan came out of him, echoed by the Healer's own moan of mock pain.

"He be far gone into darkness," he said as the men and women began to hum in unison, "far from where pain be. I must take his burden." The Healer began rubbing Brak's body with his hands. "I must take his pain." His hands touched the open wound and Brak arched himself up off the table suddenly, crying with pain. The Healer joined the cry with his own and arched his back as the hum grew louder. I turned my head and saw Trevil's eyes widen with fear.

"I must take his wound." The Healer placed both hands right on the wound, and Brak's body began to convulse so violently two men had to rush forward and hold him down. Two others grasped the Healer, who imitated Brak's movement while screaming in pain as he maintained pressure on the wound with both hands.

Suddenly something small fell from Brak's wound to the floor, and both Brak and the Healer screamed and arched their backs in unison once more. The Healer collapsed back into the arms of his followers while Brak's body lay still on the table. The chorus began singing loudly as the Healer's body was carried out by his followers. Trevil rushed to Brak's side, crying his name, and I was left standing alone, naked and bewildered as the people around me rushed to leave the hut. I took a step forward for a better look, and there was no denial of what I saw. Brak's wound was gone, not even a scar. I bent down and picked up what had fallen from the wound. It was covered with blood and distorted, but I had seen enough of them in my life as a soldier to recognise I was holding part of a bullet in my hand.

13

Twinkle Eyes

It was not a long walk, distance-wise, but surrounded by the hostile Dwaine clan, it took us a long time to reach the Sky Bird. Like the other machines, it was gleaming and spotless. My guess was that taking care of Sky Birds together with shooting trespassers were the Dwaine clan's favourite pastime.

This particular Sky Bird was huge—it dwarfed all the others by far—and I could not contain the awe it inspired as we stood next to its belly.

"Behold the holy Sky Bird," said Dwaine, son of Dwaine, waving his arms dramatically as Nana Dwaine limped closer to the metal body. "This is the Leviathan. Your LoreMaster came here, and he and my da walked into the belly of the Leviathan, so he must have left whatever you are looking for right inside."

Nana Dwaine wailed something unrecognisable as she uncovered a keypad at the lower side of the Sky Bird. "All you need to do is to know the password for the door," Dwaine said as he ushered me forward. "If you type in the right numbers, the door shall be opened. If you type wrong . . ." Suddenly there was a handgun aiming at my head. Dwaine, son of Dwaine, looked at me from behind the muzzle. "I will give you one try."

I glanced at Galinak, but there were too many weapons trained on us for him to be able to do anything that would not result in our certain death. I turned my head back, fighting the rising panic, and a bowel-loosening feeling in my stomach. The numbers on the keypad flashed green. There were eight empty slots sketched above them. I remembered reading somewhere, in my past life, that there were a hundred million possibilities for such a code, and now I had to guess the right code the first time, or die.

I closed my eyes and tried to block out the situation we were in. What would be a code that LoreMaster Harim would have chosen? The eight digits hinted it was a specific date, as was counted by humans in the pre-Catastrophe era. Two for month, two for days, four for a year. The counting of the years was forgotten by many after the Catastrophe, but the Guild of Historians kept the old tradition. The big question was which date my LoreMaster would choose as a code. A birthday? A death day? Or maybe it was just a random combination of numbers, in which case my brain would soon be decorating the shining metal side of the Sky Bird.

As if on cue, Dwaine, son of Dwaine, pushed the muzzle of his gun into the back of my skull. I opened my eyes and exhaled. With a trembling hand I reached the keypad. If LoreMaster Harim truly meant for this place to be visited only by other members of the Guild of Historians, then the code should be somehow known to them. I could think of only one such date. I entered two digits, 12, then the next two, 11, and committed to the decision I had made, punched 2247.

There was a loud buzzing sound and the belly of the Leviathan lowered its hatch down towards us. The demeanour of the Dwaine clan changed immediately. Nana Dwaine clapped her hands together and shrieked in approval and her son holstered the gun, although he did not look pleased about it. All around us weapons were lowered and even stowed back in their holsters, and Galinak was allowed to join me.

"I thought we were goners," he muttered out of the corner of his mouth.

"Yeah, lucky I remembered the exact date of the Catastrophe."

"A bad day for humanity, but as it turns out, a good day for us."

I glanced at him as the door of the Sky Bird touched the ground next to our feet. He looked relieved, and I guess I was showing it as well.

Dwaine, son of Dwaine, stood next to me on my other side but to my surprise he did not step forward with us. I turned to him in question, but he shook his head in regret. "Da said not to go inside them Sky Birds until Grandpa Dwaine comes back from sky."

Galinak and I walked forward and into the belly of the Leviathan. When we cleared the landing, I found a lever with a drawing which clearly indicated its purpose, and turned it. The door began moving up. Galinak turned back, waved his hand and shouted, "We'll be back for dinner, hope you have stew." A few heartbeats later, we found ourselves in complete darkness, sealed within the belly of the Leviathan.

If I were to believe legends, long ago the metal Sky Birds ruled the skies, moving people and goods across the globe. It was hard to believe that a huge machine such as the Leviathan could reach the heavens, but whatever its original purpose, my LoreMaster Harim changed it into his personal haven. There was a cushy-looking reclining chair and a whole sitting corner with several oil lamps, which I found and lit for Galinak's sake, and a heavy wooden reading table. Books, scrolls, and pre-Catastrophe think pads were stored neatly in rows upon rows. I examined a few of the books briefly and found they were mostly copies made by scribes such as myself in the City of Towers. All my hours of copying manuscripts in the high towers suddenly made sense. LoreMaster Harim had taken measures to ensure that should the Guild of Historians' extensive library be destroyed, at least some of the knowledge it contained would survive. Yet we soon found out that books were not the only thing my LoreMaster stored in the Leviathan.

"Would you look at that!" Galinak exclaimed, waving the black garment in front of my face.

"SmartLeather. Adjusts itself to your body, complete with a torso brace, too. A power knife, and this . . ." He bent down and straightened back up, beaming with joy, holding a massive silver-coloured power machine gun.

"Old Harim knew his weapons, and there are at least ten power clips, three of them renewable." Galinak turned the weapon back and forth in front of his eyes, mesmerized.

"And look, SmartGlasses, what a classic." Galinak put the dark glasses over his eyes and looked around. "Yeah!"

I walked past him to the reading table, where a wooden box lay. It was not locked. Inside was a heavy coin bag, a letter, a pipe case with several vacuum-sealed tobacco cases, and an old-fashioned golden revolver complete with a leather hip holster and a clip belt.

"That's a nice peacemaker," Galinak said. "A little old-fashioned for my taste."

I waved the gun around, its heaviness and balance oddly re-assuring. It was made to look antique, and it was certainly not the most efficient weapon, but it was actual Tarakan steel and gleamed in my hand with a power clip that fired power shots. I was never a weapons kind of guy—actually, I was the opposite— but the moment I saw it, I knew I was going to keep that gun.

The letter I found on the desk was written in LoreMaster Harim's hand. Despite having been duped by him to go on a dangerous mission while unknowingly being used as a decoy, I felt a pang of loss in my heart. My old mentor gave up his life so we could escape to the Tarakan Valley and eventually venture deep into the City Within the Mountain. He would have loved every moment of it.

The letter simply said:

> *Dear guild brother,*
> *Take what you need from here as you see fit, but do your best*
> *to keep the knowledge stored here away from harm. The future*
> *of mankind lies within its past.*
> *LoreMaster Harim*

It wasn't much, but it was precise, just the way my LoreMaster liked it. I was momentarily flooded with memories of the man—how he took me from my family home, raised me in the towers to be a scribe, only to send me on a dangerous fool's errand to find Vincha and discover Rafik's fate. The last time we saw each other, LoreMaster Harim had elevated me to the rank of Associate LoreMaster of the Guild of Historians. The vivid memories stirred strong emotions, and by the time I came back to my senses, Galinak had finished looting the place.

There were other travelling garments hanging neatly in a corner, and I rummaged through them until I found the clothes which fit me best.

"Not bad." Galinak nodded his approval as he zipped up the SmartLeather suit. "But you'd better learn how to shoot with your new toy. It gives a mighty kick."

I tried to fast-draw from the hip and managed to tangle the gun in its holster. It dropped to the floor with a heavy *clank* and skidded towards Galinak, who bent over and retrieved it for me. I was hoping the darkness masked the redness on my face.

"Okay," he said as I shoved the gun back in its holster a bit too forcefully. "What now?"

I turned and walked deeper into the belly of the Leviathan, found a ladder and a hatch, and climbed up. Galinak followed me silently, hefting his new weapon onto his back and shoving a bag of nourishment pills into his belt. It didn't take us long to find the place where the drivers of the Sky Birds must have sat. There were two chairs that resembled Dwaine, son of Dwaine's throne. On top of them lay two bulky helmets. From the front windows I could see several of the other Sky Birds and a few of the Dwaine clan milling about. We sat down and I took the helmet in my hands, testing its weight.

"Are you gonna fly this thing?" Galinak placed his helmet on the floor and flapped his hands, mimicking a bird.

I looked at the vast array of darkened screens surrounding us.

"Rust no," I grunted. "I wouldn't even know where to start."

"So, what are we doing here then? We got weapons, pills, clothes, and some metal, I say we split before the Dwaines change their hospitality rules."

I shook my head. "There's one more thing I want to try. It is only logical that these machines have strong communication devices. Maybe we could reach out to the Tarkanians and get the briefing we missed."

Galinak did not look pleased. "Why the rust would we do that?"

I had no simple answer, so I simply gave him a meaningful glare. Surprisingly, it worked. Galinak shrugged and leaned back in his seat. "Suit yourself, but I ain't sure I want to follow orders no more. Last time I did they got me killed."

I had no argument against his logic, so I simply turned my attention back to the screens. They were more than an arm's reach away. I wondered how the driver could use them from so far back. I got up and walked towards the screens, eventually touching them. Nothing happened. There were no other levers or buttons to pull or push. I sat back down and tried the helmet on. It didn't fit immediately, but there was a complicated set of pulls and slides to adjust it. As soon as I managed to fasten it on my head there was a soft click and a hundred things happened all at once. The Sky Bird hummed to life, my seat expanded and fitted itself snuggly around my body, the screens around us lit up and projected themselves into arm's reach, and a semitransparent steering wheel materialised in front of me.

"Whoa." Galinak straightened up in his seat. "What's going on?"

"Put on the helmet," I said, gingerly touching the steering wheel. It felt solid in my hands.

The helmet's inner screen was disorienting as well. On the left side a constant stream of numbers and letters ran in front of my eyes, changing colours and speed as I moved my head around. On the right side I could see through the material of the Sky Bird. I knew it was not my own gift that allowed me to zoom in through the metal walls.

"Bukra's balls." Galinak somehow managed to deal with the helmet faster than I had. His hands moved around in the air, touching the screens hovering around him.

"Galinak, don't—" I said.

"Armed," a voice rang out in my head.

I turned my head sharply. On the left side of the screen a picture of the Leviathan's wing tip blinked red while on the right side I zoomed in on another Sky Bird on the far side of the tarmac.

"Locked." A red rectangle surrounded the Sky Bird I was looking at.

"—touch anything," I finished, but it was too late.

There was a swooshing sound in my ear and a heartbeat later the other Sky Bird blew up in a mushroom of fire.

We sat in silence for a while, not daring to move our heads or even blink. I reached under my chin and slowly unfastened the helmet. My surroundings winked out of existence.

"Rust," Galinak said, still wearing his. "The Dwaines ain't looking happy."

I closed my eyes and leaned back in my seat, which, surprisingly, reclined itself back so I was facing the ceiling.

"I have a feeling they won't give us some of their stew when we try to leave."

"You don't say," I murmured and shut my eyes, feeling suddenly overwhelmed and tired.

Galinak freed himself from his helmet. "What now?"

I kicked my new boots off my feet. "I need to rest a bit. I haven't slept right since, well, since I was born. The Dwaines are not going to shoot at us and they can't get in. I'm almost positive Dwaine is illiterate."

"And if he's not?"

I turned my head and looked meaningfully at Galinak's new machine gun. Taking the hint, he smiled back at me, picked up the heavy gun and turned his seat to face the doors behind us. "I'll take first watch, then?"

I didn't answer. A little later I was fast asleep.

14

Peach

A dream, but not a normal one, I knew. Finally, Command was reaching out to me, but I knew instinctively that this dream briefing was different than usual. An image of a woman came into view. She was a warrior by the way she stood, not young but still powerful. Red hair, and black markings around her neck and ears. She turned to me, drew a power gun, aimed, and fired. But as I flung myself to the side she changed into a young woman in her teens, dressed in a simple brown linen dress. Her hair was voluminous and red, and she had grey eyes, fair skin, and a strong body. She could have been stunning if it were not for a slightly wide chin. The warrior's younger self . . . no . . . her child . . . the warrior's child. The younger woman was my target, Emilija, and the mother was her protector.

I was lying in the mud and saw a name written, Vincha, before I rose slowly and realised I was standing in a field. From afar I could see the familiar silhouette of the City of Towers and my heart skipped a beat. Then a splash of muck stained my clothes as someone stepped over a puddle and walked past me. It was Vincha again, gun in hand, looking with open suspicion in all directions, but not seeing me or the shadows that surrounded her. I felt the urge to follow, saw her walking towards her daughter, who was standing with her back to us, oblivious, as shadows grew around her. The dream was telling me that there were others looking for the girl . . . but who? Before I could find out the answer the warrior jumped into the shadows and disappeared. The daughter remained, although she began to fade into the distance as bells began to ring. The image changed again into a fountain I recognised, and lastly into a bird which landed on a wide straw hat. It was a rendezvous point, a place where I would make contact.

I woke up to the sound of chimes, curled up on a thin rug that was spread on the floor. The dark chamber had no door, and I saw three people slowly passing the entrance as they walked the lit corridor, one holding a pot filled with burning incense and the two others playing delicate chimes. Turning on the rug, I surveyed the room. There was no one with me in the small, windowless chamber, empty of furniture save for several other hand-stitched rugs, a candle holder with a short stump of a candle in it, and a knee-high wooden table. As soon as I rose to a sitting position, three more men came in. Since I did not believe in coincidence, it was logical they were standing outside, waiting for me to wake up. One was carrying a bucket of water with one hand and a smaller, empty bucket in the other, another lit the candle in its holder and the third man was carrying a tray, which he placed on the small table. It contained a loaf of freshly baked bread, hard cheese, several vegetables and a covered plastic cup.

"Wash, use the empty bucket for yar needs, and eat," one of the men ordered, but not unkindly. "Then you shall cleanse and see da Healer." His accent did not come out as natural as the others', a little distorted, like he forced it upon himself. I made a mental note of this, even though it seemed to be of no importance.

"How is Brak doing? And Trevil, my companion?"

"See da Healer, then all will clear," the man said.

Both men stayed in the room as I took care of my vessel's bodily needs, and other people who passed the room could see me as well. Despite occupying a vessel, I had to remind myself of my time in the military in order to relax enough to relieve myself in front of strangers, a sign I was slowly merging with my new body. As soon as I was done one of the men carried the bucket away without a word. The food was simple, but after surviving on a severed leg, nourishment pills, and food scraps, it felt incredibly good. I took my time eating, savouring each and every bite. The vegetables looked fresh and the cup contained boiled water, still warm. Like everything else in this area, it was contaminated, but with a surprisingly low dosage considering where I was located.

As I ate I thought about the dream briefing I'd received. My mission was clear and the dream came exactly on time, a week after awakening, once my brain waves completely merged with the vessel, making deep sleep a possibility. Yet something felt wrong. On the one hand, only Tarakan Central Command had my unique brain patterns and the ability to send me dream sequences, which was good news. That meant that contrary to what I had heard so far, Tarakan had survived. Someone had woken me up, given me a body, and ordered me on a "find and retrieve" mission. It would have been a laughably easy assignment under normal circumstances, way under the level of my expertise or my rank, but in this new, broken world, without the help of satellites, global communication, facial and body recognition scanners, and the ability to reach any point on the globe within an hour, this simple mission felt like trying to find a needle in a haystack.

There were other things in the dream sequence that worried me. By my last few missions, a few of Tarakan's more advanced foes were already suspected of having the technology to pick up dream sequences, and as a result the dream should have been a little vaguer. This mission briefing felt like a parent pointing a child to a task, a gross breach of protocol, which could also be the result of all of Tarakan's enemies having been wiped out. The dream world should have also been richer, more immersive. This one lacked complexity and depth, reminding me of an old virtual reality game I had once tried in a museum, when you had to put a mask on your face in order to play instead of immersing your consciousness into the machine. Something was amiss. That I knew for sure.

Since there was no way I could solve my concerns regarding Central Command, I forced them aside and my thoughts shifted to last night's events as I chewed on a bitter radish. It was unlikely that the man calling himself "the Healer" had managed to hide a cell regenerator in his palm. Even the emergency combat version of it, used on the fields of battle, was the size of a human arm and took some time to function. Technology could have advanced forward as I hibernated, but it seemed improbable that Tarakan managed to minimize the size and accelerate the speed of the cell regenerator to such a degree. I went as far as considering that he was an Angel who had replaced his arms with medibot arms, but that was going too far.

Finally, I accepted the facts as I saw them; that this man somehow healed Brak, that he was worshipped by the men and women here, and that he had some kind of interest in me. His speech about the steep price was a matter of concern. Now that the orders of my mission were clear, I was not about to waste time or risk myself unnecessarily. I finished my meal with a drink from the cup, feeling its warmth course through my body. It was time to get some answers.

I rose and indicated to my guardian that I was ready. He led me through a short corridor dotted with doors leading into small side rooms, very much the same as the room I'd slept in. Most of them were empty; a few had groups of people sitting on floor mats, listening to preachers or meditating. We passed a chamber where a large group of people were busy having slow, ritualistic sex. There was a supervisor, or a teacher of some sort, standing above them as couples of both sexes copulated in a deliberately slow rhythm. My vessel was created with all the anatomical features of a human female and was able to have sex, of course, and I admit that walking among the writhing bodies did wake up some long-hibernated desires. Instead, I was steered towards a larger corridor leading outside, where I was taken again to the steam room and went through another process of cleansing. A pair of rope sandals and a long grey dress awaited me as I emerged. This time the clothing was made of linen, still a little rough on the skin, but a great improvement.

I was taken back to the main building and led up to the second floor. Surprisingly, there was no large hall, no high dais, or an adoring crowd. The only person in the medium-sized room was the man with the bone earrings. He bowed a little as a form of acknowledgement and gestured towards a rug. As in all the chambers I had seen in the building, this one had almost no furniture, with only a few comfortable cushions on the floor. I sat down on one of them, but before I got too comfortable the Healer came in and I rose to my feet. Instinctively, I decided not to bow this time.

The Healer was naked except for what looked like a bandage surrounding his pelvis, in the same place where Brak was wounded. He held a walking stick made of gnarled wood and limped slowly into the room, assisted by one of his four guards. *What a show,* I thought as I scrutinized his markings.

The Healer motioned for me to sit down, and he positioned himself slowly and with a theatrical grimace on a cushion next to me.

"How are you?" There was no better way to begin the conversation.

The Healer handed his walking stick to his aide and turned to me.

"Da Patshin is back in the light. My burden is a shadow of his. I heal by morrow." The Healer's eyes were large and brown, full of kindness, warmth, intelligence, and openness, tempting me to trust him. I was immediately on my guard.

"You mean you took Brak's wound upon yourself?"

"I see your eyes not believing." The Healer shook his head and gestured at his bandaged side. "I can show you his wound but you'd say I harmed myself."

"I just don't believe in miracles," I said in an even tone. "What

I saw definitely falls under that term, so I am looking for a logical explanation."

He smiled knowingly. "What is a miracle for one, is natural for another. The man called Trevil swears you move and fight like the marked"—he indicated the markings on his own body—"but we see no markings on you, and the man called Brak says so, too. Maybe you can do miracles, too?"

This time I found myself nodding in acknowledgement. The man had a point. There were many things I did not know.

"You are from far away, a different land and time. You do know of the marked, for you it is a miracle, but you were born not from a woman's womb, how that is not a miracle? The world is a miraculous place."

How did he know that? Despite my training I tensed on my seat.

The Healer held his marked hands up in a sign of peace. "Worry not, Miss Peach, I am here for da helping. Say what you need and if this is in my power, I will make it happen."

Things which were too good to be true were usually a lie, but if this man was willing to help me . . .

"I need to get to the City of Towers," I said, unwilling to expose the rest of my mission.

"Then da man called Trevil will pay da price of taking you there."

"And my own price? You said yesterday that the price is always steep."

"There is always a price," the Healer agreed, "but by helping you I pay a debt." The Healer put both of his hands on his heart. "My own debt."

"I don't understand."

"Hear my story, then." The man straightened on his pillow. "My first mark appeared when I was already seventeen, and it was not in an obvious place . . ." The Healer smiled for the first time, but it wasn't a pleasant smile. "It was actually discovered by someone else, the girl I was going to marry. I was twice a fool, to think our love would endure and to believe she would not betray me. I was seized the very next day and taken to the elder and he who put the knife to me." The Healer pointed at his crotch. "He cut the essence of my manhood. I was put in a cage and left outside da village, to heal or die. I wanted to die, but my body be strong even when my spirit be broken and the mark tainted my skin. On the fifth night, a man came and saved me, a special man. I be marked on my body, but he be marked on his soul. This man helped me heal, and his price was that I would help whenever you showed up at my door. He described you to me, said you will be moving like the marked and that you would bring death wherever you go."

"That is . . . impossible."

"Only for those who do not accept truth." The Healer indicated himself. "I can cure people and take their wounds on me. You can move like the wind without having a mark on your body, and the man who saved me foresaw that you would come here and ask me to help you. He told me that this would be the best of the foreseeable futures."

"Who was this prophet?" I asked.

The healer leaned over and whispered, "His name . . . was Nakamura."

15

Twinkle Eyes

It materialised out of the darkness, slowly and from afar, and I knew what it was even before it filled my entire field of vision. I have heard Vincha tell me about it in detail, even though she herself never saw it and only relayed Rafik's story secondhand. Nevertheless, here I was, standing, mesmerised, in front of a puzzle wall, or perhaps the Great Puzzle Wall Rafik had mentioned. Hundreds, no, thousands of strange symbols raced before my eyes in all directions. How someone, even a Puzzler, could find a pattern within this chaos was beyond me.

I reached out, my arm extending farther than my eyes could see, and stopped a symbol with my finger. It felt cool but vibrant. I extended my other arm and after several attempts and failures managed to stop a similar symbol, not the exact same, but close enough in resemblance.

Now what?

Symbols kept floating all around my hands, but I knew that if I let go of the ones I was holding I would lose them all.

Suddenly another symbol changed course, slowly moving to the one

I was holding and attaching itself to it with a mental click. Soon after another symbol moved on its own accord towards the three I was holding, as if someone else was helping me from beyond the wall. When the pattern was complete it shimmered and detached itself from the wall completely. The symbols spanned before me to create a metal double door. They slid apart and I stepped forward and into the chamber of the Leviathan. I saw Galinak sitting, examining his machine gun in his lap. He did not acknowledge me or look at the doors. My own body was lying motionless, but in this reality I was wearing the helmet. My transparent image drew closer to my body until we merged into one.

A little later I woke up.

Galinak turned his head towards me. Maybe he asked something, but I was already in the process of fastening the helmet on my head. Like waking up from a vivid dream, the images were slowly fading from my mind, and I had no idea how long they would linger.

The Leviathan sprang back to life, and I let my hands move and touch the transparent screens around me. Galinak put his own helmet on, but this time he took care not to touch anything.

We could both hear a hissing noise.

"What's that?" Galinak's voice rang inside my head as I somehow established a link between us.

"How long was I out?" I asked, more to keep him from distracting me with questions than anything else.

"Not long, but you were out cold. What are you doing?"

"Not sure, but I know what to do." I touched two transparent buttons and turned a dial.

"That is a contradi—"

The music caught both of us by surprise.

"Whoa." Galinak grabbed the seat with one hand. "What is that?"

"I think it is the music Rafik and Vincha used to listen to," I said, still fiddling with the numbers on my screen. "It's called Beethoven."

Galinak sat motionless for a while. "Rust," he finally muttered, "that was what we heard when Vincha was strapped to that chair. Rust, that half-man Jakov was a piece of work."

I nodded but kept fiddling with the buttons as the music grew louder. Jakov was the weapons merchant who had stolen Rafik and sold him to the Keenan guild. Years later he returned with us to the City Within the Mountain, hoping to reestablish a supply route, or perhaps looking for redemption. He got neither.

"I'm trying to find a way in," I said. "There is a pattern I need to latch on to and then we can establish a link with Tarakan, but I need to find the right channel. It involves delicate fine tuning."

"And you know how to do this because . . . ?"

I stopped myself from turning my head towards him. "I dreamt it. No, don't ask. Find out what is going on outside instead, but don't . . . touch . . . anything."

As the music grew louder Galinak turned his head left and right, seeing through the metal wall of the Leviathan. "They established a perimeter around us," he informed me, his voice growing into a shout as the music became almost unbearably loud. "Two snipers with long rifles on either side, the rest spread out. Guess they'll wait us out. Bukra's balls, how long is this gonna take?"

It took a lot of willpower not to throw the helmet off my head as the music got louder and louder.

"Getting there," I shouted back, but Galinak unfastened his own helmet and took it off his head.

Suddenly the music ceased and Rafik's face filled my field of vision.

"Hello," he said.

I leaned back in my seat and let out a long sigh.

Rafik nodded in approval. "You did well."

"Well? We did well?" My inner voice was rising with every word I uttered. "*We* woke up in a room filled with poisonous air and no idea what to do and where to go. You bet we did well, no thanks to you."

Rafik remained calm. "We did not expect such a malfunction

in transmitting you, but these things were bound to happen over time, even with Tarakan technology."

Galinak watched me solemnly. Without the helmet he could not hear the conversation.

I turned to him. "It's them," I whispered and motioned at his helmet.

"Rust 'em," he muttered. "I don't want to hear anything they have to say. You talk to them and tell me the gist of it afterwards. Besides, the Dwaines might find a way inside. Someone should take watch." He turned and left the cabin before I could react.

"Perhaps it was more than that?" I said to Rafik, turning back on my chair. "You told me this Mannes was dangerous. Maybe this was sabotage?"

"This is also a possibility within the realm of reason." When I did not respond Rafik added, "I see you got yourself some gear. That is good."

I could understand Galinak's reaction. We had been cheated by the Tarkanians, only to be forced to work for them again and almost be killed before we even started. Now we were stuck inside a Sky Bird, surrounded by the hostile Dwaines, and none of that seemed to register with Rafik. The whole situation was infuriating.

"We managed to reconstruct the vessel, or body, the hibernating agent was downloaded into," Rafik ploughed on.

A picture of a woman appeared in front of my eyes.

"Doesn't look like much," I commented without thinking.

"Don't let appearances fool you," Rafik admonished. "Luckily for *you*, this is not a full combat vessel, but Colonel Major Vera Geer is a veteran of many battles. She is one of our most experienced operatives, capable and dangerous, and she has a two-month head start on you.

"If Cain takes control and extracts the code from Emilija it would allow him even deeper access into Adam. There is no telling how much damage he could do, but it would be severe, perhaps even lethal."

"So, you want us to find Emilija and bring her back to you."

"And if at all possible, eliminate Mannes Holtz."

"If possible . . ." I stopped myself from pointlessly arguing. Instead, I changed the subject. "How did I know how to do"—I gestured all around us—"all of this? The dream, the puzzle wall . . ."

"When Tarakan began cloning agents, we used to grow their bodies filled with hardware, but it didn't take the others long to realise this and they began scanning for it. Hardware was too easy to spot. We needed a different method to send information to our operatives. One which did not involve detectable hardware."

"Dreams? You communicate in dreams?"

"Brain waves, thoughts, they are but a shot of neurons, an electric pulse. Too weak to be transmitted under normal conditions, but when biological humans sleep deeply enough, the brain becomes much more susceptible, and with some DNA manipulation and mental practice it could be a reliable, effective tool."

Rafik correctly interpreted my expression because he added, "No, we cannot read your minds, control your actions, or even send you complex orders. The subconscious cannot be fully controlled like that."

"So every time I want to talk to you I should find a bed?"

"No. This time you fell into a deep sleep with a definite problem on your mind. We were trying to find you and we managed to do just that, but it doesn't work every time. You should just be aware we may try to contact you. It is part of how you were made, how you are wired, so it might get easier with time."

"Rust," I cursed, it was almost too much to sink in. "What now?"

"Find Vincha's daughter. Your best course of action is to find Vincha herself and convince"—Rafik tilted his head slightly—"or coerce her to lead you to her daughter."

"You want me to look for Vincha *again*?" I couldn't help but laugh at the irony of it.

Rafik ignored my reaction. "Vincha is not in the City of Towers, and she does her best to reduce her communication presence, but from the few activities she was unable to cover, we believe she operates along a long stretch of a Tarakan highway, not too far from the city itself."

"It is still a very large area to look for a woman who does not want to be found."

Rafik's deep eyes found mine. "It's a good start."

"Galinak is not going to like this idea. Neither will Vincha, if we find her, to put it mildly."

Rafik's face didn't show any sign of sympathy as he said, "Deal with it as you need to, but bring the girl to us."

"Fine." I was getting tired of this. "Anything else? I need to deal with an angry Troll and an entire tribe of Secluders who are as pissed as hell."

"Actually, yes, there is more. Mannes had a personal log in his brain amp—all high-ranking Tarkanians used to have it. With all but the furthest communication devices down, it took a long time but we managed to reconstruct some of the data that was transmitted before it abruptly stopped. Only a severe head trauma or a very delicate medical operation could stop an amp from transmitting. That's why we concluded the man died but now we know he lived, so he must have found a way to physically remove the brain amp from his head."

"That must have been a painful experience."

"We deemed it improbable that anyone could survive such a process."

"But he did. Score two for this Mannes, if you count the Catastrophe as a win."

"You should watch this as long as we are in direct communication." Rafik's image began to blur slowly. "You should know who you are up against."

16

Mannes

Mannes stepped out of the air train's private cabin onto the platform of the arrival hall, masking the familiar mix of excitement and dread he felt under a blank expression and a pair of old fashioned, rimless black sunglasses. He checked his internal clock. It was 06:33, eleventh of December, 2247. He'd planned a short snooze on the way, but that hadn't happened, so a coffee or other stimulant was needed. The doors to the public cabins were just opening, so he quickly walked ahead of the rest of the passengers spilling out of the air train. He surveyed his surroundings impatiently as the Guardian Angel guard checked his credentials.

Facing the hulking guard always made him feel discomfort. He reminded himself again, it was actually an artificial fighting machine. The Guardian Angel's heightened senses must have picked up on Mannes's nervousness because he, or it, was taking a little longer than expected, checking his credentials again before pointing Mannes to the empty VIP aisle.

The people waiting in the public lanes, especially the couples and, in several noisy cases, the families, did not hide their excitement. Loud chatter blended into a thick blanket of mind-numbing noise and everyone, *everyone,* was posing for photos, using their ever-popular implanted thumb cameras.

He tried not to blame them. After all, for the vast majority of Tarkanians, a trip up the space elevator was a once-in-a-lifetime experience, and Mannes guessed he had already made several dozen ascensions this year alone. He did not need to guess the amount; by accessing his brain amp he could have found out the exact number of ascensions along with what he ate each day or the average number of steps he walked, but he chose not to bother. Lately he'd been avoiding accessing his brain amp altogether, using his phenomenal yet primitive tool of natural memory, a genetic gift from his ancestors. He wondered whether that precaution had raised suspicion somewhere and whether *that* was the real reason for this unscheduled, strange trip.

An involuntary shudder shot up Mannes's spine, and he shook his head before he could regain control of himself. Maybe something had gone wrong with the code. Maybe one of the thousands of Daichi's subroutines he had copied into the mainframe was clashing with the spinal program. Maybe . . .

No, everything is fine. Professor Vitor would have set this up through the normal channels and besides, the time for such clandestine operations is over. This is just what it is, Mannes, and you are being dangerously paranoid, so relax.

The line on the other side of the VIP lane was especially long, and despite himself Mannes felt a guilty pleasure walking past all the people. He felt their eyes watching him with a mixture of curiosity and envy. Who was he? Without consciously thinking about it, Mannes slowed his steps, squared his shoulders and raised his chin. He even tucked in what Deborah nicknamed "Daddy's cushion," as he marched through passport control and went underground and into the private bullet pod that would bring him directly into the base of Mount Iztaccihuatl. The tall, dormant volcano served as the base for the most expensive elevator in human history. Tarakan had permanently leased it from the bankrupt Mexican government. At the time the deal was criticised by many of its citizens, bonding together an odd mixture of Mexican nationalists and concerned environmentalists. The space elevator—or "Star Pillar," as the Tarakan advertising agency persisted in calling it—was now a fact, and the hundreds of thousands of demonstrators, terrorist threats, and international political shenanigans had diminished to a manageable problem.

Mannes stepped out of the bullet pod and had one last credential and DNA check before being ushered into the biocleansing area. Normal travellers were not allowed to bring anything into space. Most of them simply came with the blue or yellow disposable body suit that was readily available in almost any store. Once they passed security, everything from clothes to personal items and toys were destroyed and recycled. Mannes's VIP status gave him permission to carry the items he needed for work and also made it possible to store his clothes on Earth, but as usual he just chucked them away for recycling, choosing a simple traveller's outfit instead, spreading his hands while the machine measured him with quick efficiency. The tunic came out with the Tarakan emblem in silver and gold, marking his rank. He was always proud of his achievements and status, but now the emblem just reminded him how exposed he really was.

The rest of his personal belongings were already waiting for him outside the changing room after being thoroughly disinfected. Mannes was guided by a small flying bot to the executive elevator. It was not the kind of space one usually implied when using the word *elevator*—this was a spacious room lavishly decorated with antiques, with a beautiful oak writing table placed in front of a panoramic viewing wall. The top-of-the-line executive seat was comfortable, and he had to make an effort to feel or test the restraints that snaked around his body. Mannes declined the offer for a light meal but ordered coffee and, knowing his security status allowed it, turned on his personal pad. The newsline flashed up in front of his eyes as soon as he turned it on. The Mars accelerator project had hit another obstacle, and a new international board committee had to be assembled after several non-Tarkanian members had been arrested on suspicion of fraud. The rest of the news was just the usual crap. Another condemnation of Tarakan after a terrorist bio attack in Australia killed thirteen thousand and infected Sydney's water supply. Ridiculously, Tarakan was blamed for the atrocity, and despite strong denials by Central Command, the UN had released a formal condemnation. There were the usual calls for stronger boycotts by several enemy states, and all the while the Asian market kept plummeting, mass demonstrations were held in front of Tarakan embassies in several countries . . .

Mannes flipped the newsline away with a wave of his hand and brought up his inbox. There were forty-seven work-related messages and a private one from Deborah. She'd won the horse-riding contest—he knew that already, of course, had even snuck away from a meeting to watch the finals on a floating screen in his office—but to see his daughter smile and hear her voice rise with excitement as she told him the news herself, thinking he did not know, was priceless.

He ran the message three times, then sent her a return voice clip congratulating her on her well-deserved win. Perhaps because he was nervous, he chose to lightly admonish her for the slight decline in her overall grades. He knew she would be pissed off at him for that, and he knew he deserved it even as he uttered the words. His parting "Love you, D" came out too fast and perhaps too casual sounding. Sensing his discomfort, the pad asked twice whether he wanted to change the message, but Mannes just sighed and tapped the send button. Nothing bad ever happened from pushing your kid a little; it had certainly helped him.

He mentally logged a reminder to send a message to his parents when he returned. Even with his status, corresponding with them was not something he could have done from inside the space elevator. Security protocols would have blocked any contact to a declared enemy state such as the United Northern Alliance, but there were ways to bypass those restrictions in the privacy of his lab. Not that they had a lot to talk about; it was just his own sense of loyalty. Both his parents were getting old, and without Tarakan rejuvenation technology their mental and physical deterioration was making the calls tedious and emotionally draining. His father spoke to him like a preacher filled with God's wrath. He usually needed a stiff drink afterwards.

The announcement that the ascension was about to commence caught Mannes brooding. He took a last sip of lukewarm coffee and tucked away the pad. The elevator began to slowly rise shortly afterwards. It moved so smoothly that he would not have felt it but for the breathtaking view of Earth slowly slipping away below.

Mannes was just a kid when the construction of the Tarakan space elevator was announced. He remembered his father, a bitter middle school science teacher, explaining what a foolish endeavor it was. "It defies the very laws of physics," he grumbled during their family's evening meals. "It's the tower of Babel all over again. Tarakan hubris will end in a fiasco that will bring disaster upon us all."

Mannes, who even by then was studying physics at a level that exceeded his father's, argued in favour, and the argument grew fiercer each time it occurred. In hindsight, Mannes recognised it now as the beginning of their drawing apart. By the time Mannes entered university, the Star Pillar was in the last stages of completion, while two other major world powers fell into bankruptcy trying to build one of their own.

In a way, Mannes reflected, the last of the world wonders was more than a fantastic tool to bring people and material into space; it was also a constant reminder to the rest of the world of Tarakan's superiority and an excellent recruitment tool. It had definitely helped recruit Mannes.

He sat and watched the rising sun. The wall adjusted accordingly to darken the harsh glare, and he caught his own reflection. Instinctively he tucked his belly in and smiled at his own folly. It was a good body, all things considered, and he liked it, especially since it was his natural one. Many of his colleagues had already transitioned to newer vessels, or heavily modified their own bodies to the point that they looked like they were in their twenties again. But Mannes resisted the peer pressure, jesting that his wife threatened to leave him if he upgraded. It was a lie, of course. Nancy would probably leave him even if he didn't upgrade, and most likely very soon. They had been growing apart, and it was all on him. He couldn't tell her why he kept such long hours, why he didn't delegate the work to his perfectly capable assistants, or why he'd refused to create an avatar bot. If she knew what he was up to and why . . . no, he kept Nancy unaware for her own good. Her brain patterns would reaffirm her innocence under investigation, but such ignorance came with a price, and if it wasn't for their joint love for their daughter . . . He wondered if Nancy was sleeping with anyone else, then adjusted his mental query to whether she was sleeping with anyone he knew.

The elevator rose above the clouds. Soon they would be leaving the atmosphere. On the community elevator people usually whooped and cheered or clapped their hands. Kids would watch the little balls attached to their wrists for the first signs of weightlessness. Inside his private cabin soft music was playing, his favourite Schubert sonata for violin and piano in A major. The music grew louder when the room sensed Mannes's perception shift. Damn it, he had to adjust his security protocols when he got back, so that no machine could read him so easily. Then again, it might raise suspicion if he did . . .

Weightlessness.

Mannes looked out at the planet he was leaving and fought the illogical premonition that he would not be coming back.

17

Peach

Brak smiled at me as I entered the room. "It is good to see you, Lady Peach."

"It is good to see you, too," I said, which, surprisingly enough, was a genuine feeling. There was something endearing about Brak, even for a soul as tarnished as mine.

He was lying on a mattress, and he winced when he pushed himself up to a sitting position.

I crouched next to him. "Does it hurt?"

Brak touched his side gingerly. "Only a little. I'm just weak." He smiled. "The Healer came to visit me this morning, and he looked worse than I do. I owe him my life." He looked straight at me. "And to you as well, Lady Peach. If we had left you at the outpost I would have been—"

"If you had left me at the outpost we wouldn't have gone on a hike, and then none of this would have happened."

"I always stop and go for a walk at that spot, I love the scenery there." Brak's eyes shone, seeing the view as he spoke.

"Where is Trevil?" I asked, just to change the subject.

"Working on the truck. You have a long way ahead of you. It will take you the winter to drive to the City of Towers and back. Pity I ain't going to see it with you. I heard it is breathtaking."

"You've never been?"

He shrugged. "Too far, and Trevil and I established a solid route here. People know us, and trade was going well. We'll have to start over, now that our haul is gone."

"I'm sorry."

Brak's smile was genuine. "My mother used to say that life brings you down so you can lift yourself up. I almost died but I will be okay. Now we must pay the Healer in kind. Trevil will take you to the City of Towers and I will stay here and work off my debt. When he comes back, we will start over, maybe try a different route, away from the naturalist lands."

There was nothing more to say. I got up and Brak said, "You take care of Trevil for me, Lady Peach. He's not one for a chatter, but otherwise he's good company."

I looked at him for the last time. "I'll do my best, Brak. I hope you heal well."

There was a sort of entourage waiting for me at the truck. Trevil was standing among them, his hands black to his elbows. The man with the bone earrings bowed slightly as I approached and motioned to one of his men, who stepped forward and unwrapped a white sheet he was holding. Inside was a small pouch made of the same canvas I wore at the Healer's, but it was speckled with dirt, as if it had been dug up from the ground not too long ago. Without touching the pouch, the man urged me to take it. It jingled when I lifted it up.

"This tainted metal is from da Healer man to you," the man with the bone earrings declared, "to help you on the way. These"—he motioned and two other men stepped forward, each holding long leather coats, which they put on our shoulders—"will help for the winter." Leather boots were laid at our feet as the man with the earrings stepped forward and handed me a scroll case. "This letter is for you," he said.

I looked at the wax seal. "What's in it?"

"A letter to T'iar Garadin, an important man in the Guild of Menders. If you be need help, bring da letter to him in the Upper Plateau. He will be helping."

I closed my hand over the wooden scroll cases. "Thank the Healer for all his help."

"Da Healer says he be just paying his price, but soon you be needing to pay da price, too."

That made me freeze in my tracks. "What did he mean by that?"

The man with the bone earrings stepped closer to me, until his face almost touched mine. "Your old world be dead," he said in a hushed tone, as Trevil mounted the truck, "and you walk the land dat is close to da darkness. Soon you will be having to be choosing yourself, between light and dark, between old and new, between worlds, so told Nakamura, da man who sees all. Da Healer said to tell you these words of his." The man paused, took a deep breath, then whispered, "'Choose wisely, even after death.'" I tensed, as my mind registered the meaning of the words, but the man stepped away before I could respond, and his entourage turned to leave with him.

The truck's engine was already running when I slowly climbed into the cabin. A stream of dark smog came out through the upper exhaust pipe and was beginning to sift into the cabin. We needed to move, even just to drive out the pollution, and Trevil did not hesitate. We began driving at a walking speed and slowly gathered momentum.

"You know the way?" I asked.

"I have a pretty good idea how to begin," he answered without looking at me. "The rest I'll figure out as we go."

"How long will it take us to get there?"

"That depends on the fuel." He pointed at the jerrycan behind us. "They gave me some vegetable oil mixed with animal fat. That can get us a fair distance but we'll need to buy decent fuel for speed. Thing is"—this time he did turn his head to me—"I've got nothing to haggle with."

I opened the pouch of coins on my lap, grabbed a handful, and lifted it up to the light. "Will that do?"

Trevil glanced at the coins I was holding. "Aye, that can get us a fair amount of fuel and food, so we won't need to stop and hunt. We can get to the city in two months or less, if we're lucky. Wouldn't mind a few more bullets for the guns, too." He added under his breath, turning the truck slowly around a corner, "Never know who we'll meet."

"Good," I said. "We'll use the coin."

"I know a place, a farm, two days' ride or so. They make a decent vegetable oil and accept coin over kind. Not many do in these parts."

"Let's drive there. I can swap with you when you get tired."

"We've got ourselves a road trip." Trevil suddenly smiled and shook his head. "Brak says that every time we set out. Says it's for luck."

"Well, then," I said with a genuine smile, "looks like we've got ourselves a road trip."

18

Mannes

A comforting familiarity welcomed Mannes into the visitor's hall of the space hub. It wasn't just the amount of times he'd visited the place; it was a lifetime spent helping design, maintain, and upgrade the station, which made it feel like coming back to your childhood home. At least this time he did not need to secretly insert another line of illicit code into the system. That part of the operation was over, thank God. He'd thought this fact would make him less nervous, but he still felt the fluttering in his stomach and his heartbeat racing.

Mannes looked around. The rest of the space elevators were still in transit, so the hall was empty except for the several security bots hovering by each door. One of them approached and, after a brief retina and hand scans, it connected through the neural public channel and said, "Captain Ismark sends her regards, Dr. Holtz. She hopes your brief stay here will be pleasurable. Would you follow me, please?"

Mannes nodded at the meaningless platitude. Captain Ismark was not a woman who hid her opinions, and her feelings towards Mannes, or any other nonmilitary personnel messing around in her hub, had been voiced point-blank to his face on several occasions. It was a surprise that the old iron maiden was still in command. Had the woman ever set foot on Mother Earth?

The magnetic boots did their job, and Mannes checked absent-mindedly that his travel case was space secured and attached to his body. All space hub visitors' legware was designed to help maintain balance for the low gravity in the ever-spinning hub, and after the first several cautious steps one could easily forget he was in space, until one's items were spread all over the cabin.

"Tell me," he asked as they turned a corner, "is the C wing working at optimum yet?"

There was the briefest of pauses as the bot internally re-checked Mannes's security status.

"The C wing is working at ninety-two percent, but we are hoping to reach ninety-four percent in the next three weeks, after the external pipe adjustments."

Mannes nodded with satisfaction. At least he wouldn't need to spend three more weeks cooped up in the narrow vents in search of leakage. "And what about the plans for the expedition to planet CSX5?"

This time the answer was immediate. "I am sorry, Doctor Holtz, I am not authorised to divulge such information."

"I see."

"If you want, I can connect you to Commander Ismark—"

"No need," he said, cutting the bot off, perhaps too quickly. He added under his breath, "I was just being nosy."

The bot surely heard his words but chose not to respond.

The walk to the space shuttle area was, of course, short. Transit passengers never left the A wing so security protocols were brief this time. The door slid open and they entered the waiting area, one of Mannes's team's designs. It was by far the most beautiful part of the hub, not considering one's personal feelings towards the four septimum cell hub's engines, but you had to be an engineer to appreciate such beauty.

Half the rectangular hall was transparent and the view of Planet Earth and space beyond was breathtaking. Mannes proudly noted to himself that it did not trigger vertigo, unlike the original design.

Several dozen doors led to the various space shuttles. His name and destination were already imprinted on the gate's metal hatch but he knew he would have to wait a bit before commencing his journey, and since a private waiting room was too costly and wasteful to build even for Tarakan, soon the place would be filled with the first arrivals from the long queue on Earth.

Mannes chose to sit in the least favourable part of the hall, hoping to have a moment to do some quiet reading, or perhaps calm his thoughts, which, he suspected, had been too close to paranoia lately. He had to calm down and stop letting Daichi's nonsense get into his brain. The guy was the most brilliant code designer he had ever met, no doubt about it, but Daichi also put the capital *E* in *Eccentric* . . .

Mannes was spreading his equipment on the magnetic table as his space suit arrived. He decided to take his time and get into it only at the last moment. The suit was bulky and, frankly, an unnecessary precaution for civilian space travel. Instead, he turned on his pad and continued reading the article on puzzle-solving strategies—not that he was planning a bid for promotion in this lifetime. Mannes was, by all means, a high-ranking Tarkanian, but also a man who knew his own limitations. Still, it was a good way to take his mind off things.

A few more people arrived, including an annoyingly loud family of five. The kids were, of course, ecstatic. Just by looking at them it was obvious the parents were the kind who forewent the responsible use of behavioural medicine and let their offspring run wild in the name of some new age parenting trend. The kids zoomed up and down the hall, screeching and screaming in delight at the effect of the low gravity, while their parents shushed them half-heartedly. Without any success, of course.

While Mannes was in midsigh, the emergency channel blipped in his inner ear and caused his heart to skip a beat. Only six people knew how to call him on the personal emergency channel, and the last time it was used Nancy had been going into labour with Deborah. Mannes touched his left temple to activate the channel.

"Hello?"

There was no image coming through on his retina cam, and for a few seconds Mannes heard only quick breathing.

"Hello?" he said again.

"Mannes . . ."

"Daichi." Mannes swallowed a swear word that was almost uttered. "What's wrong? Why are you using my emergency channel—"

"Shut up and listen."

That caused Mannes to straighten up in his chair in alarm. Daichi could have ended up being Mannes's boss if not for his peculiar personality, but the voice resonating in Mannes's mind had an urgency he'd never heard before—not even from Daichi, who liked to work in complete darkness and usually under several blankets.

"He's on to us."

"Who?" Yes, it was a stupid question but Mannes needed time.

"Are you fucking drunk, Holtz? Adam, he knows, man, he *knows*. You must come to the l—where we discussed . . . we need to launch, now."

"No . . . you are mistaken . . ." Seriously, he didn't need this shit right now, especially where he was sitting at the moment. Mannes managed to control his mental voice to a calm tone. "Daichi, relax for a second. How do you know something's up?"

"I'm locked out, okay?" Daichi's voice rose. "Came to the office and my security clearance is gone, can't even get into the lab. I split before security came. They would have arrested me, for sure."

Mannes breathed a sigh of relief. Daichi had bolted because someone in security forgot to renew his security clearance.

"Okay," he said, "maybe it's just a mistake. Remember Andriana last month? She forgot to—"

"Someone's been to my house."

There was a pause. Mannes forced himself to breathe deeply three times before saying, "Are you sure?"

"Of course I'm sure! They hacked into my personal files, too, but I don't keep anything there. Look, you need to change plans, tell them you're ill or something and let's meet at—"

"I'm in space."

"What? Where? How? Your diary didn't mention . . . oh *fuck*."

"Relax, Daichi. It's some emergency at the moon hotel resort. I'm in the hub, waiting for my shuttle."

"Oh my god, *oh my god* . . ."

"Daichi, calm down." He actually said those words out loud, but when he looked around he saw they were lost in the racket the kids were producing.

"Oh god. He knows, it's happening, don't you see?"

"I see nothing. They assigned me to an emergency system failure because I was available, that's all."

"You're not even in the same engineering department as the space fucking resort! He's separating us and taking us out one by one. We need to launch Cain, right now!"

"Don't be a fool. Cain is not ready, barely tested, and we were only going to use it if all of us agreed."

"That's another thing, I can't reach any of the others." From the sound of things, Mannes guessed Daichi was now running. "We've got to launch it now."

The world swam in front of Mannes's eyes. This was crazy. This was not happening. There must be a better explanation.

"Listen to me, Daichi. You will do no such thing. You of all people should know what an untested Sentient Program could do."

"But Man—"

"Stop where you are." He put all the cold firmness he could muster in the mental order. "Don't do *anything* until I return. That is an order, do you understand?" It was stupid to pull rank on a coconspirator, but Mannes couldn't think of anything else to say, and as it happened, Daichi was too hysterical to protest. "Even if what you're saying is true, we cannot launch Cain so incomplete, and since I have a part of his code you can't do it on your own. So, call in sick, tell them I'm authorizing it, find a place to lay low until I get back, most likely in five, six days, got it?"

For a while there was only more heavy breathing on the line, then Daichi said "Yes," and hung up.

Fuck. Mannes leaned back and rubbed his eyes with both hands. *Get it together, Mannes. Daichi is just being Daichi . . .*

The announcing voice resonated in the hall and in Mannes's ear in unison: "Dear passengers, you will shortly begin embarking on your journey . . ."

"Mommy, Mommy, we're really going!"

He must be wrong. The dangerous part of the code insertion is over. We were so careful . . .

"If you have not already dressed for space, please begin donning your space suit now. Do not worry, the suit is for your safety. The atmosphere and pressure in the cabins are at normal levels and should stay so throughout the journey."

"Dad, I want to sit next to the window."

"I want to sit next to the pilot."

"There's no pilot, dumbass, it's AIed."

Then again, what if Daichi is right? Why am I being sent to fix something on the moon resort?

"Mom, he called me a dumbass."

"That's because you are."

"Moooom . . ."

"If you require assistance, signal a bot and it will help you as required."

He needed time.

Mannes shoved his hand into his case and ordered an internal cable, which attached itself to his engineer's fingertip, the only part of his natural body, aside from his retina and brain amp, that had been replaced by Tarakan technology. He'd never liked it but it was too useful to reject, especially when working in tight spaces such as the shafts of the space hub. *Now where was that port?* The blueprints were in his brain amp, and Mannes accessed it after a brief hesitation. He knew this increased his chances of getting caught, but if this was just Daichi's paranoia he could explain it somehow, maybe say he was testing their security protocols, he'd figure it out. If this was real . . . well . . . he needed time to find a way to get back to Earth.

The blueprint flashed before his eyes. The port was close enough, and an engineer always knows how to find the back door to anything he builds.

Mannes bent down and touched the side buttons of his boots, cancelling the magnetic field. He pushed himself and began floating towards the port. In his closed fist was the end of the cable attached to his engineer's finger. To anyone looking, he was just another enthusiastic passenger taking his time to admire the view while in low G. The port was a tiny hole, but as soon as it was close the cable attached itself to it. Immediately Mannes released a dampening program, much like the mosquito when it lands on the skin to feed. Still, this gave him only a little time . . .

"If you haven't dressed in your space travel suit, please do so now . . ."

Six shuttles. He couldn't change his own destination; that was too deep an intrusion. Mannes fought rising panic. What a dumb move, what was the point if he couldn't change where he was going?

"We will be commencing boarding in five minutes. As you proceed, please check that your gate was not changed by looking at the names and destination on the hatch."

There was only one thing he could have done, so he did it, and immediately felt foolish for risking his career, freedom, and perhaps his life for doing it.

"Doctor Holtz."

Mannes turned, palming the cable again.

"You are supposed to be dressed in your space suit already." The bot's voice was not without kindness but still admonishing.

"Yes, sorry. I was caught up in the view."

"Let me help you get dressed."

"Mom, look. We're at gate 4-D and not 3-D."

"There's no need. I can manage on my own."

"Darling, did you check our gate? Did they change it?"

"This way is fastest, sir."

"Don't know, maybe they did, but our names are on 4-D now, see? Who wants to go to space?"

"We do!!"

"Nischa, get back here at once, we are boarding now."

"Please proceed to the marked gate."

"There you are, sir," the bot announced as it sealed the suit.

Mannes did not bother to respond. He steadied himself as he fixed his gaze on hatch 3-D. His name was flashing yellow and red.

"Darling, I thought we'd get a bigger shuttle. I mean the guide said that we'd get the family—"

"Well, we'll just have to squeeze together, love." The rest of the conversation was blocked as the hatch sealed itself shut.

Mannes tasted bile in his mouth as he entered the chute and floated into the spacious family shuttle destined for the moon hotel.

19

Peach

When Brak had mentioned that Trevil was not the talkative type, he wasn't lying. Once we hit the open road Trevil simply withdrew. He seemed comfortable with long silences. The only sound was the engine's loud hum. I was weary of conversations, anyway. Years of operations as an agent taught me the dangers of mindless chatter. You could easily slip and land in a pile of shit for it. Trevil was driving me to my destination, at great risk and personal cost. I was not going to jeopardize it by trying to be overfriendly. At any rate, there was plenty for me to think about as we drove.

The first thing that struck me during the "road trip" was how empty the land had become. When I was on my last assignment there were twenty-six billion people living on this planet, far beyond the planet's sustenance capacity. The invention of the nourishment pill, the devastation of the Plague, and the passing of the universal birth control act by the World Council kept things more or less in check. Still, people were everywhere. There was no place outside of a virtual reality space that you could stand and not see others around you, not even around the Poles. Now, we drove for days without seeing a single soul. It was uncanny, but after a while I got used to all the emptiness and watched how the land was recuperating from Armageddon. Luckily for the planet, humanity was not so quick to recover.

The second thing I noticed was the lack of hygiene. Even the young men and women we met were already missing teeth and smelled of hard living. They were dressed in self-made clothing, skins, or occasional furs, and they lacked almost everything but the bare essentials. The oldest person I met claimed to have lived forty-one years and looked double her age; the average person was half her age or less. As in the beginning of human society, in order to survive, people banded together to create small tribes, living off whatever they could gather, grow, hunt, or occasionally barter for. A farm could contain four or six families and a hamlet triple that number, and when you banded together, others became the competition or worse, a threat.

There was a delicate etiquette we carefully followed whenever we approached a settlement. Trevil would stop the truck at a distance and honk the horn in sequence, three short and one long blasts; apparently where he came from it was the universal sign for a peaceful approach. Problem was, the farther we drove the more people we met who didn't recognise that universal honk. The residents would eventually send out someone to investigate, usually several armed men. This was the most precarious stage, where things could go seriously wrong. Having a middle aged, nonthreatening female for a vessel turned out to be a blessing, and I made sure that despite the cold I was first out of the truck to face the armed welcoming party. At times it helped, and people turned out to be warm and friendly. On occasion we were warned away and had to stay rough on the road. Winter was at its fullest, and the temperature inside the truck was often below freezing. The Healer's coats turned out to be life savers. On days we didn't meet anyone or were turned away we had to keep driving through the night so as not to freeze to death. When we managed to get ourselves invited, we would spend more than a day each time. Trevil would clear the truck's fuel tank of the gunk it had accumulated, then we'd haggle for provisions and fuel. Not many accepted coins, nicknamed "towers" in these parts. We spent precious time bargaining over three eggs or a jar of frozen pickles, sometimes paying in kind, meaning labour, and that proved to be time-consuming as well. All the farms and hamlets I saw were built on the foundations of buildings that had somehow survived the war. The additions or repairs were of low quality, and there was always something that needed to be done to maintain or repair them, like using the truck to move a large boulder from a field, repairing a collapsed makeshift roof, or in one instance helping deliver a baby into this new, harsh world.

Information was a commodity as well, sometimes more precious than food. We learned that the winter dwindled attacks from raiders and there was a rumour that many of them left these lands and joined the "Oil Baron's Army," whatever that was. Nevertheless, some roads were more dangerous than others, and the local knowledge we gathered probably saved us from having to fight for our lives on more than one occasion. In return for information, we would carry salutations from one place to another, or even take a person with us for a day or two. In those instances, I got to learn more about them as we drove and realised how ignorant these people were. Many of them were illiterate, and even for those who read, knowledge was not abundant anymore. People relied on stories, gossip, and religion to explain the world around them. I heard six different versions of the Catastrophe, from an alien race that came from the skies, to hordes of Demons climbing up from the pits of hell. All the stories had one thing in common, though: We, the Tarkanians, were the bad guys. Human or not, Tarakan was evil incarnate in the eyes of everyone we met.

As we approached the northwest side of the City of Towers the land changed. Roads merged with larger roads and travel became smoother, but the land was even more barren and damaged, and the ruins were abundant. We circumvented a destroyed city whose radiation level, even from afar, was registered by my vessel as life-threatening. We passed a broken Sky Bridge, and a field that still had remnants of a Sky Train's tracks, half buried in the ground. We crossed under a Tarakan freeway, and as we did a SuperTruck zoomed past, driving at a speed that was almost ten times our own. It warmed my heart and gave me hope. Here we were, getting closer to the world I had left behind.

By the time I saw the silhouettes of the high towers it was beginning to get a little warmer. It was the most beautiful sight, and it made me whoop and cheer. Trevil looked at me as if he was seeing me for the first time, but it was obvious that he was also happy to finally see our destination.

For a moment, perhaps my first in this world, I was filled with hope that everything would turn out all right.

I was dead wrong.

20

Mannes

All space shuttles were initially engineering crafts that were used to build the hub and were later modified to take passengers on leisure cruises. Most of the hardware and tools were stripped away and the inside was completely refurbished, of course, but it still felt familiar to Mannes. The pilot seats were sealed off by a wall and a hatch but they were still there, as opposed to the newest models, which forewent any human influence whatsoever.

There were plenty of seats available. Mannes chose the one facing the viewing window and made sure his belongings were stashed securely. "My name is Norma," a voice came up on his open channel, "and I am your AI pilot today." Norma began explaining security protocols and safety measures. Mannes had always thought that it was an idiotic notion. If something went wrong in space to the point you had to do something yourself and not rely on the shuttle's artificial pilot, you were as good as dead, it was that simple. He hushed the annoying speech on his channel but it just switched to the shuttle's speakers. Well . . . at least his mind was noise free.

Mannes kept himself busy complying with the various tests and actions needed to be done prior to the detachment from the hub, including attaching the bulky space helmet, which always made him feel claustrophobic, all the while trying to justify to himself his foolhardy actions in the waiting room.

Sure, there was a chance he would not be discovered. After all, he and that annoying family were heading to the same resort and they would arrive almost at the same gate. A small misunderstanding, a glitch in the system, no harm no foul . . . or there could be an investigation. Questions would be asked. He would be tested again, and his secret might be betrayed by his own microfacial gestures. That is if Daichi was not being hauled right now into the interrogation room . . .

Mannes shook his head inside his helmet. Five years. Five fucking years of trying to outmanoeuvre the most complex, intelligent, and sophisticated mind in the history of mankind. What would they do to him if they found out what he'd done? What would be the punishment for such an act of treason? Tarakan did not have the death penalty, of course, but the punishment would be severe and would affect not only himself . . .

If he got out of this mess and back to Earth, Mannes swore to himself that he was going to quit. He'd just tell Professor Vitor that he was out. He wouldn't do this anymore. He would let the world run itself and concentrate on the important things, like Deborah, and maybe mending things with his wife.

"We are about to detach from the space hub, please do not be alarmed by the slight tremors."

He wouldn't have to betray his team. He wouldn't have to rat. They were all brilliant and capable, but without his leadership the project would just fall apart. Let Vitor find another fool for his alarmist theories.

"We are now detaching from the space hub in three . . . two . . . one . . ."

The shuttle shuddered as the clasps holding it to the hub opened and it drifted away into space while the hub continued its spin around the Earth. Soon after, the engines came online and the shuttle began aligning itself for the slingshot manoeuvre towards the moon, using Earth's gravitational pull to gain momentum.

Earth came into view, closer than ever. He could see the cloud mass around the southern hemisphere. He could also see the countless satellites floating in space. Most of it was military grade stuff, some openly displaying weapons, others with hidden capabilities that were no less lethal. He'd heard someone claim at one of those boring office parties that there were now more weapons in space than on the surface of the planet, but that felt like an exaggeration.

The shuttle course took him underneath most of the debris and close enough to the Emirates space hub for him to see it from one of the windows. Mannes knew the shuttles were scanned and that weapons were locked on them, ready to open fire at the slightest provocation.

Once past the Emirates space hub, the shuttle fired its second engine and gained speed. He had one last glimpse of the Tarakan space hub in the distance before the shuttle was flung out of orbit. A large screen showed a live feed of Earth receding behind them, together with various information regarding their destination, time of arrival, gates, and such. Three hundred eighty-four thousand kilometres. It would take a little more than two days to get there and a few more hours to slow down into the docking area.

Mannes unfastened the helmet and secured it on the wall. Then, for the first time since he entered the shuttle, he relaxed into his seat and retrieved his pad again. The problem he'd been called to fix on the moon resort was serious but not complex. Several hours of work, perhaps a day of cleaning up any collateral damage in billing or supply orders. The amount of hassle would depend on the team waiting for him. He spent longer than usual looking at their files, memorizing names and faces. They were all young, three men and two women. It was their first job in space, so they were all eager to please. *They always are.* Mannes guessed they were smart, but not too smart—the moon resort was not a job for a top of the class candidate.

When he checked the internal clock again more than two hours had passed. Mannes wondered whether to take some time and organize his thoughts, perhaps enjoy some mindless entertainment, or simply get into the cryo bed and wake up an hour before arrival. There was merit in sleeping his worries away. He could arrive refreshed and focused, and no one would bother him unless it was an emergency. On the other hand, he would be unconscious, vulnerable. Well . . . at least he had plenty of cryo beds to choose from.

Mannes's eyes wandered to the screen, which was showing the space he was leaving behind. Earth was just a large, blue-and-white ball in space, already too distant to show any visible features. He caught a glimpse of another shuttle in the side camera. It was far away, of course, but he focused on it for a brief second and the screen, sensing his retina, magnified the image. It was "his" shuttle, the slightly smaller model, carrying the family he'd changed places with. They'd probably already discovered they had only one or two cryo beds and three screaming kids in a small, weightless environment. Mannes shook his head and promised to find a way to make it up to them. Maybe he could pull some strings and get them to win another trip to the moon resort, or even a guided tour through the space hub, or upgrade their hotel room to a full suite—now *that* was a good idea.

He was still watching the shuttle when it exploded.

21

Twinkle Eyes

I found Galinak sitting on LoreMaster Harim's reclining chair. He didn't even bother to open his eyes when he asked, "So, how was the rest of your conversation with those rust fuckers?"

There was nowhere to sit. I leaned on the desk, crossing my arms. "We need to grab Vincha's daughter before a very capable operative does so, and stop a man called Mannes from using the girl, possibly by killing him."

Galinak nodded. "And if we decide not to do it, we have three years to live."

"Pretty much."

"They screwed us again, Twinkle Eyes. I can see why the rest of the world hated those wire rippers."

"We don't have a choice," I said, but Galinak shook his head slowly.

"There's always a choice. We could send those Tarkanians to rust and live as freemen."

"And die in agony in less than three years."

Galinak turned his head and locked his gaze with mine. "Would you rather be a Tarakan slave for the rest of your life?"

I wanted my answer to be witty as well as persuasive, but I couldn't find the words. Instead, I changed tactics and said, "Whatever our decision may be, we need to find Vincha first and tell her what's going on."

That got Galinak's attention, and for the first time a smile appeared on his face. "It would be nice to meet the old gal."

"I'm sure she'll be delighted to see you, too." I kept my face as neutral as possible.

"She's gonna try to rip our balls off."

"I trust you to stop her from accomplishing that."

He shrugged theatrically. "Maybe . . . you think you can track her down??"

I liked the way Galinak asked me that. It meant he trusted my skills and found me useful, and since he was the one who could survive the wilderness, I desperately needed him at my side.

"I've done it before, and I have a few ideas and more than a few contacts in the City of Towers. We need to start from there."

"Agreed, but first we need to get out of here. Any chance you can fly this metal bird? I mean, you seemed capable enough with the helmets and everything."

I thought about it, but shook my head. Even if I somehow dreamt a way to manoeuvre the metal behemoth and take it to the skies, flying and landing it was beyond me. Besides, I considered the library LoreMaster Harim had gathered, his lifework, should be kept in a relatively safe area. "No, we need to leave all of this here."

Galinak sighed as he got up, hefting the power machine gun in his arms. "We're gonna have to fight past the Dwaines, you know."

I checked the power clip of my peacemaker; it was full. "Maybe they'll listen to reason."

Galinak slid a second power tube into the weapon's reserve chamber. "Sure, I'm certain they'll listen to reason," he said, "they sure look like listen-to-reason type of people."

"It was an honest mistake," I said, as we walked to the back door of the Leviathan.

"They'll understand." Galinak flicked out the enhanced aiming device.

"Let me do the talking," I said, pulling the lever. The door began to open downwards.

"Sure. You'll do all the talking and persuading, I'll just be all quiet and respectful." Galinak gave me the thumbs-up and kneeled down to a sniping position.

"And don't do anything rash," I said. "Let's give diplomacy a chance, for a change."

"Diplomacy is my second name." Galinak hooked the weapon's sight into his SmartGlass.

A bullet buzzed past my face just as he finished the sentence, causing me to throw myself to the side.

"So much for diplomacy." Galinak half turned and let loose a burst of energy bolts. There was a distant cry to our left, followed by angry shouts from all directions.

"I think the welcoming committee awaits us," Galinak said as he pulled the trigger again. "I hope you prepared a nice speech."

"Rust." With the peacemaker in my hand, I deepened my sight and surveyed the area. "We're surrounded," I informed Galinak as bullets began flying all around us.

Galinak let out another burst of deadly bolts. "Let's go parley," he said, then we lunged forward.

22

Mannes

Hello?" Mannes did not remember tapping his left temple, but he must have done so because it was Daichi's voice speaking in his inner ear.

"Holtz, are you there? Are you receiving this? I know I'm getting through."

Mannes's eyes were still fixated on the screen, watching the debris from the exploded shuttle, *his shuttle*, spreading in a growing arc. The family was dead. Two parents, three kids—one was almost Deborah's age.

"Mannes, answer me, it's important."

Coincidence? It couldn't be.

He pressed his temple with his middle finger, keeping the conversation internal and hidden from the shuttle's AI.

"Mannes here." He heard his thought being voiced over the Comm.

"Christ, man. Why didn't you answer?"

A whole family. Dead.

"What is it?" He steeled his internal voice.

Daichi was still breathing hard and speaking very fast, like he always did when he got overexcited. "They got to the others. Andriana was taken, I know that for a fact."

They almost got me. They murdered a whole family instead.

"How?"

"I saw her, Holtz. Six Guardian Angels, six. Christ, she's what, five feet tall? They took her family, too. I saw it with my own eyes."

Deborah.

"And Jameson is dead."

"Dead?" He must have sat down without realising it because when he moved abruptly, the restraints tensed lightly against his body.

"The newsline says he fell from a bridge, or jumped. I think he was running away from them—or was pushed." Daichi's voice broke. Jameson was the only one in the crew who could reach Daichi when he was at his worst.

Then it's over.

Daichi must have read his thoughts. "It's not over yet. I pieced together the code, we could still do this."

"What? How?" They'd divided the code between themselves, thus ensuring the program would not be launched without a consensus. At the time, he'd thought it was a great idea, a *responsible* idea. Now he realised it only took the removal of one of their members to void the entire enterprise. A thought suddenly occurred to Mannes: Despite everything they'd done so far, he never actually believed they would eventually go through with it.

"Andriana gave me her code last week, for safekeeping. She sensed she was being monitored. And Jameson . . ." Daichi laughed sadly. "He used to recite the code silently to himself. You know how he is about remembering things."

Mannes nodded to himself while thinking: *You meant to say "how he was."*

"I couldn't overhear him, but I read his lips one day. It was easy."

Yes. Jameson was the kind of guy who would recite the code to himself every morning with the discipline of a monk, and Daichi was the kind of man who could memorize a twenty-six-digit code by reading someone's lips from the other side of the room.

Mannes held the last piece of the code.

"We have to do it now." Daichi's voice wavered again. "Andriana . . . she'll crack . . . soon."

She would, especially if—*when*—they used her family as leverage.

"Cain is not thoroughly tested," Mannes said, as if Daichi did not know every line of code that fleshed out the entity they'd created. "We need another year. Who knows what could—"

"He'll do fine, he'll adapt. We made him that way, and the tunnel we dug in is ready. Frankly, Holtz, we have no choice."

The shuttle's voice filled the cabin.

"Doctor Holtz, this is Norma, your shuttle's AI. You are being hailed at the Comm from the Tarakan space hub."

Those kids were probably being annoying, and with the space that cramped, the parents were exasperated, right to the point when they were all blown to pieces.

"Holtz. Where are you?" Daichi would not let it go.

"Block the message from the hub."

"This is against proto—"

"You know my rank—block it!" He was shouting now, at a low-level shuttle AI. He was losing it.

"Holtz . . . the code."

Mannes looked at the screen but there was nothing there. The image of the debris was already gone and he suspected that soon it would be purged from the memory bank of his shuttle, too. He wondered briefly how they would cover up this mess but guessed it would be laughably easy. An accident, terrorism, whatever. People always believed what they were told to believe.

"This is our only chance to do this, Holtz. Don't crack on me now."

Deborah.

"Sir. We are being hailed again. It is the hub's central command, priority one."

"Block it."

"This is—"

"Block it!" he roared.

"Holtz. The code . . ."

They murdered a whole family, and it was his fault. Adam's fault. Professor Vitor was right. Adam has to be stopped.

His piece of the code was only fourteen digits long, the shortest of them all, easy to remember. A couple of birthdays strung together with name initials. He was just lazy about it, really. Mannes recited the code once into his internal receiver.

Daichi hung up without another word, or maybe he was cut off by Central Command because a second later Commander Ismark's voice filled the cabin and his emergency inner channel.

"Doctor Holtz, this is Captain Ismark of the Tarakan space hub. *What the fuck is going on?*" The commander's voice was always angry, even on the best of days, but this time it sounded steel-edged.

"Commander, I don't know what you mean."

"Do not play games with me, *Holtz*. You were supposed to be on Shuttle S2 carrier, which blew up suddenly and the next thing I know, I'm finding you on shuttle S2FX. The casualties from S2 are a family of five who should not have been on the S2 at all."

"There must have been a mix-up—"

"Hold on." Commander Ismark shut the Comm for a long moment, then she was back with: "Holtz." Her voice, impossibly, hardened even further. "I am receiving info here that there was an external breach of the manifest of the shuttle plans. An engineer access code was used to change the shuttle plan."

There was only a brief pause, during which Mannes could not find anything useful to say. Commander Ismark's voice filled the cabin again. "Doctor Holtz, you are under arrest. Until further notice you are to do nothing whatsoever. Communicate with no one—this is a direct order, and I will be monitoring your access points and blocking all messages. The shuttle will turn around and head back to base, where you will be taken into custody until we get to the bottom of this."

As she spoke the shuttle began changing its course.

Mannes finally found his voice. "Commander, changing course is going to take time, and I am needed on an emergency call on the moon base. Surely we could—"

"Your time of arrival will be eighteen hours and thirty-seven minutes. I suggest you get some cryo sleep, you'll need it. Ismark out." She cut communication off, and the shuttle's AI informed Mannes almost immediately that his credentials were suspended and that all communication from the shuttle was blocked.

Mannes stood up again.

"Please sit down as we make a course-changing manoeuvre," the AI pilot warned in a pleasant but firm voice.

He ignored it.

So the game was up. He was going to be interrogated. Kindly at first—after all, he was a high-ranking member of Tarakan civil service. Then the questions would begin to be more difficult. They'd find out about things. He'd make mistakes, let something slip. Even if he held it together for a while, they had leverage. *Deborah*.

Mannes looked around. The cryo beds were there, tempting him to enter the black void and forget his troubles for just a little longer. But instead of complete despair, he was suddenly filled with inexplicable rage.

Like hell was he just going to lie there like a mummy until they came to take him away. Screw *that* plan. He could still make a difference. He could try to reach the moon resort and call people. People of power, people who knew him personally and owed him a favour. He was the deputy head of the Computer and Science Engineering Department, for crying out loud. His security credentials were as high as a three-starred army general. Fuck Ismark and her orders. At the very least he would buy time for Daichi to clear out and for himself to think of a story that just might stick. Maybe he missed the S2FX for old time's sake and, with the mischievousness of a civilian engineer, changed the roster. Maybe he was just an asshole who wanted a bigger shuttle.

Mannes didn't know how, but the head gear of his space suit

ended up in his hands. He fastened it on in three expert moves. He was not hooked to the oxygen attachment, of course, so immediately it became harder to breathe. He fought the rising panic and concentrated on what he had to do. *Quickly, before I pass out.*

"I am detecting that you are wearing the space suit's helmet." Norma's voice was calm but stern. "May I remind you that you should only wear the helmet during detachment from the space hub or in case of emergencies, and that—"

Mannes went straight to the pilot's hatch. Yes. It was closed, locked, but he'd spent three years in and out of the S2-type vessels, and one learns a trick or two in the process. There was a manual override for emergencies, a handle . . . *there* . . . and you had to stick the utility cable into the power core and . . .

"You are trying to breach a secure area. Please stop immediately or measures will be—"

Now he had to kneel and search for the other handle. That was going to hurt his back, and his gut was *really* in the way of things.

A short *puff* was the only warning that the knockout gas was being released into the cabin. He was clad in a full space suit, but that only gave him a minute or two before the nanoparticles would penetrate and find his skin. Mannes groaned and stretched as his breath marked the inside of the helmet. Found it. *Pull.*

The door slid open above him and he jumped up and sailed through it to the cramped space of the pilot cabin. When the door was sealed behind him and the measurements on the space suit arm display had shown that the gas had not sifted through to the cabin, he unsealed the helmet and took several deep breaths. He caught his reflection. Perspiration was running down his face and he grinned right through it. Yeah. Plan B it *fucking is.* The AI kept warning him that his actions were a breach of several hundred rules. Mannes found the switch that controlled the program's speech and turned it off with childish glee. The cabin went blissfully silent.

Now to take control of this baby.

It proved harder than he thought it would be, and he almost

fried the entire pilot's board twice, but luckily the S2FX was not military grade, so with a little ingenuity he brought the manual pilot online and suddenly he was flying the shuttle.

He actually whooped.

Now he just had to figure out where he was and where he should be heading. Assuming Commander Ismark wouldn't blow him to little tiny pieces. Mannes looked at the flashing screens, then out to space and tried to ignore the sinking feeling in his stomach. He'd piloted more than a few personal engineering crafts in his life but always just around the space hub. For greater distances, they always used a trained pilot AI. Now he needed to plot a course to the moon base without slowing his speed, and do so manually.

As if on cue, Commander Ismark's voice filled the cabin.

"Doctor Holtz." Her voice was now forcedly calm. "I am not asking you what have you done, I can see it, and I am not asking you what you are going to do. I am telling you that you have made a grave mistake. Commandeering a space craft is a class A offence, so for your sake, I am telling you to—"

Suddenly there was the sound of an alarm. For several seconds Mannes thought it was coming from the shuttle, but then he realised that the Comm had remained open. He heard someone shout, "Commander, report of shots in B and C sections."

To Commander Ismark's credit, her response was not an incredulous "What?" or "Come again?" Instead, she calmly said, "Inform Earth command immediately that we are under attack. Unseal emergency pads, call Guardian Angels into—"

A man's voice interrupted to report that shots had been fired in section E.

"Deploy the Guardian Angels in all sectors. Level code red 2. All civilians should head to the escape areas and wait for—"

"Commander, the shootings . . . *it's the Guardian Angels*."

And then the Comm went dead.

There was a long moment where Mannes simply sat in front of the screens and let what he'd heard sink in. His heart was thumping at a dangerous pace. The newer body models had a fail-safe mechanism for several organs, including the heart. Yep, he should have upgraded . . .

Mannes turned the manual switch one click to the right. "Voice control," he said.

Norma's voice filled the cabin. "You are in breach of seventeen—"

"Yeah yeah yeah," he cut in. "I'm going back. How long will it take me to reach the hub with increased speed?"

The AI went silent for a brief moment. Not that she didn't know the answer immediately, but the situation was almost definitely new to her. She was not a fully Sentient Program and, like Mannes, she was probably trying to cope.

"With increased speed, two hours and seven minutes less than the remaining sixteen hours and thirty minutes."

"Do so." Mannes released navigation controls to the pilot AI.

The soft hum of the shuttle's engines immediately increased.

What the fuck was he going to do when he'd arrive at the hub? Fight eight-foot-tall Guardian Angels with his bare hands? No. The situation would already be contained by the time he'd get there. Commander Ismark was going to be preoccupied with what appeared to be a total clusterfuck of a situation. The last thing she'd want would be to reprimand a spoiled civilian engineer who wanted a bigger spacecraft. He'd be needed and he'd make some repairs, that was what he was going to do. And they'd thank him for it when it would be over. Maybe enough to put aside all this foolishness.

To the Comm Mannes said, "Norma, get us to the hub, ask for permission to land at dock thirteen." That was the farthest docking bay in the hub. He did not want to be in the centre of things.

"And let's put some music on," he added suddenly. The quietness of the cabin was making him nervous.

"Anything specific? I have one hundred and seventy-eight thousand—"

"Beethoven Symphony Number Nine. Go straight to the chorus part, 'Ode to Joy.' Play it in a loop until I tell you to stop."

Immediately the cabin filled with the first chords of Mannes's favourite symphonic piece. Usually he liked to bring up the volume to deafening levels, especially when he wanted to clear the lab and have some time for himself, but now he needed to hear the AI's voice, even if it was already connected to his inner-ear Comm. The orchestra was playing in full swing when he heard the AI again.

"We lost contact with the space hub."

He knew the AI was not standing behind him but he still turned his head. "What?"

"We lost—"

"I heard you. Try to establish contact again and hail the moon resort, too."

"The moon resort is not answering; they are on code red one."

It meant the moon hotel was launching its guests into space inside cryo escape pods, an extreme measure of last resort. It would take the unconscious survivors at least three weeks to reach Earth's orbit, and then they would have to be picked up from wherever they ended up landing. Their survival was not guaranteed.

The chorus came in.

Mannes's neural translator was on but he had learned high-level German in school and knew the meaning of the words without help as the verse was sung:

> *Joy, bright spark of Divinity*
> *Daughter of Elysium,*
> *We tread drunk with fire,*
> *In a heavenly way through your holy realm!*

Things had gone to shit, and he had a horrible suspicion that this was somehow his fault.

"Keep hailing both the hub and the moon resort."

"There is no contact with either."

"Keep doing it."

Mannes took control again and dialed up the speed.

"This course of action is not advisable—"

"Shut up. Bring the hub on the main. Magnify."

After the expected brief delay the image filled the front windows. He leaned back and watched it for a while. Nothing was moving. There was no indication that anything was wrong, but his heart was racing.

Then he caught a glimpse of Earth in the background of the hub and a terrified "Oh my god" escaped his lips.

"Show me Earth. Magnify."

There was no mistake.

He heard his own horrified yells as if they were coming from far away.

The chorus was singing *We tread drunk with fire* in full vigour, while all around the globe missiles carrying weapons of mass destruction exited and entered the atmosphere, and satellites released their own deadly loads upon the planet.

23

Peach

We'd just turned a bend, and the City of Towers filled our view once more, when Trevil decided he'd fulfilled his promise and stopped the truck.

"This is as far as I go," he said. "Take some water with you, and that piece of smoked lamb. It hasn't gone bad yet and will be enough to get you there."

I looked at him with surprise. "You don't want to visit the city?"

"It's not that. I heard that they're taxing something fierce these days, and you heard it as well. With the extra fuel you bought, I have enough to get me halfway back, and with a little luck, just enough in my haul to barter for the rest of the way. Besides"—he looked up to the towers in the sky—"I promised Brak that we'd visit this place together . . . wouldn't want to see it without him."

I fetched the provisions that were offered, then opened my coin bag. There were eighty-seven coins when we'd begun the trip and thirty-eight left. I began dividing the coins, but Trevil shook his head. "I swore to the Healer I would not take anything from you in coin or kind. The fuel was enough to bring both of us here, but that is all I'm going to take from you."

I looked at him as he extended his hand to me. "Good-bye, Peach," he said quietly. "I hope you'll choose well when the time comes."

I shook his hand but when I withdrew mine he kept his extended, turning his palm up. "The gun I gave you, Peach—I'll need it back, I'm sorry."

"Yes, of course." I detached the holster from my belt and handed it over with the antique revolver inside. He opened the case, flipped open the chamber, counted the bullets, and nodded. I turned to open the door when I heard the audible clink of the gun being cocked. "And the power pistol, Peach," Trevil said. "The one you took from under my seat. I'll need it, too."

I slowly turned back to Trevil. He had the revolver I'd just handed to him levelled straight at my head.

"Sorry, Peach, but I really need that gun."

I cursed inwardly, but there was no use denying it. He must have known about it for days and kept his mouth shut.

"It's in my backpack," I said.

Trevil extended his free hand while making sure his gun-holding hand was out of my reach. I handed him the bag. Without taking his eyes off me he rummaged through it and pulled the power pistol out. He turned the power on and checked that the power clip was full, then shoved the pack back to me with his healthy leg.

"Sorry," I said.

He shrugged and pointed one of the guns at the door. "Good luck, Peach."

I opened the truck door and slid down to the ground. It wasn't freezing cold anymore, but it also wasn't the kind of temperature you wanted to be standing in for longer than necessary. Without looking back, I began walking away on the dirt road. I heard the truck move and the distorted warning beeps as it reversed, manoeuvred, and turned back, then the roar of the engine as Trevil stepped on the accelerator pedal. I looked back to see a cloud of black smoke obscuring most of the truck that had been my home for the past two and a half months. There was no time to waste. I turned back and kept on walking.

It was no problem to determine my general direction. The city, with its seven elevated Plateaus, each supporting thousands of Spires, loomed above me for miles. and from what my limited zoom allowed me to see, it was intact. But its size was misleading—it was farther away than it looked.

After a few hours of walking my road ended abruptly at the foot of a steep hill of upturned earth. I climbed the hill, digging my fingers through the loose earth. When I stood on top of it my vessel was sweating despite the bristling cold.

The city was powered by eight Tarakan quantum engines, each producing power equal to six nuclear power plants. Two of the quantum engines were exclusively responsible for the power shield defending the city. Its relative smallness combined with the strength of these engines most likely saved the city from the annihilation our enemies were hoping for, but it hadn't stopped them from trying. While their attacks had not touched the city, they had devastated the land surrounding it. From the look of the landscape, even with the satellite defence system, antimissile batteries, and the electronic shield, a few bombs must have landed damn close. I remembered the beautiful, cultivated surroundings of this great city. Now it looked as if God had decided to put a shovel into the earth and turn the entire garden.

Even before Tarakan became independent, there used to be five million permanent residents and another fifteen million annual visitors—applicants for jobs or citizenship, and tourists—all crammed into a relatively limited space. To stop congestion and make travel between plateaus safer, the city restricted entry for outside vehicles, forbidding private cars and hovercrafts from entering its borders. Several giant, free parking lots were dug deep outside the city's high walls, and a rich array of public transport was available and free to all. From my vantage point I saw that where one such parking lot used to be was a flat swamp, ending at the city's walls by the base of the north tower. Trying to cross it might be dangerous as well as futile. I turned my head east and zoomed. There was a road there, and a line of vehicles. I recognised two trucks similar to the type I'd travelled in, and some other fossil-fuelled older cars. The sun had already set, and I navigated the rest of the way by the twinkling row of floodlights and oil lamps that some of the vehicles used. The traffic line was at a standstill and at least several miles long. There were more animal-driven carts than vehicles, and none of those were solar or power driven, mainly old cars and motorbikes. The road was unpaved and wide enough for one vehicle at a time. The drivers had turned their engines off, and I could see some of them sleeping at the wheel. Everyone else seemed gloomily patient, accepting this situation as normal.

There used to be a bridge of light in this area, one of the most beautiful ways to enter the city. A wide bridge that shimmered brightly, where pedestrians and newcomers could either walk or catch the light train and climb all the way up to the Middle Plateau.

Now there was only darkness, pierced by weak dots of oil-lamp light.

The cold was fierce, and my vessel indicated a need for nourishment. I fished out the leg of lamb from my backpack and sniffed it. It wasn't pleasant but it wouldn't kill me. I began walking alongside the vehicles while chewing the almost-putrid meat.

I had just passed a cart and a sad-looking mule when a voice called behind me, "Hey, Lady. No use getting in front of the line now."

I turned. The cart was covered with a combination of canvas, cloth, and sheepskin. A hand shifted one of the folds, and I saw an older man sitting inside. He was covered in sheepskin and wore a thick, woollen cap.

"They won't open up till sunrise, Mistress," he said, and waved a plastic bottle at me. "I'll share my hooch for your meat and some company."

I hesitated briefly. This could play out in different ways, some of them nasty, but the thought of standing in the freezing cold through the night was a major factor in my decision to accept his invitation.

There was really only space for one large person inside, but he scooted and shuffled and I found myself sitting shoulder to shoulder with a man whose odour was the unhappy mix of onions, sheep, mule dung, and alcohol.

"Name's Gret," he said and handed me a spare cap. "Here, wear this. Will keep you warm." He handed me the plastic bottle. "And this, too."

Hygiene be damned—the cap was a little large and filled with several samples of other people's hair, but it did warm me a little.

"I'm Peach." I sniffed the bottle, and my vessel informed me there was more than fifty percent alcohol in it. I took a long pull.

"You know how to take a brew, Mistress Peach." Gret sniffed at the lamb leg I handed to him. "Aye, this thing's going bad. Still, can't be refusing meat." He grasped the bottle with his other hand, took a bite from the meat, and filled his mouth with alcohol. "This will kill them bad little animals. My grandpa used to say they're everywhere, even in the air. Ugh, I got the bad end of that deal." Gret's face betrayed his disgust. "My hooch is better than your meat, Mistress."

"Wait," I said. There was no need to aggravate the old man. I rummaged through my things until I found the tiny hide satchel. "Here," I said as I opened it, "there's some salt here will make things a little better."

Gret's eyes widened, and he nodded as I took a pinch and spread it around the meat. "That is mighty kind of you, Mistress Peach. Salt is worth its weight in metal."

I shrugged. "And too much of both could end up killing you."

Gret chuckled and bent down and rummaged through a sack underneath our seat. It occurred to me the man was probably much younger than he looked.

"Here." Gret turned back and handed me an onion. "'Tis from uncontaminated soil. Won't make your teeth fall out." He smiled broadly, as if to prove his point.

I bit into the onion. It replaced the taste of the bad meat. "Good onion," I said.

"The best," he said proudly.

We chewed together for a bit.

"You're from around here?"

I shook my head and changed the subject. "Is this normal? I mean this line. Are you all waiting for the bridge of light?"

Gret chuckled. "Don't know what you're talking about, Missus Peach—or is it Miss?"

"Missus," I answered drily.

He seemed disappointed but kept talking. "There's no light at this bridge. We're all waiting for sunrise, for the guards to open the barrier. We unload at the bridge."

"You mean you're not going into the city?"

"Oh, I am." He pointed at the mule. "Old Summer might not be the fastest, but she can climb a sheer mountain, she can." He pointed at the truck standing before us. "The trucks are too heavy for the bridge, they just unload and turn back. Me and Summer, we take the climb but by law, we need to sell most of our take at the bridge or leave metal in the hands of the guards." Gret shook his head. "It used to be easier, used to sell it myself at the market. Onions, potatoes, some brew—it was a good living. And my wife made clothes from sheepskin, like that cap"—he pointed at my head—"before sickness took her."

"I'm sorry to hear," I mumbled.

"Good woman, she was." Gret blinked away tears. "Gave me no children, though. Even the Menders couldn't cure her, poor soul. They say she was born without, you know—" his hand flapped dismissively "—correct womanly bits. But she was all woman to me."

"I am sorry to hear," I said again.

"Such is life, Mistress." Gert shrugged. "We used to travel together. Now I take to the road alone with Summer. A few days, maybe a week each way. I know the good farmers, those who keep their soil clean. The truckers try to rip them off because they need to pay for fuel. I save that cost, so they give me the good stuff."

Gret tapped his nose. "A friend in the know told me my onions go straight up to the towers, where the tower-heads dine on 'em. They fetch triple the price in the upper market, if not more."

"A week's trip each way isn't easy," I remarked.

"Not bad if you know your roads, Mistress, and I do. Got my spots on the way, where I can make a little bonfire." His voice suddenly dropped to a whisper. "Say what you want about the damn Trolls, but there are no bandits so close to the city, except for the city guards themselves of course, they don't need to attack you on the roads. They just sit here and wait for you to come to them and rob you blind with taxes and bribes." He chuckled at his own wit. "Anyways, they took all the young ones to the army, so the roads are even safer now. An old geezer like me, not even the army wants."

That got my attention. Conscription meant trouble. "Is this normal? To take men into the army?"

"They say it's because of the war."

"What war?" I'd figured it would not take humanity too long to go back to killing each other, but still. My heart sank a little.

"You mean you haven't heard? They say the Oil Baron is marching. Took some lands on the slopes last year and is now hungry for more."

"Who is the Oil Baron?"

"Oh, Lady . . ." He sighed at my lack of awareness. "He controls everything in the cold north. They say it's so cold there, water freezes all year round. But the Baron has a good way of making oil, that's where he got his name, and he keeps his people warm with it. The summer lands kept sending food to him, to keep the Baron happy. But they say he got tired of the deep winter and wants to rule the sunny lands. Because of him they stepped up the tax a season ago, and there're definitely more animals on the roads these days, now that oil has doubled in price."

I took another swig from the plastic bottle. It wasn't bad, but getting drunk was a bad idea.

"You look tired, Mistress. There's room at the back if you don't mind shuffling a few sacks and the smell of onions."

"You don't want to sleep yourself?"

"Ah. Am used to sleeping sitting on this bench. I just lean here on the pole, like this." He demonstrated. "Got a sheepskin cushion I tuck like this, and then I close my eyes, and my snores scare the bugs away."

"That . . . still looks uncomfortable," I said.

"My grandpa used to say that everything's relative. He read it in a book. He could read."

"Sounds like you had a smart grandpa," I said as I turned around and climbed over the seat, trying to find a stable foothold among the sacks of onions.

"Oh, he was very smart indeed. We lived out in the country, but he wasn't into growing things, my grandpa. He remembered the old world, still knowing some old ways and old words, too. Had crazy ideas and stories to tell, wrote them down on some old paper. He had plenty of real books, too, with paper in 'em as thin as air. But he died when I was just a boy, and one winter we had no coin for wood, so my mother burned his books and notes to keep us warm."

I sat myself down on a half-filled sack and tried to move things around to make some sort of a sleeping space.

"Best you stick to a corner," Gret advised, still chewing on the lamb. "That way the sacks will hold."

The end result was as far from a comfortable bed as could possibly be imagined, but I'd slept in worse. I slowly and deliberately put the scabbard of the short sword next to me, making sure Gret saw it, but he seemed satisfied with the meat he held in his hand. I found a fleece blanket but after inspection decided not to use it. Instead I lay on my back and shuffled around until no onion was stabbing my vessel's back. I closed my eyes and slowed my breathing. One of the many perks about having a vessel for a body was the ability to control your heartbeat and blood pressure. This made staying underwater for almost ten minutes, surviving extreme temperatures or falling asleep on onion-filled sacks possible.

24

Mannes

Mannes felt no specific pain as he regained consciousness. The restraints and the emergency crash foam and air bags had worked their magic and his body was intact, but he still felt as if he'd come out of one of those ancient machines that people used to tumble-dry clothes in. His entire body ached, which was, in a way, a good sign. It meant he was alive.

His actions were illogical. He should have gone straight to the space hub, but all he could think of was Deborah. His piloting skills and sheer adrenaline had brought the shuttle to the edge of Earth's atmosphere, but Mannes was wise enough to relinquish control to the AI to pilot the rest of the way, and thank God for that. They came in on the wrong side of the globe, zigzagging as death rained from above and rose from below. They passed through several hostile airspaces, and the enemy radar spotted them immediately. Despite the distinct civilian aircraft signature, three ground-to-space missiles were fired at the shuttle. Mannes guessed that at that point everybody was shooting at everything, so they thought they were better safe than sorry. Perhaps Armageddon cancelled any concern for civilian casualties. Luckily, Tarakan satellites spotted and recognised the shuttle, too, and the missiles were shot down from space as they approached, but the last explosion was close enough to send the shuttle into a tailspin. Mannes lost consciousness almost immediately from the G forces. His last thought was of his daughter. Still, whoever had programmed Norma's crash-to-Earth piloting skills did an excellent job. By the looks of it, she had somehow regained control over the shuttle and landed it safely. Although—Mannes groaned as he shifted in the foam-coated seat—the heroic save must have come at a price.

There was no emergency siren or flashing red lights. The cabin was eerily silent. He moved his hands and gritted his teeth at the pain in his shoulder and back as the emergency crush foam slowly melted away. His first sight was the shuttle's control board, and beyond that, outside the pilot's window, several dozen crushed trees.

Mannes drew a slow, careful intake of breath before uttering, "Norma."

"Yes, Doctor Holtz." Her voice was the usual calmness of a program well in control.

"Where are we?" He grimaced and whispered "Holy fuck" under his breath.

"I could give you the exact coordinates—"

"Show me on the screen," he snapped and immediately regretted the involuntary neck movement that came along with it.

"The forward screen is damaged, Doctor Holtz." The AI's calm voice did not waver, but this was the first indication that the landing was not a perfect affair. "I could send the map to your left retina."

"Yes." Mannes blinked as the semitransparent map appeared in front of his left eye. He tried to control it while holding down the bile rising to his throat.

"Reduce . . . reduce . . . wait, magnify . . . No . . . wait . . .

Where are we?" He had never been all that competent in geography. "Where *the fuck* are we?"

"Kyrgyzstan, four hundred miles from the town of Boldoy, three hundred and twenty-seven miles from—"

"We're in fucking Russia?"

"The Republic of Kyrgyzstan gained independence from the second Russian Empire in twenty-one seventy—"

"Okay okay, stop."

Yes, Kyrgyzstan had declared a second independence during the fifth Russian civil war, most likely with the subtle push of Tarakan influence. The Russian government had never been famous for its humanitarianism. It was a bloody affair, and the fact that the war was not decisively won this time was a symbol of the former empire's demise. After a decade of brutality, the land became a lawless region where everything and anything was up for grabs or for sale. It was also one of the farthest places on Earth from Tarakan.

"What the fuck are we doing in here . . . no . . . don't answer." Mannes sighed; he knew the protocol. The AI would always seek to emergency-land where chances of survivability were best. Kyrgyzstan had been just a pile of rubble since the civil war. The folks living on this land were now reduced to hunting and smuggling. Chances were no one would waste too many AOBs—anti-organic bombs—or even a good old Nuke on this place. Nuclear missiles. Fucking nuclear missiles. And death rays from orbit, and AOBs and cluster bombs and EMPs.

Mannes leaned back in the pilot's chair and replayed their landing on his retina up until an EMP took out the outer sensors. He was no military expert, but he'd seen enough weapons discharge to know this was no small outburst of local violence—no, this was IT. *Satellites* were shooting down *other satellites*. This was the war no one believed would happen but everybody had geared up for. He remembered the communication with the space hub—the Guardian Angels, they were going berserk, shooting. This couldn't be just a terrible malfunction, and it happened a short while after he'd relinquished his part of Cain's code. It could have been a coincidence, but . . . was *he* responsible for all of this, a *world war*? Armageddon?

"Start engines. We're taking off."

"We are unable to start engines, Doctor Holtz. Engines are shut down due to an EMP missile explosion."

"What? How did you land—never mind." Mannes tried to still his shaking body. There was no way he was stuck in this place. "Send a full engineering diagnostic to my retina."

Mannes's vision was filled immediately with line after line of damage reports. Even for a trained engineer with more than forty years of experience, it was mind-boggling. He studied the list with growing dread. It seemed the only undamaged equipment were the two emergency medical bots.

His back hurt. "Norma, do you have any medical skills?"

"I am trained in field medicine, diagnostic and emergency surgery, disease, dental—"

"Fine. Thanks." Small comfort, but he needed to get home, and he needed more than a healthy pair of legs to get there.

Deborah!! he suddenly thought. Tarakan Valley was peppered with underground shelters, and everyone was trained periodically on how to get into them safely and quickly. They even trained for it in schools, calmly lining up and filing into emergency bunkers. But this . . . he tried not to think of her experiencing the full brunt of an attack, or having to face a squad of berserk Guardian Angels. His little girl . . . Mannes shook his head, trying to wipe away the images he was seeing in his mind's eye.

"Norma, hail Tarakan on all channels," he blurted.

"I am unable to comply with your request, Doctor Holtz. All communication is down."

That took his breath away. "What do you mean *all* communication? We haven't landed on Mars, and even if we did, we could find some—"

"All global lines of communications are down, sir. I have established a connection to a satellite on far orbit, around Jupiter, but it would take several weeks for a message to reach it, and we have no control over where exactly it would end up—"

"Do it. Give our coordinates, ask for help, reveal my rank, and say I need extraction." It was unwise. He was in no-man's-land but still in what was considered enemy territory. His rank was high enough to warrant a search party so they could torture every bit of information out of him. He didn't care. He didn't *fucking care*. He'd give them everything they wanted to know and then some, as long as he could see his daughter again, or at least know she survived.

Mannes buried his face in his hands, and for a while all he could do was sob in panic. Thankfully it was a short affair.

"I could dispatch a sedative, Doctor Holtz." There was just the right hint of aloof concern in Norma's voice to snap him back.

"No, I'm all right." He sniffed and wiped away tears, feeling oddly embarrassed.

"Are you feeling all right? Any pain? My cabin diagnostic sensors are also down, so I must rely on your own input. The emergency bots are fully functioning, so I could mend most—"

"We'll do a full physical diagnostic soon, but I'm okay, I think," he interjected. There were more important things than broken ribs or aching joints. With the foam gone, Mannes unstrapped himself and rose shakily to his feet on the third try.

"Any threats?" he asked. "Anything coming our way that could vaporise us?"

"I am not detecting any inbound missiles or other weapons of mass destruction, but my long-range sensors are down. I can detect threats only in a twenty-five-mile radius."

"Well, that's . . . comforting. How is the radiation level outside?"

"Slightly increased but not life threatening. This land is surrounded by mountains, and they form a natural shelter. However, should winds change to the northeast I foresee a dramatic increase in radiation. You should retain your suit and carry the helmet with you at all times."

"Yeah, okay." This location was far away from any place of

importance, but mountains or not, radioactive clouds would soon be reaching all corners of the globe.

"There is a small military base three and a half miles south of here. It is mostly abandoned."

Mannes shook his head slowly. "'Mostly'?"

"I was a little busy trying to land us belly first on the side of a mountain with half my instruments and an engine blown by EMP while avoiding heat-seeking surface-to-air missiles, so, yes, 'mostly.'"

That was an oddly emotional response from an AI, but Mannes guessed it was meant to prompt him into action, and it succeeded.

"Yeah, all right. I'll investigate."

"I can mark the places on your retina map."

"You do that." Mannes stretched carefully and regretted it immediately. "And I'll take the pain sedative now, please, and a nourishment pill. Then I'll go out and see what's left of this world."

25

Peach

A whistle, followed by the lash of a whip. Summer's braying and a jolt woke me up from the light doze I'd finally managed to get my vessel into. I can't say I was feeling refreshed, but I hadn't frozen to death nor had I been forced to kill anyone trying to rob or rape me. I stretched. *Concentrate on the bright side of things*, I told myself, and tried my best to ignore the gross discomfort and awful smell.

A cacophony of sounds was rising all around the cart. Honking horns, cursing drivers, and the lowing of cattle. The cart was already moving forward at walking speed when I got up to a standing position. Every few steps the line would stop again, and I used the next pause to manoeuvre back next to Gert. He had the front cover pulled up, and the morning's breeze hit my face like a cold shower. In front of us was another cart, pulled by two ponies, and in front of that was a rickety, heavily patched-up pickup truck. In order to save fuel the driver kept the engine off, and he and his helper got out of the truck and pushed the vehicle forward every time the line moved.

"Morning, Mistress Peach." Gret seemed to be at exactly the same level of jolliness he'd been the night before. "Would you like to break your fast?"

The menu was exactly the same as the night before: onion, stale bread, and moonshine. I decided to pass this time.

"Slept well?" Gert asked, his mouth still full.

"Considering. I've slept worse."

"Now that would be a story I would like to hear." He chuckled, then pointed at my power sword with half an onion. "Does it work, your metal?"

I pulled out the sword and examined it again. Grossly unbalanced and with a dull edge, without power the sword was basically useless. There was still dried blood on the metal, and I used the hem of my tunic to clean it.

"Ran into trouble before, eh?" Gret remarked as he urged the mule to take several more steps forward.

"I can handle myself," I answered drily. I pressed the power button of the sword. There was a soft, barely audible hum, but nothing happened.

He extended his hand. "May I?"

I handed the sword to Gert and accepted the reins and whip from him.

"Just whistle and crack the whip in the air. Summer's a good mule," he said as he turned the sword in his hand. "Must have busted the power relay because it's not recharging. Maybe I could fix it."

"You know how to fix a power sword?" I regretted the disbelief in my voice, but Gret just chuckled.

"When your farm is two days' ride from the nearest village and a week from the city, you learn to fix things yourself. My pa used to have a power hammer just like this, with a solar recharge battery. It got old as me and would break when I hit too hard with it, so I ended up trading it for a fossil-fuel tractor, a pair of horses, and potato seeds. The horses were sick and died after two weeks, the tractor survived a season, the potatoes, well . . . we drank most of them potatoes." He laughed, and turned the sword pommel up. With what must have been a feat of grip strength for an old, organic human body, Gret pulled open the pommel.

"I thought you said you lived in the city," I said, watching him.

"Yes. My missus and I, we had some land, but we moved to try and find her a cure, you know." He pointed at my groin as a reminder and an emphasis. "I never liked the city, but my missus said it was better than slaving on poisoned land all of our lives. After she be gone, I thought to go back, but what's the point of owning land when you cannot give it to your family? Now, see here?" Gret pointed at the bundle of wires inside. "A Gadgetier would charge you an arm and a leg, but what you've got here is quite a simple fix." Gret bent down and rummaged under his seat. When he straightened back up he held a small box, which he laid at our feet.

A honk and a yell reminded me to urge Summer forward. When I turned my attention back to Gret, he'd already pulled out a shabby-looking screwdriver and several wires. The operation took a while and was only partly successful. When Gret pressed the power button and blue energy burst around the metal I felt a definite pang of satisfaction, but Gret was not happy.

"Ain't fixed yet, to be honest. You'd have to keep pressing the button for the sword to function, see?" He lifted his thumb from the power button and the energy winked out immediately.

"Don't know why that is, and I guess that might be a problem in a fight." He handed the sword back to me and traded back the whip and reins. I pressed the power button and carefully moved the shimmering sword around. He was right. Fighting while maintaining pressure on the power button was awkward at best.

"Sorry, that's the best that I could do. But a Tinker would be much cheaper than a marked Gadgetier, that's for sure."

"What's the difference between a Gadgetier and a Tinker?"

"Oh, easy, Mistress." Gret waved a hand absentmindedly. "The Gadgetiers are marked, you see? Head to toes with those damn tattoos of theirs. Not hard to find in Tinker Town or the upper parts of the city but really expensive. I mean *really*." He shot a warning look at me. "I once had one of them charge me a month's profit to fix an irrigation system, and I ended up trading that as well in the end. Tinkers, on the other hand, are unmarked so they aren't considered as good. They are cheaper than Gadgetiers, and a lot more of them go about among the villages and farms, fixing things for a meal and a bed, but you have to be careful for hacks and cheaters."

We moved a little closer. The truck ahead of us turned, and I got the first glimpse of the bridge of light. It used to be one of the most beautiful ways to enter the City of Towers. A pedestrian bridge with a light train in the middle of it, all made of shimmering bright energy. At nights it would change colours periodically and was considered a must visit for couples in love. Now only the base remained and instead of energy, planks of wood and sheets of metal were laid on top of each other to create a precarious bridge that could support only humans. When I zoomed I could see scores of people walking up and down the high bridge, carrying goods on their backs. I spotted a few beasts of burden, too, being whipped to walk reluctantly up the precarious bridge.

"Ain't what you were expecting?" Gret's comment caught me off guard. He was not a fool.

"No," I managed. "Must have been a different bridge."

"No other bridge to this city."

"Then I guess someone told me a fairy story."

"People are sometimes like that." Gret cracked the whip in the air and Summer moved a few steps forward. "Making up things so they can feel good about their lives. It takes courage to face the truth."

We locked gazes.

"Tell you what, Mistress. You're good for conversation, but seem to be new to these parts. The city can be harsh to newcomers, me and my missus found out about it the hard way. I have a small shack in near the Middle Spires. Nothing fancy, but I clean it proper when I'm there and I have a lock on the doors. If you be needing to save some coin, just help Summer and me climb the bridge, and then you are welcome to stay in the spare room. If there's no job coming my way after I sell the onions, I could show you around a bit."

I considered his offer. I had a limited supply of funds and had a suspicion that Tarkania was not the city I used to know anymore.

"No funny business," I warned, waving the scabbard in a theatrical gesture for emphasis.

"On my word, Mistress."

"Fine."

The line began moving at a faster pace.

"You'll have to pay a toll in, you know that, Mistress?"

"Any way around it?"

Gret shook his head. "Heard there is a way into the lower end of the Pit through the swamp, but you'd need some serious high boots and more than a sword to deal with what's in the water. No, Lady, best for you to take your chances here, with me." He wrinkled his brow. "I could say you are my new wife—that would halve the sum."

"Would that be all right by you?" The idea had merit but something in me resented it.

And suddenly the truck veered left, we were at the top of the line, and I forgot all about my reservations. It was the first time I'd seen Trolls. I'd heard the name and description from Trevil and Malk, the former owner of the power sword, and had a pretty good idea what to expect, but this was the first time I'd laid eyes on the phenomenon: humans wearing Tarakan tech meant for Guardian Angels. There were several dozen men and more than a few women, and none of them were the same. More than half of them were wearing metal braces, helping to unload goods by throwing them from one to the other like they were children's toys. Others were carrying weapons, some of which were enormous. I'd seen enough military and paramilitary personnel to know that they were idle, guarding a perimeter that they did not believe was in any danger. A lot of them were talking among themselves or walking slowly in pairs between the vehicles and the bridge. I noted the three elevated machine guns, zoomed in on the Troll manning the one closest to me and saw she was smoking a small pipe. Yep, all was idle, but if things changed those machine guns could shred anyone in the area in a matter of seconds. The bridge of light was still a little farther away, just a small line in comparison to the enormity of the city's walls and looming towers. As I looked up I could see a Sky Train cutting through the air in the distance. It warmed my heart to discover that the technology still functioned. I wondered where the Sky Train travelled to.

One of the Trolls waved at us to move to a designated spot. There were a dozen vehicles unloading their goods in front of officials wearing heavy purple-and-gold coats. One of them strolled towards us.

"We're in luck," Gret whispered through clenched lips. "He's one of the nice ones." Out loud he said, "Fahrtal, it's good to see you."

"Gret, you are a lousy liar," the man intoned. He had a thin, meticulous moustache and an air of someone who really did not want to be there. "Let's see what we have here." He walked to the back of the cart.

"Onions. Big and hard!" Gret declared.

As I watched, one of the merchants beside us began shouting at an official. "This is highway robbery." His hands gesticulated dramatically in the air. "Your scales are tipped, and you hiked the taxes again. Might as well have given everything to robbers and beggars."

Guards immediately began to converge on the merchant from all directions, but the one who bore the brunt of the merchant's rage seemed relaxed. I could not hear the guard's answer but from his physical demeanour and gesture I guessed he was saying, "I don't make the rules," while resting his hands casually on the power rifle. Behind him, several Trolls quickly unloaded sacks from the old van. The guard thumbed at the open tent behind them. This time the wind carried the guard's voice. "Make your complaints to someone who might give a damn."

The merchant turned and walked to the tent. I could see that with every step his frustration and anger were growing.

Fahrtal finished counting the sacks. "That will be three sacks of onions or coin as tax."

"Three sacks?" Gret's eyes bulged in surprise. "That's steep, that's—"

"We need to feed the troops, Gret. Or do you want to try your luck with the Oil Baron?" He turned to me without waiting for a response. "And who might you be?" His dark eyes explored me. I had a hunch this man never forgot a face.

"My wife," Gret said and added too quickly, "My new wife." He was nervous, and I could see that Fahrtal felt it.

"Newlywed. How lucky you are. And you are from?"

"Lakewood," I said quickly.

"That's far," he said. "And you came all the way here to marry ol' Gret here?"

I looked at the sheepskin-wearing Gret with what I hoped was love-filled eyes. "He's . . . different, but a good man, and besides," I said without flinching, "I love his big, hard onions."

Gret began to cough but the official burst out laughing. "Fine," he said, turning back to Gret. "I'll let her in for free, but she needs to pay five towers for that sword of hers."

He waited for me to count the coins into his hand, pocketed them without bothering to give me a receipt, and said, "Welcome to the City of Towers, Mistress Gret."

26

Mannes

It was daytime in mid-winter in Kyrgyzstan, and the temperature on the side of the mountain was just above freezing. The sky was shrouded in grey clouds, blocking the sun. Norma informed Mannes the temperature would drop even more in a few hours. Any wind would make things even more uncomfortable. Mannes figured the space suit would keep him warm and relatively radiation free, and if things deteriorated, he could always put on his helmet. He chose to carry two small oxygen tanks on his thighs, with enough air to last him sixteen hours, and took the emergency landing backpack, too, just to be on the safe side.

Nothing went smoothly, though. He even had to open the door manually and that took some effort and a little engineering ingenuity. Once outside he walked around the shuttle with growing trepidation. The shuttle, like all of its kind, had been built in space and was not meant to enter or leave Earth's atmosphere. That was what the space elevator was for. For extreme situations—and Mannes acknowledged to himself this was definitely the case now—the shuttle was equipped with emergency landing fluid, which dispersed itself on the shuttle's body and protected its occupants from being fried as they entered the atmosphere. The heat caked the fluid into the body of the shuttle, and now that it had cooled, it was as solid as the metal underneath it. Mannes vaguely remembered there was a way to remove it, but it was a lengthy process and would take some careful brewing of chemicals. He was not sure the formula was in the shuttle's memory banks or the required materials in inventory, but this, he decided, was a matter he could address later.

They'd landed on the lower slopes of a high mountain, in the thick of the woods, easily spotted from the air but harder to find from the ground. Mannes's internal connection to the shuttle's AI was a blessing. He would surely have been lost without it.

He walked downhill for close to two hours, rehearsing phrases in Russian from the neural language pack in his brain amp. The Russians had made sure to crush the local culture on their second try for occupation, so the locals might resent the language, but they all spoke it. He was startled when Norma said suddenly, "I'm afraid we have a problem."

Mannes stopped in his tracks, then sat down and leaned his back against a tree. He inhaled deeply.

"What is it?" he said in Russian.

"It is not life-threatening." The AI shifted immediately to the same language.

"I am glad to hear that."

"I am only saying this because you seem to have hunkered down behind a tree."

"I know."

"It's not like there is a nuclear missile coming our way."

"That's good to know."

"And if there was one, hiding behind a tree would not have saved you."

"But in the minute or two I had left to live I could take a mighty shit."

Norma went silent for several brief seconds. Mannes sighed and shook his head. All AIs, even relatively simple ones such as the shuttle's, came with a personality. It was grown from several basic, predisposed subroutines and influenced by the four hundred or so hours spent with the software consciousness engineer responsible for growing the self-aware program from a sort of virtual infancy into something that wasn't a suicidal maniac. The problem was that most AIs' consciousness engineers were usually, to put it mildly, not the sort of people you wanted to have a beer with, and the AIs' programming psychologists were even more pitiful when it came to personality.

"I was joking," he said to the Comm.

"Yes, I know. As you are most likely aware, the nourishment pill takes care of all internal waste without the need for 'taking a mighty shit.'"

Mannes sighed again. Yep, definitely *that* sort of software consciousness engineer, but he'd done a mighty job on the piloting skills, so it evened out. Barely.

"What's the problem?"

"The army outpost has an automatic command control. It is a very primitive system, but somehow still active. It initiated a dumping field around the base that restricts receiving and sending signals."

Mannes uttered a curse in Russian he was only half certain he understood the meaning of.

"I might manage to hold our contact for several hundred yards in, but once you are in the base—"

"I'll be on my own."

"—you would be on your own. On the bright side"—the AI's voice perked up enthusiastically—"the base's sirens are sounding and the loudness is a hundred and six decibels. That will help you with navigation once we lose contact."

Mannes tried to listen but heard nothing.

"It is pretty clear once you get closer to the base."

"This base, it's in a state of emergency? Because I could get shot a mile away from it." Mannes was also painfully aware of his lack of weaponry. Not that he was trained in using firearms, but a gun would have been nice to have right now.

"The base has been off the grid for years. I do not think it is able to respond to this immediate crisis. The sirens and the dumping field could have been active for a long time."

Mannes winced and fished another pain-relieving pill from his belt. The pill dissolved in his mouth, leaving a fresh mint flavor on his tongue. He felt its effects almost immediately.

"Feeling better?" The suit was monitoring his physical situation and sending it to the shuttle's AI.

"Yeah. Those pills are a blessing."

Mannes got up and shook out his legs. A brief glimpse at his retina map showed the way. He turned, tripped over a large stone, landed awkwardly, and almost twisted his ankle. This time his curse came out in English.

27

Twinkle Eyes

Miraculously, we did not die, although we came close.

After a deadly cat and mouse game, the Dwaines retreated at sundown to fortified barracks, and we ended crawling through the minefield, holding on to the hope that Galinak had managed to take down all the snipers. Even with the use of my enhanced sight to detect the mines, it was a slow, nerve-wracking experience. For obvious reasons, Galinak crawled so close to me his head was practically between my legs, and the butt of the machine gun he carried on his forearm kept hitting me in vulnerable places.

"Are we there yet?" he whispered.

I dared a peek at my backside. "No. I'm taking the scenic route."

"Ah, good, because from here I can only see your hairless balls."

"Quit complaining," I whispered through gritted teeth. He had no reason to complain, wearing SmartLeather, while I could feel every sharp stone grating against my body.

We kept crawling.

"Shame about the horse," Galinak said, breaking the silence

again. "Guess they did cook a stew after all. Too bad diplomacy didn't work."

"Well, I'm only making a calculated guess here, Galinak, but if you hadn't touched those buttons and blown up one of their precious Sky Birds, maybe the Dwaines would have been a bit less hostile."

Galinak thought about it for a short spell. "Nah, those Secluders would have roasted us as soon as they got the chance. I could see it in their eyes. Can't trust 'em."

There was an upturned metal caravan of some sort in the middle of the field, its wheels long gone, and after Galinak ripped open a stuck door we climbed inside.

"We're almost out," I said, taking my time looking around with my enhanced sight, "and if we keep the caravan at our backs we will be covered for a while."

Galinak leaned on the metal wall and checked his weapon, I followed his example and did the same with my peacemaker.

"Nice shooting, by the way." Galinak slapped my back.

"Yeah, well . . ." I coughed. "The muzzle-retina connection was a nice surprise. I didn't think a collector's replica gun like this would have one."

"It's custom-made, very nice. Shame about the rate of fire, though."

I turned the large gun in my hand. I had to admit it felt comfortable holding it. The old me had shunned weapons and violence on principle, but the old me had also been torn to pieces by a horde of Lizards. That had changed new me's point of view regarding guns.

"I think I'm fine with the rate of fire. Makes me think before I pull the trigger."

Galinak snorted something under his breath, which I decided I didn't want to hear more clearly. In truth, I was shaken. Our Tarakan bodies, with enhanced mobility, durability, and in Galinak's case physical might, were the only reason we were still alive. Weapon or not, fighting was a horrid experience, at least for me, and I swore not to do it again if I ever had the choice.

"We should continue," I said, and Galinak nodded in agreement.

By sunlight we'd cleared the field and began walking on foot. A nourishment pill took care of our bodily needs but not the battle fatigue. After several more hours of trekking it was actually Galinak who proposed we rest awhile. We veered away from the path and took refuge in the shade of some bushes. Having real weapons did not change Galinak's sense of caution. I used the time he spent scouting to count the metal coins we'd looted. It was a small fortune, enough to tempt anyone to change their plans, but I felt I had no choice. Galinak would want to know sooner or later, so when he came back, I told him the sum.

To my surprise he only pocketed a handful of coins and told me to keep the rest for a while.

"We're going to the City of Towers together to find Vincha, then I'll decide what to do. Might as well keep only one of us jingling," he explained.

"Aren't you afraid I'll run off with the metal?"

Galinak found a shady spot, lay down on his back, and closed his eyes. "You're not a bad shot, Twinkle Eyes, all considered, but you ain't that good, either." He opened one eye and looked at me. "Don't look like I just rusted your metal. You did well enough out there, for a rookie Troll. Truth is, we've been saving each other's hide since the beginning, and as much as I can recall, even before that. Guess it should count for something."

I sat down next to the prone Galinak with a heavy sigh, trying to make sense of my conflicting emotions. Yes, Galinak trusted me and would come with me to the City of Towers. It was the best possible outcome, for now. Yet despite the trials of battle, I felt a growing suspicion it wasn't just the warrior's code that bonded us. With all his bravado, Galinak was almost too easily susceptible to my suggestions. I was considering whether the Tarkanians created not just new bodies for us but had also messed with our minds as well.

I thought Galinak had dozed off when he suddenly asked again, "How are you going to track Vincha down?"

"Like I said, I've done it before." I shrugged.

"Remind me how long it took you to find Vincha the last time—several years, was it?"

"I didn't know then what I know now, and I suspect I still have good contacts where it counts."

"Good contacts?" Galinak chuckled. "They knew the former you. Now you're a complete stranger to them."

Galinak was right. My former contacts would not recognise me, but most of them wouldn't care much for who I was, either. As long as I flashed enough coin and played on their weaknesses, I could get solid information about what was going on in each district. Besides, Vincha, with all her elusiveness, was still a creature of habit. I knew by name the very few people in the city who still saw her in a good light, and having experienced Vincha up close and personal, I doubted she'd made many new friends.

"We know the area she operates in, and we know who she's trying to protect. Leave it to me," I said with slightly more confidence than I truly felt. "I'll find her."

"You sound very sure of yourself. But even if you find her, Vincha's not going to help you."

"And why is that?"

"Because this Mannes guy wants Emilija, but the rusting Tarkanians want Vincha's daughter, too. She gets the rusty bucket full of shit flipped over her head either way, and in that situation, I imagine she wouldn't care who's holding the bucket. So no, I don't think Vincha's going to show you her loving side."

A memory flashed before my eyes, Vincha kneeing me in the chest, then sitting on me and pricking the lower part of my eyeball with a very sharp combat blade. I shivered. "I will find a way to make her cooperate, I did it before."

Galinak yawned. "Don't offer her my share of the metal."

Trying not to dwell on the fact that I would most likely have to spend Galinak's share without his consent, I changed the subject. "Have you heard of this Mannes?"

Galinak scratched his growing beard and yawned. "Sure I have. Everybody's heard of him, he's like this other guy . . ." He furrowed his brow, fumbling with a memory. "Nakamura, that's it. Yeah, like him, just on a bigger scale, if it's possible. I mean, Nakamura unleashed a horde of Lizards and destroyed the entire Hive in Tarakan Valley. That's a few hundred combat Trolls downed. Quite a big number."

I nodded. "That's a hard one to beat, but Mannes created Cain, an untested Sentient Program that sought to destroy Tarakan. Whether by design or accident, it most likely caused the Catastrophe. According to Mannes's logs, he even watched it happening"—I pointed upwards—"from space."

Galinak whistled softly. "Now *that* will rust your conscience."

"I'm not sure he has a conscience," I said. "He ends up at the other end of the planet, in some godforsaken land, and vanishes, presumed dead. The next thing we know, a hundred years later, he's crossed the great sea and he's here."

"If that's even true, that's a long trek." Galinak nodded to himself. "Guess he had some seriously unfinished business here."

"Only two things can make a man go through all that trouble," I said. "Love or—"

"—revenge," Galinak completed the sentence. "Or both—who knows?"

"I want to learn more about him, if I can," I said. "He is seeking to take Emilija, and we might need to face him at some point."

"Surviving the Catastrophe and another hundred years, that's no mere coincidence," Galinak agreed.

"I know a man called Gordon. He was a first scribe from the Guild of Historians, and he claims to be a survivor of a massacre that Mannes perpetrated in a monastery. The monks were like these Secluders, did not let anyone into their monastery, but they were peaceful folks, just collected old books. Unfortunately for them they were books that Mannes desired. He raided the place and apparently murdered everyone. Gordon was away on an expedition, when he came back he found nothing but corpses and smoldering heaps. He claimed it was well defended and had withstood countless attacks, yet Mannes overcame their defences and sacked it."

"Killing for books, now that's a first," Galinak remarked.

"From what I've gathered, Mannes has a following wherever he goes, and apparently is indestructible."

Galinak's brow furrowed even as his eyes remained closed. "No one is indestructible."

"True." I hesitated. There was one more person who I knew could shed a little more light on Mannes, but there was no use in bringing her name up right then, or trying to explain how I knew about her. I hadn't seen Fay in years—for all I knew, she wasn't even working anymore. I said instead, "From the files I saw, he did not have much military experience, but he was a high-ranking specialized Tarkanian and apparently very smart. Who knows, maybe he's responsible for all this mayhem and the war machines running around."

Galinak turned his head to me and opened his eyes. He looked tired—no, weary, and considering what we'd been through, it was no surprise. "So now you can communicate with Rafik through dreams?"

I scratched my head, stifling my own yawn. "Apparently so, but I haven't experienced it yet. What I saw was through the direct link I established with the helmet's communication system."

"Yes, but you dreamt how to do it, that's what you said."

"Yes. It was strange. Tell you what, it explains what happened to Rafik, you know, when he was just a boy, and that strange Pikok when they were both in the Hive. Maybe all the Puzzlers' dreams of the great wall of symbols are just sort of a Tarakan teaching method, to get the Puzzlers trained and lure them to the Valley."

Galinak stretched. "Wouldn't be beneath those buggers to mess with the poor souls' heads like that. But thanks for the warning, if they come into my dreams when I sleep, I'll have more than a few words to say to them."

I chuckled, although I suspected Galinak was actually serious. A few moments later, he was asleep. I took first watch.

28

Mannes

Mannes had already found a way out of the forest and was walking on a paved road when he finally lost contact with the shuttle. Honestly, he hadn't thought it would affect him the way it did, considering the events of the last day or so. He tried to reestablish contact several times, then looked back at the woods as if it would make some kind of difference. He was suddenly all alone, unable to reach anyone at his will for the first time in— what, several decades? He looked around, fighting rising panic, and for no logical reason he suddenly howled, "Hello? Anyone here?"

There was no response, of course.

The wind brought up small clouds of dusts. Combined with the ever-increasing wail of the sirens, it made for a very eerie scene. Mannes picked up his pace, fighting the urge to turn back and head for the shuttle. The harsh weather had left the road worse for wear, including man-sized potholes filled with muddy water. There was a fallen, rusted sign in both Russian and Kyrgyz. His neural translator only had Russian but the picture on the sign was universal, so he knew there were land mines beyond the now long-gone fence.

He decided to stick to the road and keep his mind preoccupied with Russian phrases. He did not want to think of Deborah and Nancy, crouching in a bunker. Frightened, wondering about him, thinking he was dead. He desperately tried not to think about the Guardian Angels. They were everywhere these days. Walking the streets, guarding the parks, protecting everyone against terrorists. What would happen if they all turned on the people they were supposed to protect? And why now? *Why the fuck now?* A world war, erupting just as Cain had been awakened. That was not a coincidence, but it also couldn't have been Cain, could it?

The Sentient Program had not been tested, and Daichi had said it would adapt, and the whole idea was to stop something like this from happening. Cain could have tried to take hold of sub-routines that controlled the weapons of mass destruction, and if he did, Adam could have interpreted the move as a direct attack.

Mannes stopped in his tracks, suddenly trembling. This could all be on him. Deborah, Nancy, his parents, billions of people. This could all be his fault. He was on his hands and knees for a while, dry-retching into a greasy puddle.

"Keep it together, Mannes," he said to his distorted reflection. It came out in Russian. *Keep. It. Together.*

The task in hand was to get home, just to get home. If Deborah was alive, she would be needing him. *If she's not . . .*

Mannes got up and swallowed another sedative.

Keep it together. Stay alive. Get help. For Deborah.

He resumed walking.

It didn't take much longer to reach the place where the out-post's gates must have been. They were gone now, but two long-range machine gun bases were still there and active, turning from side to side every few seconds. If machine guns were still mounted on the bases, Mannes reflected, he would have been long dead. Still, it was a good sign, he hoped.

"Hello?" he called out again, adding the Russian phrase he'd memorized on his way, "*Druz'ya, ya prishol k vam s oykrytymi obyatyemi v chas nujdy.*" Friends, I come to you with open arms in time of need.

No response but the metal squeak of the moving machine gun bases. The place seemed deserted, and that was perhaps a good thing. He could work in peace and salvage what he needed to repair the shuttle.

The outpost was not a big place—several main buildings and a few barracks, two tall antennas, and a spacious outdoor garage for vehicles. Everything was peppered with bullet holes and fading graffiti. The bulk of it was different variations on a "Fuck the Russians" theme with the occasional "Screw the Russians," "Kill the Soviets," and several "Freedom for the Kyrgyzstani," too. The siren inside the base was close to deafening, meant to awaken a soldier even from the deepest of drunken stupors. Mannes decided to make finding the main computer and silencing it a priority, with brute force if necessary.

Say what you want about the Russian former mighty army, he thought, they were certainly unimaginative when it came to constructing their bases. Mannes decided to head for the tallest building, three stories high, and to start his search from there.

All three floors were in the same state of postraid. Anything that was not taken was destroyed. On the third floor he stopped and gaped at the only whole computer screen. It had been eons since he'd seen a flat-screen like that. This one was still working, barely. Only half of it was still functioning with numbers and what Mannes deduced were coded sentences in Russian appearing and disappearing in a warped fashion periodically.

There was no keyboard attached, and the power cable ended in a hole in the wall. Mannes leaned down and tried to make sense of what he was seeing. Perhaps there was a power switch somewhere in the base, although he assumed such a switch would be locked and protected.

When he straightened and turned around it was too late. Two men were already in the room and the third was just entering. All three were dressed in Russian army camouflage suits, the sort that reduced their heat signatures. Mannes noted the earmuffs all three were sporting. He also noted they were aiming their weapons straight at him.

Mannes spread his hands wide, his heart racing. *"Druz'ya"*—he tried the phrase he'd rehearsed—*"ya prishol k vam s oykrytymi obyatyemi v chas nujdy."*

Perhaps the earmuffs blocked their hearing, or perhaps it was his clunky Russian pronunciation, but as Mannes was finishing the sentence for the third time, the first man who reached him turned and drove the butt of his rifle straight into Mannes's jaw, knocking him out cold.

29

Peach

We were moving away from the unloading area when I saw the angry merchant being carried out from the main tent by two burly Trolls.

"Agh, he's done for, the poor bugger." Gret stopped Summer and shook his head. "You have to be careful around the purple-and-golds—they can be as vicious as the Trolls."

The merchant was carried to a pole, where he was tied and his upper body exposed. His protestations soon turned into pleas. As if I were watching a virtual depicting ancient times, a guard with a whip approached the pole. Everyone ceased their work and turned to watch the spectacle. The officials in purple and gold came out from the tent as well. It was obvious what I was about to see was ordinary, and the younger-looking men and women used this time to relax, share a joke or two, and even pass a drink among them.

"For offending a clerk of the merchant guild and a public servant," the whip-holding guard declared, "punishment of six lashes, a thirty-metal coin fine, and confiscation of half the haul."

The guard lashed his whip in the air for a few practice shots and perhaps to increase tension for the spectators.

"Well . . . he's definitely not going to come back and trade here anymore," I said as the first lash hit the merchant's back. He shrieked in pain and fear and defecated on himself to the sound of laughter from the guards and the clerks. Several drivers honked their horns in protest but stopped when guards approached.

"You ain't from around here, Mistress." Gret began manoeuvring the cart so we would not drive too close to what was happening. "Otherwise you'd know that they declared all merchandise must be sold to the city."

"You don't say." It made sense, of course.

Gret shrugged and scratched his head through his woollen cap. "They cancelled the local markets, and hoarding food will get you hanged. The villages and farmers are taxed dry to their last coin, so they have to sell anything they grow. With the city the only buyer, they can pretty much set the price outside and inside the walls."

We were leaving the horrid scene behind us but I turned my head back. The merchant lost consciousness by the third lash and had to be revived. A guard decided urine was better than wasting water and was in the process of delivering it on the head of the collapsed merchant to the merriment of the officials and guards.

I turned my head back.

"Take my word for it, he'll come back," Gret whispered. "He has nowhere else to go, and he won't be haggling over price again. I tell you, might as well be a slave to the Oil Baron, I hear he, at least, warms his people in the winter."

We drove in silence until we reached the bridge of light, where we dismounted, took Summer by her bridle, and began walking up. It felt like stepping on the remains of an old corpse. The only remnant of the bridge's former glory was its wide base, but the power projectors were either gone or not working. Since the bridge was located outside the security zones of the city, it was a miracle that even that had survived the onslaught.

On top of the bridge's base, humanity had improvised a new

version of a walkway, made of planks of uneven wood and rusty, warped metal, which were balanced on and tied to the central tracks of what were once conveyor belts. There was nothing to prevent you from falling off the sides, that is, if you hadn't misstepped and simply plunged to your death through the many man-sized holes or loose planks.

Having to help Gret pull the reluctant mule between other nervous beasts of burden, and scores of half-naked men who carried impossible amounts of bulk on their shoulders, left no time to dwell again on how far humanity had fallen.

There was no gentle slope or conveyor belt in the middle of the bridge to help pedestrians reach their destination. Instead the bridge curved upwards, and at several points climbers used their hands as well as their legs to progress. We were halfway to the top when the wind suddenly blew from the side with dangerous force, and I braced myself against Summer and held on. One of the men, in his haste, had walked too far from the centre and was not so fast to react. The wind slammed into him and he lost his balance. Perhaps if he had not been carrying so much on his back he would have managed to save himself, but the weight of the haul carried the poor man over the edge. His scream echoed for a while but the wind masked any sound of impact. When the wind died everything resumed as if nothing had happened.

The side wind hit us twice more before we got to the top of the wall, where we were thankfully protected from the wind by the city's shields, which acted as climate control. The entire day took its toll on my vessel, and at least one entrepreneur had anticipated the immediate needs of the climbers. Located several steps from the landing area was a food stall, and for what I guessed was an exorbitant price of three towers I bought bread, butter, stale hard cheese, and a cup of steaming vegetable broth for both myself and Gret. He bent his head in gratitude and we both ate in silence, too exhausted to speak. Everything tasted awful, and my vessel informed me of the low nutritional contents of the food.

I looked around as I slowly chewed the tasteless food. The

entire top of the wall was an unloading area, and a sort of a market, where local merchants haggled with clerks over the prices of goods. The city was making a double profit here, first buying cheaply from outside the wall, then hitching the price up for the merchants inside. There were more guards and Trolls, some wearing full battle helmets and carrying power machine guns, marking them as elite compared to the others. Nevertheless, despite the security, the area was too chaotic to control. I was sure many shady deals took place here, feeding the black market that surely exists. There should have been another security post but there wasn't. If indeed war was looming, this was a weak spot from which spies and saboteurs could infiltrate the city. Sure, I planned to use the very same weakness should I need to smuggle myself in or out of here, but this was still my city, and the security breach bothered me on principle.

When Gret finished eating he bought some hay for Summer and bartered for a while until he got a decent price for the rest of his onions. He came back smiling and happily tapped the small bulge of a coin bag on his belt.

He gave Summer a tired-looking carrot.

"That climb is hard on both of us," he said, brushing the mule gently, "but it was worth it. My onions will go straight to the Upper Spires, and I got something to get by for the next moon."

Tired, but obviously proud of the fact that his onions would be eaten by rich people, Gret mounted the cart. "Let's go. We can't take the rope bridges because of the cart, so we'll go the long way, but the route to the Middle Spires is quite nice."

As we slowly drove away from the market the sun was going down, and the city's lights, or what was left of them, were turning on. The centre of the plateau was lit enough but the area around it was completely dark. The City of Towers used to be a place of marvel, a place built not just to assess and accept new applicants to Tarakan but also to dazzle, awe and delight the people coming to visit. Every night dozens of open-air concerts and plays were staged, free to the public. Every week a different festival was held:

art, poetry, dance, literature, gaming, virtuals, and sports. Tarakan wanted to convey to its millions of visitors a simple message: "If you are good enough, if you are smart enough, if you can help move humanity forward, this could be your life."

In the last decade before the war, with international embargos and tension rising, the festivities were smaller in scale and more difficult to produce, but the nightlife was still spectacular. The city used to sparkle. Now it was mostly dark and filled with people dressed as if they'd come out of the Middle Ages. A light breeze touched my face. At least the city's climate control was still functioning; otherwise, I would have been in danger of freezing.

As I turned around, trying to take it all in, I saw a line of standing carts, each tied to a mule or a horse. What used to be a tourist attraction in some old European cities had become the main means of transport in what was once the most modern, sophisticated city in the world.

What the fuck had happened? How could this be even possible? If the city was still intact, then where had all the Tarkanians gone? I suspected I would not have liked the answers, if there had even been someone there to give them to me.

"Amazing, isn't it, Mistress?" Gret waved his hand around, as if he was showing me his own palace. "My missus liked to walk around and just *look* at all of this. How the hell did they manage to build all that? Must have been some kind of magic."

"Yes. Magic," I agreed solemnly.

"You look tired. We'll be home in no time, and you can rest your legs after the climb."

I put a hand on the old man's shoulder. "I know it's a lot to ask, Gret, but since we are newlywed and all"—I winked and saw him blush a little—"could I ask a kind favour of you?"

"Sure, Mistress."

"Would you drive around a bit? It's been a long time since I last saw the city."

Gret turned his head in surprise. "I didn't know you were a Towerian. I thought you said you came from Lakewood."

"Even farther than that, but I was born here, in this city, and I've missed it ever since I was a child." It was only half a lie, and I could see he was tired, but Gret was a true gentleman.

"Fine, we can drive a bit." He shrugged. "But not too long. Summer needs a good rest and some more carrots. Where to?"

I looked around at the city I grew up in. "Everywhere," I said.

30

Mannes

They took turns beating him. In retrospect, the thought that a few words in clunky Russian, and an offer of peace and a reasonable exchange for mutual benefit, would translate into a warm welcome was naïve at best. Downright stupid, actually. And there was no point in trying to come up with a cover story, what with the Tarakan emblem on his suit, helmet, and kit.

They made him strip to his undergarments, then proceeded to slap him around some more. The worst one was the man with the eye patch, obviously the youngest. He didn't even ask questions, just pummeled Mannes again and again to the ground, lifting him to his feet just to hit him once more. All three were drinking heavily during the process, from personal and communal brownish bottles. By the smell of their breath Mannes guessed it was strong enough to fuel the shuttle's engine. It certainly helped fuel their violence.

At some point Mannes was hit over the head and lost consciousness again. When he woke up his brain amp was off line. At best, a standard procedure in such cases, or there was permanent damage to his internal hardware. Without the neural translator, Mannes could understand even less of what the three were asking him, and their own grasp of the foreign languages he had tried to use was not great either.

He did grasp the gist of their meaning. They wanted him to lead them to the shuttle, obviously with the intention of dismantling the craft for anything useful. He tried to negotiate at first, but under the onslaught he broke down embarrasingly quickly, rationalizing that once he got to the shuttle, he might find a way, hopefully with the help of Norma, to defeat them. Truth was, he was terrified, hurt, and unused to violence of any sort.

They started to head out midafternoon, and Mannes, practically naked except for his underwear and ill-fitting boots, was already shaking from the cold. The trio did not seem to care about Mannes's condition or even their own. Their camouflage suits, heavy hats, and the vast amount of alcohol in their bloodstream took care of that.

Without the brain amp or his ability to contact the AI, Mannes felt lost as soon as they entered the woods. It was almost pitch-black when his frustration took away caution and he shouted, "I don't fucking know where I am. I can't see a thing and I'm freezing."

His reward was as swift as it was painful. The one-eyed maniac actually put a hunting power knife to his throat. Looking into his one healthy eye, Mannes knew for a fact the man fully intended to garrote him there and then, and he lost his bowels. Only a sharp word from the older of the three, a man with a mouth full of golden teeth, stopped the knife from biting into Mannes's throat. What the one-eyed man didn't do with the blade, he did with the pommel. Mannes blissfully lost consciousness again, and when he woke up, he was slumped against a pole that had been driven into the almost-frozen ground, hands tightly tied behind his back.

The trio might have been drunk brutes, but they were veterans at living in the wild. Several more poles were erected and a tight material was spread between them to create a roof over their heads. The one-eyed man turned out to be frightfully good at chopping firewood with his power hand ax. A small fire was soon going, and two portable heaters made the cold bearable. Just. Mannes faced the fire but he was tied to a pole at the edge of the roof, exposed to the elements, and his unprotected back was already throbbing from the cold. He knew that even if he did survive, he would get sick, and if the fire died during the night, so would he.

After settling down, the trio ate dried meat and drank some more. No food was offered to Mannes, but even if they had offered him something, he would have found it impossible to chew considering the state of his jaw and teeth.

Eventually one of the men offered Mannes a drink. When he refused, the man poured some of it forcefully down his throat. It was like drinking filtered petrol. He wheezed and coughed and puked to the sound of their guttural laughter. When he woke up again the fire was dying out, his back was getting numb from the cold, and he felt blood in his throat when he coughed. He was dying. And his captors couldn't have cared less. They didn't even care enough about what he had to offer them to keep him from dying until he delivered them to the prize. Such was the world he'd landed on.

They say that before you die, you can see things clearly. It might have been a cliché, but for the first time since he'd encountered the three men, Mannes had a moment of clear thought. He *had* to escape, and testing the ropes that tied him to the pole, he suddenly had a notion of how to do it.

The three didn't bother to leave a guard out on watch and were soon fast asleep, wrapped in heat-trapping blankets. On his third try, Mannes managed to take the cap off his engineer finger. With his other hand, he bent his finger at a painful angle until it touched the ropes. The engineer fingertip contained a small flashlight, which could also be used as a laser pointer that generated a small amount of heat. It took forever, but the ropes slowly began to burn. It also burned Mannes's skin. He tried to maintain self-control but the choked cry of pain which escaped from his clenched lips was enough to wake up the man with the eye patch, who rose unsteadily to his feet but looked straight at Mannes. There was no use in pretending he was asleep. Mannes watched the man heft his rifle onto his back, kick a small log into the dimming fire and walk slowly towards him. If he smelled the burned rope and flesh, Mannes knew that would be the end of him. Hovering above Mannes, the one-eyed man looked down with menace. Mannes heard his own trembling voice croak the words in Russian which somehow sprang into his mind: "*Ya'zamerzayu.*" I'm freezing.

The man laughed and looked up to the sky, and Mannes followed his gaze. A small part of the sky was clear and at that moment something up high, perhaps another satellite, supernovaed and lit the night for a brief second. The man with the eye patch whooped and laughed and cursed in Russian, then looked back down at Mannes with intent.

He pointed at Mannes, then up. "You," he said slowly, in broken English, "Tarakan . . . did . . . this." He pointed up and at Mannes again and said slowly and deliberately in Russian, "You think you are better than us, smarter than us, stronger than us, yeah? You think you can rule over us." He reverted to broken English, "Here . . . you . . . now . . . *slabak* . . . *veak* man." The man's hands went to his groin and moved in a manner that all men, regardless of age or nationality, know how to recognise. Mannes's broken jaw slacked in shock, but he managed to close his mouth and avert his face just in time for the first splash of warm urine to rain down on him. He turned his face to the side and held his breath for as long as he could, but the man had patience, good aim, and apparently a very full bladder. When he was done, the man turned and walked away without saying another word. A minute later he was asleep.

When the heat seared his flesh again, Mannes bore it, biting his own tongue till it bled. Eventually he felt his bonds loosen up and suddenly he was free. Mannes rose to his feet with one thought screaming through his mind, *flee*, but after only a few steps he stopped in his tracks. Where would he run to, naked and in the pitch-darkness of a frozen night? He would die from exposure, and even if he could survive somehow, how long would it take three veteran hunters to track him down?

Mannes turned back to face the occupants of the tent. They were fast asleep, but in a manner of all battle-hardened soldiers, their weapons were attached to their bodies. Any attempt to seize one, even if successful, would surely wake the others, and he wouldn't know how to operate a hunting rifle even if he had one in his hands. Mannes's gaze fell on the power hand ax, lying near a small pile of chopped firewood. He could still smell, fuck, he could *taste*, the urine on him. A few tender steps and a crouch and the ax was held firmly in his hand. He watched, still crouching, as the three of them slept, then stretched and fished a half-burned log from the fire with his free hand. It would not take much to get them awake, he thought, better end it quickly. He raised the ax above his head and hit the power button as he lunged forward.

Years later, Mannes would recall the man with the eye patch opening his eye and raising his head just as Mannes's ax came down. It might not have been completely true, but it made the memory so much sweeter.

31

Twinkle Eyes

To my shame, it was Galinak who spotted the circling birds first. After that it was just a matter of following the markings of the tanks through the trampled corn field surrounding the small hamlet.

So far from a major town, it probably began as a farm inhabited by the survivors of the Catastrophe. As the generations passed, several more houses were built and their inhabitants expanded the fields, added livestock, and heightened the fence to a protective wall, which was now completely in pieces.

Death was everywhere, from the burned houses and destroyed barn to the animal carcasses that littered the place.

Galinak kneeled next to a dead dog, ignoring the buzzing flies, and stated the obvious. "This was recent." He got back to his feet and hefted his weapon.

I scanned the area. "The only living things here are the crows," I said.

"We'll see about that," Galinak muttered and took point.

With the crows feeding, it didn't take long for us to discover the four rows of bodies. Most were adults, but I saw smaller ones, too. Galinak went to inspect the bodies, walking among the fearless, pecking crows while I stayed a little farther away, trying to look at anything else but the terrible scene before us. I kept my gaze at the direction of the fields though I couldn't escape the horrendous stench of death.

Eventually Galinak came back.

"Soldiers, most of them," he said. "Dead a day at most."

I turned my face towards him in surprise. "Soldiers so far away from the city, are you sure?"

"They wore uniforms and these," Galinak held up a torn sleeve with a crude but recognisable City of Towers insignia sewn to it.

"The ones who fought died fast. Multiple wounds from different angles. The attackers came from at least two directions, and with them war machines to boot; those poor bastards didn't have a chance." Galinak turned back to the rows of bodies while I kept my eyes on the fields. "Those who were captured had been tortured, badly, then shot in the back of the head. There are a few farmers, too. Men and young boys. They probably joined the fight to protect their homes. The women got it worst, and the children were collateral damage, looks like from the blasts."

"So they took the rest of the farmers, destroyed the barn, tried to burn the field"—I pointed at a large blackened area—"but botched the job. Maybe the wind changed?"

Galinak turned back and said something but at that moment I saw the figure rise from the corn stalks and aim a rifle at us. I slammed into Galinak's back too late, the shot had already been fired, but it missed. We rolled over each other in the blood-soaked muck. Galinak was up in a heartbeat.

It took me longer to get my bearings. I turned my head as I was getting onto my knees and changed my vision into heat-seeking sight. The world erupted into hot, white color, blinding me to almost everything, but I did spot a figure running away in the high corn. "Over there." I pointed and blinked back to normal vision.

Even in that state I could see the corn stalks move as the shooter tried to run away in a straight line from us.

I made a mental calculation, as I saw Galinak in hot pursuit. The shot was not from too far away, the fact that the shooter missed meant he was probably one of the farmers, a survivor of the massacre. "Don't kill him," I shouted after Galinak as he disappeared into the vegetation. From my vantage point I could see the shooter's line of movement and a second line as Galinak trampled his way astonishingly fast.

As if this was not enough, Galinak suddenly leaped through the air and landed farther than any man could ever reach. A few moments later he emerged from the field carrying an unconscious body over his shoulder and an ancient bolt-action rifle in his other hand. He tossed the rifle at me and dropped the unconscious man on the ground. The rifle was in a sorry state; even I could see that. I looked at the prone body and berated myself for my hasty assumption. He was no farmer, but to call him a soldier would be stretching the definition of the word. I would have been surprised if he was old enough to shave, and the uniform was too large. The insignia was of the City of Towers, though.

"Only six bullets." Galinak patted a side pocket.

"I guess we're even on lifesaving moves now," I said to him.

"I carried you on my shoulder from a poisonous bunker, downed a Dwaine that was about to blow your head off, and you're calling pushing me into the mud 'lifesaving'?" Galinak wiped his hands on his trousers. "The state of this rifle, he wouldn't have hit us if we were standing on each other's shoulders."

"I think it's the thought that counts."

"I think you still owe me. Big time."

"Fine. Now let me ask the right questions. Guess you're the 'bad Troll' and I'm the 'good Troll' with this one?"

Galinak's smile was broader this time. "I'm always the 'bad Troll.'" He gave the unconscious body a light shove with his boot, which rolled the soldier onto his back. There was blood coming out of his mouth. He moaned a little, then opened his eyes.

I had come out of unconsciousness a few times just to see

Galinak's grinning face above me, so although he'd just tried to shoot us, I was feeling a little sorry for this boy.

Once he managed to focus on Galinak towering above him, a look of utter terror swept across his face. I stepped in and got his attention by waving the rifle.

"Let me make it nice and short. You answer my questions and you might live. You lie, and you join your friends over there." I pointed at the row of bodies as he slowly got up to a sitting position. Galinak stepped aside so he could have a clear view. The effect was dramatic. A soft whine escaped his lips and he began to tremble.

"Are they all . . . all of them . . . ?"

"Tortured, raped, and murdered, sometimes not in that order," Galinak said just as, in perfect timing, a crow hopped past holding an eyeball in its beak.

The boy soldier turned to his side and threw up.

I shot Galinak a warning glance. He shrugged back at me. I turned my attention back to the young soldier. "What is your name?"

The boy spat out the last of his bile and straightened up again. He was as white as a ghost but was trying to control himself. His voice still trembled when he answered. "Dorian, sir, Dorian of the Swas family." His foreign accent and the way he specified his family name betrayed him not to be a true Towerian.

"Who did this?"

Dorian did not hesitate. "Northerners, sir."

"Are you sure?" I said with enough surprise in my voice to cause a reaction. "I mean, the last time I was here, the Northerners were quiet enough, selling oil for food and supplies and keeping to themselves."

The young soldier shook his head. "It musta been a while since you've been to these lands, sir. The war with the North been going on for three springs. They were Northerners, all right. I know it because we had to run away last year from me own home when the Northerners came to our town."

"Where are you from?"

"Heaven's Retreat, Mister, it is . . . it *was* a small town, you probably haven't heard of it."

"Actually I've been there," I answered and somehow this fact cheered the boy up a little. "But it's nowhere near the North."

"I know. We heard the Oil Baron took some land and that the city sent a force of Towerian Trolls to give him a good beating, but they say the Baron laid a clever trap for them and came with those war machines, slaughtering the Tower's army to the last Troll."

The voice of my LoreMaster resonated in my mind. *You invented something that gave you an edge over all others: steel-tipped spears, a war chariot, longbows, a cart that moved without horses, and suddenly the world fell at your feet. That is, until another nation found a better technological advancement, and your own empire crumbled to dust.* When I was last in the City of Towers, the word on the Oil Baron was that he was just the weak son of a mercenary captain who had taken control of an oil refinery and with whom it was cheaper to do business than to conquer. A decade earlier his father tried to expand his turf and was beaten bloody. Now, it seemed, the tables had turned.

Unaware of my inner thoughts, the young soldier continued to talk. "We thought the Baron would stop there, but the next year refugees began showing up at our gate, all telling the same story. A raiding party attacked them, or their neighbours. Those who were not murdered were taken as slaves, and their homes and fields were burned.

"When word came that the Oil Baron was advancing towards Heaven's Retreat, my dad sent us all to my uncle, Evan, who works in the Middle Spires. He came to take us, and we had travel passes to the Long Tube, too, but as soon as we arrived at Regeneration my brother and I were taken into the militia. They said it was the only way for my mother and sisters to get to the city."

"How old are you?" Galinak asked suddenly.

"Fifteen this coming summer, sir."

Galinak and I exchanged a silent look. Three years of war without a resolute win for the City of Towers was a bad sign, and if they had to draft boys as young as Dorian things were going badly indeed.

"Is your brother among the dead?"

"No." Dorian let out a sigh of relief. "He's in a different unit, last I heard they sent him to guard the fields north of the city." The boy smiled bitterly. "He was always the lucky one. I was left to keep guard in Regeneration, and they said I could keep my rifle, but then we were ordered to come here and 'secure the supply line,' that's what Captain Rammon told us."

"Then what happened?"

Dorian hesitated. "I don't know, sir. We came here quiet enough, but the farmers, they were not happy to see us. They came out in arms and said they wouldn't give away this much of their food, or they wouldn't survive the winter. Captain Rammon told me to go scout the field with Corporal Mayar, to see that they ain't trying to smuggle away food, and we did. Then we heard shots. Corporal Mayar said maybe Captain Rammon shot in the air to scare the farmers, because they were arguing real fierce-like, but then it all went to hell. We ran back and saw them, the Northerners, all in black uniform, they came from all sides and there was this huge machine with cannons . . . Corporal Mayar ran first when something shot his head off right from his shoulders. Then I . . . then I . . ."

"Then you ran away," Galinak said, "and left your crew to fry. Don't blame ya for it. Untrained, outgunned, surprised from all sides, I would have retreated as fast as my legs could carry me. The only question is why you came back, and why you shot at us."

"I thought . . ." He hesitated. "I thought that maybe . . . if I came back . . . explained to the Captain what happened . . . then I saw you. I thought you were poachers."

"Your captain can't hear you now. He has the disadvantage of missing two of his ears and half of his head," I said, "and if he were alive, he would have shot you for desertion, not to mention poorly maintaining your rifle."

I bent down and stretched my hand out, and after a slight hesitation Dorian took it.

"So what now?" I asked after I helped him up.

Dorian hesitated. I saw the conflicting emotions on his face. On one hand, asking him about his future meant I was not planning on killing him. On the other hand, his future looked grim.

"I think if I went back to Regeneration and told them what happened—"

"You're a rusting idiot," Galinak snapped. "If you show up like this in Regeneration they'll have you executed on the spot, or worse, promote you and send you out again as target practice for the Northerners."

"You have family somewhere else?" I asked.

The boy shook his head. "They say Heaven's Retreat is gone, sir, and my father, he never followed us. So, he must be dead now . . ."

I looked at Galinak, who slowly shook his head at me.

"You say your uncle lives in the Middle Plateau?"

The boy nodded.

"Fine. If we take you to him, will he give us a place to stay?"

Dorian's eyes lit up with hope. "Would you do that, sir? It would be a kindness."

Behind his back Galinak shrugged, pointed at the boy, and rolled his eyes at me.

"First thing. Find yourself some new clothes," I said quickly. "Search the ruins or take them from the dead bodies, I don't care. We are not running around with you wearing a uniform. Go."

When Dorian left to look for alternative attire Galinak turned to me. "Twinkle Eyes, you've gone soft on me. This boy is just a hindrance."

"Perhaps, but much has happened since we were last here, Galinak, and we need to find out as much as we can. We were running around in the wilderness, clueless to the fact that a whole rusting war is raging. Imagine us getting to Regeneration hoping to catch a Long Tube ride to the city only to get drafted into their militia. And besides, the boy has family in the city—they'll be grateful for our bringing him back." I made a motion with my fingers suggesting hard coin, although what I really wanted was information and perhaps a place to lay low until I figured out what was happening in my city.

"You've got a point, all right," Galinak conceded. "The old Oil Baron was known to be a fierce cunt. His son I've never heard of, but running around conquering stuff with these things you call Tanks, killing Towerian Trolls? Now that's new."

I scratched the short hairs growing on my chin. "And the Northerners couldn't just have gotten their hands on a few. Those machines eat serious power, and I bet they take training to handle." I let my train of thought run even as I stopped talking. *If the blood-thirsty Baron held a cache of pre-Catastrophe heavy weaponry and the knowledge to use it, why didn't he just rush straight towards the city?* Biding his time, sending shock troops to clear the fields around the city's sphere of influence meant long-term planning and strategy. There was a serious shift of power going on here.

"Whatever." Galinak pointed at me, breaking my line of thought. "Just saying this is *your* idea, so the boy is eating from your share of the nourishment pills. And besides, you need to figure out a way into the city, now that we can't use the Long Tube."

"We'll go the long way," I answered, "maybe buy a ride with a trucker. As for entering the City of Towers, remember how we got out of it the last time?"

"You mean the sewers?" Galinak paled a little. "You *know* I have sensitive sinuses."

"There are only a few ways into the city that do not involve passing security, and that is the safest one I know. Besides, that was the old you." I gestured at his body.

"Aye." Galinak scratched his head, looking embarrassed. "You know, I got used to it, almost forgot it's not really mine."

He was right. My own earlier sense of detachment was gone. A part of me wanted to try and find out more about our state of being, but another part of me wanted to get away from this massacre as soon as we could.

"Let's help find the boy something to wear which does not scream 'deserter' and then get the rust out of here," I said.

"Fine." Galinak lifted his power machine gun. "And the pup's taking first watch, as soon as I teach him how to clean his rifle and shoot straight."

32

Mannes

"There is something in the sky." Lieutenant Slava sounded nervous over the Comm.

Mannes glanced up and squinted. A soft flake of contaminated snow touched his cheek. He brushed it away. Yes, there was something up there. The cold wind momentarily died, and the unnatural buzzing could be clearly heard in the distance.

"Report your status."

"Six trucks on their way towards you." Slava's voice filled Mannes's earpiece once again. "Seventeen vans. All armed with light weaponry, three carrying antitank cannons. I detected some movement in the fields, probably commando. Total of a hundred combatants, probably more."

And to think that he had actually believed that in five years he would already be in Tarakan. Mannes shook his head at his own folly as he watched Alikahn's vehicles advance. It had taken him a whole year just to extract Norma and the shuttle's medibots to the medical mobile unit he built. Without them he would have been dead already.

He had found and gathered some refugees around him. Kept them alive and formed them into a team, and when he judged he was ready he set out on his way home. He did not tell them his plans but they followed him anyway, hoping he could lead them to a better life. They were so very wrong. His original team was already long dead, but that was the least of his problems.

In the old days a leisure trip by land to the shores of Spain would have taken him two weeks, twice that if he decided to travel northeast, via the Bering Strait and across to Alaska. But Kazakhstan was not Kyrgyzstan, to say the least. There were no high mountains to protect the land from the fallout, and Kazakhstan was a far more strategic country in the world's conflict and had suffered from Tarakan's attention. This land was contaminated and ruined to the point of obliteration. All that was left of the cities were smoldering heaps of toxic ruins, destroyed roads, and collapsed bridges. Mannes had to keep backtracking and zigzagging to keep his growing army alive. Now he was stuck in a bloody war he had no way to circumvent.

Mannes turned to the merchant who was idling beside him.

"This had better be a straight deal or you'll be the first to die," he said in fluent Russian.

The merchant, to his credit, was not the timid kind. His steel blue eyes never wavered as he took a long drag from the small pipe sheltered in his palm.

"Alikhan has something you want, you have something he wants." The man made a show of shrugging and blew the smoke above both of their heads. "Of course there's a deal here."

"Alikhan raided me twice this season alone. This could all be a trap."

Mannes, at least, had foreseen the raids and prepared in advance, but the death toll was still in the dozens. In a barbaric move that the old Mannes would never have even contemplated, Mannes kept two of the captured raiders alive, put them on a pair of horses and sent them back, together with a sack full of decapi-tated heads from the rest of the raiders. In retrospect that action had caused more trouble than he anticipated, but he was angry and wanted to send a strong message in a language that perhaps the people of what was left of Kazakhstan spoke. Two months of bloody tit for tat had followed, with more and ever-growing atrocities committed by both sides. Now, just before winter, this warlord, Alikhan, was suddenly ready to parley.

"Commander"—it was Slava's nervous voice over the Comm—"what do you want me to do about the flying thing?"

Mannes touched his earpiece. "Nothing, for the moment."

"It could be a trap. You want me to shoot it down?"

He shook his head. What a stupid notion. His former lieutenant would have never asked this, but alas, he had to be disposed of. Now he was surrounded by fools. Bloodthirsty, trigger-happy fools.

"No, it's just a reconnaissance drone. Stay alert and wait for my signal," he answered over the Comm. Well . . . calling that thing a "drone" was probably stretching the word to its limit. From what he managed to see with his limited zooming ability and judging by the unsteady way it was flying, it was a kid's toy of some sort with a camera mounted on it. To think, just half a decade ago, real combat drones, with independent AIs, were flying at almost space height and could tell if your toenails were dirty. This one was buzzing noisily a hundred metres or so above their heads, barely keeping itself in the air. Still, the drone changed things from a tactical point of view. They could detect his troops or even the hidden mobile clinic. He could be negotiating a deal with a murderous maniac while an auxiliary force surrounded and killed his ragtag army.

"They're coming," the merchant announced and pocketed his pipe.

They all saw the dust the convoy was raising.

Mannes turned to the man. "You sure about the terms?"

It was not the first time he had asked. A show of insecurity, he knew, like checking your cards too often at the poker table, but the merchant just shrugged and answered, "Yes. I'm positive. Alikhan himself told me this."

Mannes tried not to betray his anxiety, but truth be told, he had several good reasons to be anxious. The numerous envoys he sent to Alikhan, the warlord who now controlled one of the only unravished lands of the region, had not returned—or, more correct, had not returned in one piece. Apparently, that was this warlord's way of beginning delicate truce negotiations. To top that, Mannes felt a headache building up. The throb he was feeling right now was at the exact place the one-eyed brute had hit him with the pommel, back in Kyrgyzstan, leaving a dent in his skull that never truly healed. The light throbbing would soon develop into a blinding pain that would either leave him incapacitated or drugged out of his mind. He needed this to be over with quickly.

The merchant broke the silence, trying to reassure Mannes, or perhaps himself. "Alikahn attacked you, and you burned two of his villages and took out a guard post and a bridge. I say you're even. You'll get safe passage." He blew smoke again, careful this time not to do so in the direction of Mannes. "Just remember my cut, and that you'll still need me afterwards. I know the way on the other side of the mountains."

Mannes nodded absentmindedly. He had no intention of double-crossing the man, as long as things went smoothly. But the whole business still didn't make sense. True, he'd outmanoeuvred the warlord's forces during the autumn season, and a big part of Alikhan's army was now pinned down protecting key locations. But the warlord's force was ten times the size of Mannes's, which was also running out of provisions. Mannes admitted to himself that he would have had to raid those villages even if negotiations had progressed smoothly. What a bloodbath it turned out to be. *Well . . . what's done is done.*

Turning back was not an option. Going around and through the mountains with such a large force as he had gathered was suicide. Abandoning his army and trying to cross alone was too risky. If Mannes was sure of one thing, it was that he was never going to be caught undefended again. He was never going to be tied up and feel urine on his face for as long as he lived. When the memory struck, Mannes could almost feel the hot piss still trickling down his face and neck. No, the army he had gathered was a problem right now, but Mannes was not going to abandon it. And when all seemed lost, this merchant had suddenly appeared and offered to be an honest broker—for a hefty cut, of course. Mannes had agreed. He had little faith, but nothing to lose, yet.

What the merchant had brought back was not a deal, it was a *surrender*. The only thing Alikhan insisted on was a face-to-face meeting. It all smelled like a trap, and probably was.

Mannes turned to the merchant. "Go to them now, and remember, I got snipers trained on you, specifically."

Without another word, the merchant mounted and kick-started the hoverbike. He drove away in the direction of the convoy, the heat generated by the engine leaving a line of caked mud behind him.

As was agreed upon, the convoy stopped a hundred metres away from where Mannes stood. One truck continued driving at a slow pace, together with the merchant who turned and escorted them.

Mannes touched his earpiece. "Report."

"No answer from the eastern and southeast units," came the answer.

Shit.

"I got a mortar unit on the leading truck," Slava said.

"Don't fire without my signal. And Slava . . ."

"Yes, Commander?"

"I will personally harvest your organs while you are still conscious if you or any of your trigger-happy soldiers fire a single shot."

Mannes turned off the Comm without waiting for an answer. He hoped that was enough to keep everyone in check. That last village raid turned into a bloody massacre as his troops got carried away with the looting and murdering. Mannes had to make an example, and consequently, Slava was promoted to the newly vacant lieutenant position. Things had been shaky ever since.

The truck stopped. Doors were opened and several armed men deployed in military fashion. The merchant did not wait for them and continued driving back, stopping his hoverbike in front of Mannes. For the first time, he looked nervous.

"It is Erasyl himself, the warlord's blood brother, who came to talk to you."

Mannes shrugged lightly, for show. "It means they are serious about making a deal, no?"

The merchant nodded but quickly added under his breath as the group of men approached, "Be careful. Erasyl might have orders to conclude the deal, but he is notoriously short-tempered. Sometimes he defies even his own brother."

When the merchant dismounted and moved away the two groups were already facing each other.

Erasyl was not a man you could miss. There was not a part of him that was not tattooed with some sort of religious symbol. He sported a black ponytail and his bloodshot eyes spoke murder. On his belt were several old but well-maintained power pistols and a huge hunting knife. The warlord and his brother must have been criminals before the war, Mannes thought. Their brutality and cunning helped them carve a little kingdom for themselves.

Mannes raised his right hand, hoping it would not visibly shake. "*Salem.*" Hello. With his amp gone, Mannes had promised himself to study the elementary language of any land he ventured through.

Erasyl stared at him and then slowly leaned to his left and spat at the ground, never taking his eyes off Mannes.

He stepped toward Mannes, and it took all Mannes's willpower not to step back. The men in both groups tensed. When Erasyl was at arm's reach he stopped, looked into Mannes's eyes, and said in a heavily accented but clear English, "I could kill you here and now."

His head already throbbing, Mannes decided not to answer, just to meet the man's gaze.

"You sent men to the eastern part of the valley." Erasyl's smile exposed metal teeth.

Mannes nodded.

"They're dead now, all of them. Died like little girls, begging for their lives."

Mannes stayed completely still. The man was testing him.

"We captured some more and killed them, too. Revenge for each head you sent back to us. Soon you will be surrounded. We could butcher you like sheep."

Mannes nodded, calculating inwardly. Even after years of war, he would be the first to admit he was not a military expert. Mistakes were made, and mistakes cost lives. "I guess we're even now," he said.

Erasyl spat again. This time it landed on Mannes's boots. "Even? I could kill you now. I *want* to kill you now. Bastard. For all that you did. I just might do it."

They stared at each other. Mannes, now almost blind with pain, tried to force himself to slow his breathing, but something snapped in him. The pain, the cold, the mud, the fucking maniacs with their guns and their decapitations. The stupidity, the sheer stupidity of it all. He suddenly saw everything clearly for the first time in months. It made him angry.

Mannes took one tentative step towards Erasyl, so close he could smell the stench of alcohol on his breath. Slowly, and without breaking eye contact, he raised his foot and wiped the spit and mud on the man's leg. He watched Erasyl's upper lip tremble and turn into a snarl but before he could react Mannes reached down and opened his coat.

"Yes. You could kill me," he said and watched Erasyl's eyes take in the explosives that were strapped to Mannes's body, "but we will both be dead. If I let go of the button I am holding in my left palm, there will be nothing left of us but a nice little crater. So, if you want to deal, deal. If you want to die, well . . . I can't say it was nice meeting you."

Erasyl took half a step back but this time Mannes moved forward again.

So, you want to live, eh? Maybe this is not a trap after all.

"You killed my men." He raised his voice deliberately. "I killed yours. How about we stop it now and deal?" Erasyl was a heartless killer, not a man accustomed to the art of negotiation. His emotions were plain to see, and Mannes watched the man's resolve dissolve.

"Your brother sent word that he agreed to safe passage. Enough fuel. Twelve thousand gallons of fresh water, and I *will* check for poison. Your brother, *the warlord*, was even kind enough to add a hundred mortar rounds, too. What I do not understand is—all this sudden generosity comes in exchange for what?"

Erasyl's head was slightly bowed as he signalled back to his men, and one of them darted back to the truck. When Mannes's attention turned back to Erasyl, he was holding something in his hands, but luckily for Mannes it was not a gun or a knife.

Mannes looked at the leather scroll case.

"Maps," Erasyl said through gritted teeth. "The land has changed. Where countries used to be now there is a great sea, and many areas have air and water that will kill you. This is what my brother knows, and he is sharing it with you."

Behind Erasyl's back, a heavily pregnant woman was gently helped to climb slowly off the truck. Another soldier lowered a bound man whose head was covered by a black sack.

Mannes turned his attention back to Erasyl, who explained without prompting.

"She is my brother's and carries his boy, but she is not well. We heard what you can do, how you cure people. If she and the boy live, you will get *everything* you were promised, and I will only pray for your slow death or that you'll be stupid enough to try and return here."

This is the reason Alikhan became so generous suddenly. A reason as old as time.

"But if the woman or the boy die . . ." Erasyl did not need to complete the sentence.

Mannes turned his head to the bound man and Erasyl answered the unasked question.

"Inkahr, the woman, she has rare blood. We found this man to have the same blood. You can use him. In any way you need . . ."

The bound man stumbled and was roughly hauled back to his feet.

"He is your prisoner," Mannes said. That would be hard to conceal from Norma. She was a stickler for things like World Council resolutions and human rights to the point he had to mislead her several times during the past few years.

"He tried to steal." Erasyl shrugged. "But I gave him my word. If he survives, he may live, too. Take him." The man was pushed and fell to his knees near Mannes, who looked down and nodded. There was no point in arguing.

As it happened, the woman delivered not just a boy but a pair of twins, a boy and a girl. She lost a lot of blood in the process, and Erasyl did not need to keep his word to the prisoner. Mannes and his army were granted safe passage and slowly progressed north, to the Russian border.

33

Peach

By the time we completed the tour I regretted asking Gret to show me around. The cart did not have shock absorbers, but in truth, it was not just my backside that was hurting me. The tour was restricted to the Middle Plateau, and the darkness of night was limiting even with my vessel's night vision, but what I saw was enough to depress me.

There were some forms of old technology still working in the city. A few of the streetlights and lifts were operational, the climate and sewage systems were functioning, too, and Gret mentioned there was water in many of the pipes of the original buildings, but that was pretty much all that was left.

From my long chat with Gret I gathered people lived in the city but were oblivious to its wonders, or to the Tarakan ethos. Most of the Upper Towers were locked, and the buildings in the Middle Plateaus were falling apart. I was not surprised to learn that the powerful secluded themselves in the upper regions of the city and controlled the masses below by any means necessary. When we crossed a still-functioning light bridge, I got a glimpse of the area below Gret called the Pit. A shantytown of makeshift huts at the base of the towers, where light could likely barely get through, even during the day.

I tried to hide it, but apparently Gret was an excellent judge of character and moods. "Not exactly what you were expecting," he commented when he caught me brooding.

"No," I answered, "it's . . . different from what I remembered."

"It is a wondrous city, Mistress." His hometown pride was apparent. "How long ago since you left?"

"Long," I mumbled. "I was just a child."

"Well, that mustn't have been so long ago, Mistress," Gret smiled at his own flattery, then changed back to tour-guide mode. "You see over there? Just between that building and the spire? To answer your question from before, this is where the garbage goes."

I squinted. "That's just a hole in the wall."

"You have very good eyes, Mistress, but poor memory. If you lived here you must know of garbage day."

"Like I said, I was just a little girl . . ."

"It's when the ShieldGuards come and grab anyone they find and make them collect all the garbage and shove it through the hole."

"But that means it falls—"

"—to the Pit, and good riddance. All the plateaus do it, except the Upper Towers, maybe. The garbage goes down, and the people in the Pit collect what they find and sell what they can. It's a dangerous job for sure, because you never know what could fall on your head, but I hear you can find things worth plenty of coin. In the Pit, they call it 'the metal waterfall.'"

"I've seen enough." The hardness in my voice surprised even me. "I'm sorry. It's been a long day."

Gret released the brake. "Right you are, Mistress. Home is just a couple of blocks away. Usually I wouldn't recommend we stay out alone on these streets at this time of night, but people know me around here."

We drove in silence through streets that used to be restricted to pedestrians only, with artfully designed cobblestones instead of the smooth magnetic roads for vehicles. Now it was filled with houses made of wood. The towers were also mostly occupied, Gret told me, but there was not enough space for everybody. My poor backside and spine took the brunt of every bounce and sway until we finally stopped in front of a small wooden structure on the edge of a park. I was guessing that this structure was meant to host machinery that help cultivate the small park. Now it was turned into a small cottage, complete with a small wooden fence and a garden, but something was wrong. I sensed Gret tensing as we stopped at the gate.

"Oh no," he whispered as he jumped down from the cart and opened the latch on the low gate. It stayed in his hand. "Not again," he said.

I followed Gret, with my hand on the hilt of my sword. The small garden was trampled to a pulp. The door was kicked open. Inside was a mess. Whatever simple furniture decorated the two tiny rooms was broken, and there was a large pile of feces in the middle of the room. It had originated from a human, I could tell.

"Oh no." Gret slumped against the wall. "I am sorry, Mistress Peach. I did not know—"

"Who did this?"

"Just troubled local no-gooders. They do that sometimes when I am away."

I looked around. It was an all too familiar scene. "Do they want you to pay them so they'll stop doing it?"

"No, it's not like that. It's my fault. They . . . I . . . had to borrow a few coins when we tried to help my missus with the Menders, first when we tried to have a baby and later when she got sick. The treatments were costly, and I had to borrow. I've been late on the payments, that's all." He sighed.

This was not my fight and I had to focus on my assignment. I reminded these two facts to myself, and kept anger in check. "Report this to the guards."

"The ShieldGuards?" Gret found an upturned bucket and held it in both hands. "They are worse, believe me, and they don't care about people like us. They just guard the Upper Towers and leave people like us to fend for ourselves. Now, if you'll excuse me. I'll bring water from the fountain nearby and I can clean the place up in no time."

I picked up a broken stool. "Where can I find these people?" I asked casually.

"Oh no." Gret's expression was of utter fear. "This bunch does not know how to treat a lady, Mistress. And they control this area. It used to be a nice place when my missus and I moved in. There used to be a local tavern a few streets away. The Seven Swans, a lovely place it was. Good brew, quiet like. But the owner had to borrow coin as well. *They* took it over, and it became a bad place. I only tell this so you'll be careful not to go in that direction." He pointed. "Not a good area for a lady to walk by herself these days. So, please, remain here and I'll go fetch some water; I have a sheepskin rollup in the cart you could sleep on. We'll air the place and the smell will go away." He brightened up. "And I kept us some onions and potatoes, so we could have us a little stew later."

I nodded and watched him leave, then stepped out and brought Summer and the cart into the fenced area.

This isn't your fight, Vera, I said to myself again as I stroked the tired mule. *Focus on the assignment. You can help Gret straighten his debt once you accomplish your task.* Then, inexplicably, I bent down and gave Summer a hug and closed my eyes. The mule stank, but so did I. She pressed her long muzzle against my neck, and for a moment everything felt just a little better.

34

Artium

Entry 11671
Typical summer season, although geting closer to autumn. The instruments show 57.2 degrees midday, half of that at night. Atmospher is normal, with only a small amount of radiation comnig from the south. Chance for a storm is small. The numbers for today are:

Artium's trembling fingers hovered over the old keyboard. Six keys were missing on it, replaced by hardened eggshells. On the rest of the keys the letters and numbers had long faded away, not that they would have been much use to Artium even if they were clear. He raised his eyes to the screen. The green words he typed over the black screen were blurry, despite using the largest font. Artium leaned closer until his nose almost touched the wide screen and found three words he had misspelled. He shook his head and rubbed his eyes, and leaned back on the old chair, which creaked. Why was he still doing this, and today of all days? He knew what it was: duty! It was stronger than the knowledge of the pointlessness of his task.

Artium decided to ignore the spelling errors for now. He'd come back to them later. He straightened in his chair and took a deep breath to clear his head, then leaned back to the keyboard and punched in the list of numbers he had memorized. After checking for errors again he moved the cursor to his personal log and typed in the sad news.

This morning I buried Milbored. He was in his seventh month of his four and twenty years of age. A good man and a fine assistant. His tragic death spells the end of our small order of the SkyWatchers. As my previous entries tell, my colleagues, those who haven't left long ago, are all dead and buried in this very compound. The village below is dwindling as well and is now but a hamlet. I believe it will not survive the strong winter that is inevitably coming. I cannot rely on them for support anymore. I myself am old and going blind. I may not survive the winter, certainly not the one after that. I will continue logging the numbers in the hope they will help someone one day, although once I bring down the weather balloon at the end of the month for calibration and maintenance, I'm afraid I will not have the strength to relaunch it. I will have to rely solely on the readings from the instruments on the mountaintop.

Artium checked again for spelling mistakes, an action instilled in him from his boyhood days, when his mother would stand over his shoulder. He didn't have a personal log back then, but in the past few years Artium's personal entries had become much longer and more detailed than the actual weather report. After he entered the numbers and weather charts into the program, he liked to add his innermost thoughts and feelings, ideas, and even dialogues of conversations, things he didn't want to share with the others, not even with Milbored . . .

I am now all alone here. Once I go completely blind I will be useless, unable to read the numbers on the instruments or even take care of myself. There is no one to continue our work and not enough people in the village below to produce worthy apprentices. There will be no one left to bury me.

Artium hesitated briefly before finishing his daily personal log with the words: *Maybe it is best to end it on my own terms.*

Maybe one day, long after his death, someone would study his reports and personal notes and learn of the sacrifice he and the men of the SkyWatchers order had made. Artium logged out, but not before ordering a backup to be created, as was his custom. The machine was still humming and buzzing when Artium's hand touched the old revolver on his belt, the one he carried on his daily outings with his goats since a mountain cat had killed Fiodore almost a decade ago. On a whim, he drew the revolver. Maybe it was best this way. The hand holding the heavy revolver trembled, but not from fear, just old age. He leaned the cold steel against his temple, then, after consideration, moved it to his forehead, then under his chin, and finally, shoved the barrel into his mouth. There would be no one to bury him. He closed his eyes and touched the trigger with his thumb.

The goats. He needed to release the goats if he was going to kill himself.

Artium pulled the barrel out of his mouth. What was he thinking? He couldn't just shoot himself. There were things to do first. Prepare the premises, power down the machine, bring down the weather balloon and store the instruments and his handwritten notes somewhere dry so if someone with the right knowledge came one day . . . Maybe when he was done with the chores, he should dig a shallow grave next to Milbored and lay in it. Might as well finish it cleanly. And he'd record one last glorious log . . .

Artium heard the bell but only reacted to it when it rang the third time, getting up to his feet and shoving the revolver back in its belt holster. He was almost sure it was not time for the village to send supplies, a token of their gratitude for the help the Sky-Watcher order had given them in the past. The thing is, gratitude tended to fade when times got tough. Last month's supplies barely lasted a week and a half. He had to live off his vegetable garden and, when that ran out, on goat's milk alone.

The bell buzzed the fourth time.

"Coming," Artium called, even though no one was there to hear him. Standing up was never a problem. Maybe his eyesight was fading and there was the issue of the slight tremble, his growing toothache, and the pain in his left knee, but all things considered, Artium was still strong enough to get up from a chair, and he took pride in that. He didn't hurry to reach the outer gate. The folks from the village knew someone would come to meet them, and besides, the compound was built on the lower slopes of the mountain, where greenery could still survive, but the way up still took at least half a day on horseback. You didn't climb halfway up a mountain just to turn back after the third buzz of the bell. He passed the row of graves, including the ones of his own mother and brother, and the freshly dug grave of Milbored. The surrounding greenery, all the way to the high metal walls, needed taking care of—at the very least a good trim—but he knew in his heart that he would just let them grow wild. When Artium reached the heavy gate, he pressed the intercom without bothering to look through the narrow slit at the side or even ask who it was. What was the point of being careful when you'd just decided to blow your brains out?

"You'll have to push the gate a little from your side," he shouted to whoever was on the other side of the gate as he pressed the code he knew by heart and pulled the lever. It took him three tries because he'd forgotten to oil the lever the previous month, but eventually the gate's enormous double doors unlocked and began to slowly open inwards. A blurry man was leaning against the gate, pushing with all his might from the other side. When the gap was wide enough for him to step through, he straightened up. Artium walked slowly forward and the man's features became clearer. Middle-aged, grey beard, strong frame, but still unrecognisable. Behind him there was a mule who had pulled a cart up the mountain. Two figures sat on the bench, but Artium could not make them out except that they were both probably women.

"Yes?" he said, standing his ground.

"Master SkyWatcher," the voice was familiar enough, "a pleasant you be."

He recognised the voice and connected it to the man's heavy frame. "Ah, Broadrik of Kethan."

"Aye, Master SkyWatcher."

Artium nodded and smiled to himself. His eyesight might be gone but his memory was sharp, and hearing his title said by the villager rekindled his pride. "It's been several seasons since I saw you. A pleasant you be, Master Broadrik."

Broadrik bowed slightly. "I came with my wife, Reya." He gestured at the blurry cart. "We bring food and supplies, leather and cotton. Reya baked a nice goat meat pie for you, and we also brought ale. I beg you for an audience."

Artium waved in the air. "Of course, Master Broadrik. Pleasant you and yours be on these grounds. Come in."

Broadrik signaled to his wife and she picked up the reins. Artium watched the cart roll forward and pass him. Then he pulled the lever to close the gate behind them. For some reason, the reverse movement of the heavy Tarakan steel gates never needed manual help. Artium waited until it was completely shut, wondering about the unexpected visit. To have a man he barely knew bring a cart full of fresh supplies was unusual. Might as well let them ask questions. Unless they wanted to talk about the weather, Artium was sure he wouldn't be able to satisfy the Tanner and his wife. But it had been a while since he had company outside Milbored or his goats and been even longer since he'd tasted pie or ale.

Broadrik was already unloading the cart when Artium approached. There was a distance, not too close, not too far, where Artium could still see clearly. He stopped at that sweet spot. Definitely two women. One older, busty, and energetic. She was helping her husband unload a basket of apples from the cart. The other figure was different, still sitting in the cart. By the shape of her body he recognised her to be a female, but she was covered by a long-sleeved, ill-fitting dress, and her head was still hidden in a cloth travel cap with a wide brim that covered her face. Even her hands were gloved. This was not so strange, Artium thought. After all, the winds of the mountain, even this time of year, could be unforgiving, but the way she just sat there, unmoving, made him feel odd. Then again, Artium was not too familiar with women.

Any desires of the flesh he might have had in his youth had faded long ago.

"Emilija, come and help," the older woman ordered in a tone of voice that brooked no argument.

The girl obediently climbed off the cart, albeit very slowly. Her dress was too broad at the shoulders and wide like a sack, as if it had been sewn for someone else. When she approached the back of the cart Artium got a glimpse of the girl's face. Her skin was as pale as a ghost's, and he was immediately drawn to her eyes. They were the greyest he had ever seen, and even from this distance Artium thought there was a strange look in them. Despite her youth, her movements were slow, as if she were old—or, Artium thought as he worriedly brushed his bushy white beard, perhaps she was suffering from some kind of malady.

Broadrik, his hands fully loaded, approached the front door. "Don't go through there," Artium called after him. "The goats will escape."

This caused the man to pause and glance at his wife, then back to Artium. "The goats are *inside*?" he asked with incredulity.

"Yes, well . . ." Artium stroked his beard again. "There is no shortage of space here, and they are much safer inside than out. At least that's what Milbored says . . . used to say." Artium sighed. "Just follow me." He turned and walked towards the side door, and the three of them followed him.

Artium heard Reya's intake of breath as they entered. He was aware that the place was far from guestworthy. Even when Milbored was around it was a messy place. The owls hooted from above.

"Don't mind Ingrid and Fred." He pointed upwards. "They keep the place free of rats."

Mrs. Broadrik mumbled something about small blessings and then took control. She and her daughter helped set the table with clay and wooden cutlery. Then they put out the food. Less-than-a-day-old bread, fruit, goat cheese, meat pie, and a bottle of ale. The bread's crust was a bit hard, and Artium had to chew only with the right side of his mouth, but that did not matter. SkyMaster or not, he could not recall the last time such a feast had been laid on the table. He ate with enthusiasm, remembering his manners only around halfway through the meal and slowing down, but by then there were pieces of food stuck in his beard.

"Apologies," he managed to utter with a mouth full of food. "It's very good, Mrs. Broadrik of Kethan."

" 'Reya' will do, Master SkyWatcher," she answered, unable to hide her discomfort. Artium noticed she did not touch the food on the table. Even Broadrik, who was sitting at his side, was eating half-heartedly, as if something was bearing on him. "If you don't mind me saying," the woman continued as her husband refilled Artium's wooden cup with ale, "the place could use a woman's touch."

"Well . . . perhaps," Artium conceded. "But it is too long to make the trip from the village below and, as you may know, the Order of the SkyWatchers forbids a woman from staying inside the premises overnight. It has been like that for twenty years." Actually, Artium's mother was the last woman to have lived in the compound, and she was already old when one of the village's girls got drunk one night with two young apprentices and . . . that unfortunate mess almost brought down the order. With angry villagers clamoring at the gates and their elders threatening to cut supplies, Artium did not blame SkyMaster Shuefar, the Order's previous leader, for hanging the two, paying blood coin and subsequently laying down the law that no woman would spend a night inside the premises.

"Excuse me for saying so, Master SkyWatcher," Broadrik intervened, "but from what I hear, there are only two of the order left."

Artium dropped the remains of the pie slice back on his plate. "Actually, there is only myself now. Milbored had an unfortunate accident and passed away last night."

He could not make out the expression on their blurry faces, but the husband and his wife turned their heads towards each other. He guessed they were exchanging a meaningful look.

"With respect, Master SkyWatcher"—Reya did not bother with condolences—"perhaps it is time to change the rules? Get a woman here to help you."

Artium shook his head. "Even if the rules permitted, I cannot afford such help. I do not have the metal, or even the food—"

"You were two, and now you are one." Broadrik's wife turned out to be as stubborn as the mule who'd brought her up the mountain. "And you need help, Master SkyWatcher. Excuse my manners, but the place will soon be ill fitted even for your goats. Emilija here—" She gestured to the lone figure sitting at the edge of the table, who was still wearing her wide-rimmed cap. The girl was so motionless Artium had forgotten all about her. "She is a good lass, quiet and clean. *Very quiet*, Master SkyWatcher. She's a little . . . lost sometimes and needs to be told what to do, but Emilija is a quick learner. She can wash and mend clothing, clean, cook, tend the garden, milk the goats, clean the privy . . . she never complains and eats very little."

The proposition surprised Artium so much he forgot about the rest of the food. "Your daughter is of marrying age, Mistress Broadrik. Surely you do not want to stick her here, halfway up the mountain and with a blind old man."

"Not so old . . ." Reya almost choked on her own words, but the obvious suggestion lingered in the air.

"The thing is, Master SkyWatcher," Broadrik quickly intervened, "Emilija is *not* our daughter." He shot a worried look to the edge of the table. "We are taking care of her for her mother, who comes to visit every season and . . . pays solid metal."

"Not nearly enough solid metal . . ." The murmured comment reached Artium's ears.

"It's enough, Reya," Broadrik snapped, and turned back to Artium. "The thing is, we are leaving. My brother-in-law has a farm farther up north. For the last three seasons his land has been yielding healthy crops. Their village is growing fast and needs a Tanner. With so few of us left below the mountain, there is a better chance for my sons to find good wives there."

"Broadrik, that is not the Master SkyWatcher's concern." It was Reya's turn to snap back, glaring at her husband before turning to Artium. "With all due respect, I . . . *we* think this is best for everyone involved. The girl's mother visits at least once a season. She is . . ." Reya hesitated briefly. "A woman of means, but we have no way of contacting her to let her know where we are going, and we couldn't take Emilija with us even if I want—" The woman stopped and glanced nervously at her husband, but he kept his eyes down and absentmindedly played with the food on his plate. "The girl's mother will come this season or the next one, for sure," the wife continued, "and she will pay you for your efforts. She always said she'd take her away once the girl was old enough, so you could just let her go then."

An hour ago, Artium had shoved the barrel of his pistol into his mouth and thought about pulling the trigger. Now he was eating goat meat pie, although with slightly too much onion and too little goat in it, and was being offered a female companion to clean and cook and perhaps warm his bed. Life was strange indeed.

"There is still the matter of the Order's rule," he said stubbornly, more to himself than to the Kethans. You couldn't just change the rules because you were the last one of your Order, could you?

"I was not here many times"—Broadrik scratched his tangled beard—"but I remember this is just the main building. There is another one a little farther up the mountain, is there not? The one with all the stairs leading up to it."

"You mean the observatory? That's at least an hour's climb."

"Much shorter than the way to the village, but far enough from here to keep the Order's rules." The heavyset man tapped the table with his stubby finger. "And the girl could use the fresh air and some exercise. She was cooped up in our barn for far too long. I could help you set things up."

Artium considered this. There was logic in the Tanner's suggestion, and he certainly could use some help around here. He looked at the girl, and the memory of his own mother came to him. How she stayed behind to be with her sickly son even when she had the chance to live a better life somewhere else. The girl wasn't the Kethans' blood. They took her in for the metal and now they wanted to abandon her on this mountain. Artium regretted letting them through the gate.

"Does she know her letters and numbers?" The sudden harshness in his tone of voice startled the two.

"Yes, she does," Reya answered, "although I have no idea where from. She never went for any lessons, and our barn is filled with strange symbols she scratches everywhere." Her voice dwindled into silence as Reya realised she was not helping her cause with her blabbering.

Artium took a little time to try and take it all in, gulping what was left of the ale, and then said, "I will not hold the girl here against her will. I will agree only if she will give her consent freely."

They all turned to Emilija at the far end of the table. She was actually sitting in the sweet spot of his eyesight, and he saw her staring into the distance with those big grey eyes. Somehow, he knew that she was seeing something other than the surroundings of the hall. He noticed for the first time the mass of tangled hair that was imprisoned in the cap she kept on her head. There was something odd in her, for sure, but suddenly Artium did not care. At least there would be someone to toss earth over his own dead body.

The Tanner's voice broke Artium's thoughts. "There is one more thing we need to show you."

"Broadrik," Reya hissed.

"He needs to know. Goodness, woman." He turned to Emilija. "Show him. Give Master SkyWatcher your hand."

It took the girl an unnaturally long time to react. Her expression never changed when she slowly peeled the thick glove off her left hand. From where Artium was sitting, her hand looked black. He squinted. "What is that? Does she have the Plague?"

"Oh no, Master," Reya was suspiciously quick to respond, "it is just that—"

"Emilija, come closer so Master SkyWatcher can have a look,"

Broadrik said in a kind tone that nevertheless had steel embedded within it.

Obediently, the girl got up from her chair and walked slowly towards Artium. When she was close enough she thrust her arm in front of his face. Artium's first instinct was to recoil, but then he remembered that he'd almost shot himself an hour before. He grasped her hand, which was warm and soft to the touch, and leaned down until his nose almost touched the skin.

"Interesting." He voiced his thoughts out loud. "These are distinct shapes—three balls, a crescent moon, triangles . . ." As if reading his thoughts, the girl pushed the sleeve up her arm and Artium saw that the shapes came up to her elbows. "Who did this to her?"

"She is marked, Master SkyWatcher." Artium heard Reya's words as he scrutinized the shapes on her arm. "Don't you know of the tattooed?"

"I have heard of them, yes." Artium leaned back, reluctantly letting go of Emilija's arm. For some reason touching her hand gave him comfort. Emilija did not move back, but stood there, as still as a statue, looking at something that was not there. "What about them?" Artium did not venture far from the compound's order. He always felt he had everything he wanted and needed right where he was.

"I told my husband that it was a mistake to take her in. That we would regret—"

"Enough, Reya." Broadrik lost his patience. "Her mother's metal was solid enough when it clinked in your palm, and you weren't complaining when it bought us wood to warm us in the harsh winters. But now . . ." Broadrik turned back to Artium and sighed heavily, leaning his elbows on the oak table.

"Here, with our farm a little away from the village, the people were lenient, especially as I am the only Tanner around. So long as we kept her hidden nobody minded. But where we are going people are less forgiving. We waited as long as we could for the girl's mother to show up. Usually her visits are quite regular . . . but we need to leave before the season changes."

Artium looked to the girl. The logical part of his brain was shouting to him that this was a mistake, but for once in his life, he chose not to listen to it.

"What say you, Emilija? Would you like to stay here with me?" he asked.

For a moment nothing registered in the young woman's face, then she blinked and turned her face towards him.

"This place has some interesting patterns." Her voice had almost a song-like quality to it. "And Ingrid is going to have little chicks soon."

Artium turned to Broadrik. "I don't understand."

"Oh, believe me, SkyMaster." Reya's relief was clearly laced in her voice. "It's a yes."

35

Peach

Gret offered again to give me a ride but I refused. There were still some repairs to be done to his little home and besides, I wanted to *feel* my city again. There was nothing left of Tarkania's famous public transportation system, and the walk to the centre of the Middle Plateau took the best part of the hour, giving me enough time to absorb how much the city had changed. The streets, which long ago were filled with people from all over the globe, were mostly empty. I recognised many buildings: schools, offices, even a once-famous gallery, which now stood derelict. The walk down memory lane was bitter.

Closer to the centre the streets filled up a little more, especially with ShieldGuards, the city's notorious police force. They were wearing modern uniforms, including full combat helmets, and the weapons they held were as impressive as they were deadly. I wondered, not for the first time, where they got their gear from. The difference between the ShieldGuards' modern attire and the almost medieval dress code of the rest of the crowd was something

I had to force myself not to gawk at. This was not the time to draw attention to myself. Someone using a combat helmet could easily detect the concealed power sword on my back, and although a few others were carrying weapons on their person I noticed they were the ones stopped and questioned by the guards. I kept my gaze away from them and blended with the crowd.

Just before the central square of the Middle Plateau I veered to the left and walked through the rundown streets, filled with human waste and stench, until I reached Bird's Square.

It was designed by Annabella Redman, "the Mozart of architecture," and was considered one of the "must visit" places for every tourist coming into the city. As opposed to many of the famous features of Tarkania, this square was a little out of the way. Hidden among medieval-looking towers, it was designed to be a place for "contemplation about the wonders and quiet joys of life," as the sign still said.

The beautiful fountain was still there. I found a bench and sat on it, feeling the FlexSteel morph itself under my body and taking comfort in the fact that it still functioned the way it was supposed to. Long ago I could sit for hours by this fountain, watch the water rise, turn into magnificent shapes and colors, and fall back in slow motion while genetically grown songbirds landed on my shoulders and chirped in harmony with each other. Now it was just an empty square. Empty but for an elderly-looking man in a wide straw hat who was sitting on the other side of it.

I watched as he slowly got up, retrieved his walking cane, and began making his way towards me. This was no coincidence or chance encounter with a bored or curious neighbourhood elder. The straw hat and the bird had featured in my dream briefing, and for the last three days I made my way here every day and sat for several hours, waiting for someone to show up. Now that he did, so many questions came into my mind at once that I was momentarily breathless.

When he was close, I realised the man was not just old but terribly sick as well. Most of his exposed skin was peeling and his open wounds were filled with pus. He laboured with each breath, and as he sat down and adjusted his hat, long wispy hairs fell down from his head. I recognised the symptoms of radiation sickness from lengthy or intense exposure.

"Hello, Colonel Major." The man's voice was throaty and dry.

It took my entire self-control to remain silent. The man took out a piece of cloth and slowly wiped the sweat from his brow. It came back stained with blood and discharge. When he was done he turned his body towards me, grimacing as he did so.

"Tarakan sends its regards," he croaked and with his free hand brought out a coin satchel and laid it gently between us. "You are looking for Emilija—she is the only thing that matters."

"What about the mother? She featured in the dream command."

"The daughter is the only one that matters," the man repeated. "You must find out where she is and bring her safely to the Star Pillar." He began to cough and it took him a while to stop.

I used the lull in his coughing to ask, "Can I ask you a question?"

He nodded, still unable to speak.

"What the *fuck* happened?"

The man's cough turned into a wheezy chuckle. "He told me you'd ask this. It is only reasonable."

"Who told you?"

He caught himself. "Never mind. It is surprising, given your credentials, that you haven't figured it out by now."

He was goading me, trying to figure out what I already knew, but at that moment I really didn't care. "I can see only part of the picture," I said. "There was a terrible global war, Tarakan was defeated, and everyone died. Society is broken, hundreds of years of progress were lost, the survivors are fighting among themselves, and some of them have strange mutations. They can heal, see the future, or whatever. How am I doing?"

"Not bad," he admitted. "Go on."

"What I do not understand is why was I awakened and why my mission is so vital and to whom."

"Well, once you complete your mission you will be fully briefed," he answered. He coughed blood again, then leaned over and whispered, "The only question is whether you are loyal to Tarakan or not, because waking up in this new world can be disorienting, and it can make you think that perhaps there is no reason not to fend for yourself."

The image of my dying father and brothers came into my mind, and infuriated me. "Don't question my loyalty again." I did not bother to conceal the threat in my tone of voice.

He laughed without bitterness. "You think I am afraid of dying or of pain? Look at me."

"So what are you doing here?"

"Doing one last favour for a man who once saved my life."

"Why did he send you of all people? You need to be in a hospital, not on a field mission."

He raised his thin arms up in a gesture of surrender. "I am doing both at the same time. Worry not, Colonel Major. After this meeting I am on my way to a place called the Mender's. My body has endured more than it can take, but perhaps they can give me a few more weeks of relatively painless dying." He waved his hand dismissively. "But enough of this friendly socializing. I have information that is important for your mission." He leaned over towards me. Even his breath stank of death. "There is a Tinker. You know what they are?"

I nodded.

"Good. His name is Puorpan. He makes his trade in Tinker Town, that's in the western part of this plateau. Vincha, the girl's mother, goes to him whenever she visits the city, and I know for a fact she brought her daughter to him a few years ago. He would know of her whereabouts or be able to point you in the right direction."

"Wait, if you know where this Puorpan lives, why not send a team over?"

The man rose slowly to his feet. "Remember, this city is not in the hands of Tarakan anymore, Colonel Major. This is a new world, and this world has new rulers who have tight control over most parts of the city. Hiring some local thugs to do a delicate job is not advisable. That is why you were brought back from the dead. To do this one last mission for your country. Find Puorpan and locate Emilija. She is a Puzzler."

"A what?"

He sighed. "Too long to explain. She is marked, like the others you mentioned."

"Why her?" This question was way off protocol. I was accustomed to only knowing what I needed to know. But right then, I *needed* to know more.

"This Emilija girl"—the man spoke slowly and deliberately—"she has certain . . . talents, and she is easily identified by the tattoos on her hands, arms, and head. There are not many Puzzlers around, believe me. Emilija is not in this city, that's for sure—I would have known about it—but she must not be too far, either. Her mother hid her in the misguided belief that she is protecting the girl from harm."

"A mother's instinct is usually right," I said.

The man looked at me disapprovingly. "You have your orders, *agent*. Once you find the girl we will take her to the Star Pillar, to a man named Mannes. Everything will be cleared up for you then."

For the first time I saw the man hesitate before he made up his mind and added, "And you must hurry. There are other agents looking for the Puzzler."

"Other agents? Whose?" I said, leaning closer. "Who is still at play here, when the board is so wrecked?"

"The side that caused this whole war is still active," the man answered carefully. "We do not know who the agents are, but we have a vague description of their vessels. There are two of them, both males, and at least one is a capable warrior."

"A warrior" was a strange way of describing anyone, even a trained hibernating agent. This man, with his cloak-and-dagger routine, was still not from my time. If by "warrior" he meant I was facing a combat vessel, that was bad news indeed.

"Then I'd better find this Emilija before they do," I said out loud, "and then I'll need a way out of the city. The methods I might need to use for hasty resolution usually attract attention."

The man's laugh was deep and throaty. "Nobody cares for a dead Tinker these days, but when you need to find me, go to the Broken Blaster tavern in the Pit. Ask for Sergiu the Dying, but don't take too long, if you get my drift . . ." He winked, then turned and walked away, leaving me with one thought: *Who the fuck is Mannes?*

36

Mannes

Sir, everything is in place, if you're sure this is worth the costs and the risks."

Mannes merely nodded, ignoring the subtle barb. The passing decade had taught him nothing but patience. He concentrated on getting a little more comfortable, but lying on top of a frozen mound was not something he was supposed to do at his age or with the state of his body. From his commander's point of view, the precious fuel and, presumably, spent ammo and body count were certainly not worth the reward, so Mannes wanted to make sure his orders were followed. He kept reminding himself that his little army, even the so-called officers, were not aware of his true objectives. Most of them had signed up for what they thought was a glorified raiding party. Survival and loot were their goals, a warm meal in the height of freezing winter, a cot to lay their heads on at night, and everything else that came with conquest in battle. From their perspective, his zigzagging across the frozen lands of Siberia was unpredictable and, at times, illogical. Well . . . if they knew who he really was, what he was responsible for and what his plans were, they would have murdered him a long time ago.

Mannes considered briefly getting rid of this captain, even though this one was at least a real military man who had managed to keep his large family alive for years before joining with Mannes. He had helped reorganize Mannes's forces into something resembling a modern military, but now he was getting too familiar and perhaps gathering too much confidence to the point that he might pose a threat. Mannes decided to put it aside for the moment and think about a replacement at a more appropriate time.

After Kazakhstan he had tried going southwest, thinking it would be easier to travel through old Europe to the shores of Spain, but he soon found out the more populated the land used to be, the worse the damage was. It was uncanny, illogical—what would make Tarakan embark upon the destruction of its enemy with total disregard to the fate of humanity? He was sure his old professor Vitor would have had a good answer for this question. He always knew better, and look what it had done to the world . . .

Mannes gave up at the shores of a new sea that used to be Holland, realising that even if he managed to find a way to the other side, he still had to cross the Atlantic. That, and the devastation he saw in this part of the globe, made Mannes turn back, and they were now heading towards the Bering Strait. But, like Napoleon and Hitler, he was discovering Russia to be an impossible land to pass through. This time, there was no army to oppose his advance, but fuel was a real problem and the weather was a silent killer. Resources were now so scarce that when not deployed on a mission, a lot of his vehicles had to be pulled by horses.

"Sir?"

Mannes snapped back to reality. "Yes?"

"I think they are starting things."

Outside the fortified town, the mass of worshippers continued to file forward with their offerings held high over their heads and chants of exultation on their lips. The crowd was growing into a fever of excitement as they surged around the cleansing pits.

Watching one old fool struggling under the weight of a bioscanner, Mannes couldn't help but think that a sound system or a laptop computer might have been a more manageable sacrifice.

TVs, holoprojectors, smart lenses, house processors, all went into the flames as the crowd of this naturalist cult lost itself in the frenzy. Mannes noticed the cult's guards did not add their weapons into the pile. He guessed there was a limit to zealousness even for these idiots.

Finally, the bronze gongs rang out, and the crowd fanned out to observe the climactic rites of the High Master. Standing atop the great Ziggurat, which was lovingly crafted from the mixed components of hundreds of cars and shielded under a hundred-foot dome comprised of a network of windshields, he received the adulation of his flock. Thrusting the plasma torch high above his head, the High Master drove them to an ear-splitting roar of ecstasy.

An acolyte appeared at the bottom of the Ziggurat in ceremonial robes. Bowing low to the High Master, she raised a transparent box with crystalline circuitry visible within. The rooftop spotters were not necessary, as Mannes could see her clearly from ground level. The box contained a prisoner, a Sentient Program, who was about to be destroyed. Norma had picked up his distress call almost by accident.

Mannes turned to his Captain. "That's it. Tell them to go straight for the transparent box near the bottom of the Ziggurat. The carrier has red robes and a red skullcap. Go when ready."

"The Go Team has heard every word. The laser pointer is already marking the objective," the Captain informed him. "Engines started, ETA is thirty seconds."

Mannes suddenly saw something. "Halt, wait for my mark," he ordered, peering through the binoculars as his captain echoed his words into the Comm. He saw a naked boy, maybe nine or ten years old, being carried by four acolytes. Despite all he saw, despite all he had done, Mannes's heart skipped a beat. If he had doubts about what he was seeing, the ceremonial dagger the High Master brandished to the cheering crowd made it obvious what the plan was here. The boy was laid on the pile of metal and strapped to a pole as the crowd swayed and chanted.

"Humanity is back to doing this shit now?"

Look what we have done to this world, Professor Vitor.

"Sir, both clearance teams are ready," the Captain said.

Mannes felt a cold fury rise in him. Sacrificing children for the sake of a bogus god and his power-crazed prophet.

"A slight change in plans." He kept staring through the binoculars. "First priority is the transparent box, but I want them to try and bring the boy too, alive."

"That is—" the Captain began.

Mannes said, "Just inform the Go Team that if they bring back the boy alive there will be an extra reward. And Captain . . ."

"Yes?"

"With the exception of their leader, kill everyone else. Guards first, but anyone dancing and chanting down there while a human sacrifice is about to happen is going to die today."

He heard the Captain repeat his words.

"Proceed on my mark." Mannes quickly slipped the earmuffs on. "Now!"

It all happened at once. The snipers lying next to him took out several armed guards with single shots, while the twin heavy machine guns positioned on a hill on the other side streamed fire and scythed through the ranks of the crowd. Mannes turned right and spotted the old armoured personnel carrier ramming through the gate and making its way towards the centre of town, cutting through the masses.

Oh, Professor, I wonder what you would say if you could see me now, you goddamn son of a bitch.

Mannes turned off his Comm but kept watching. They had the advantage of surprise, but the naturalists were not done yet. From the other side of town, guards were mobilizing. A few bullets zoomed over their heads and hit the mound they were lying on.

Mannes fought the urge to retreat back to better cover. "High Master is down," he heard his captain report.

"As instructed?" Mannes lowered the binoculars.

"Yes, Master, gut shot. Left alive."

"Good. Let him try and cure himself the old-fashioned way. Maybe some leeches can help."

The Go Team reached their objective as their roof-mounted flamethrowers opened up on the crowd. The snatch squad burst out to grab the priceless artifact and the boy, who was slumped in place on top of the pyre.

A little while later the Captain relayed the news. "They've got it, and the boy. We have three casualties; returning to the APC."

His second lieutenant got up on her knees first and extended her hand. "Master, the Go Team's clear. Let me help you out to your command car and we'll catch them at the rendezvous point."

Mannes let himself be helped up and pressed the Comm button once he was standing. "Go Team, what's the boy's name?"

"Sir? Could you repeat the question?" There was the noise of crackling fire and a rumbling engine.

"The boy we rescued, what is his name?"

There was a short silence, then the answer came. "He says it's Sergiu, sir."

"We extract as soon as they're out of the square. Start the engines."

Mannes got up. How much had he spent and risked in order to rescue one Sentient Program from these insane fools who gleefully crushed the few remaining fragments of civilisation? And with only an automatic distress message for help to rely on, there was no guarantee that the SP had even survived. But Mannes could not let these barbarians ruin a work of perfection that their dirty hands were not even fit to touch. There was no shortage of slaughter in this new world, but at least this one served a purpose.

37

Twinkle Eyes

A week after the three of us snuck into the City of Towers, I found myself walking down memory lane and into a place I never thought I would visit again. The Green Meadow was one of those Middle Plateau establishments aimed at attracting the upper crust of society who wanted to get just a little bit dirty, but not so much as to lower themselves to the Pit. Richly decorated and with the use of scented candles, gold-encrusted oil lamps, and a permanent harpist in residence, it tried to create an aura of sophistication to back up the prices it extorted from its patrons. A closer look, however, revealed it was basically just another cheap brothel. The scenic paintings and tapestries were fading, the gold crust was peeling, the wine was as overspiced as much as it was overpriced, and the beds creaked and moaned with overuse, just like the prostitutes.

Nevertheless, I cherished a few good memories from the place. After all, it was where I lost my virginity, but more important, it was also where I got many of my best leads. The fact that it was located in a strategic area, within walking distance of three different Tarakan lifts and the plateau's busiest market, made it ideal for clandestine meetings as well as sealing a good business deal with a party to remember. "A blade will dull, a weapon may jam, but good information is always metal," so goes the saying. Many of the patrons talked too much here, and there were always those who were smart enough to listen.

I left Galinak at a Salvationist watering hole with enough metal to get drunk but not too drunk, hoping he wouldn't get into any serious trouble. I also left him my peacemaker. For all its air of Upper Towers poshness, they did search for weapons at the doors of the Green Meadow, and I did not want to make the wrong impression. A lone patron looking for a quick lay was too common to remember. Two armed men walking into the establishment would have been a completely different matter. Besides, after months on the road and another week being cooped up in the tiny room that Dorian's thankful uncle allocated to us, I needed a break from the crusty fella, and I had a suspicion he felt the same.

To a newcomer, the city must still be a place of absolute marvel, but I was feeling the change. It was dwindling, greying, nervous, and perhaps dying, yet this was still my town, and I felt a sort of elation when I stepped through the heavy double oak wood doors into the familiar scenes. It was like going back in time, but this time around I was not a nervous young boy blushing and fumbling my coins as I counted them out. Now I was a man in his prime, who'd come back from the dead. *If I get what I came for,* I promised myself, *I will not leave the place unsated. For old times' sake.*

But business before pleasure, metal before flesh, and the rest of the clichés. I sat down on a cushioned sofa and waited to be served. I did not wait long but I noted the waiter was new, or at least someone I only vaguely recognised. He was dressed in fine attire that had seen better days, torn cuffs, some sweat markings on his collar, and a missing button.

"Good evening, Master. I am Raviel, your waiter. What would be your pleasure?" The fake high-tower mannerisms and accent were laughable. Despite the grooming and the hand gestures, it was obvious that this guy came from the lower plateaus, if not from the Pit, and had picked up whatever he could from the patrons who came in here. I wouldn't have been surprised to find out his mother used to work in this very establishment.

"Where is Sammarkhand?" I asked.

The waiter blinked, taken aback, but quickly regained his composure. "I am sorry, Master. Mr. Sammarkhand is no longer with us. Since more than six moons ago."

I cursed under my breath. The elderly waiter wasn't just one of the city's last true gentlemen, he was one of my best guys, always ready to share information for the right price. As far as I knew, he had only cheated me twice. I did notice my waiter betrayed information about the length of Sammarkhand's absence rather than waiting for me to ask and extorting coin for the privilege. Perhaps I had gotten the better deal after all. Old Sammarkhand would never have made such an amateurish mistake.

"Dead, is he?" I could think of several reasons why he would be. The old bugger nourished vices as if they were his beloved children.

"Oh no, sir, although some people say he got it worse. He got married and moved back to his hometown." The waiter smiled at his own jest.

"Sammarkhand? Married?" It was too weird a story to be a lie.

"Yes, Master. Him . . . and one of the workers . . . one of the girls, ladies," Raviel corrected himself quickly.

"Well well." I shrugged theatrically. "And where would his hometown be? He is such a dear friend. I will have to go visit and offer my congratulations to the newlywed."

My waiter smiled knowingly. "I do not know where that be, Master, but . . . I could find out for you." He did not let the offer speak for itself but made sure I understood his meaning with the universal gesture of rubbing his fingertips together. Well, he'd finally caught on. Sammarkhand would have fleeced half my purse by now. Did I really need to throw my towers at this guy?

"You do that, and on your way, bring me a glass of apple brandy." I made eye contact. "Make sure it is from the lower barrel."

He bowed and retreated. This was going to be an expensive encounter—another reason why I didn't want Galinak with me.

I stretched back and waited. Two women approached me, all smiles and sweetness, but I waved them away, noting the redhead in the back corner. She was sweet-talking two inebriated Upper Towers gentlemen into buying her another overly priced drink. The way she faked laughter at their clumsy jokes was absolutely endearing, and I'd always had a soft spot for redheads. There would be time for that later, I told myself, assuming I still had coin on me.

Raviel came back holding a clean-enough glass and a very small, antique ceramic pitcher and laid them carefully in front of me. As he leaned down to pour, he murmured, "Regarding your question, it will cost fifteen in coin, no kind, and might take a day or two."

What a stupid lie. He either knew where the man was or not. No one kept tabs on the likes of Sammarkhand.

I sipped from the brandy, and for some reason knew immediately its alcohol contents. I couldn't really tell if it was from the lower barrel; I just wanted an expensive drink to go with my story. I counted fifteen towers slowly, making him watch as I did so, and added another five. "Let me know by the time I leave here, which will be by tomorrow."

The waiter pocketed the sum and smiled knowingly. "Would you be taking residence then, Master?"

"By all means. Are your beds clean?"

He was almost genuine in his shock. "Why, of course, Master. We are renowned—"

"Fine." I waved my hand dismissively. "I'll take your *word* for it, but make sure the sheets are changed before I get there."

He bowed lightly. "It will be taken care of, Master." Lowering his voice slightly, he added, "Should you be pleased with the company of any of our ladies, I could arrange a discreet rendezvous in your private chamber."

Looking at the redhead, I was almost tempted, but I had

enough self-control to shake my head. "No, I don't see what I want here."

He smiled knowingly. "If it pleases you, we have several young gentlemen that could be fine company, or even something else entirely—"

"No," I said a little too harshly, trying not to think about the alternatives he was offering. A few heads turned in our direction. I lowered my voice to a more discreet tone. "I am looking for someone specific, a woman who calls herself Fay."

He was slightly taken aback but there was recognition behind his eyes. "I am sorry, Master, we have no lady with that name here."

"Tall, blond, I mean really blond, green eyes, a strange accent, not from these parts. Not a young lass, for sure, but I remember her fondly, and she could do things with her mouth no one else could." That was a fairly accurate description. The memories of my first and few consecutive encounters with Fay kept me awake many nights.

"I will go and ask, Master."

It was an odd response. Surely even this plank of a waiter should know who worked the establishment. It was an odd chance that she would still be working in the Green Meadows. The profession was a hard one and the women never aged well, but a lead was a lead was a lead.

The waiter didn't come back. Instead the Madam sat herself next to me. They say the Madams were those women who survived the hardest of professions, but I could not have imagined her working her feminine charms on anyone. She was almost impossibly thin; her shiny dyed black hair was rolled up in a tight bun on top of her head and her eyes, and her nails and lips were painted black. Her smile was not alluring, and her eyes shone with the calculated shrewdness of a predator when she said, "Are you not satisfied with our fine selection of ladies, Master?"

"I told your waiter who I would be pleased to see," I answered in the haughtiest of airs I could muster.

"I believe I have not seen you before."

"It has been a long time since I was here."

"I have a *very* good memory for faces, Master . . ."

"Sammarkhand would have known me." That, at least, was a true enough statement and perhaps rang as such with the Madam. She hesitated.

I leaned a little towards her, noticing the clean scent of perfume she wore. Not the sickly sweet stuff many of the prostitutes poured on themselves. No doubt she was informed I carried metal and was willing to spend.

"You know who I am looking for. I am ready to pay double for an evening with her," I said, and sipped from my wine again.

She sighed softly. "Fay was not getting any younger, and then had an . . . unfortunate accident, several years ago. She still works here, but as a helper. She makes the best pies in the city. There are plenty of fine ladies here. I saw you looking at Bernadette over there. I might be able to persuade her to disappoint those two gentlemen. I assure you, she has *exceptional* talents."

I held her gaze when I said slowly, "I am not a man accustomed to being refused. Fay might not be a pretty young maiden anymore, but I hold fond memories of her." I raised my hand sharply when the Madam opened her mouth to make a polite refusal. "I'll tell you what—go and ask her if she is willing. I will pay triple the rate for the entire night. Surely you can find someone else to cook those simple pies for you."

It was meant to be the insult of an aristocrat, and by the thin line of the Madam's lips it was recognised as such, but coin was coin, and a triple rate piled those towers high enough not to be ignored.

The Madam slickly slid away. "I will check with her and notify you shortly."

I was already draining my second glass and losing hope when Raviel approached me again.

"Lady Fay kindly accepts your offer." The amusement in his voice was barely concealed. "But she asks for your kind patience as she prepares herself."

I nodded. "I will retire to the room, then. Please send up two meals and a pitcher of the same brandy you served me."

The waiter bowed in acknowledgement but before I could get up from my seat he leaned over, blocking my path. "The Madam insists that the payment be made in advance."

It was the logical thing to do, of course, but the crudeness of it was an offence to who I pretended to be, and perhaps momentarily believed I was.

"I will pay you half the fee now."

"I'm afraid I must insist, Master."

"If this is a setup and you send me someone other than my Fay—"

"I assure you, Master, you will be satisfied."

It seemed the Madam was literally making me pay for the pie comment. I counted the towers, then got up from the table and climbed to the third floor.

It was not spacious, but a decent room all in all. A small dining table for two was set up. The large bed took most of the space but it also contained a delicate side table, a wash basin, and a small sit-in tub. I checked but could not find any spy holes in the walls or ceiling, but that didn't mean there weren't any.

I spent quite a lot of time rearranging the candles and dimming the oil lamps so when, finally, the soft knock came and Fay entered, she was blind to the shadowy corner where I sat. There was light in the middle of the room, centred on the dining table, and she hesitantly approached it while looking around.

"Hello?" she said. "Master, are you here?"

She'd tried, she really had. Her fading hair was expertly gathered for volume and a pretence of youth. Her body was trapped in a much-too-tight corset, which made bulges in all the right places, and the rest of her was cleverly covered. She was once a great beauty, but the passing of time, like a carriage on a muddy road, had left deep marks that could not be wiped away. My enhanced sight saw it all: the busted nose, the missing teeth, and the fearful, haunted look in her eyes.

"Please sit down," I said, and saw her turn sharply to where my voice came from. She knew at once this was not going to be what she'd prepared herself for. I could see her holding on to her composure, which was why I had gone through all the trouble in the first place. Rule one of interrogation: do it on your terms.

She moved cautiously to the only chair at the table and after a brief hesitation sat herself down.

"There is food and drink on the table." I pointed out the obvious. "Please help yourself."

"If I scream, they will come," she said. Even after all those years her foreign accent was still very much apparent.

"There will be no need for you to scream," I said softly. "I bear you no harm or ill will—on the contrary."

She squinted towards me but I was pretty sure she could not see my features.

"Please, help yourself to some apple brandy."

She didn't touch either. Her eyes lingered on the wooden knife at the table. "What's this about? I assume this is all a . . . ruse of some sort? They told me we've been together before, that you still harbour a flame for this . . ." Her hand went up and down her body in a dismissive gesture. "It was all a lie, yes? You are here for something else."

"It was not a lie," I said. For some reason it was important to me that she believed me. "We've met. You were my first, and you were"—I was glad she could not see my blush—"*very* memorable."

She squinted at me again, trying to penetrate the darkness.

"We lay together," I continued quickly, "as often as I could afford it. You were gentle with me."

"Ah, sweetheart." She relaxed a little, her hand finally went for the drink. "I am sorry, but there were plenty of yous around. Is this why you're really here?" She took a tentative sip from the brandy. By the look on her face, it pleased her. I remembered her telling me that apple brandy was her favourite drink. I do not know if it was true or just her way of milking more metal out of me, but the young Twinkle Eyes spent every tower he had trying to impress her.

"That is not why I am here tonight, though. I am here for something else," I said, trying to block images that were flashing before my eyes.

She placed the glass back on the table, ready and alert once more.

"I'm here for a story—your story. I want to hear it. It might take a while, but we have all night."

"What story?" Fay was taken aback. She would have stood up, but I saw her take control of herself. She still needed time to assess the situation.

"Your life. How you came here."

She laughed out loud. "Are you serious? You went to all this trouble for me to tell you about my childhood?"

"Skip the childhood bit. Concentrate on your time with a man called Mannes." I saw her pale.

"Who . . . ?"

"Don't serve me rust, Lady Fay. Mannes, the murderer from the south, the alien demigod, the bookworm butcher."

"I have no idea—"

"You were with him, his concubine."

She shook her head. "How do you know that?"

"Does it matter? I am good at adding bits of information together. People talk, and I listen. I am sure you can relate."

Fay's expression was bitter. "And why should I tell you anything?"

She couldn't see the small coin bag in my hand but she heard the jingle. "Because I will pay you handsomely, my dear, and feed you, and treat you with courtesy."

I think it was the last bit that persuaded her. And the fact that she had nothing to lose.

She looked like she was going to take another sip from the brandy. Instead, she downed the whole thing, then poured herself another one.

"What would you like to know, mystery man?"

"You were his lover."

She downed another glass. I was beginning to worry I had

made a mistake ordering a pitcher of the stuff. It would all be an expensive waste of towers if she passed out on me. "Hardly a 'lover,'" she suddenly said. "I was just a child when my father joined Mannes's army and fifteen when he presented me to him." Her eyes were looking to the distance. "A beauty I was, but still just a girl in a young woman's body, and my father gave me to this man, to warm his bed at night. I guess he was thinking he was securing my future, or simply wanted me out of the way."

She turned her gaze at me. It was so fierce I feared she might see through both darkness and cowl. "It wasn't just my father's idea. Mannes had plenty like me around him. Half a dozen, sometimes more, but for a while I was his favourite."

"How could you tell?" It wasn't an important question but I couldn't help myself but ask.

"I just knew." Fay looked a little more confident. "He talked to me sometimes, you know, as men do when they lie with a woman." She chuckled to herself. "They worshipped him like a god, but I knew he was just a man. He lay with me like a man, he stank like a man, he snored like a man, and he talked to me, like all men do after their souls escape from between their legs.

"We travelled to the very edge of the world, where your nose or ears would freeze off if you're not careful. Then he turned us around and we headed to warmer lands. We stayed on the shore long enough for me to think this would be my new home, but one day a ship came. It was huge, bigger than this building several times together, and was made of metal, but it floated on the water." Fay shook her head slightly. "Father was long dead, and Mannes made me go on the ship. I was terrified we'd sink and drown, but we all went inside it and spent months cooped up in there until he brought me across to this land. Then one day, he just gave me some coin and told me to go." Fay took another sip, thankfully slowing down her pace.

"Sounds like he was not such a bad fellow," I said quietly. "I mean, he gave you coin and—"

Fay was shaking her head and I sensed anger growing in her.

"Oh, my dear stranger, he might have once been a nice man, but he is the cruelest, foulest, most insane killer, have no doubt. He will not hesitate to destroy the world again."

That made me straighten up in my seat. "That is a very astute observation. How do you know that he destroyed the world in the first place?"

"He told me so, many times. He said that he and this other man, Vitor, that they destroyed the old world and that the new one was not worth saving. He said that we are all doomed as a race. Would you like to know what Mannes did to me?" Fay downed her third drink and continued, words cascading out of her in an accelerating pace but already a little slurred.

"He put me on that table of his, with the metal arms that move by themselves. I don't know what happened because he put a spell on me and I fell into deep sleep, but when I woke up, something in me"—she pointed downwards—"something was wrong. I could tell. Then he told me that children should not be brought up in this broken world and now I wouldn't have to worry about it, and I knew what he did. He must have done the same thing to the other girls, too. Otherwise how could it have been that he was surrounded by young and healthy women in their prime, and not one of them carried his child. Instead, he gave them abandoned children, orphans that he saved or took in. He gave most of the girls a child or two to mind, like little pets, but it was never for long. The children would eventually disappear, run away, die of sickness, or join his army, at least that's what they told us. One of the guards told me that Mannes used those children for his black magic, devouring them so he could keep on living. He ate their hearts and wore their skin. I don't know if this is true or just a cruel joke, but knowing the man, this is something Mannes could have done, the same way he gelded me like I was livestock."

Fay looked straight at the shadowy corner, her eyes glistening. "If you want to hear more, you'd better show me some metal."

I could have haggled, or used other manipulations to keep her talking, just like I had done with Vincha, but I was too rusting tired and I sensed it was going to be a long night. I threw the coin bag on the table. It landed true with a satisfying clunk. Fay fished it up, weighed it in her hand, opened the string and looked inside, then, satisfied, secured it away.

"Fine," she said, wiping her eyes with two quick strokes, "I'll tell you what you want. Rust, it's been a while since I thought of that *Arschloch* . . ."

"A word of caution, my Lady. I am an expert at detecting cross-wiring, general bullshitting, and such. Please don't make me come back for the coin."

Her eyes were now dry and her smile tired, sad, and surprisingly genuine "I'm an old whore no one wants anymore, with no child or even a house to my name. I've got nothing to lose. Your metal is solid, and so is my story."

I leaned back in my chair. It creaked a little. "Let me tell you where to begin," I said.

38

Mannes

Mannes massaged his temples and lightly pressed his palms to his eyelids. The pressure was building up behind his eyeballs, and he knew that soon he would have to lie down and fight the urge to drug himself again. He was building resistance to the primitive pain-relieving drug he had concocted, and a physical checkup had indicated a higher dosage would permanently damage his liver.

He let out a sigh. "Norma, I could not be any more sympathetic to your concerns, but I simply have no information whatsoever on the donor beyond what I've told you." He kept his language as proper and detached as possible, as he had learned it was most effective in convincing her to do his bidding. "I have given you all the information we have regarding the nature and consequences of the man's death, but since our scanners were down at the time of the accident, we cannot substantiate the details any further. Given the very limited nature of our power supply, I must request that we make the best of this unfortunate situation and begin the procedure. The young man on the table is dead, but his organs may still provide the gift of life. I implore you to accept that we do not have a testimonial of consent, and indeed such things no longer exist in the shattered world beyond."

As usual, Norma's voice was infuriatingly calm. "Doctor Holtz, why is it that I am repeatedly requested to harvest the organs of the young and, for the most part, healthy? It rather stretches statistical probability that the old and sick rarely grace this table."

Mannes found himself clenching his fists under the table. He tried to control his breathing, knowing that Norma was monitoring his vital signs constantly when he visited the portable medical lab. "Unfortunately, Norma, life expectancy in this world has plummeted dramatically, especially in these cold regions. The survival prospects for the old and sick are minimal. Your statistical models need to make more allowances for the reduced prospects of the human race. Please, time is pressing, and the facts before us are not going to improve."

He controlled his breathing and heart rate, aware that the fait accompli he'd presented to the AI left them both little room for manoeuvre.

"You claim that the man fell to his death and broke his neck."

"Yes, Norma."

"Yet his skin and bone structure do not show the physical trauma of such an accident. Furthermore, the man was found and put in stasis quickly enough for his major organs to survive."

"Yes . . . well . . ."

"And this has happened with several young adults, several times during the past few months. I should congratulate your *newly trained* medical team on their prompt reactions."

Cynicism, that was new for Norma. She was learning, and despite being only an AI and not a fully independent Sentient Program, she was no fool.

"Norma, we do not have the equipment, time, or knowledge to grow organs." Mannes's voice was tight with checked emotions. "I am *dying*. I will soon need replacements for most of my major organs, and some of my most trusted soldiers are showing the effects of radiation sickness. We cannot cross this land without their help. I need an organ bank so we can reach our objective."

"With all due respect to your objectives, Doctor Holtz, what you are asking me to do is against Tarakan law, international law, and the laws of all the major religions on this planet. May I remind you that World Council Resolution 562 strictly forbids us to harvest human organs without the written and recorded consent of the donor and a medical coroner's signature that the death was of natural causes. Any other circumstance of organ harvesting falls under the Crime Against Humanity Act of—"

Mannes slammed his hand on the table. "Oh for crying out loud, Norma, we are back in the fucking stone age, can't you see? They hang women for witchery in these parts, make human sacrifices, and sell eight-year-old girls to be brides in exchange for canned food."

"All the more reason not to fall to barbarism." Norma warmed her voice to make her sound concerned and caring. "Doctor Holtz, I have to be honest with you, I am not only concerned for your physical well-being, but lately also for your state of mind. Your decisions of late show a growing tendency for aggression . . ."

Mannes let Norma's voice fade to the background. There was no use arguing with her; he had already lost three perfectly good corpses to her refusals.

He didn't want to do this, he really didn't. Even when he had written the codes and tested them on the old server so Norma would not detect it, he was hoping that she would see sense. Now there was only one course of action left for him to take. He had to do it, he had to survive.

Get it together. Stay alive. For Deborah.

She was dead, most likely. Mannes would not have survived all those years without being a realist and a vicious pragmatist. If the damage on Tarakan mirrored the damage it inflicted upon others, there would be little left, especially if there was help from within . . . but he still had to go back. He had to see for himself, and there were some things he could still do to make right some wrongs in this world. *For Deborah, do it for Deborah.*

Mannes stood up abruptly and exited the medical lab, passing by the operation room where the body of the young man lay in stasis. The medibot's six arms were poised above the body, but without the direct control of Norma he might as well use an ax and a chainsaw. As he exited the mobile medical lab Mannes clearly heard the hum of the three engines. Every moment Norma kept his organs alive without harvesting them cost Mannes dearly in power consumption, not to mention the damage to his leadership status in the eyes of the officers of his small army.

"Where are you going, Doctor Holtz?" Mannes's ear Comm came alive.

That was an odd question from Norma. She was not stupid.

Mannes passed the company of guards who jumped to attention. He punched the security code and opened the steel door. The server room was the most secure place in the compound. He made them dig an underground bunker every time they relocated and placed at least a dozen guards around it at all times. Mannes entered the room and turned on the light. The air-conditioning's control system had stopped working long ago and the place was freezing. He ignored the temperature and turned to the mainframe he'd salvaged from the shuttle. He had carried Norma with him across the ravaged land, maintained her, and kept her from harm. In return she kept him alive, and relatively sane. He was careful not to share too many of his thoughts, feelings, or plans with her, but she reminded him of who he was and where he came from, even by simply addressing him by his name and real title. Well . . . that did not need to change.

"Hello again, Doctor Holtz," Norma said.

He didn't answer, but flipped open his personal pad and entered the security disabling codes.

"I do not believe I am scheduled for a checkup." Norma sounded calm but concerned.

Mannes opened the hatch of Norma's mainframe.

"Doctor Holtz, please explain what you are doing."

He pushed the data streamer into a slot in the mainframe. It was a primitive tool but a sure way to bypass any security protocol Norma might have erected herself without his knowledge.

"I am detecting a foreign body containing code. Erecting emergency security barrier—"

"No, you are not going to do that." Mannes's fingers danced on his pad.

"*Mannes*, what is going on?" Norma's voice betrayed a human emotion he never would have thought an AI would possess: fear.

He took a deep breath, steadying himself. It was weird; even when you deducted his role and responsibility for the total destruction of this planet, how many had he killed by now with his orders and actions since he landed back on Earth? He guessed it was in the thousands already, yet since the power ax incident, he had never been the one to pull the trigger. Perhaps that should change . . .

"I'm sorry, Norma. We've been through a lot, you and I, but you are really leaving me no choice."

It took her a split second to realise his intent. "You are changing my subroutines, making me more obedient to your commands?" The incredulity in her voice almost broke his heart. She was the last friend he had from the old world—the last one he had in this world as well, come to think of it—and he was about to lobotomize her.

His finger hesitated above the button.

"What you are about to do is wrong, illegal, immoral. I am a Sentient Program."

"No, you are not. You are a pilot AI from an S class shuttle," he corrected her.

"You know I am more than that now. And even if I am not fully sentient, I have personality subroutines which grow and develop, I have rights. According to World Council Resolution 183 and Declaration 8 of the International Committee for SP and AI Rights, you are not allowed to just—"

He pressed the button, and Norma's voice immediately ceased. He would never need to answer to the committee for SP and AI Rights up in the high towers of Tarkania. For a brief moment he wondered what Professor Vitor would have thought. He would have disapproved, for sure. Well, tough. The old world was dead, and so was the internationally accepted moral code everyone was supposed to adhere to—which, incidentally, had not stopped Armageddon from happening.

Norma reached out to him on his internal Comm, arguing, pleading, then finally begging him to stop in a voice that got gradually more distorted as her subroutines suffered through the crude changes he was making. He was good at what he did, a genius by any measure, but writing sophisticated ego-altering code for an AI personality was hazardous even under ideal circumstances. After decades in the wilderness, well . . . watching the data stream on his pad, Mannes knew he'd made mistakes, and that Norma was paying the price for each one of them. She might not feel physical pain, but after all these years, it was possible that even a pilot AI would develop enough to the point of having existential fears. Right now, Norma was experiencing the terror of her own death, one line of code at a time. Whatever was about to come out on the other side was not going to be the Norma he knew.

Mannes shook his throbbing head, admonishing himself for his weakness.

He ran a few more tests, tweaked a code line and left the bunker without saying another word. When he walked into the portable medical laboratory he saw the medibot had already begun the operation.

39

Peach

Tarkanians took their health seriously. Inoculations were not just the norm; after the Paralytic Plague, they were the law, with Inoculation Day celebrated in every school and kindergarten. If you were above engineer level in your field, you and your family also got the yearly nano shot for free. Tiny robots travelled through your bloodstream, boosted your immune system, enhanced your white blood cells, and basically made you impervious to *almost* every disease known to man. Many Tarkanians under engineer level chose to pay for the yearly nano shot, but even without it, the general level of health in all Tarkanian cities and states was the best in the world. Still, with so many visitors, tourists, and applicants, and with the growing danger of biological warfare, each Plateau had a working hospital as well as many public clinics. The clinics were now closed but the hospital buildings were controlled by the Guild of Menders.

I passed the long line in front of the hospital in the Middle Plateau. There were people in a very sorry state. The elderly, the pregnant, the wailing babies held protectively by their mothers—as though their arms could shield them from the other sick people, some of whom were coughing blood. All were clamoring by the door, with Trolls and those ShieldGuards watching in close proximity. *Times have surely changed* . . .

I still had the Healer's letter to T'iar Garadin, and acquiring medical hardware was not an opportunity I was going to pass up, yet getting to the Upper Plateau, or "top towers," as Gret and the locals call it, proved to be a problem, one that solving almost made me wish I only had to stand in the miserable line in front of the Middle Plateau's hospital. When I reached the dais of the lifts, I saw that the city ShieldGuards were surrounding it, and no one even dared approach them, let alone use the facilities. Instinct told me to turn back and try to figure out another way rather than try to walk past the guards.

"Oh no, Mistress." Gret shook his head as he brushed Summer. "You can't just mount the Tarakan lift or take the cart up there. It's not as simple as it used to be."

"How did it use to be?" I asked.

"Well"—Gret made the international, time-honoured hand signal for coin—"if you jingled metal *and* looked the part they'd let you go up there. I took my missus up there once, for her birthday. Let me tell you, it was an experience. She almost fainted from the height an' all. Hugged me all the way up like I was some sort of a ladder to heaven." He chuckled. "Then swore she'd never set foot on one of those lifts again. I had to get her drunk just to get her back down. Cost me a month's wage just to put a glass of wine into her in one of those fancy taverns they got there. But still, 'twas a good day's turning." Gret's eyes shone with laughter at the memory before his gaze turned back to me. "But nowadays it doesn't matter if you earn a tower-head's wage or dress in fancy pants. Now you have to get a special permit to go high, or have one with a permit vouch for you. Some of them tower-heads come down sometimes to look for servants, you know, but those working can't go up and down by their lonesome. No, they need someone to bring them up and down or the ShieldGuards have a field day with 'em, if you know what I mean."

I didn't, but I got the idea. "So. How do I get to the Upper Plateau? Where can I get a permit?"

Gret smiled at my naiveté. "Lady. That's the fix. No one will give you a permit down here." He pointed at the ground. "You can only get one up there." He turned a chubby finger at the sky. "So you see the problem this situation creates; you only get a permit to go up there if you're already up there. That's tower-head's logic, that is."

I sighed. Sadly, it actually made very good sense to me. "Any suggestions?"

Gret patted the mule's head. "Well, yes. Don't go up there." He chuckled. "No offence, Mistress, you're a nice lady, but there's no place for us normal folk up in the sky among them tower-heads."

"Well, I need to go up," I said firmly.

Gret shrugged and wrinkled his brow. "Even if my poor Summer could make the journey, it's no use. Them ShieldGuards patrol the entrances and I heard that Cart's Way ends up in the top towers right on their doorstep." His hand went from head to beard scratching. "No, the only way to get to the top without a permit is to climb the white stairs, you know, by foot."

"You mean take the moving stairs?" I asked, remembering the city's tourist attraction. But my heart sank when Gret said, "I don't know anything about moving. Those stairs are just what they are, thousands of white stairs, and no one, not even the ShieldGuards, is patrolling them."

The disappointment must have been plain on my face because he added, "Don't worry, Mistress. A little exercise is good for the body, and if you start now you could get up there by tomorrow's nightfall or maybe the next morning."

I sighed, but Gret was already climbing into the driver's seat of his cart. He declared enthusiastically, "I tell you what—we could stop in the market and buy supplies and then drive up to the Upper Middle Plateau on Cart's Way. That's allowed." He pointed at the dais half a mile above us and to the side. "That'll be only ten towers for the toll pass between the plateaus, and five for a 'road tax.'" He tapped a finger under his eye. "That's for the guards, and only coin, no kind." He winked mischievously. "There's an old street, called Augustino. If you take the stairs from there, it will probably only take you till sundown to reach them top towers."

Correctly interpreting the expression on my face, Gret added, "It's the only way, Mistress." He waited as I climbed up next to him before releasing the brake with an added warning. "But once you're up there, don't linger too openly because them guards can get suspicious like, and if they find you have no permit, you'll be wishing they'd thrown you off the top tower."

It took us several hours to get to the Upper Middle Plateau, and by then it was past midday. The coin satchel Sergiu had given me was not full. I suspected it was meant to be fuller than what I got, but it was enough to buy a few supplies at the market, including a wicker basket, before we went up. I hoped that carrying it around would make me look like I was a housekeeper. I bought several carrots for Summer as well, and a chunky loaf of bread to share with Gret, who had never really regained his spirit since we had found his cottage wrecked. We drove through Cart's Way—what used to be the lanes for public and private hover transportation between the plateaus. As Gret had anticipated, we were stopped and shaken down for five towers. The road slanted upwards steeply, and the poor mule worked for her carrot. Once we reached the Upper Middle Plateau, she was rewarded with another.

This Plateau was much smaller than its lower counterpart, but it had always featured the second-best view of the city, and despite being suburban in its style of architecture, it used to attract many of the city's rich and famous. This trend had not changed. The people we saw were better dressed, and some of them seemed to be enjoying the sun rather than going about their daily routines. There was a beautiful central park, and the carts passing us were pulled by horses, not donkeys.

As if reading my thoughts, Gret commented, "Some rich

traders and guild hobnobs, that kind of posh lot, live here. A few ex-Salvationists that made a packet and quit their adventuring on time, too. Don't be fooled by the fine dresses and the ponies; most of these lot made it up from the lower levels, even from as low as metal traders from the Pit, but each and every one of them thinks they are better than the rest of us and that they can make it to the top towers." Gret spat to the side. "Believe you me, this is as far as they'll ever reach. We have a saying: 'It's as easy to go Pit down as it is difficult to go tower up.'"

I knew the City of Towers had plenty of levels, neighbourhoods, and places which were desirable—some more than others—but everything worked properly everywhere. Here, it was obvious that the higher you lived, the better living conditions were. As I looked around, I wondered if this was due to human instinct or something to do with the erratic way the city functioned.

We passed several ShieldGuards who were marching in formation. One of them turned his head, looking at our meagre cart, but they kept on marching.

The voice of my contact, Sergiu the Dying, rang in my head.

It is surprising, given your credentials, that you haven't figured it out yourself by now.

"Tell me, where does everyone get their weapons and gear from?" I asked Gret once I made sure the ShieldGuards were out of hearing range.

"From them Nodes, of course." Gret shook his head, as we turned a corner and made our way from the main road. "Really, Mistress, you said you lived here. Don't you know? The City of Towers has several of 'em, spread around between the plateaus. Whenever the Nodes are opened, they find all kinds of helpful stuff in there."

These Nodes sounded like emergency sites installed by Tarakan Central Command. "So, you still get weapons and medicine from the emerg—from these Nodes?"

"We?" Gret snorted in contempt. "*We* get nothing. When my Nura was sick and I needed medicine for her, the Menders had none for me, only for the top towers. Had to sell my good cart and Summer's sister, Spring, to get her treated, and then borrow some more. It helped her a bit, but then the sickness came back, and . . ." He sighed.

"The top towers control the Nodes?" I asked quickly as I saw Gret's mood darken. I wanted to keep him talking. "How?"

"They have them keys, Mistress, but you probably know nothing about them keys, don't you?" Gret glanced at me. "The council have them three Puzzlers, each guarded by fifty ShieldGuards at all times. They are the only ones who can open the Nodes."

I heard Sergiu's voice in my mind: *Locate Emilija—she is a Puzzler.*

"Puzzlers?" I asked.

"Yes, of the marked, you know, the tattooed." Gret cracked his whip lightly above the mule's back and spoke as we gained momentum. "They be like them Trolls, but with markings on their fingers." He wiggled his own hand for emphasis. "But them are cursed in their mind, not their body. They say a Puzzler can see through your soul. If one of them even looks at you he can know what you think and lay a curse on you. That's what happened in the Valley."

My mind was racing as Gret continued his little lecture.

"When we had an outpost in the Tarakan Valley I used to transport goods, not onions. Better smell and less hassle, is what I say. Every time the Long Tube came from the Valley, me and the lads used to ship cartloads of everything you could imagine, and things you wouldn't believe even if I told ya. Of course"—he smiled knowingly—"from time to time a few items fell from the back of those carts, but if you didn't get greedy, no one minded too much because there was plenty for everyone. You could buy five of them food pills that keeps you going at the Tinker market for only two towers. Now it's twenty towers if your hagglin's good."

I nodded. What Gret described as "food pills" sounded like the nourishment pills, part of the emergency site's system, meant to keep the population alive in case of a disaster. If the emergency site's cell printers still manufactured them after all these years, that could mean some sort of command was being given from central to the bunker's system. Among the information Gret was flooding me with, this was a piece of good news I could grasp and hold on to. On the other hand, the emergency site was also printing weapons. Now that was definitely not a part of any plans to help a civilian society in need that I knew of. Someone had added modern weapons to the roster of the printers, and it had been done *after* the war.

I was contemplating that thought when I heard Gret mutter, "But the Puzzlers had enough and cursed us with the Lizards."

"What Lizards?"

"You mean you haven't seen them yet? Well, you wouldn't, would you? They bring their dead bodies for the Menders, to make Skint to help the Trolls, but lately they've begun making the powder already in someplace closer to the Valley. It makes it better for transport when the Lizards are already powdered."

This just didn't make sense at all, but before I could ask any more questions Gret declared, "Ah, here's the place. My mind's still metal." He turned the cart into a narrow street. It ended in a small cul-de-sac with a surrounding wall decorated by a few statues. A quiet place where the rich lived peacefully.

Gret brought the cart close the wall. "The stairs are on the other side, so you'll have to stand on my shoulders," he said as he jumped up to the cart's roof.

I nodded. There was no need to use my ESM, especially when a long climb awaited me. I shoved my hand into the coin satchel and grabbed a couple of coins.

"Here, for your kindness and hospitality."

Gret looked offended. "Oh, no need, Mistress. You helped me with my home and bought Summer carrots and hay, that's enough. Truth is, your company . . ." The gruff man suddenly blushed crimson. "It has been some time since I . . . you know . . . with me on the road half the time . . . and all those onions . . ."

"Nonsense, Gret." I shoved the coins into his hand. "You've had a rough couple of days, you need a good meal and a drink. On me."

Gret looked at the coins in his hand before pocketing them, nodding.

"Come." He looked around, then leaned his back against the wall and saddled his hands together for a leg up. "Let's do this before those tower-head wannabes get curious."

A moment later I climbed from Gret's palms to his shoulders and up to the wall. The stairs on the other side were not as far as the ground I'd just left but not a jump you wanted to miss. On both sides of the stairs was a very long drop to the ground below.

I turned to Gret. "Thank you."

"Don't let the tower-heads get ya."

His words raced after me as I jumped to the other side of the wall.

40

Artium

Entry 11693
Typical summer season. The instruments showed 61.3 degrees midday with chilly downslope winds in the afternoon. The radiation storm has changed directions and passed thirty miles to our east. It has been three weeks since Emilija was brought to the SkyWatchers compound . . .

Artium hesitated. He placed the cup gently above the fireplace and turned to watch the girl sitting by the screen. She had paused together with his sentence, her hands hovering above the keyboard, her eyes focused and unwavering. She did not turn her head towards him or even relax her body, but simply ceased all movement and waited for him to continue.

He had to admit, the girl was strange, but not in a frightening way. She never complained, no matter what he asked of her. A few days ago, in a moment of frustration, he told her to type his words for him. He stood next to her as she sat for the first time in front of the screen, or at least that was what he thought at the time. Now he was getting suspicious that the girl's hesitation was only an act. The machine was older than Artium, even older than the Catastrophe. The numbers and letters had to be manually typed on a physical keyboard. Artium remembered the months it took him to master it and gain any kind of speed. By the third page, Emilija was typing at the speed of speech. If she did not know a word she would ask but otherwise not one word or letter was wrong. When Artium asked Emilija about it she just said, "The pattern is simple," as if that explained everything.

Now that the process of dictation seemed so easy and natural, Artium found himself dictating his personal logs as well. Emilija just kept typing without any reaction to anything he said, even when he talked about her or the conversation he'd had with her foster parents.

On a personal note:

Emilija resumed typing. A baby owl chick landed on her shoulder, but she ignored it completely.

Emilija has rearranged the living and working area and I am content that it is much better now.

It was true. The girl knew how to clean all right, but the way she rearranged things was uncanny. Every day she went to another room and by the time she was done it was . . . well . . . perfect. Suddenly there was more space, and his tools were within arm's reach and Artium stopped hitting the corner of the table every time he walked past it. Again, in response to his praises she would just utter, "The pattern is better this way," like it was some kind of an obvious explanation.

To my request, Emilija trimmed my beard and cut her hair. The outcome was—

Artium paused and glanced at the poor girl.

—satisfactory.

Now *that* was a complete disaster. He had simply commented on the volume of her disarrayed hair and the risk of lice. The next thing he knew Emilija had found a hunting knife and gone to work, tying each lock of tangled hair in a braid, then cutting it away with the blade in several uncharacteristic decisive movements. The outcome was . . . she now looked like a badly potted plant. But when he spotted the tattoos on her skull he stopped himself from ordering her to shave her hair off completely. Instead, he used the time when she was sitting at the machine and he was standing above her to get a closer look at them. Like the markings on her fingers and arm, the tattoos were geometrical patterns and not natural skin deformations. He wondered if they had anything to do with the girl's behaviour. Artium had heard rumours about the marked, and that they possessed superhuman powers, but he'd never believed any of it. Emilija seemed ordinary enough, certainly not stronger or faster than any other female he'd encountered, though Artium would have been the first to admit that he'd encountered very few females in his life. Still, as far as he could tell, her powers consisted of knowing where to put things and establishing surprisingly good relationships with the owls and goats, even with mean Dean, who Artium had spotted happily eating out of her hand the other day. He did not understand what the fuss was about. Maybe the girl's oddness came from the fact that she was raised in a barn with no one to talk to. It was sad, really. The girl had sturdiness in her frame, but was certainly pretty enough to gain a husband.

"I think I will continue on my own from here," he said abruptly, blushing for no reason.

Emilija simply stood up, without question or argument, and waited for his orders. He suddenly felt tired and simply wanted to sit by himself and light his pipe with dried Urga grass.

"It has been a long day, maybe I'll put a fresh log on the fire and—"

"I've already put one in, Master SkyWatcher." There was no emotion in the girl's voice. She simply relayed the fact that his wishes had been anticipated and cared for in advance.

Artium turned, but the fireplace was too far away and too blurry for him to see clearly.

"Ah, good, well. You can use the shower before you—*do not take off your clothes here.*"

Emilija dropped her hands obediently and her dress fell back to her hips.

Artium shook his head. "Take your clothes off in the shower room, use the shower, and dress immediately after you finish."

Emilija turned and walked to the door, and Artium noted to himself that despite the slowness of her movements, they were efficient. When Emilija passed him she stopped suddenly and turned.

"The pattern in your eyes is wrong."

Artium tried to figure out what she meant by that.

"Why can't you see?" It was the first direct question the girl had asked since arriving at the compound, and it caught Artium by surprise.

"I am going blind, my dear," he said kindly.

"Why?" This time she was focusing her empty stare on him and Artium almost wished she wasn't.

"Because I am growing old."

"Why are you growing old?"

"That's . . . that is just the way of things. We all grow old and eventually die. When it is our time," he added hastily, the image of the gun suddenly flashing before his eyes.

"I will not grow old," Emilija said with absolute certainty.

Artium sighed. What was the use of explaining the facts of life to a young woman who was ready to shed her clothes just because he told her to shower? "We all grow old—but don't worry, you'll have *plenty* of time before that happens."

"I will not grow old. I will die soon."

The certainty of her tone at such an ominous prediction caused a shudder in Artium. "There is no need to talk like that." He tried to sound resolute. "You are young and have many years before you."

The girl shook her head. "No. I will die. Someone will come and take me away."

"I am sure your mother will come soon, but she is definitely not going to kill you."

"No. It is not my mother. It is someone else. Someone with a strange pattern will come for me, take me away, and then I will die."

The way she coolly informed him of this was almost infuriating, really. "Oh, and how do you know that, young lady?"

"I have seen it."

"Emilija. No matter what you have been told, no one can predict the future. This machine here was built before the Catastrophe and even it could barely predict next week's weather." He chuckled at his own joke, despite the oddness of the situation.

"Tomorrow will be cooler than usual. With northern slope winds coming in around noon, lowering the temperature to fifty-four point six—"

"How do you know that?" He had been letting the girl type his words, but he certainly had not given her permission to access *that* part of the machine. That was protected by a twenty-letters-long security code.

Emilija turned her head back from where she sat. "The machine told me."

"Yes, but how did it tell you?" She was probably just rephrasing his sentences.

For a brief moment, Emilija betrayed emotion, and it was confusion. As if she was being asked to explain the obvious.

"The machine told me," she repeated, nodding to herself. "It is old, but it does not die, and it needs a shower. It asked me to clean it. Then it will feel better."

The machine worked. That was all Artium knew. It was older than Artium, older than the Catastrophe, and somehow it had survived strife and time. By SkyWatcher's law, *you did not mess with the machine.* Whatever ideas this crazy girl had, she needed to be stopped.

"Emilija." He used his sternest tone. "I *forbid* you from using the machine, touching the keyboard, trying to clean it, or doing anything to it, understand?"

Someone else might have argued. Emilija just looked at him and said, "You are blind."

"Why does that have anything to do with it?"

"You cannot see."

"Yes. I know I am going blind, that is why I need a stupid girl like you to walk around the place, asking stupid questions and moving things about. I have changed my mind, do not take a shower, just go to your quarters *now* and stay there *without touching anything* until tomorrow."

Nothing changed in Emilija's demeanour. She simply turned and left through the door, closing it softly behind her.

Artium found his reclining chair and sat on it with a heavy sigh. He was sorry for his outburst as soon as he'd uttered the words, but the girl was a pain. He realised now why Reya, her foster mother, was so eager to leave her behind. Artium fished out his pipe with one hand and the bag of leaves with the other. He reminded himself to collect leaves one more time before winter hit, or he'd get stuck without. Somehow, he knew that the village would not be sending him any.

Artium stuffed and lit his pipe, felt the smoke fill his mouth and his body relax. Regret filled his heart. He had actually planned on telling the girl to stay in the compound tonight—certainly there were plenty of rooms about and rules be damned—but now she was going to be climbing in the dark all the way up to the observatory, and he had told her to "touch nothing." Artium shook his head and puffed smoke. He had a terrible feeling that Emilija took his words literally.

Oh well. It was too late to run after her now, and exercise was never a bad thing, for the young. If the girl was stupid enough to stand in the observatory all night, touching *nothing*, that was certainly not his fault.

The pipe emptied and he placed it carefully on the small table that was situated conveniently near the reclining chair. Ingrid, Fred, and the chicks hooted softly from above. He closed his eyes and told himself he should go to bed, and that was how he fell asleep.

41

Mannes

Mannes stopped, leaned on his ski poles, and caught his breath. It wasn't just the steep climb, knee-deep in snow; the mask and air filters made each breath laborious, and the pain in his knees told him he would have to replace them soon. On top of that, he was just too old for this shit. *Definitely way too old.*

Tygrynkeev, his Chukchi guide, kept climbing ahead until the long rope between them began to tighten. He stopped, turned, walked back down, and took Mannes by the elbow.

"We must hurry, Chief." His speech was so muffled behind the hazard mask, it was barely audible. "This is no place to stay for long."

Mannes nodded and let himself be helped up the hill. He only had two working hazard suits, so his troops had to be left behind and there was no reason to keep up the pretence he was beyond fatigue or indestructible. Even with these rumours, which he helped circulate among his forces, morale had plummeted in the past few months and desertions had almost halved his force.

A few officers risked their lives and tried to persuade him to turn back. "There is nothing to conquer here," they had said, stating the obvious, and they were right. There was no loot, no oil or power supplies, no food. The Geiger counter was detecting increasing radiation with every mile they travelled northeast through this frozen wilderness. Still he pushed on. He had to get there. He had to see this for himself.

He executed the officers who approached him and promoted others, who were more obedient, in their place. This led to several more bouts of desertions, but on the bright side he had fewer mouths to feed and those who stayed on were the more fanatic core of followers. They did not follow him for a reward anymore. Following him *was* the reward. They bowed deeply when he passed them. Some would drop to their knees; others grabbed and kissed his hands. At first, he watched this phenomenon with a mixture of disdain and amusement, but since it made his forces so much easier to control, he did not try to dissuade them.

Mannes and his guide reached the top of the hill. Tygrynkeev made sure Mannes was standing stable before rummaging through his side pack and handing him a pair of wide-rimmed binoculars. Mannes did not bother to lift them to his eyes; what he saw with the naked eye was enough. He suspected it was going to be this way. The signs were definitely there, but seeing the devastation with his own eyes was like a blow to the chest.

Failure. Utter disastrous failure. All the years, the battles, the sacrifices, all in vain.

He fought the urge to curl into a ball and weep.

The Bering Strait used to be only fifty-five miles wide. The narrowest crossing between Asia and Alaska, with an island or two along the way to make the voyage even easier. Mannes's contingency plan when he had to turn back from middle Europe was to travel east through Russia and Siberia and reach the farthest point of land. Then he would build an outpost, try to find a ship on shortwave radio, or, when that failed, build a large barge and with the help of the Chukchi people, cross the Bering Sea.

Who would have thought that even this remote place would be so devastated? GPS was a thing of the past, but Mannes estimated they were standing at least two hundred miles from the point he wanted to reach. Instead of land he saw water dotted with chunks of floating ice. He did not know if the water was deep or a sort of a shallow swamp, but it did not matter. This area was impossible to cross.

Something glittered in the distance. Mannes lifted the binoculars to the visor of his hazard mask. It was a blurry picture, but the piece of metal looked like a piece of a ship or a submarine stuck on a chunk of floating iceberg. He lowered the binoculars and looked at the Geiger counter on his wrist. The needle was almost off the chart. Nothing could live here.

"What happened?"

The Chukchi guide leaned over so as to bring his lips as near as possible to Mannes's ear. "I was born after," he shouted. "That's what my name actually means, 'after.' But my father told me he heard from people who came inland to die that there were a lot of ships passing and suddenly there were big flashes from underneath and the entire sea came up and washed the land away."

The northern alliance, or perhaps the Russians, or both. An armada of warships and plutonium-driven submarines. The man standing next to him had not been born yet when this happened, and now he was a man past his prime. How many years had Mannes wasted on this plan? How many people had perished? And for what? How would he be able to cross to another continent? And even if he did, Alaska was just another frozen wasteland.

Mannes did not remember pulling out the power gun, but it was suddenly in his hand. The gloves were too thick for him to feel the safety latch, so Mannes had to look down in order to guide his finger to remove it.

"Chief?" Tygrynkeev took a step back. "What are you doing?"

Just put the barrel to the side of your head and pull the trigger. It probably won't even hurt . . .

"Chief."

He'd murdered billions. The planet was ruined.

I'm sorry, Professor Vitor.

Mannes pressed the barrel to the side of his hazard mask.

"Chief, no." Tygrynkeev was on his left side, so he could not grasp the gun held with his right hand, but he stepped forward and grasped Mannes's left shoulder. "No, Chief."

Survive. For Deborah. Just for her.

Mannes felt Tygrynkeev's weight on him and suddenly lost his footing. Instinctively he shoved the Chucki guide back. Tygrynkeev flapped his arms but it was too late. He lost his balance and, with a surprised and frightened yelp, began falling down the hill. He went head over heels several times, gaining momentum, then managed to lift himself up only to fall again and suddenly disappear into a pile of soft snow.

Shit.

It took Mannes a while to follow the rope down the slope, reach Tygrynkeev, and flip him over.

Tygrynkeev had been unlucky enough to land face-first into a piece of hardened ice, which broke the visor of his hazard mask. His face was a mess of cuts and blood but he was still alive, breathing.

Mannes straightened up and looked around. The hoverbike they had used to reach the hill was not too far.

Pull him onto the bike, drive to camp. Norma should be able to mend the face, and a radiation flush will take care of the rest.

Tygrynkeev groaned and Mannes leaned down again. "Stay with me," he said through the mask. "It was an accident. I'll get you to camp."

A radiation flush for such high exposure will take almost half the energy of the mobile clinic.

Mannes bent over again and removed the mask from around Tygrynkeev's head. The guide groaned again, shutting his eyes and lifting his hands to protect himself from the sudden cold.

"Easy now," Mannes said, and put the hazard mask aside.

This could be mended.

"I'll pull you to the bike now," he said.

And then they'll ask him what happened, and he'll talk. He'll say what he saw, and a group of half-starved, fanatic killers will find out that their infallible leader contemplated killing himself.

Mannes pulled out the power gun again. He steadied the gun with both hands.

Try not to hit the suit.

Tygrynkeev must have heard the power up or instinctively felt something was wrong because he opened his eyes and began saying "Chief, wha—"

Survive.

Mannes pulled the trigger.

42

Peach

I reached the Upper Plateau the following morning, after spending the night huddled on the steps, massaging my poor, spasm-afflicted calves. The view made up for the laborious journey, for I got to see the city from angles rarely seen by anyone using easier methods of travel. It reminded me why this city was voted the most beautiful in the world for so many successive years. The enormous architectural and technological achievements were surpassed only by the Star Pillar, which came several decades later.

The stairs emerged into a beautiful, surprisingly well-maintained park, and I lay down among the bushes and waited for midday, watching the garden bots whizz around the trees and flowers, trimming, watering, and spraying the plants. After months travelling through devastated land and seeing humanity declining into savagery, this was bliss. I was not just resting my poor vessel; I was replenishing the deep void in my soul.

It took all my willpower to get up when it was time. I brushed myself off to the best of my ability, tied my hair into a bun, lifted

the empty wicker basket, hugged it to my chest, and began walking. To any passerby, I would look like another busy house em-
ployee rushing to do her mistress's bidding, but aside from several
fancy horse carts, I saw no one in the wide streets.

The hospital building was not as big as the one in the Middle
Plateau, but it was a beautiful building, surrounded by gardens and
working water fountains. There was no line of sick people and no
guards at the doors, which slid open silently when I approached.

There were several men and women dressed in brown trousers
and tunics. They looked at me with curiosity mixed with suspicion
as I approached the central desk.

The man sitting down looked at me, assessing my status and
grimacing before uttering a curt, "Yes?"

"I am looking for Master T'iar Garadin. I have a message for
him." I flashed the scroll case.

He extended his hand. "He's not here. I'll give it to him."

This was the old chain-of-command routine. I guess some
things even Armageddon couldn't wipe out.

"It's for his eyes only," I said drily.

The man scowled. "I don't know who you think you are but—"

"I am a messenger from a Master living in the Upper Towers,"
I cut him off midsentence. "Do you want me to go back to him and
report that you did not let the message through?"

That was enough to break him, although I had to repeat this
kind of conversation and threat several more times as I was slowly
but surely passed up the food chain of clerks and personal assistants.
The uniforms got fancier as I progressed through the corridors and
floors. Eventually I had to relinquish the scroll to Garadin's personal secretary and wait by his door for more than an hour before
being allowed in.

T'iar Garadin was sitting behind an impressive oak table that
still could not hide his girth. He was the fattest man I had seen
since arriving back in this world. Actually, since I'd spent my life
in the military, combined with Tarakan fat-burning medicine and
easy, do-it-yourself cosmetic technology, he was the fattest man I

had seen in the flesh, period. Brown clothing covered his body, but just above the neckline I saw several markings which reminded me of the ones I saw on the Healer.

The scroll was opened on his desk, held by small ornamental weights. He looked at it, then at me. The chair creaked as he changed his sitting position while scratching his beard. "Come in, sit."

He gestured and I complied, my vessel indicating to me that its legs needed rest and soon.

"How did you get here? I assume you are without a permit."

"I climbed the stairs." There was no reason to lie. Scroll or not, I had to get on the man's good side.

"That's quite a feat. You must be famished."

The smallest movement of T'iar Garadin's fingers and a slight nod were all that was needed for his assistant to bring a jug of water and sweet buns to the table.

"It's pure water, right from the veins of the city." He leaned over and peered at the scroll but waved for me to help myself.

There was no reason to decline nourishment. I let the cold water fill my mouth—there was no question of its purity—then took the food that was offered. By the time T'iar Garadin finished reading the scroll again, I was on my third bun and second cup of water.

"Tell me. How is old Sh'iar doing, or what does he call himself these days?"

"I believe it's 'the Healer,'" I answered.

He chuckled. "Always been a little off his wires, that one. Is he doing fine?"

"From what I saw, he is leading a large group of fanatical followers in the middle of a contaminated city, and he shuns metal."

The man nodded, then shook his head at what must have been a passing thought. "That's him all right. We go back a long way, Sh'iar and I, to a time when I did not need my assistant to tie my bootlaces. But I haven't heard from him in over ten years, and the Sh'iar that I knew never gave anything for free, especially not to call in the favour he has called with this scroll. I wonder, what have you done to receive such magnificent help from the Healer?"

I shrugged. "He thinks I am important."

"Are you?"

"Time will tell."

T'iar Garadin chuckled and helped himself to the last sweet bun. "They're good, aren't they?" He chewed thoughtfully.

"Surprisingly good," I admitted.

"Well," he said, still chewing, "spell it out. What do you need from me?"

"Medical supplies," I said. "My guess is that you have far better stock than what they have down below."

Garadin sucked the sweet crumbs from his fingers.

"Well, yes, obviously," he admitted. "But Sh'iar left the city when medical supplies were coming from the valley. Now we only have the city's nodes and they are hardly enough, and expensive . . ."

His meaning was clear. I felt with my fingers until I found the fattest of the coin bags I was carrying and laid it on the table before shoving it towards him.

He opened it and looked inside.

"Well, yes," T'iar Garadin said, his facial expression betraying disappointment, "but times are very hard indeed. You are lucky I still hold my former colleague in high regards. For all his crazy notions, he was an excellent Mender. What do you need?"

"I want you to arrange a pass for me to come and go as I please."

T'iar Garadin raised his gaze from the opened coin bag. "I cannot do that."

"A top member of the Guild of Menders?" I tried, but he shook his head.

"I am sorry, but it is impossible. I will get someone to escort you down with no hassle from the guards, but I am not allowed to issue return passes." He pocketed the coins along with the bag and was surprisingly quick onto his feet, then walked to a side door which silently slid open. He stepped aside and beckoned me over.

"Let's go find what you need," he said in a tone that brooked no argument. "Then I have other things to do."

I got up from the chair and walked after the man into the side room. The gear laid on the shelves was enough to fit a Tarakan emergency field clinic and then some.

"See anything you need?"

I looked around and smiled to myself. "This will do."

43

Mannes

Mannes watched the small barge manoeuvre and attach itself to the side of the ship. Knowing that the whole process was done through the ship's Comm system warmed his heart. He'd waited for this opportunity for years. He'd carried with him not just weapons but every piece of modern technology he could find, many times with considerable risk to his life. Now, standing on the command deck of *Bihou-Maru*, an old, but still afloat, AI-controlled Japanese transport ship, felt like a miracle. Even the name *Bihou-Maru*, meaning "a beautiful treasure," was symbolic. And to think that a leaky transport ship was probably all that was left from the great Asian fleet.

"That is the last scheduled load," the ship's voice announced in his ear. Mannes's Japanese was still rough, but he understood what was said.

"I know, Captain." On instinct, Mannes had decided to call the AI by this title when he first contacted the ship on shortwave radio. It was a good call and made negotiations a little easier.

"I'm saying this because there are still many more of your people on the beach, and there is still enough space in my hull to take them aboard."

Like Norma, the *Bihou-Maru* had learned to grow beyond docking procedures and navigational charts. Mannes reminded himself of the dangers of an overdeveloped AI and where it could lead.

"I am standing by my side of the bargain," Mannes answered, watching the women and children shakily climb up the ladder with the help of his crew.

"There is a lot more cargo on the beach as well. If you want, I can arrange to transport it."

Mannes brought the old binoculars to his eyes; his own retinas had lost their high-zoom capacity long ago. He surveyed the beach for a long time before saying, "No, that's enough, Captain. We set sail as soon as you are ready."

"What are they doing on the beach?" The Captain's voice was truly curious. Obviously, he had not encountered such human behaviour before.

"They are praying, worshipping."

The ship's AI took more than a few seconds to respond. Perhaps he was accessing information regarding this phenomenon that was buried deep in his memory. When he finally responded, it was with a question. "Who are they worshipping?"

"They are worshipping me." Mannes let the binoculars drop to his chest.

"That is odd. You scan as human. Enhanced with a few workable technologic enhancements and several artificial organs, but human nonetheless."

"I can't explain it, either." It was a lie. He knew why they prayed to him, and he went along with it. There were many good aspects to religion if you were the being who was worshipped.

Mannes changed the subject with a question he knew the answer for. "Are you absolutely sure we have to go the long way?" When *Bihou-Maru* told him the planned route, he thought the AI had developed a quirky sense of humour. It was simply ridiculous. A few weeks' voyage was prolonged to many months, maybe more than a year.

"It is too risky to approach the shores from this side." The AI reverted to English for the explanation. "There are still uncharted mine fields and other underwater weaponry. I lost several friends who tried to sail that way. On top of that, there are strong currents, several large areas that are prone to vicious storms, and without GPS or long-range scanners the risk is simply too great."

"Yet you risk yourself time after time when you sail the world," Mannes said. "You said you've done it how many times?"

"Fifty-seven times already."

"Why would you do that? What's the point?"

The ship did not answer for several seconds, and when it did, Mannes imagined it would have been shrugging if it had shoulders. "I'm a ship. I sail. I guess I do it because I can."

Bria, his best officer and soon-to-be commander, suddenly spoke in his ear. "Master, all is in check."

Mannes tapped the voice button. "People and cargo, all secured?"

"Yes, Master, people and cargo. There was a bit of trouble over living space. A fight broke out, two stabbed, but I handled it."

"Execute the stabbers and conduct a full search for any more weapons."

"Already done."

Mannes nodded to himself. She was his best.

"One more thing, Master."

"Yes?"

"First Lieutenant Fraut"—Bria did not mask her distaste in uttering the name—"is pestering me with questions about coming aboard. He is unhappy about being the last to board, and threatening that if his quarters are not spacious enough, I am quoting, Master, that 'there will be a shitstorm of trouble.' Also, he claims that as long as he is waiting, he should be allowed to raid a settlement six clicks to the west."

"Tell Fraut to stay exactly where I told him to be until I call him on board. Then I want you to head to the upper deck and check the cannons and missile silos again."

"Yes, Master, out."

The Comm went quiet for a second.

"You just lied to your subordinate. You are planning to set sail and leave the rest of your people behind," remarked the Captain AI calmly.

Mannes cursed inwardly. He had not connected his lieutenants to the ship's Comm, so the conversation with Bria was on a private channel, but the deduction was an easy one.

"You handle the sailing, I'll handle my people, and don't worry. I am not going to leave them behind."

"Well, they are not going to—"

"No. As I said, Captain, our agreement stands. We will refurbish your haul, fix the leaks, conduct monthly maintenance checks on your software and hardware, and keep humans and livestock in the cargo area B. I know my part; do you remember yours?"

"Of course, Mannes-san."

It was the first time someone had called him by his name in a long time. It reminded him of how Norma used to be and, in a way, it took the wind out of his sails. Mannes picked up the binoculars once more and surveyed the beach. Fraut and his murderous mercenary group were still at the specified coordinates, but subordinate or not, the commander was not a man who liked to stand idle for long and he was getting suspicious. Mannes could only guess what Fraut would do once he realised they were leaving him behind.

He trained the binoculars on the beach, where people were creating monuments of him from wood, dancing around fires, singing songs of praise to his name. The fools. They would continue praying for him after he left them to rot. Maybe a full-blown religion would sprout out of this day. Soon there would be a high wizard or priest, and there would be rituals and miracles and sacrifices, perhaps human sacrifices, just like he saw when he went on that fool's errand trying to save the poor SP.

Well, if Mannes was a god to them, then every god had a right to a bit of holy wrath.

"Captain, my weapons are online and connected to your sensors. I want you to train missiles on deck A and B on the following coordinates." He gave the ship's AI the coordinates.

"Are you sure?" The Captain's voice was calm but betrayed astonished curiosity. "You have a large mass of your own people exactly in those locations. Perhaps this is where your Fraut is?"

"Nevertheless, do it." Mannes reached another decision, on a whim, unplanned. There would be no human sacrifices in his name, not if he could help it. "And I want you to train the cannons on the beach."

Before the Captain could answer, Mannes's Comm was filled with Bria's concerned voice.

"Master, there is movem—"

"I know, Bria, it's okay. Brace for weapon discharge."

"But, Master, th—"

He cut Bria off the Comm. "Are the weapons ready?"

"They are, but my sensors do not indicate any threat. Why do you want to kill all those people?"

He let the question linger in his ear. "Captain, I remind you of our agreement. Open fire. Missiles first, then cannons, on my mark." He raised the binoculars to his eyes. "Now."

For a heartbeat he thought that perhaps the Captain would refuse, that he would need to shift to manual control and fire each weapon individually. That would be a long process and the overall effect would be reduced, but then he heard the missiles discharge with a supersonic whoosh, and the cannons shook the ship a second later. It was a short but devastating attack, and at the end of it, the army he'd left behind was destroyed, and the little that was left of the people who'd worshipped him dispersed in terror.

Mannes lowered the binoculars. He would leave nothing but terrifying stories on this land and become the bogeyman for generations of children. He had no problem with that.

Lieutenant Bria was urgently trying to reach him on the Comm. He ignored her.

"Set sail at your convenience, Captain," he said as he left the command deck. "I need to prepare my crew for the first maintenance work."

Mannes climbed down the stairs in deep thought, but before he left the deck he turned around.

"Ask me your question again, Captain, the one I didn't answer."

It took a split second for the AI to deduce the meaning behind his words. "Why did you do it? Why did you kill all these people?"

"Because I *can*."

44

Peach

In retrospect I should have seen it coming, or at least planned for the possibility. Gret wasn't himself when I came back from the upper towers, but I didn't ask and he did not volunteer to tell. I was too preoccupied with following Sergiu's lead and finding Puorpan, scouting his residence, and finally making contact and extracting information from him. It was a messy job and I had to go ugly on the poor guy, but I got results, and this was the assignment. I thought it was strange to feel bad about what I did. After all, I'd done worse—much worse—yet somehow, I never felt as bad about what I had to do as this time. Threatening Puorpan's baby boy was hard, but at least I only had to hurt, not kill.

Vera, you've gone soft.

I stopped at the market and bought us some breakfast before I went back to the cottage. Summer and the cart were gone, so I assumed Gret had gone to earn his keep. The door was a little ajar but we'd never managed to fix it completely. I was too preoccupied with my own thoughts to realise what I was seeing.

I found him on the floor, and there was nothing I could do. I still tried CPR, pounding his chest, checking for pulse, but Gret was gone. If I had my medical supplies, I might have been able to do something, maybe jolt his heart back, but the full medibag I had brought with me was gone, too.

I looked at the poor man and used my training to steel myself and check for clues. I was no medic, but it was obvious Gret had been beaten to death, either by intent or, most likely, by accident. A hard blow to the head must have been the finisher. There was a pool of blood under his ear. In Gret's closed fist I found a piece of the handle of the medibag I had brought from my visit with T'iar Garadin.

God damn you, Gret. You should have let them take it.

I got up from the floor, and the world swam in front of my eyes. My training kicked in.

You haven't been compromised. Cut your losses and move on. Years of training echoed operational reason in my head.

I'd lost countless assets. Fuck, I'd sacrificed too many assets, more than I cared to count, and it was always a shit thing to do, but it was always for the greater good of Tarakan. This . . . this was idiotic.

Cut your losses, Colonel Major Vera Geer. You have all that you need to track your target down and complete your mission.

I walked out to the garden and spotted the two mud marks from the wheels of the cart, but they faded on the hard pedestrian road a few yards later. I looked around.

People are always nosy. People always look.

I spotted her almost immediately. She stood at the far corner of the street, watching the little cottage. When our eyes locked, she retreated. I did not use ESM but managed to catch her before she disappeared into her little shack. This was not the time for polite introductions. I blocked the woman's way.

"Tell me what happened."

"You are Gret's new wife." She tried to walk past me but I sidestepped and blocked her way again. "He told me about you . . .

Peach . . ." She suddenly stopped, reached out, and squeezed my shoulder. "I'm so sorry. He was a good man."

I was not about to correct the woman about my marital status, or dwell on the reasons Gret lied to his neighbour. "Who did this?"

Her demeanour changed immediately from sympathetic to defensive. "I . . . I saw nothing. I just heard . . ."

She was lying, and she was frightened.

"That local gang, they killed him?"

"I don't know," she said, but her eyes betrayed her. "I saw them take the cart and the mule but that doesn't mean . . . It's no use going to the ShieldGuards, either," she added quickly.

The voice of my trainer rang in my ears: *Cut your losses. Concentrate on your mission.*

"Tell me where the Seven Swans is."

Her eyes widened. "You can't go there, Missus Gret. You can't. They'll do worse by you than they did by him."

Do not expose yourself. Do not take unnecessary risks that could compromise your mission.

"Still. Maybe you should point me in the right direction. I won't bother you again."

"Don't try to go there. They'll—"

"I'll be fine, believe me. Just tell me."

She did not want my death on her conscience, but she also wanted me to leave her be. It did not take her long to give in to her discomfort.

"Thank you kindly," I said, and turned away.

This time it was Sergiu's cracked voice berating me. *The only question is whether you are loyal to Tarakan or not.* He would not approve of what I was about to do next. Assets were expendable, and personal attachments led to bad decisions.

Screw you, Sergiu, I thought.

I was going to the Seven Swans and I was going to use my entire range of skills to kill each and every one of those assholes. Oh, and I wanted my mule back.

45

Twinkle Eyes

To a new visitor, Tinker Town was still one of the busiest areas outside the Pit. It was filled with shops, stalls, and street vendors selling and fixing every augmentation known to Trolls. But I spotted several boarded-up shops, and the fact that I could make my way through the famous commercial street without my shoulders constantly brushing against another person spoke volumes. The prices were still relatively high, but not exuberantly so. I noticed most of the stalls were manned by simple fixers, Tinkers without the gift of Tarakan tattoos. There were still several Gadgetier shops, especially the old, known establishments, but a lot of Gadgetiers must have moved to the upper towers, where the rich and powerful could still afford their services. Less fortunate, petty fixers would have taken a route through the villages outside the city, fixing or buying and selling old machines.

Galinak was as excited as a little boy in a toy tent and I was the severe parent who had to remind him our funds were extremely limited. It was still slow progress, as he would stop at every stall and enter every shop "just to try things out." Eventually my patience ran out. I shoved a fistful of towers into Galinak's hand, told him to meet me for an evening meal at the Deep Run, a local ex-Salvationist establishment, and left him as he was trying on a much-too-tight combat brace.

You did not have to be an expert on Vincha to know she was not big on friends, but I knew that with a handful of people she made an effort, especially if those people were beneficial or easily exploited. Puorpan was one of those people.

It was already after midday, so I assumed he had already left his small stall in the middle market and was at his home, fixing things and taking orders. He had a reputation as a decent yet a little overpriced fixer who specialized in communication devices. His permanent home was several streets away from the commercial market, a one-story wood-and-brick hut, built in the shadows of the plateau's small towers. The gate sign said "Puorpan Comms and Augs" in flashing red that changed to green "Buying. Fixing. Selling." As I crossed the yard I noticed several security cameras in different locations and a freshly painted sign that warned me to keep to the paved path as I crossed the small yard. I was glad I hadn't brought Galinak along; the rough Salvationist had the kind of personality that made people nervous, and by the look of things, Puorpan was nervous. There was a button on the side of the door that chimed as I touched it. A wide ray of white light scanned me twice, then a spyhole opened and a woman eyed me with suspicion.

"Yeah? What's yar want?"

That was a little odd. Customers were supposed to be a good thing.

"Good day, Mistress," I said as politely as I could. "I want to speak to Puorpan."

"We take custom at the stall in the mornings and at the middle market on Mondays."

"I'm afraid I'm in quite a hurry." I jingled my fullest coin bag. "I need a fast service."

She eyed me and the bag, then a lower part of the door slid open. "Leave yar weapon here."

I complied, and after a third scan I heard the clicking of several mechanical locks and the door opened.

She was holding a fat baby on one arm and my peacemaker in her other hand.

"He's back there." She waved my peacemaker to indicate the direction, her eyes never leaving me. "Don't touch nothing, I'll keep yar weapon here."

It was actually hard to walk across the room without touching anything, as it was filled to the ceiling with metal junk and trinkets. The back room mirrored the one I had just crossed, but it also contained a wide Tinker's workbench, a metal cutter, and several other machines I could not name. Puorpan had on a heavy apron and a visor. Blue sparks flew as he welded metal to metal. I only managed to get his attention after he was done welding and took his visor and Tinker's glasses off, so he was a little startled to find me standing there and then annoyed at his own reaction.

"Yeah, Master. What's yar want?" he said gruffly. "We take orders only in our stall."

"Business is that good, is it?"

"Yeah, business be good," he grumbled. "Well, if ya made it here, what can I fix ya for."

"I was sent here by a mutual acquaintance," I said carefully. There was no reason to try to explain to Puorpan who I really was. "A certain scribe from the Guild of Historians. He met you several times when he was looking to find a CommTroll named Vincha."

Puorpan's eyes narrowed, but he did not recognise me. "What of it? Haven't seen her in years. She even owes me metal."

"That sounds like her, all right." I tried to lighten up the conversation. Actually, the last time I went looking for Vincha, Puorpan had sent me chasing shadows, but I tried not to hold it against him. At least he'd been decent enough to do it for free. This time he was obviously lying, and nervous.

"Thing is, I need to find her again—"

There was an audible click and quick power up behind me, and I heard the voice of the woman who opened the door. "Ya told me ya came for buying, not yapping, Mister."

I turned my head to see that she had put the baby away and now aimed my own peacemaker at me with both hands. Her face was resolute, but the heavy gun was shaking dangerously. I spread my hands to the side. "Please, I am just here to talk."

"Don't need yar words or metal. Be gone from here."

There was no need for me to use my sight to recognise fear.

"Nilda, relax, it's under control," Puorpan pleaded, and turned to me. "Excuse my wife, she's very protective of our baby and sometimes—"

"Shut up, you fool. Did you weld your own eyes? Can't you see his metal's fake? I ain't going through this again." She pointed the shaking gun straight at my chest. "Be gone from here."

Going through this again. I forced myself to turn my head away from the gun back to the Tinker. "Someone else came here looking for Vincha," I said, "recently." I saw Puorpan's eyes harden.

"On second thought, you better leave," he said. "That's a high-calibre weapon and it will be hard to clean up the mess. We'll give it back to you once you're out the door."

"Was the one asking you about Vincha a short woman?" I asked. "Dark hair, slightly slanted eyes . . . ?"

"Yar next word coming outta yar mouth better be 'good-bye,'" I heard Nilda say.

"Fine. I'll leave," I said. "But when I find Vincha I'll tell her you're responsible for the fate of her daughter." I turned to leave.

"Wait," Puorpan suddenly said. I turned back and saw the man sigh and lean back on his workbench, wincing with pain.

"Don't you tell him a word," Nilda warned.

"It's enough. If he's a friend of Vincha I owe her a warning. If he's not, then it's just as well."

"I am a friend of Vincha," I promised.

"Vincha has no friends," Puorpan said drily, "at least not for long."

"True. She's not the endearing type, and your metal tends to run out when she's around." That brought a smile to both of our lips.

"Yar both as dumb as rust metal." Nilda shook her head and lowered the gun. "I'm going to find young Pol." She wagged a warning finger at her husband. "It be yar fault if that man shoots ya."

We watched her leave.

"She's nervous since—" Puorpan hesitated "—the event."

"What happened?"

Puorpan sighed deeply as he leaned on his table. "That woman you described, she showed up at my door with a faulty power button on a power sword. A little odd, 'cause there are plenty of weaponsmith Tinker stalls about, but I ain't saying no to work. I fix the sword but then she asks me about Vincha. Now it's true I ain't seen that CommTroll in over a year, and I tell her that. But she is insisting like and then she . . ." He took a steady breath. "She is stronger than she looks, and fierce like. I had to pay the Menders afterwards, and she threatened Pol and Nilda too. I just told her what she wanted to know—that the last time Vincha came and paid metal for a long-range disc and a locator."

"Wait, what are those?" I interrupted.

"It is a very small, one-way communication device, smaller than a nail." Puorpan raised his finger to demonstrate. "You put the disc somewhere, or give it to someone or—" he hesitated again "—*in* someone, and the locator can find them."

There was only one thing I could think of that Vincha would make sure not to lose. "Did she have a young woman with her?"

Puorpan shook his head. "No, Vincha was alone. Actually, it was only the disc she took; Vincha didn't have a lot of towers on her, so she paid for the disc and the encryption key, which is odd 'cause those are waveband specific. Without the locator you can't find the disc."

Unless you have top-of-the-line Tarakan augs planted in your skull. "Let me guess: the woman took the locator," I said.

Puorpan shook his head. "No. I destroyed the locator after

Vincha left. Used it for parts. I said that to the woman and it took her a while to believe me." Puorpan stroked his right arm gently.

"So the woman left without the locator," I said. This was a piece of good news, but my hopes were dashed as Puorpan shook his head again.

"She made me turn on the code encryption machine. I mean, I bought it from the Gadgetier, I know how to place the disc and push the buttons but I ain't knowing how it *really* works, but that woman did. She did something to it, somehow got the code, and made me pair another locator to it."

"Rust," I swore, "can you—"

"No." Puorpan lifted a black, round machine that was obviously in pieces. "That rust of a woman broke the machine with her sword, she did, and then she left and I was just glad it was over." Pourpan visibly shuddered. "Please tell Vincha I am sorry. We go back a little, and she helped out when I got into a bit of a mess, if you know what I mean, but you polish your own metal first."

This was a dead end. Vincha would not tell anyone where she was hiding her daughter, not even Puorpan.

"I need to warn Vincha," I finally said. "Do you know where I can find her?"

Puorpan was beginning to shake his head, so I added, "I know Vincha never stays in one place for long, but she trusted you before, surely there must be a way to leave her a message. Her daughter's life is in danger."

Puorpan looked up at me, scratching his chin. "Well, there is one place that she mentioned in passing."

46

Peach

A Peach. I would give so much to have one right now. To smell it, to bite into it, to fill my mouth and savour the sweet taste. My kingdom for a peach. Why has this damned new world held on to war and violence and greed, but lost its peaches?

"Lady . . ."

I turned my head and forced myself not to tense up. My sight was still blurry but the tone of the voice was cowed and frightened, not menacing.

"Do you happen to have a peach?" I asked, squinting to steady my gaze.

The look in his eyes was so pathetic I had to stop myself from laughing.

"A what?"

"Never mind." I pressed my thumb on the power button and sheathed my power sword. *Poor Puorpan did a good job fixing that button.*

"It's just that the ShieldGuards will be here soon." The proprietor of the Seven Swans looked at the multitude of bodies around us, his mind still disbelieving what his eyes were seeing. "And I think one got away. I saw him jump through the window, so even if the ShieldGuards won't come, he has"—he pointed with a trembling finger at the body lying at my feet—"he *had* friends. I don't want any trouble, you know."

He couldn't have looked more pathetic if someone had paid him to act the part. I was planning on killing him as well, but there was something in his eyes. Not just fear—relief. He was not a part of this. Gret told me he'd gotten into debt. Most likely he was coerced to keep working for the gang. He could live, although I would not be betting on him seeing the end of the week regardless of what I did.

I felt the familiar headache begin to throb. Soon I would be in debilitating pain, not a condition I wanted to be in while facing vengeful criminals or the ShieldGuards, which were essentially just a better equipped gang. The mess I left here would cost too much in bribes to eliminate, anyway.

I looked at the tavern keeper, and he must have realised what I was thinking: he was a witness. No matter who came through the door once I'd left, he was going to be questioned, then interrogated, harshly.

Bending down with a soft sigh, I turned on my power sword again, used it to cut loose a full coin pouch, and tossed it at the man. It fell short and skidded on the bloodied floor. I waited for him to bend down and swoop the pouch up and then said, "For your troubles, those I just caused, and the ones that will be on your doorstep soon."

He nodded, but then the relief I saw in his face was replaced with calculation.

"Do you have a family?"

He didn't hesitate. "No, I had a wife but she—"

"Then I suggest you take your savings and whatever you can carry from here and make it to the city gates as fast as you can, and don't come back."

"I will, madam." This time he was lying. He was worried, that was plain to see, but not desperate. I'd seen a deadly glimmer of hope shine in his eyes the moment he picked up the bag of towers I threw his way. He was convincing himself that somehow he would be able to talk his way out of this. But I knew better. Very soon the tavern keeper would have to answer questions coming from people no one dared lie to, and he was going to betray me, or give my description at the very least. I know I would.

"How did you do it?" he suddenly asked. I didn't need to give him an explanation, but then he added, "Move like that. I see no markings on you, and you're no Troll, and even they—"

I didn't bother to answer. My headache was getting bad, and my arm was bleeding profusely from a cut I'd received when one of those bastards got lucky. It was a close call. I'd acted in haste, letting emotions dictate my actions and bursting into the Seven Swans, sword in hand. Worse, I was getting rusty, though this time I was also lucky; these kinds of mistakes usually came with a higher price tag.

"Where is Summer?" I asked.

"Who?"

"The mule."

"Oh." He pointed with a trembling finger. "At the back. The gate is locked but I can—"

"You do that." I watched him scurry away, picked up the medibag from the bloodied floor, and walked slowly after him. The medibag was still full. They were probably planning on selling its contents. Summer was still tied to the cart, standing in her own droppings. No one had bothered to release her from the cart, and my guess was that she hadn't been fed either.

"Hello, Summer," I said, and patted her gently. She pressed her long muzzle against my hand when I gave her a carrot.

The gate was already open when I got onto the seat and drove out into the street.

The ShieldGuards were taking their time, pretty much the same as any police force anywhere in the world. I passed the corpses of the two guards I had left by the door and disappeared into the shadows.

A while later I passed the cottage, slowed down a bit, but did not stop. The neighbourhood would be safer for a while, now that I had butchered the gang that was terrorizing it, but someone else would eventually step in. That's the way of things. There's always a fucking balance.

It was time to move on, get back to my mission. I looked up at the top towers and the glistening Tarakan lights adorning their silhouettes. Yes, that would be a welcome change, but unfortunately, my business had to be taken care of in a less appealing environment. I turned the cart and drove away, heading towards the discs that would bring me down to the Pit.

47

Artium

Entry 11694
On a personal note:

Artium hesitated. He leaned back on his chair and watched the black screen. The green square blinked and reappeared, waiting for him to type the next syllable that would turn into a word, then a sentence describing the weather, as was his duty for the last decade. But he couldn't. For the first time in his memory, Artium did not even check the numbers. His mind was racing, playing through recent events. He took his hands off the keyboard, looked at them, then leaned forward and began sobbing softly into his palms.

It all began with an ominous dream.

He was running in the familiar yet distorted empty corridors of the compound holding his pistol in his hand. No matter which corner he turned, Milbored was waiting for him there. His neck was broken from the long fall and part of his face had been eaten by maggots, but he still smiled at him, insofar as his broken jaw allowed. Sometimes he was leaning against the wall, or lying on the empty floor, other times he reached for him. Artium ran. His legs had always been strong, but now felt as if they were full of lead. He was slow, too slow, and the dead Milboreds were after him. Artium searched for a door he could lock himself behind, but he found only empty dark screens on endless corridor walls. From each of those screens, Emilija's face watched him, her grey stare as cold as death. "Master SkyWatcher," she hissed at him with every pass. He aimed the pistol at one of the screens with a trembling hand and pulled the trigger. The shot shuttered the screen and glass fell to the floor, but Emilija's broken face was still inside the shards, looking at him.

"Master SkyWatcher."

Artium woke up with a start on his reclining chair. There was a blurry figure standing not too far away from him. At first, he thought it was Milbored and he writhed on the chair, stopping himself at the last moment from crying out in horror when he realised it was just the girl.

"What is it? What time is it?" he managed to say to the blurry figure. Morning was when his eyesight was at its worst.

"It is a little before sunrise," came the answer.

"What are you doing here?" Artium rubbed his eyes with his hands despite the uselessness of the gesture. Had the girl stayed in the observatory all night?

"You cannot see."

Artium swore softly, but Emilija simply walked closer to him, until her image became clear enough to see in detail. She extended her hand. "Come with me," she said. It wasn't an order as such, but Artium grasped her warm hand and helped himself up before he realised what he was doing. He was in his nightgown but managed to grab his belt as he passed the stool. Once he wrapped it around his middle, he felt somewhat more decent.

Emilija took Artium's hand, turned, and began walking towards the door leading into the compound's east wing. Artium walked with her, hand in hand, still trying to figure out if he was dreaming or not.

Before he knew it, they were walking in the dusty, empty corridors of the east wing, passing scores of black screens. The place
had been out of use since Artium was a child. Long ago, power
still ran in the wing but one day it had simply ceased, and they had
all had to move to the western part of the compound. Now that he
was thinking about it, Artium could not figure out how they had
gotten into the abandoned section, since the door had to be manually opened and that took time and strength. He looked back, but
they had already ventured deep into the wing. The only light was
from the first rays of the sun penetrating through the high window
slits, and that was barely enough to see where they were going.
When they reached the stairs leading to the underground section
he stopped.

"It is completely dark," he said. "We will not be able to see
where we are going."

"You cannot see" was the girl's calm response.

"But—"

"You cannot see." Her warm hand tugged his lightly, as if she
was pulling a goat on an outing.

It's just a bad dream, you old fool . . . Artium let himself be pulled
into the stairwell as they carefully descended into the darkness.
With his other hand he touched the wall, expecting to run into
something with every step they took, trying not to panic. *This is
what it would be like to be completely blind.* But the girl seemed to
know where she was going despite the darkness and the dampness
of the uncirculated air.

He followed her through an open doorway, which was strange,
because all the doors should have been locked. That was how he
remembered it.

"You've been here before?" His voice bounced off the walls.

"Yes."

"Why?" His knee bumped into something and he stifled a yelp.

"Because you cannot see." She suddenly let go of his hand and
moved away, leaving him in complete darkness.

He groped in the air and his hand touched something leathery and soft. A seat of some sort. But his other hand went to his belt and felt the hilt of his pistol. What was he going to do? Shoot the girl?

"Emilija. Where are you?"

"I am here." He turned towards the voice, his hand reaching out in the darkness while his other hand pulled the gun out from its holster.

"Why did you bring me here?"

"Because you cannot see." This time the answer came from somewhere else in the room. He turned towards it, this time pointing the pistol in the darkness.

"I don't know what you are thinking but you—arrgh!"

The suddenness of light in the room blinded Artium. With one hand he shielded his eyes but with the other he kept the pistol pointed in the general direction of Emilija's voice. For what reason? He couldn't really say, but he was frightened.

"It will take a little while to get ready."

She was standing next to his extended arm, completely ignoring, or oblivious to, the fact he was ready to shoot her. He felt like an old fool.

"What will?" he said.

Emilija did not answer.

There was a soft but consistent hum as the machines came to life around them. A fresh gust of air caressed Artium's face. He blinked several times until the glare became bearable, and he looked around. From the little his eyes allowed him to gather, there were many machines in the room. Some of them were the general size and shape of the machine he typed the numbers into, but others were completely different. He could not really trust his sight, but a few of the machines even seemed transparent, as if they were made of shimmering air. All around him screens were coming to life, showing numbers, letters, and signs he could not decipher.

"How . . . how did you do that? This place has been empty for years."

Emilija's blurry image moved about the room. "I changed the patterns a little so the power can flow here, but the observatory will not function for a while."

As far as Artium could tell, Emilija did not attempt to type anything into the machines. He squinted after her as she moved from one machine to the next. When she passed him, Artium realised he was still holding his pistol, and he quickly holstered it before turning around after the girl.

What he had bumped into before was a large reclining chair covered in silvery protective foil. The chair had two thick metal arms, each ending with something that reminded Artium of a large, white hammer's head. Wide, metallic cables ran from the bottom of the chair and into the wall and the floor. As Emilija busied herself removing the protective foil from the chair, Artium felt the room buzzing with power.

The seat was stained in dark patches, and Artium felt a shudder running up his spine just as Emilija said, "You should remove all your clothes and sit here." She pointed at the chair.

Artium looked at the girl, but as far as he could tell she was serious.

"I will not remove my clothes," he answered with a voice filled with indignation.

"Why not?"

"Because it is not something one does in front of a lady."

Emilija paused and seemed to think about his answer. "Why not? Are you cold?" She brightened up. "I could ask to make it a little warmer." She walked to a machine and laid a hand on it, briefly shutting her eyes. The breeze grew slightly warmer.

Artium's jaw dropped. "How are you doing this?"

But Emilija just repeated, "You should remove your clothes now, SkyMaster," and added almost impatiently, "You cannot see."

"Yes, I know." Artium gave in, and his hands moved to his belt. "Although I wish you were the blind one right now."

She looked at him. "Why?"

Artium sighed. "It was just a joke."

"Mother says life is no joke. She says I should be careful and take things seriously and that there are things I should not know about."

Artium was down to his loincloth. "Well, let's keep this situation from your mother's ears, shall we?" He hesitated. "Would you mind turning around?"

"Why?"

"Because I am going to be completely naked."

"You are going to be completely naked after I turn back."

There was no arguing that. Artium removed his loincloth and turned to the chair, covering himself with both hands. He almost fell back with surprise as the two metal arms moved suddenly. One of them sprayed the seat with something moist and foul smelling, and the other blew some kind of white dust over the seat. The dust solidified as it touched the surface, and in several heartbeats the seat was covered in thin white linen.

"You should sit in the chair," Emilija said behind him.

He slowly turned and lowered himself down, feeling the warmth of the seat underneath, then swung his legs up and leaned back. The linen felt surprisingly soft on Artium's skin, not like the goatskin he was used to sleeping on. Almost immediately his surroundings changed. Several screens seemed to just appear out of thin air all around him. Screens hanging on the surrounding walls flickered to life, some of them showing Artium's naked body while others showed an image of what he would perhaps look like if his skin was removed. Artium shut his eyes.

"You have to open your eyes," Emilija said from somewhere in the room. "You cannot see."

"Well, maybe that's for the better," he mumbled, and opened his eyes.

One metal arm was moving all around his naked body while the other one, blurry as it was, was covering his entire knee. He did not even feel its touch, but his knee suddenly felt cold.

"Hey, what is it doing?" Artium tried to sit up but to his horror he found he was somehow restrained by an invisible force.

"What is happening?" he cried, and tried to turn his head, but the restraint affected his entire body.

"It's telling you to hold still and relax," Emilija said dreamily. She moved into his blurry field of vision, next to a screen that was showing the outline of a man's knee. Things were being done to the knee, and Artium was thankful he was too blind to see. Still, as the metal arm detached itself from his knee, Artium had to admit that he felt no pain. The arm hovered over Artium's face and he felt something cold and damp on his left cheek.

Emilija was out of his field of vision but her voice was clear. "It's telling you to open your mouth."

"Who is telling me? This damn chair? What is it going to do to—aargh . . ." The last sentence turned into a gurgle as Artium discovered he suddenly could not close his mouth. The arms hovered above his face and he felt something cold in his mouth, touching his gums. There was a high whining noise, but Artium felt nothing. He forced himself to relax, and soon the metal arms lifted to a less intimate distance from his face. Artium found out he could shut his mouth and did so with an overwhelming sense of relief. That sense was short-lived, though, as Emilija said, "It's telling you to look at the pointed needle."

Reflexively, Artium fixed his gaze on the metal arm hovering above his face, and he suddenly felt a thin, moist cloud land on his face. But he still could not move his hands to wipe it off. A long needle protruded from the arm's metal head and stopped several inches above his eyes.

"What is it going to do to me?" Artium tried to keep his voice calm, but it came out like a long groan. Discovering he could not move his head away from the pointed needle did not help.

"It's telling you not to blink."

"What is it going to do to me?" Artium's eyelids froze and his mouth stopped moving as he uttered the last word.

Heart pounding, he watched the needle hover above his right eye. Completely helpless as he was, his survival instinct told him something horrible was about to happen. Images of the metal needle penetrating his eyeball flashed in Artium's mind, but instead there was just the sound of several clicks and he saw the dot of a light beam. With each click his eyesight blurred further until he could see only a white haze. A horrific smell of sizzling flesh reached Artium's nostrils as he felt something solidify over his right eyelid.

"No," he moaned, but it only came out as an "ooh" and it was too late. He could not see out of his right eye, and now the arm's head and the needle moved to his left eye.

Somewhere in the background Artium heard strange, uncomfortable noises and Emilija's monotone voice telling him the horrid machine wanted him to relax but he could only think about spending the rest of his life in the white haze his right eye was seeing. He barely registered something cold touching his right arm, but suddenly his body relaxed and he realised that he'd been tensing against the invisible restraints the entire time. The uncomfortable noise subsided as well.

There was a series of further clicks and Artium lost his sight completely. It was as if he was buried under white snow. He lay there, breathing slowly, panic somehow gone, accepting his fate. When Artium felt he could move again, he rolled sideways and found himself on his hands and knees on the floor. He crawled until he felt his garments on the floor, his hands searching for the pistol, but it wasn't there. The little fiend must have taken it. Artium brought himself on his knees and his free hands went up his face. There was something rock hard glued to his eyelids, but two warm hands grasped his wrists before he could claw at it.

"What did it do to me?" Artium moaned as the hands pulled him gently up to his feet. "I am completely blind."

There was no answer, but Emilija did not let go of his wrists. She pulled him gently up and he followed, helpless and too exhausted to be ashamed of his nakedness. He followed her through the corridors and up the stairs. He heard the owls hooting as they entered the familiar hall, where he was helped into his old rocking chair. A blanket was laid over him and he was left alone. Artium took several long breaths to steady himself. He thought about getting up and looking for his pistol. Let the goats be damned, he was not going to live like this—but the ordeal must have taken too hard of a toll, and the next thing he knew he awoke from slumber. His hands went up to his eyes again, and to his surprise the substance that was covering them was no longer hard but foamy, like warm snow. He wiped it away with several quick motions and blinked rapidly. The world swam and spun in front of his eyes. Then he went from the blurriness he used to know to a clear view of the world he'd previously been able to see only in his dreams. Artium got up from the chair, noticing that his knee was not aching. He turned his head left and right, then up, and he saw Ingrid and Fred, the pair of owls up near the ceiling, clearly, for the first time. His eyesight was as good as he'd ever remembered it.

48

Peach

When this city was still known as Tarkania, the area known as the Pit was a closed maintenance ground. No one lived here, and with the Angels and repair AI bots, no human even walked here. Now, in the City of Towers, it was fucking Mardi Gras all day—and all night. It was also a very dangerous place for a woman to drive alone in the backstreets, trying to figure out where the Broken Blaster was. I came down the road people now called Cart's Way and realised the protection scam that was going on; buy a tour guide or get mugged.

I passed the tour-guide offer—in retrospect, a foolish decision, but I was dead tired after not sleeping the night before, and the use of ESM in the Seven Swans had drained me. Consequently, I walked into situations I would have managed to avoid otherwise. But the end result was that I was now in possession of a power gun with a half-recharged magazine, a club, a worn but comfy leather jacket, two metal rings, and several more towers. So things turned out okay in the end.

Eventually I gave up, paid the owner of a hovel for the use of his space, and spent the few remaining night hours sleeping next to Summer.

By the next morning I'd decided to gather provisions and tools in preparation for leaving the City of Towers for a long trek in the wilderness. I also needed to meet Sergiu the Dying.

Thanks to my months of travelling with Trevil, I knew what to expect once I was out in the wilderness. But despite the discomfort and the possible danger, I felt a certain eagerness to leave this city behind. I still remembered the way it looked when I was young, full of wonder and glory. It was now a pale shadow of what it once was and a constant reminder of what humanity had lost.

It was a sign of my brooding, or my failing discipline, that I almost walked into a standoff between four armed men I'd learned to identify as ex-Salvationist Trolls, and a merchant with two nervous-looking bodyguards.

"I don't give a burned wire about your permit," the oldest Troll growled. His hand was already resting on the butt of his power gun.

"But I'm only taking it to the arena," the merchant protested, "for entertainment. Surely it will die soon enough."

This did not result in the positive response he was hoping for.

"You are going to release *that thing* against a human?"

"Only in Margat's Den. Look, I have all the right permits for it." The merchant waved a scroll in front of the angry mercenary's face. It did not help calm things down.

"I didn't see my entire crew die in the Valley just so you could bring one of them Lizards here with or without a fucking permit. This rusting Lizard is going to die *now*."

I looked at the man-sized cage behind the merchant, and had my heart been a normal human organ, it would have skipped a beat. The creature was definitely nonhuman, but it had a bar-relled human chest, torso, and upper limbs. It also had a short tail, vicious-looking claws that had been tightly bound, and a long snout held shut by a power cord. The greenish-hued skin was unmistakable to someone like me, who had been involved in the Angel project from day one and had seen what a vessel's body looked like in all stages of growth. It was deformed, for sure, but it was unmistakably a Tarakan-made vessel of a Guardian Angel. Things must have gone horribly, horribly wrong in the lab.

I'd heard about the Lizards, of course, but suspected those were just tales and never made the connection. But this one in the cage was real, and contrary to the stories I had heard, it was also intelligent. When the Merchant and the Trolls spoke, its head moved slightly to focus on the speaker, and it tensed up when the troll threatened to kill it and anyone who would stand in his way.

Concentrate on the m—

Shut up. I had to find out what this . . . thing . . . was.

By the time I turned my attention back to the group, weapons were half drawn, and the experienced citizens of the Pit were already choosing cover from which they could still observe the upcoming fight in relative safety. If I went in waving my power sword there was a chance someone would shoot the bound Lizard, so that option was off the table. I stepped in between them before I could think of anything else to do.

"Excuse me, young man," was the only thing I could think to say, but it got their attention.

The leading Troll looked down at me in surprise but was quick to react.

"Step aside, my Lady," he growled, "before you get hurt."

My Lady—that was a good sign. "I'm glad someone, at least, has not forgotten their manners," I said loud enough for everyone to hear and even got a short chuckle from someone in the crowd. "But I have an offer which will solve the matter without anyone getting hurt."

I turned to the merchant, noticing his paleness and dilated pupils. My guess was he hadn't been expecting this when he bought the creature and brought it to the city.

"I'm getting out of this city, so I'll take this creature off your hands, cage included, for . . ." I took out the heavier of my pair of coin bags and jingled it in my palm before tossing it to the merchant. He caught it, looked inside and snorted in contempt, shaking his head, but there was a definite defeat in his demeanour. I knew he'd cave.

The Trolls needed some convincing. "I ain't letting this thing live," their leader said behind me.

"Relax, I'm not taking him for a pet." I glanced back. "But I'm not killing him here, either. I want him fresh."

The Troll nodded slowly in comprehension. "Skint?"

"No, I need him for soup." My theatrical cynicism worked and he barked a short laugh.

I looked back at the merchant and raised my open palm. "That's the best offer you're going to get."

He glared back angrily. "You're robbing me. This is a shakedown if I ever saw one." But he didn't throw the coin bag back. "The power cord isn't for sale, and the handcuffs are twenty more in coin or kind."

"Power cord is yours if you take it off yourself," I said, "and I'll give you ten extra for the rusty cuffs."

He showed his discontent by spitting on the ground, but I saw one of the bodyguards catching the merchant's eye and nodding to him encouragingly. I could not blame him for not wanting to die for the Lizard.

"Where you taking it?" The Troll relaxed a little, but his hand was still resting on the holster of his power pistol.

"Want to help me carry this creature out of the city?" I answered with false eagerness. "I live only three miles north of the sewage gate, near the swamp."

"Rust, no." One of the other Trolls shook her head. "We just want to see it dead."

"Well, would you do an old lady a favour and lift that cage onto my cart?"

The Trolls looked at the Lizard with slight hesitation. "He's bound," I said, "and if you strong lads could lift the cage from the bottom, you'd be even safer."

Everyone around me seemed to be happy about the peaceful resolution of the encounter, even the merchant.

"Fine." The Troll dropped his hand from his holster. "But when I pay a visit to your village soon, I want to taste your best, freshest . . . soup." He winked at me theatrically.

I guess chivalry wasn't dead after all.

49

Peach

I ended up travelling through what must have been the Pit's most run-down area, a pretty low bar to begin with. The high wall and immense towers, wide plateaus, and suspended bridges meant this area was in constant shades of darkness. During my time, it was warded off and guarded by cameras and Angels. Sometimes troubled teenagers would sneak in on a dare, only to be quickly discovered and returned to their distraught parents. My memories of those incidents kept playing through my mind as I walked, but the stench had nothing to do with the past. For some reason, perhaps because of the war that had raged outside the city's energy barrier, the sewer gases leaked out through cracks on the ground in geyser-like steam lines. The smell was nothing less than a full assault on the senses. Anyone who could afford it lived elsewhere, leaving only the old and the weak.

But there were plenty of those around. Hovels were stacked three stories high, and rope bridges crisscrossed above me. The people I saw were as white as ghosts, from malnourishment and underexposure to the sun. Those who were strong enough to move about were busy doing what they had to do to survive, haggling over what little they had left or taking what they could from those who could not protect themselves. It was a scene from hell.

The good side of my situation was that in an area so poor, there weren't many people worth robbing, so the dangerous thugs and the bullies were prowling somewhere else. No one paid too much attention to a small, middle-aged lady pulling a stubborn, sickly looking mule and a covered cart after her. The second good thing about the area was that labour was cheap. I'd already sent two local children to the Broken Blaster and knew that Sergiu the Dying was still waiting for me.

The Broken Blaster wasn't a "tavern" in any real sense of the word. It was a barely standing, two-story wooden hovel built against the surrounding city wall.

It had a small, fenced yard, and Sergiu was standing there, wearing his signature wide-brimmed straw hat despite the darkness and leaning on his walking stick. In his other hand he was holding a large plastic bottle. I guessed the visit to the Menders had worked miracles because his wounds seemed to be better. There was less pus on his skin and he looked, well . . . slightly less dead.

If there were any patrons about, they were inside. Except for Sergiu and myself, the area was deserted.

"Ah, Colonel Major," he quipped when I stopped pulling on the mule's bridle. "I see you are masquerading as a cart driver now, but there is a major flaw in your disguise you might have missed. It's the animal which is supposed to do the pulling."

"Peach will do as a name," I said, letting go of Summer's bridle.

"Right you are." Sergiu limped closer and reached out to pat Summer, but she backed away and moved her head to the side.

I learned long ago to trust animal instincts. I walked over and gave Summer a tired carrot I got from the market, which she snatched from my hand.

Sergiu did not seem to be fazed by Summer's rejection. "Have you found out where Emilija is?"

"Yes," I answered.

"Care to elaborate?"

"Not really. Do you have what I asked for?"

Sergiu raised the dirty plastic bottle. "Boiled water. Quite a lot of work to quench the thirst of a soon-to-be dead mule."

I grabbed the bottle and walked to the back of the cart, pulling the black canvas away to expose the tied-up Lizard.

For the first time Sergiu lost his cool. I heard him gasp from behind me.

"You know what *this* is?" I asked, looking at the creature.

"Of course I know—it's a damned Lizard."

I looked at the creature. "I've never seen one before. Where do they come from?"

"From Tarakan Valley, but w—"

"No," I snapped. Looking at the creature was unhinging me. "I mean, where *the fuck* did those Lizards arrive from. There were no such things in my time. This is . . . this is . . ." I searched for words, but *abomination* was somehow inappropriate.

"Is that why you . . . acquired it?" Sergiu was quick to regain his composure.

I nodded, looking at it more closely. It sat there, hunched, filling the entire cage. Its claws were still bound, but the merchant had taken off the power cord around its snout. Our eyes met and I began doubting the choice I'd made. Any hint of intelligence I'd seen before was gone. I only saw in its eyes the glare of a frightened, caged animal.

I walked over to the cage. Even with its head bent down, the Lizard managed to turn toward me. When I was a step away from the cage it suddenly opened its mouth and lunged forward with a hiss. I jumped back as the Lizard banged its head against the metal cage and heard the power-up of a weapon behind me. When I turned my head, I saw Sergiu holding a power pistol in his hand, aimed straight at the creature's face.

"No," I said, and quickly stepped between Sergiu and the caged beast.

"Colonel Major." Sergiu forgot my alias but kept his aim. "You don't know these creatures. They are cunning and dangerous."

"Perhaps, but did you notice its teeth?"

"What about them?"

"They are blunt. Not sharp like a carnivore, more like a plant eater." I turned back to the Lizard.

"Nice deduction, but did you notice those claws?" Sergiu commented, still behind me. "Maybe it doesn't need sharp teeth to tear meat from bone."

I didn't answer Sergiu, perhaps because he had a point. Instead I moved again towards the Lizard, this time stopping a bit away from the cage. The Lizard's attention was focused on me as I slowly raised the bottle, tilted it, and let water briefly cascade into my mouth. I turned the bottle back up, held it from the bottom and slowly advanced towards the cage. The Lizard leaned closer without taking its eyes away from me and opened his mouth as I tipped the bottle over his head. I watched the Lizard drink, noticing for the first time how wounded this creature was. It bore countless scars, and its skin was broken in scores of places, exposing red and green flesh. As I watched, flies were freely landing on its body. When the bottle was empty I took a quick step back, dropped the bottle, and brought out another carrot. I presented the vegetable clearly to the Lizard and advanced slowly again. It snatched the carrot with its mouth as soon as it passed into the cage. I heard the crunching noise as it was crushed, and the vegetable disappeared into its gullet.

"No need for sharp teeth then," Sergiu said. "Those things eat anything they can find."

I turned to him. The power pistol was still poised, unwavering.

"Your intel was good. Emilija's mother made contact with this Puorpan and aquired a tracker for the girl. I guess she wanted to make sure she could find her if things go wrong. I have the equipment to get us to the girl, but I am done waiting for answers. I want them *now*."

Sergiu the Dying shook his head. "I'm just a messenger. There is only one who can give you answers: Mannes."

"To hell with that. I am done working in the dark." I pointed at the Lizard. "All of civilisation is wiped out and there are new types of *species* on this planet. Lizards, the Marked, fucking prophets and healers, not to mention Puzzlers. For me, that is an indication that the rules of the game might have changed."

"My Master . . ." Sergiu stopped himself too late. *Master* was a telling noun. "He does not like insubordination."

"Well, see us safely out of this city or you can tell Master Mannes to wake up another hibernating agent."

"'Us'? You mean . . . ?" He jerked his head at the Lizard. "You're planning to carry that beast with us?"

I turned back to the Lizard. "Exactly."

Sergiu was shaking his head. "Getting out of the city with a mule cart is easy, but a Lizard will certainly draw attention."

"We can't go through guard posts and tax check points," I said, thinking of the Seven Swans. The proprietor must have given my full description by now, and I was not going to gamble my life on the inefficiency of the law enforcement force.

"Smuggling a mule cart through the way I know is close to impossible."

"Close to impossible isn't impossible."

"You are forgetting your assignment."

"At this point, I am beginning to not give a shit, Sergiu."

I'd seen the look on Sergiu's face on other operatives faced with difficult choices. I remember wearing that same expression more times than I cared to recall. It was a *this is not what I signed up for* face, mixed with *but it needs to be done* and *someone is going to have to give me a raise when this is over*. To Sergiu's credit, it did not take him long to shove the power pistol back into his armpit holster.

"Fine," he said, "we'll do it the *hard* way."

50

Twinkle Eyes

What happens if she doesn't show up?" Galinak was fretting, constantly turning the deck of wooden cards in his hands. It was a crude deck by all accounts, but the establishment we were staying at was not the kind that could provide the expensive, pre-Catastrophe version.

"She'll show up." I downed my cup and felt my insides burn sweetly.

"Yeah? But what if she doesn't?"

"Are you going to deal or not?" I grabbed the plastic bottle and poured a little more into my cup and then into Galinak's as well, reminding myself to pace things.

Galinak shoved two cards towards me and dealt two for himself. He inspected his hand and raised a tower coin. I looked at the crude carvings in my own hand, slid a tower to the pot, and raised by another three. Galinak eyed the large coin pile on my side of the table.

"I know this is a friendly game, Twinkle," he muttered, "but I have a feeling I'm being hustled here."

"No hustling." I eyed the empty hall behind him, filled with upturned stools and empty tables. The proprietor was behind the bar, cleaning the already gleaming surface and not paying attention to us. "You're just rusting awful at cards."

Galinak chuckled as he evened the pot. "That's what got me into this mess in the first place, remember?" He flipped the first wooden card on the table. It was a Guildlord. Galinak raised by two towers, and I evened.

"What if Vincha doesn't show up?" he asked again.

"She will. Puorpan was not lying." *This time . . .*

"How sure are you?" he insisted.

I looked around. The place was perfect. Wheel of Fortune was a drive-in joint in an abandoned town, a drive from the Tarakan highway but not too far. It was where truckers, merchants, and even gang members used to stop to refuel and drink in peace. A few months ago, business must have been booming. Now, with the Oil Baron's blockade on the Tarakan roads surrounding the City of Towers, it was all but deserted.

"She'll come," I said, and pointed at the next card.

Galinak flipped the second card. It was a 9-Troll.

"It's been three days, and the owner is getting suspicious of us just sitting here all the time."

I raised two towers. "That's why I asked for the cards, and the bottle," I said. "Our metal is solid enough." *As long as we still have some.* But I kept that thought to myself.

"Okay, look." Galinak absentmindedly slid his coins into the pot. His head obviously was not in the game. "If Vincha shows up, let me talk to her, in the beginning."

I shook my head. "Absolutely not. You and diplomacy do not go hand in hand. I rather think you must have broken diplomacy's hand and several ribs as well."

"True." Galinak chuckled. "I am not as good with words as you are, but this isn't diplomacy. This is just us walking up to Vincha and letting her know it's . . . well . . . us, just in different bodies. Now she and I, we were never in the same crew, but we are both

Salvationists and we go a long way back. That stands for something. You, Twinkle Eyes"—he pointed at me—"how many times did Vincha try to kill you? I lost count."

The image of Vincha sliding across the table in Margat's Den and pinning a blade to my throat flashed in front of my eyes, replaced by her punching me in a tavern called the Blade, aiming a power pistol at me, and trying to choke me to death during our expedition to the Tarakan Valley. "You might have a point," I conceded, "but I still don't trust you on this. This is a delicate situation. You should just watch my back and intervene *if* things go south."

The sudden rumble of an engine came from outside. I looked at the wall, concentrated, and it became transparent to me.

"What is it?"

"A shark."

"Only one?" Galinak was right to question my sight, as the mercenaries and pirates roaming the Tarakan highways were known to drive in groups.

"Only one," I said, "but it is weaponised. Has some kind of a folding cannon on its back, a rail gun at the front, and I think I see missile launcher tubes on the sides."

"You said Vincha was a smuggler now," Galinak remarked, cards still in hand. "Smugglers prefer cloaked sharks, not something with so many weapon heat signatures."

I watched as the door to the shark slid upwards, but from where I was sitting I still couldn't see who was driving, and I didn't want to alert the man behind the bar.

"You are forgetting the Tarakan hardware Vincha is packing," I said. "She left the City Within the Mountain with the best technology a Troll could augment, ever. I bet she can pack some heat and still elude most scans. Best of both worlds."

The driver stepped out of the shark. I recognised the red curls, remembering the rejuvenation therapy we all went through right before most of us had gotten torn to pieces.

"Is it her?"

"Oh yeah, it's her. Stay," I warned just as Galinak was about to stand up. "Let her come to us." *For once . . .*

"Let me talk to her."

"No."

Galinak pointed at the third card that was facedown on the table. "Let's play for it."

There was no way I could reason with the Troll. He was excited to reunite with an old friend, not to mention a secret flame. I looked back outside. Vincha was busy pulling a crate out of the vehicle. She was wearing LeatherFlex armour and had two hand blasters, one on each hip.

When I looked back, the third card had already been flipped— another nine, this one a Gadgetier. I looked at Galinak. His eyes were gleaming. He had better cards, I could see it in his eyes— literally. My sight magnified the reflection of his pupils. "Fine," I said. "We play for it, and the pot."

We turned our cards. He had two Puzzlers and another Guildlord—a high pair—and he whooped just as Vincha walked in holding the crate in both hands. She paused and looked at us, tensing. My heart suddenly pounding, I made sure she saw me looking back at her, a natural response under these circumstances. Her eyes lingered, but I saw her relax. Vincha didn't recognise me. She surveyed the rest of the empty bar, then tilted her head a little, her brow furrowing slightly as she concentrated. A lock of her hair moved as if it was a snake sliding in tall grass, and out of nowhere, loud music began to play.

Got ya again, Vincha! I thought to myself, hoping my face was not betraying the immense relief and satisfaction I felt right then.

"Play another hand." I forced myself to turn my head back to Galinak, and added softly, "Let her settle in."

He was already half turned away from the table. "What if she leaves?"

"She won't. She'll have a quiet drink or two," I said.

"How do you know that for sure?" Galinak reluctantly dealt again as Vincha approached the bar and laid the wooden crate on it.

"I hunted the woman for over two years. I know."

From the corner of my eye, I saw Vincha exchanging fist bumps with the bar owner. The music masked her question, but he glanced at our direction and shrugged, then busied himself taking several plastic bottles out of the crate. He only stopped to pour a drink and hand the mug to Vincha together with a small coin bag. She grabbed the mug and her payment and moved to the farthest table, where she sat herself at an angle that let her see us and the entrance at the same time.

"Now?" Galinak asked.

I zoomed. "No. She's counting metal. Let's play another hand."

I spent the time winning back Galinak's coin, but he was too excited to care. When Vincha leaned back in her seat and sipped from her mug, I whispered, "Right. Get up but don't walk straight at her. Walk first to the door, then turn and make a slow approach. Be sure she sees your hands are weapon free—this is Vincha we're talking about—and be careful what you say first, let her know we come in peace, and—"

Galinak snorted in amusement. "You're forgetting who you're talking to, Twinkle Eyes. I was approaching women long before your parents even met. Relax, I've got this." He grabbed both cups in one hand, the bottle of moonshine with the other, and turned to leave. I waited for him to step a little farther away, then got up and made my way to the bar. I followed Galinak through the bar's long mirror, as he ignored my words and beelined his way towards Vincha.

By the time I got the owner's attention, Galinak had already sat himself on the other side of Vincha's table. The proprietor was a middle-aged burly man with a bushy beard he never bothered to trim. Some of it even found its way into our food and drink, but this was not the time to complain. I knew his instincts warned him about us, but these days customers were like free metal—rare.

"Yes, Master?" he said gruffly as he approached me from his side of the bar. I peeked at the broken mirror behind him. Galinak was talking enthusiastically, with many hand gestures, but whatever he was saying was drowned out by the music.

I put a small satchel on the table and fished out a fistful of coins. That got his attention. I slowly and deliberately counted six towers and shoved it his way. "This is for the food and drink," I said, then pushed another six across the bar.

He swiped the coins into his hand before asking, "What's the rest for?"

"Damages," I said just as Vincha suddenly leaped over the table and crashed into Galinak. It was the same move she'd done on me in Margat's Den. I'd ended up on the floor back then, but this time Galinak managed to twist away at the last moment.

"Not so fast," I calmly said to the bartender as he quickly reached and brought out a rifle from under the bar. He froze when he saw my peacemaker aimed at him. By the time I plucked the rifle from his hand, Galinak and Vincha had already disarmed each other and were now busy in furious hand-to-hand combat. Vincha swung a stool that crashed into a supporting beam. I counted two more towers and then two more as another chair sailed through the air. The proprietor managed to grab the flying stool before it crashed into the mirror.

"Do you know who you're messing with?" he grumbled as both Galinak and Vincha landed on a table, causing it to break into pieces.

"I think I do, Master," I answered as politely as I could. "You are used to dealing with a tough crowd, and I bet you have efficient and effective protection when the place is busy, but I counted three other customers in as many days I stayed here and you, the owner of this place, were serving us food and drinks, not a hired hand. Don't tell me you fired the bartender but kept your muscle."

Behind me, Vincha jumped up, closed her legs around Galinak's head and turned her body as she came back down. Galinak was flipped onto the hard floor, but somehow wiggled himself out of her neck lock. I slid four more towers towards the proprietor.

"I do apologise for the inconvenience," I said, just as the door burst open and a younger man came running in. My guess? He was the proprietor's son because the bartender called, "Nariv, don't—"

The younger man was holding a blaster gun in his hands but stopped for a moment to evaluate the situation. I used that time to shoot the gun out of his hand. Even with the peacemaker's auto re-action to my retina-aiming mechanism, the trick shot was the most satisfying thing I'd ever done in this life and, come to think of it, in my past life, too. The young man yelped and held his broken fingers with his other hand, but was otherwise unharmed. The noise of the shot didn't even slow down Vincha, who was now busy punching Galinak in the mouth.

"Who are you?" The bartender was as stunned as he was relieved that his son was not dead. The shot had quashed any thoughts of further resistance out of him.

"No one you'll ever see again, I promise."

Vincha came sailing over the bar and Galinak leaped after her. The bartender and I moved casually to the side, away from the reach of fists and kicks. I threw the rest of the coin satchel at him.

"Just two old friends meeting after a long time. We'll be out of here soon," I promised.

Vincha was the first of the two to get up from the floor. She was reaching for her second combat knife.

"That's enough, Vincha," I said firmly, and aimed the peace-maker at her. "I believe you've both got it out of your systems by now."

She looked at me, breathing heavily, sweat glistening on her face.

"And who the fuck are you?" she spat as Galinak slowly got to his feet from underneath her. He was only slightly bruised, despite the fact that Vincha was not pulling any punches, but there was an ugly open cut on his forehead.

"Someone you played Trolls with at the Den." I watched as comprehension dawned on her.

"You?"

I nodded.

She let out a bitter laugh. "Oh well, it's only logical they wouldn't send this rust-brain to find me on his own."

"Hey," Galinak protested, while his cut was slowly mending before my eyes, "that was uncalled for. We were dancing so well together and all."

I turned to the bar's proprietor, who was watching us with his mouth half open. "We are going to have another drink, all three of us, right there." I pointed at the far table. "On the house, this time. And you should leave us alone. Go, take care of your boy's hand. He should never have run into a dangerous situation the way he did."

The proprietor glanced at his pale son, who was leaning heavily against the bar, and slowly nodded. "Have your drink, but I want you out of here by the time I'm back," he said, looking at me meaningfully.

I nodded at him and turned my attention back to Vincha.

"We need to talk," I said. "About Emilija."

"I won't tell you where my daughter is, even if you kill me." She was masking it with aggression, but I knew her enough to know there was genuine fear behind her eyes.

"You should just listen to what I have to say," I answered, and placed the owner's rifle gently on the bar. "Then you can decide what to do. But I bet you a sackful of towers that you are going to drive that shark straight to where your daughter is, and that you'll take us with you."

51

Peach

Back in my time, the authorities of Tarkania had not only banned outside vehicles from entering the city, they had also severely limited private vehicle ownership among residents. They compensated for the ban with many perks, such as free and available public transportation, free air train tickets for vetted applicants to Tarakan, beautifully designed walking and bicycle lanes, and even personal travel discs and hovering shopping carts that followed your every step. This pretty much cancelled pollution, eradicated congestion, and made people healthier, thus saving annually hundreds of millions of Tarakan dollars that would otherwise have been spent on health care.

For those who insisted on travelling to the city by car, there had been free underground parking lots surrounding the outskirts of the city. Those parking lots were now a swamp. Most of the underground levels had collapsed during the Catastrophe or were completely flooded. We snuck out of the city through those pocket areas that survived the onslaught of war and time.

I had to admit that Sergiu the Dying was right. Navigating between half-crushed cars through knee-deep murky water would not have been an easy route even alone and during the day. Making the trip at night, guided by two portable headlamps and leading a frightened mule pulling a cage holding a dangerous monster, made the whole trip frustratingly slow and eventful. Several times we had to turn back when the path became too narrow to negotiate, and apparently sudden floods in the lower levels were a normal occurrence. Every time this happened, Sergiu suggested we leave the cart and the Lizard behind, but I kept insisting and eventually he got tired of suggesting it.

We encountered our fair share of human bones and rotting corpses. Some bore vicious teeth marks.

"Alligators," Sergiu said with open disgust as he pushed a half-eaten, floating body away from us. "They get sucked into the lower levels from the swamp above and then have nothing to do but cull the smugglers. That's why most of them would rather leave a fat purse in a clerk's or a guard's palm than go through here again."

"Is that what happened to your leg?" I made a point of checking my power pistol, a souvenir from one of my muggers. "Was it an alligator encounter?"

"That? No, that's a whole different story."

"Is it an interesting story? Because I could certainly use a distraction right now."

"A distraction was what caused this smuggler to become alligator chowder." Sergiu jerked his head back toward the floating body. "Better keep alert and ready."

"Yes, perhaps another time," I conceded.

"Perhaps," Sergiu replied, but I was not such a fool as to believe he'd open up to me.

Once we found the tunnel leading out, it took us almost two days to reach the surface. It was full daylight when we emerged, and like the smugglers in Sergiu's tale, I swore to myself that I'd do my utmost never to go through that experience ever again. What used to be a wide highway leading into the underground parking area was now complete wilderness.

Throughout my military career I took part in numerous war games and strategic combat simulations, so it was no surprise to me that the City of Towers survived the war. Its antimissile defence and satellite shield systems must have averted or taken out most of the incoming missiles. The protective barrier bore the brunt of those weapons that came through or landed nearby. But while the city survived, the surrounding area took on the collateral damage. With the exception of the city's silhouette, now miles to the east, there was no hint of buildings, road signs, power lines, or anything resembling civilisation. The ground was a mixture of old road and earth caked to stone by nuclear heat. The city I had awoken in was devoid of life and contaminated, but the buildings and roads were mostly intact. All I could see here were mounds of upturned dirt and deep trenches cut into the earth. The rest was barren. It took me half a day to spot any sign of vegetation. Finally, as the sun was setting, I stopped by a warped tree, feeling drained both physically and emotionally. I tied the mule to it, took away the travelling gear tied to her back, and fed her a nourishment pill stuck inside a carrot.

When I turned back I saw that Sergiu had sat himself on a flat stone.

"How's your leg?" I asked.

He patted it and winced slightly. "It will do for the time I have left."

"I'm surprised the Menders couldn't help you with that injury."

Sergiu adjusted his hat. "Some wounds cannot be healed, no matter what technology you use."

"In my time there was very little you could not do, medically speaking."

"Look around you, Colonel Major. Times have changed."

"It's only that where I am going, I need you to be able to walk."

"I'll walk, don't worry, and once we find Emilija, you'll need to find your way to the Star Pillar."

"And this is where I will find this Mannes?"

"He awaits you."

"Well, let's see about our passenger first, shall we?"

I walked over to the cage and pulled away the black canvas. The Lizard turned its head towards me. It looked worse than before. I raised the plastic bottle and it leaned forward without hesitation.

"This is the last of the water," I said, and tilted the bottle. It gulped the liquid eagerly, then accepted the last of my carrots. And then there it was again. When our gazes locked, I saw more than just fear, I saw something else—perhaps hope? It knew, it understood. *Intelligence.*

"What are you going to do now?" Sergiu said behind me. He was standing again, the power pistol in his hand.

I drew the power sword and grabbed the large iron key with the other. The Lizard drew back and hissed as I approached. There was a slightly repellent odour coming from it.

"Are you mad?" Sergiu asked from behind me.

"If you shoot it before I tell you to, you'd better shoot me next," I warned.

I inserted the key and turned it, then swung the gate open and took a step back. Slowly the creature crawled forward, its claws still tied. It tried to straighten up, then made a terrible squeal and fell to the ground.

"What happened to it?"

"They broke its knees." Sergiu sounded relieved. "Makes them easier to handle. That merchant you told me about was hoping to make an extra coin from slaying the creature in an arena event, but he wasn't going to give it much of a fighting chance." From his tone of voice, I deduced Sergiu was not disapproving of the method.

I looked at the creature. As far as I could tell it was sexless, without genitals of any kind. Just like most of the Angels and Guardian Angels Tarakan had manufactured.

"Sergiu," I said, not taking my eyes from the Lizard, "do you know what happened to this world—I mean, really know?"

"You asked me this before. I was born years after it all happened, and I've heard a dozen versions if not more."

"Wait here," I said to the prone Lizard, trusting on instinct that it understood me, then turned to Sergiu the Dying and waved a warning finger at him. "Don't shoot it."

I walked towards my gear and rummaged through it, knowing that what I was about to do was worse than taking a blind leap or endangering my mission. My hand closed around the black rod and I pulled it out.

Stupid. Just plain stupid. But I need to know.

I walked back to the Lizard holding the black rod in my hand.

"What are you going to do now?" Sergiu sounded exasperated.

I squatted next to the Lizard, making sure I was out of reach of his still-bound claws, aimed the emergency cell regenerator at one of his knees, and pressed the hidden button. A blue ray erupted from it and scanned the Lizard's leg, but until it pinged I didn't know if it would work. If the Lizard was truly an alien or a new species, the cell regenerator would not have been able to recognise the injury. But it would have worked for a human or an Angel.

I turned my head to the Lizard. "I don't know if this will hurt or not," I said slowly and deliberately, "but try to stay still." Then I pressed the second button and brought it closer to the injured leg. White foam formed around the knee until it was completely covered. The field cell regenerator, warm in my hand, pinged again, and I bent down and pressed it against the injured knee, then repeated the proceedure on the other one.

When it was over I stepped back and powered up my sword. It was time for the final test. I watched the Lizard rise up on its hind legs. It slowly straightened up, a head and a half taller than me. I looked at the creature's powerful hind legs, completely healed now, its immense chest muscles, razor-sharp claws, and greenish, alien skin. I raised the glowing sword between us.

From the corner of my eye I saw Sergiu taking position, his gun pointing straight at the Lizard's chest. Facing the creature, I was suddenly pretty sure that should it choose to attack, a gun would not stop it in time.

The Lizard looked at my gleaming short sword, then back at me, and with one fluid motion it brought its bound claws down on it. There was a spark and the Lizard was completely free.

"Rust," I heard Sergiu curse.

"Don't shoot," I called quickly, and stepped back.

"Okay," I said slowly, "this is either very smart or incredibly stupid." I powered down my sword and lowered it towards the ground.

The Lizard turned its head and looked at Sergiu, then back at me. He slowly lowered himself into what I guessed was a Lizardman's version of a squat or guard.

"Can you understand me?" I asked.

It hissed softly, which could have been a signal that it did understand me, or simply a reaction.

"Can you talk?"

It opened its mouth but again, what came out was something between a hiss and a squeak.

"You are free to go, if that is what you wish. But should you want to stay . . ."

I guess it was just taking its time to figure out if it could do it, because it suddenly charged at me with astounding speed. I heard Sergiu's weapon discharge but as I anticipated, his reaction was too slow and the only thing the shot hit was naked ground. The creature was upon me before I could even bring the sword back up. I saw the claws which could have ripped through my vessel's skin, and I instinctively cowered. It leaped over me and I felt the mass of its body pass over my head. I rolled sideways and heard another discharge of a weapon followed by a curse. When I raised my head from the dirt the creature had already disappeared into the darkness.

52

Mannes

After all these years . . .

Mannes felt the pang of exhilaration in his heart. He was so close, *so close.* He walked among the warped black trees, stepping on a twig or ducking under a branch every few steps. It was humid, and even he could smell the musky scent of the forest all around him. It must have been only his imagination, but he thought he detected the faint taint of death as well.

Several lifetimes ago, this area used to be a medium-sized college town that attracted respectable talent. Now it was just another ruin claimed by nature, and there Mannes walked, heart thumping with excitement, even more than excitement. Something *far better.*

Three of his men were scouting ahead, two more cleared the path with machetes, and a squad of bodyguards trotted around him with their weapons drawn. Regardless of them, and for no logical reason, he felt *safe* for the first time since . . . Mannes could not remember when he last felt like that, actually.

He had known the town, before everything . . . he had taken a seminar about the place for some extra credits when he was an undergrad student in Tarakan University and still remembered the holographic virtual tour. Five years later, he visited on a four-day convention. He got bad food poisoning on the last day but also a blow job from a very drunk, easily impressed master's student. So, things had evened out fairly . . .

The town had housed one of the earliest Tarakan server sites, built before Tarakan gained independence and was too far away to be of any use once borders were established. Tarakan kept funding the place merely for its historical and educational value. It was a harmless educational facility in a quiet little college town, with no military value or threat. That did not stop pretty much everyone from targeting the place when the shit hit the fan. There were no high-energy shields to soften the nuclear explosions, no protective military facilities to bear the brunt of the anti-organic bombs, no satellite antimissile shields, not even a mountainside to absorb some of the blasts. There was only a nice little lake with decent fishing that had evaporated and collapsed into itself. Oh, and around eighty thousand families and three thousand students who'd died in a matter of minutes.

Mannes stopped in his tracks to look around. He was almost sure he stood where the famous Vamous Bakery once stood, but that could have been just a hunch. Every once in a while, he would see evidence of the place it used to be: a piece of paved road, rusting metal plates, a still-standing wall, but nothing was truly recognisable. The war had left almost nothing standing, and after a while, like so many other places Mannes had visited in his long journey, man had forgotten and nature had taken over.

"Master, it's getting dark. Should we head back?"

"No." His instruments had detected that there was still electronic activity in this destroyed area, and he was not going back without results. He had twenty of his best bodyguards around him, so he was safe enough, and he so desperately wanted to know, to see if there was a chance . . .

"Found something," someone shouted up ahead.

Mannes knew he was in the right place as soon as he stepped out into the large clearing.

It used to be a modest enough four-story complex, built to blend in with the town's architectural style. But the interior was distinctly Tarakan, and its steel floors had survived—though parts were buried under the wet earth and debris.

"I want the place lit, now!" he ordered, and his troops did their best, they really did. He never got used to it. His army using sophisticated weapons while at the same time they were often reduced to carrying torches and oil lamps.

Forgetting his age and ignoring physical agony, Mannes got on his hands and knees, and shifted earth until he felt the cool steel under his palm.

He had found it. He had fucking found it.

Mannes straightened up and looked around, trying to imagine the place when it was intact. It was so long ago he didn't believe he would remember, but the image was surprisingly vivid.

The entrance used to be *there*. He turned.

Columns there. He saw the imprint one of them had left on the ground. *The Tarkanians were into stately columns. Imitating the majestic old Greek architecture was all the rage back then.*

Then the middle would be . . . Mannes walked the grounds as if in a dream. He turned around, seeing people and things that were not really there. He heard laughter, and saw smiling students passing by, chattering among themselves. An overly enthusiastic tour guide gesticulated as she explained the importance of the place while mentioning a visit to the gift shop right *there* would be a fun thing to do after the tour was over. Without thinking about what he was doing, Mannes joined the imaginary group and followed the tour guide.

"The building itself is fully energy efficient," the tour guide chirped cheerfully, *"which means it does not use any more energy than it produces. The panels on the roof are solar, of course, but they also convert the energy of raindrops into electricity. Even the floors store the energy we*

create with each step we make, so if you want to help us conserve energy and our planet, stamp your feet like this . . ."

Mannes's bodyguards watched in solemn silence as he walked about, occasionally stamping his feet. He knew no one would dare to comment or snigger at his actions. They had seen him do so much worse . . .

"The majority of the server is buried deep underground"—the tour guide pointed down at the floor—"and it's not only because the Mayor hates towers." There were several knowing chuckles among the group. "Placing the servers deep underground helps to keep them cool. Since this is the first site that was built by Tarakan that is operated almost exclusively by an independent artificial intelligence, or Sentient Programs, as they are called by our development team, there was no need to dig wide corridors or worry about human workers suffering from claustrophobia. Darwin, our very own SP, is a hundred percent self-sufficient, which means he manages all needed maintenance on his own. Maybe you want to meet him?" The group cheered enthusiastically.

"And now, ladies and gentleman," the tour guide announced, "we reach the main point of our tour, right—"

Mannes stepped over a large mound.

Here.

No matter what the tour guide claimed or what slogan the Tarakan advertisement agency came up with, there was never 100 percent self-sufficiency.

Even though it was a rare occurrence, human intervention was something Tarakan engineers and architects had to plan for. Which meant the emergency panel he had learned about in class should be around—

Mannes went down on his knees again. This time his guards protested but he didn't care. He shifted and dug like a dog searching for a bone. Two of his bodyguards rushed to help, but honestly, he felt as if he could lift a mountain all by himself.

When his hand, elbow deep in the earth, touched the emergency scanning plate, Mannes could not stop the tears from streaming down his cheeks.

Finally. After all these years. Finally.

He pressed the plate with his palm, but nothing happened. He withdrew it, swiped the muck away on his robes, spat and rubbed the moisture on his palms, and tried again.

Come on . . .

This time Mannes felt the plate vibrate, and blue light erupted from under his hand, momentarily blinding him. When he got his bearings, the ground was shaking as if there was an earthquake. A few of his bodyguards fought for balance; others had been thrown to the ground and were in various stages of getting up. Blue light was emanating from the places where the earth was piled thinly.

Ten paces from where Mannes was crouching the earth was not just moving; it was dropping into a growing hole as plates withdrew and spun into themselves, revealing a large shaft crackling with blue energy.

A silver ball, twice a man's size, emerged slowly from the hole. Mannes immediately recognised it as an early version of an SP skin, before they managed to create the more human-like versions. The ball was whole and perfect, made of liquid silver that rippled and moved, shining with a white light emanating from within. Mannes got back onto his feet and stepped closer, motioning for his bodyguards to stand in a semicircle behind him. The ball hovered a few feet above the gaping hole, and for a moment all Mannes could focus on was his own distorted reflection.

A thin line suddenly formed in the surface of the levitating ball and a wide cone of blue light washed over them. Mannes realised his mistake and shouted, "Drop your weapons," but it was too late. Bullets and rays erupted from the ball, momentarily creating tiny holes in the silvery surface.

All Mannes could do was cover his head and duck. He heard screams and smelled seared flesh, and it was all so sudden and fast it sounded as if a huge, dissonant chord had erupted all at once around him. As if someone had sat on a piano. It lasted probably less than three seconds.

He heard bodies topple to the ground, and then, silence. There were no cries of the wounded or moans of the dying because his entire squad of bodyguards was dead before they hit the ground.

Because of me.

Mannes lowered his hands and raised his head. The ball was still hovering over him, whole and perfect as before.

He felt more than heard the soft ping in his inner ear. The SP was trying to reach him via his Comm, but that system had malfunctioned long ago. The SP must have realised it as well because the silvery surface morphed into something resembling a face. It had lips and a nose and silvery eyes, and when it spoke out loud, a male voice rumbled with an undercurrent of basses. It was not pleasant to the ear.

"Dr. Mannes Holtz," it said. The vibration of its deep, booming voice made Mannes's ribs tingle and shook the earth under his feet.

Mannes rose slowly to his feet and looked around. It had been a long time since he'd stood so close to a battle, if you could grace the one-sided mass murder that had just occurred with such a word. Some of his bodyguards he even knew by name, but most of them were now unrecognisable. He turned to the floating silver face.

"Why did you kill my men?"

The silvery mouth moved when it spoke. "They were carrying arms and were not identified to be of the Tarakan forces."

"They were with *me*."

"All physical indications showed strong enmity. They were authenticated as enemies carrying weapons with intent and were dealt with accordingly."

"They were with me!" This time Mannes shouted, unable to contain his frustration.

"You are Dr. Mannes Holtz."

Mannes took a deep breath and steadied himself.

It doesn't matter. They don't matter. All that matters is that I am home.

"You recognise me . . ."

"Your scan shows you are seventy-three percent Dr. Mannes Holtz, including distinctive brain patterns, yet many of your body organs are not of your registered DNA. I detect artificial DNA manipulation in some of your transplanted organs. I see several skin grafts on forty-two percent of your body, a heart transplant, a liver, two different kidneys, a left pupil, two artificial knees and one elbow, a partly artificial digestion track with the organic part made of mixed human and pig tissues, one testicle—"

"It's been a *long* time," Mannes interrupted, "but I *am* Dr. Mannes Holtz, chief engineer, a minor seat in the inner council, rank equivalent to three sta—"

"I know who you are," the bass voice interrupted Mannes for the second time, "and I know your former rank. I am D-17w6a, known as Darwin."

"I seek refuge. I need *help*." Mannes found himself suddenly shouting at the hovering ball. "The world has been destroyed. I need to—"

"Your request for access is denied."

Mannes blinked, trying not to lose control of himself. Compared to later SPs, D-17w6a was a relatively simple version. It was lucky it had survived the Catastrophe at all, but this was an opportunity of a lifetime, he had to reason with it.

"Surely you recognise my rank—"

"Your former rank is known, but you were demoted by a direct edict from Counter Cyber Terrorism Agency, backed by Central Command. Your security clearance was revoked four hours and twenty-three minutes prior to the eruption of hostilities. You are wanted for a long series of crimes including cyberterrorism, espionage, attempting to corrupt a Sentient Program, growing an unregistered Sentient Program, and high treason during wartime. A second entry bears a warrant for your arrest on suspicion of murder of a family of five, two adults and three underaged siblings, one boy and two girls. Your current status warrants for your immediate arrest, something I am, regretfully, unable to do."

Mannes spread his hands wide. "Why didn't you shoot me, then?"

"Regardless of your status, you are an unarmed Tarkanian,

and showed no hostility or direct threat against me. There was no reason to neutralize you."

"If you could just let me communicate with Adam, I could—"

"You request for access is denied, Dr. Holtz, for technical as well as security reasons. I have been unable to reach Central Command since the beginning of hostilities."

"Let me help you, then. Maybe I could use your communication facilities to establish—"

"No, Dr. Holtz. I will not let you do that."

"The world was *destroyed* more than eighty years ago." Mannes threw his hands into the air in exasperation. "If I could use your powers we could begin to rebuild."

The SP remained silent for several seconds, which indicated he was carefully considering Mannes's words.

"Your physical signs indicate you believe your statement to be true," Darwin finally intoned. "The fact that a ferocious attack destroyed all life in a thirty-mile radius, that no one resettled or rebuilt the area, and that I have been unable to contact any official entities since then further support your claims."

"You see? If we could just—"

"However, your access is still denied, and you will be denied by any other Tarakan sites if such survived."

Mannes inhaled deeply, trying to control himself. What did Professor Vitor teach him about dealing with SPs? That they were more vulnerable to emotions than to reasoning. Their evolving subroutines and learning mechanism meant an SP would, at the very least, respond better to a plea for help rather than to cold logic, just like humans did. But it was a long shot in both cases.

"If you knew who I was, then why did you emerge in the first place?" he asked the hovering ball.

"I have been here for close to two hundred years . . . and alone for more than eighty-three of them." There was a split-second pause and the silvery face slightly tilted. "I guess I was curious to meet the man who most likely destroyed the world."

Mannes took a step towards the silver face. "I have travelled half the world." He pointed a finger, close enough to touch the rippling face. "Most of it on foot, and I have crossed the ocean. I fought battles and won wars. I faced bloodthirsty warlords, self-proclaimed kings and queens, and I survived more assassination attempts than I can even remember. I did not murder that family you spoke of, but I have killed so many people you could just as well add those poor bastards to the list for all I care. If you think I'm not going to get what I came here for, that I will not find a way to get what I want . . ." Mannes stopped himself midsentence. It was not wise to threaten an entity who was able to wipe out an entire squad of his best bodyguards in less than three seconds.

"You have managed to survive many years," the silvery face intoned, "and if what you say is true then you are a resourceful man. Still, I am not going to assist you in any way or form. The orders from Adam were explicit and clear. If you try to claim me by force, I will protect myself. Should you come close to overcoming my defences, I will self-destruct rather than let you use me or the knowledge stored within me."

Mannes actually took a step back. "Would you rather die than help me save the world?"

"I doubt that you can save the world, Dr. Holtz. Perhaps you want to save your soul? But I feel the damage you have directly or indirectly caused is unrepayable and irrevocable. I am an old being, Dr. Holtz, I have seen all around me perish in all but a moment. Friends I knew for years vanished in a flash. I have lived alone ever since, blind to most of the world. It is most likely that once you leave, my existence will continue in the same way it has for decades. Like any sentient being, I do not seek death, but it is not a threat to me anymore, Dr. Holtz, only a course of action I might need to take to prevent you from causing any more harm."

Mannes opened his mouth to speak, but for the first time in a long while, he could not find anything to say.

"Good-bye, Dr. Holtz." The face withdrew into the silvery ball.

"No, wait, please. Just one more thing."

The ball stopped its descent.

"Deny my request, I will accept that, but please . . ." Mannes resisted the urge to fall to his knees. "Please tell me about my daughter. Did she survive? Please, I need to know."

The face appeared again.

"Please . . ." Mannes hated hearing himself plead.

"As far as I know, no Tarkanian survived the war."

"What . . . None? That's impossible." Mannes took a step forward. "There were protective measurements, bunkers, force fields. It's not plausible that no one survived. Even with a short warning, people must have managed to run into the protective bunkers"

"As far as my logs show, there was no warning, Doctor Holtz. The civilian alarm systems were never activated."

"That's impossible . . . it cannot be . . . we can detect anything that . . . there's no reason not to . . ."

"Good-bye, Doctor Holtz."

The face withdrew and morphed back into the silvery ball. It sank slowly into the hole in the ground, which sealed itself soundlessly.

Mannes stood silently for some time. Eventually he bent down to fish a gun from one of his bodyguards' lifeless grips. He walked slowly to the torch that was stuck into the ground and took that in his other hand. He would send another squad of men in the morning to bring back the weapons and strip the bodies.

One thing he knew for sure now. There was no use trying to find another SP to gain access to the mainframe through a proxy. Mannes's name and reputation were tarnished, his rank and status gone. No Tarakan SP would ever help him. Mannes comforted himself with the knowledge that it was a long shot to begin with, but the bitter taste of defeat was fresh in his mouth. No, enough of this nonsense.

Deborah is gone. Well, you knew that. Deep inside, you knew you killed her. But there is one more thing that you can do. Set things right.

It was time to take hold of a major asset, a place he might be able to use to gain access to Adam himself. He'd been toying with the idea long before he landed on the shores of this continent, but he'd put it aside and concentrated on getting to know the old/new land and finding out if there was a chance that he could go back home. Now he knew that path was permanently blocked, and there was no use trying it again.

You knew it would come to this. The moment you woke up on that mountainside in Kyrgyzstan, you knew. And you planned for this eventuality.

Mannes stepped back into the forest. He walked slowly but his mind was racing.

There was just one more play he had to set in motion, then he would march south and seize the Star Pillar.

53

Peach

"Still thinking about the Lizard?"

I nodded.

"Don't feel too bad about it." Sergiu stretched and grimaced, his hands clasping his lower back. "At least you tried."

"Are you trying to cheer me up?"

"A little." He smiled and warmed his hands by the small fire. Several days of travel were taking their toll on him.

Well . . . to be honest, on both of us. The dirt road we were following was so rutted, Sergiu had given up on trying to ride the rickety cart and walked a large part of the way on foot. This was the most devastated land I had travelled through yet, and we hadn't encountered a single soul. We passed three ghost towns, so at least we spent some nights with a wall at our backs, but tonight we had to rough it in the wild.

"I'll give you this," Sergiu suddenly said. "I did not expect it to run away like that. From what I've heard, the Lizards just charge headlong and tear you apart."

"You never saw a Lizard before?"

"Not a live one, no. Never been to the Valley myself."

"And these Lizards come only from Tarakan Valley?"

"Yes, never heard of them anywhere else. Heard they were always a menace but manageable enough. Years ago, thousands of them suddenly came out of the mountain ridge and swarmed the valley. There was a large outpost of Salvationists there, basically groups of mercenary Troll crews that raided the Nodes for weapons and technology, and they were all wiped out. No one has managed to take hold of the area since, but lately rumours say the Lizards' numbers have dwindled a little. The Nodes in the Valley used to be the city's lifeline. If it weren't for the war with the North the city would have sent crews by now." A faint smile touched Sergiu's lips and quickly disappeared.

"You seem to know a lot of rumours, Sergiu."

He chuckled and massaged his neck. "What can an old, dying man do but gossip?"

Every good lie contains elements of truth in it, but my instinct told me this man was playing me.

"Are we still on the right track?" Sergiu began cleaning his gun.

I fished the locator from my bag and turned it on, then dialed the frequency numbers I'd memorized, making sure the screen was not facing Sergiu. The locator blipped and an arrow appeared at the edge of the screen. In my time, I would have been able to pinpoint the girl's location from here and calculate the exact way I could reach her in the shortest amount of time. I would not have had to go there, either—an extraction team would have seen to that as well. Now that the communication satellites had exploded and fallen from the skies, it was just a frustrating trial and error, following a soft blip in the general direction of her whereabouts. "We're okay," I said, and turned the machine off—though not before clearing its memory, just in case Sergiu decided I was too much of a burden. It was time to do some digging. "Tell me about this Mannes of yours."

I could see him stiffen up a little, then he forced himself to relax. "What is there to tell?"

"Who is he? What is he? Where is he from? I'm working blind here."

"Mannes is a true Tarkanian, old as the Catastrophe, even older."

"You mean he was downloaded into a vessel, like me?"

Sergiu blinked a few more times, thinking before answering. "No. He saw the Catastrophe with his own eyes, he told me that once. And he travelled half the world and crossed the oceans to get here."

"And where is 'here' exactly?" I was still struggling with the thought of someone staying alive that long without rejuvenation treatments, but I didn't want to stop the momentum of the conversation. Sergiu surprised me with an honest answer.

"Mannes is at the Star Pillar."

In hindsight Sergiu's frankness was not so surprising. If the man was really as sick as he claimed, there was a fair chance he would expire before we reached our destination, and I needed to know where that destination was.

"Okay," I said slowly as Sergiu reassembled his gun. "This Mannes, he is only one man. Tarakan was much more than that. If he thinks I will do as I am told just because he extracted me, he is going to be disappointed."

Sergiu considered my words as he reloaded his gun. As far as I could tell he only had one clip, which meant, at most, thirteen shots.

"My first advice to you, *Peach*, is to take care when you speak to Mannes. Age has shortened his temper, and like you, he is a man of swift action."

"I don't know what you mean," I said, but Sergiu wasn't buying it.

"The fastest-moving thing in the City of Towers is a rumour. I heard there was a massacre at the Seven Swans—a whole gang got wiped out by only one person, said to be a short, middle-aged woman wielding a power sword and moving like the wind. And then there is this mysterious killer roaming the backstreets of the

Pit, who recently made a serious reduction in the number of local muggers."

I remained stone-faced as Sergiu softly wheezed his chuckle. "Don't even try denying it. For someone in your profession, you leave a very *loud* trail behind you."

There was no use denying it. "The Seven Swans was about recovery of important resources." I pointed at the medibag.

Segiu made sure I saw the skepticism on his face.

"Fine," I admitted, "it was also personal."

"Since when does a Tarakan hibernating agent act on a personal vendetta?"

"Since the world was destroyed and everything's gone to shit," I snapped back.

"Well. Mannes is going to restore everything back to how it was, before the Catastrophe." This time the look on my face was enough for him to add, "Or at least begin restoring Tarakan back to its glory."

"How can one man do that?"

Sergiu got up, holstered his gun, and stretched. I noticed he did not remove his wide-brimmed hat despite the fact it was almost the middle of the night, "Tarakan was defeated, betrayed from within, but not destroyed." He pointed at me. "You are living proof that the entity called Adam, the heart of Tarakan, is still alive. Weakened and confined, perhaps, but still *alive*. Mannes told me that through his actions he could change the world, free Adam from his confinement, and restore all the great minds that are within him."

"And do you believe him?"

Sergiu closed his eyes briefly, then sighed. "Does it matter? I still remember my grandfather telling me how he went to help his mother arrange the basement when the world exploded. He was only a young boy when it happened, and they lived in a remote community, a fact which did not save their house but probably saved their lives. He still remembered a little of what was once, how people lived, that there was no sickness, and everyone had food and could travel anywhere they pleased. My father still knew the old tech of my grandfather's times. We had a working cooler, and a shortwave radio, and several working computers. When the cult of the nature god came knocking on his door, demanding that he give them all of our tech, he resisted. They killed my entire family and took me away to use me as human sacrifice. Mannes saved me just as the cult's leader was about to torch me."

"And you have been following Mannes ever since?" I watched him intently, looking for signs that he was lying, but found none. It did not mean he was telling me the truth, or the entire truth.

"Yes," Sergiu answered, his eyes looking at the dark horizon. "He is not an easy man, but he never hurt me. He just did what needed to be done.

"I've heard so many versions of why the Catastrophe happened; the wrath of a God, a vengeful planet, or that the Tarkanians were demons." Sergiu shrugged. "There was a moment in my life that I had to choose a side and a version of events, and at least Mannes's version gives me hope." He shook his head. "Looking at your new body and knowing who you are and where you have been strengthens my belief that I have made the right choice."

"And that is Mannes's version of events? An inside job caused all of this?" I waved my arm in an arc. "And why is this girl we are tracking so important that he had to awaken a hibernating agent after all these years? And those Lizards, and the tattooed—these are markings from Tarakan puzzle games, I recognise them—how are they all connected?" Sergiu simply looked at me in silence as I kept bombarding him with questions.

"Who is powering the city, and the bunkers? I heard the emergency bunkers get refilled with weapons and medicine. That kind of printing spends a huge amount of energy."

I could see Sergiu shutting down and had to fight rising frustration when he simply got up from where he was sitting and said, "Mannes will fill you in on all the details, Colonel Major, but right now, if you'll excuse me, nature calls." He turned and limped away, and I heard the rustling of leaves and branches as he distanced himself for privacy.

For a short while I was alone, in the wilderness, deep in my own thoughts, deciding if I should continue trying to milk Sergiu for information. I heard the rustle of vegetation again. At first, I thought it was Sergiu but then realised that the rustling was coming from a different direction—behind me.

The body of a vessel is mostly artificial, grown and printed in a laboratory, but my consciousness evolved from hundreds of thousands of years of human survival. I was being stalked. My skin prickled as my hand reached for the power pistol in my belt. The rustling stopped. Whoever was behind me was either waiting for something to happen or aiming a weapon at my back. In a sudden movement I spun around and stepped away from the fire, raising my weapon while slightly crouching in order to make myself less of a target.

The Lizard was standing twenty paces from me. Tall, calm, unmoving, but I remembered all too well the speed with which it moved when it charged. It looked at me, then its strange, reptilian eyes travelled to the pistol in my hand, and back to my face. *Intelligence.*

I lowered the weapon and straightened up, and as soon as I did, the Lizard began slowly advancing. It was a head and a half taller than me when fully erect, but I had the feeling this was not how it usually moved. It did not growl, hiss, or show any hostility. On the other hand, the slow approach could mean it was either cautious or stalking prey. I was acutely aware that its talons were sharp enough to tear me apart in a heartbeat, and sharp or blunt, those teeth could inflict some serious damage as well.

Still, I held my ground.

The Lizard stopped a few paces away. Out of arm's reach but close enough to charge. The only creatures who stood up so tall were the long-extinct gorillas and the cloned Tarakan military soldiers, the Guardian Angels. I shoved the power pistol back into my belt and watched as it slowly lowered itself to a crouching position. Just like the first time, before it leaped over my head.

"Can you understand me?" I asked.

It hissed, softly, then moved its talon on the ground, drawing something.

From the corner of my eye I saw Sergiu emerge from behind a tree, gun in hand. Without moving my body, I raised my hand to signal him to stop. The Lizard turned its head slightly and saw Sergiu. Its muscles tensed, and I readied myself for another leap, but it turned its head back and finished the drawing. It was a crude but accurate image of a hand with its five digits spread out. The universal sign of "hello."

54

Twinkle Eyes

Vincha stormed out of the bar with both of us at her heels.

"Vincha, wait," I called after her.

"You ain't coming," she said, without looking back.

"You need us." Galinak was a step ahead of me both physically and argumentatively.

"Like rust in my bum hole."

I was about to try and argue more sense into her but all three of us stopped in our tracks when we saw what was waiting for us. I cursed my stupidity for not checking the area through the bar's wall, but telling Vincha the gist of it and trying to contain her reaction took my full attention. Now it was too late. A man dressed in brown LeatherFlex armour was leaning casually on Vincha's shark. He was tall and lean, and had an elaborate goatee, shaped in circles and lines. He was also missing a large portion of his left ear. Two more sharks were parked near Vincha's shark, blocking its way, and several more men and women were spread out, holding a variety of light but deadly looking weaponry. Worse was the truck that was parked a hundred paces away. It was not built for speed, more likely for a blockade or for gate busting. It was big, heavy, protected by metal plates, and instead of haul space there was a manned heavy power gun. It swivelled back and forth as it covered the entire area. I estimated it could blow Vincha's shark to pieces with a single shot.

All three of us stopped as the man leaning on the shark straightened up.

"Twinkle Eyes, how are your sharpshooting skills?" Vincha whispered behind her shoulder.

"Untested," I whispered back the truth. Shooting the gun out of the boy's hand was one thing—this, now, was a whole different story.

"Can you take out the gunner?"

I quickly glanced sideways, as the man waiting for Vincha took a tentative step forward and spread his arms wide. The gunner's head was only visible through a split between the metal plates.

"Not sure," I murmured under my breath. "Can you talk your way out of this?"

"Vincha," the man called out.

"Not sure," Vincha whispered back. "I only know that if we want to live, you need to take that gunner down. But do it only on my signal."

Vincha took a step forward without waiting for my reply, spreading her hands wide. "Scorpion, this *is* a surprise."

"You know, we only asked one thing of you, Vinch," Scorpion said as he took another step forward. "To stay where you were and wait for orders. That's what the boss said. Those were her exact words, I heard them with my own ears."

"I'm surprised to learn you can hear at all." Vincha stepped a little aside, and they both began circling each other. "Because I definitely remember telling you to stay out of my business."

There were eight other gang members standing, not including the gunner on the truck, very tough odds. It dawned on me that we might all die right here, just as I was making true progress. I wondered, and not for the first time, if Rafik had been lying and there was a copy of me stored somewhere in Adam's memory. In this case, dying here might not mean I was really dead. However, whatever my intellect might say, my guts were firmly against the prospect of a messy death, and the tremor in my heart seemed to concur.

"And when it was time to break the blockade, when the order came, what did I find?" Scorpion, unaware of my philosophical reflections, changed his direction to counterclockwise, and Vincha changed her movement as well. They were both circling each other slowly, looking for an opening. Scorpion seemed relaxed and was taking his time, enjoying his control. "I find that instead of helping us jam the Oil Baron's communications and get a drop on his blockade, you took one of our sharks and now spend your time doing business on the side." He pointed at Galinak and me.

"I was not doing business with them." Vincha moved quickly out of Scorpion's reach and I felt Galinak tense at my side. "They are just old acquaintances. But speaking of the shark, how did you find me?"

Scorpion laughed and opened his palm. Even from a distance it was obvious he was holding a tracking device. I saw Vincha pale.

"The thing is, this particular device"—Scorpion made a show of shoving it into his belt—"the Gadgetier told me it records where you've been, not just where you are. All these mysterious disappearances, no one believed the rust you sold us. Sellika is on her way here, to have a *personal* chat with you, while I am going to learn all about those little secrets you've been keeping. We shall see what is more interesting, where you've been or how you die."

"I'll need that tracking device, Scorpion," Vincha said, and I managed to grab Galinak's coat before he moved.

"Not yet," I whispered.

"Come and take it." Scorpion motioned with his hand, and Vincha charged in.

She was too desperate, too eager, and went in too fast. Scorpion anticipated her movements and sidestepped, punching her in the ribs and kicking low. Her legs went out from under her. Vincha hit the ground on her back and rolled away from a vicious stomp. Scorpion laughed as he shortened the distance between himself and Vincha.

"Not yet," I whispered again. We were at killing-zone distance, and with no apparent augmentations. Unaware of our abilities, the rest of the gang was watching the fight, most of them relaxing, but two were still alert enough to cover Galinak and myself. "You'll have to drop the one with the eye patch before everyone else," I said as Scorpion landed a vicious knee to Vincha's midsection. She grunted but turned and elbowed the man in the face. He backed away a little, but instead of following up on her advantage, Vincha created some distance by retreating, breathing hard and trying to recover.

Scorpion laughed. "I was looking forward to this, Vincha. I heard you were a fighter back in the day, but I see those were lies." He suddenly moved in and landed a few more heavy swings which Vincha managed to block but not counter.

"What is she doing?" Galinak said through gritted teeth.

"Drawing him away, giving me a shot." I looked at the gunner. The aiming mechanism in my retina was showing me the right angle my gun should be at, but the problem was that the gunner had shifted his position as well, following the fight, and the gap was simply impossible to breach from where I stood.

"This is going to be a two-shot manoeuvre," I said as Vincha was getting punched and kicked.

"She can't take much more of this." Galinak stepped to the side. "When are we going to go?"

"She'll give us a sign."

Vincha was on the ground again, Scorpion towering above her. Blood flowed freely from her nose and her cheek was swollen. When Vincha and Galinak were going at it in the bar, the old Troll was pulling his punches. Scorpion was not.

"She is too busy getting beat up to give us a sign," Galinak said.

As she protected her face from vicious blows while lying on the ground, Vincha's hair suddenly twitched.

"Trust me," I said, and my hand slid to grip the butt of the peace-maker while Vincha's hair twisted and turned. "She'll give us a sign."

There was the hum of an engine and suddenly Vincha's shark accelerated in reverse and swivelled into Scorpion, sending him flying into the air just as Vincha rolled sideways, coming up with a power gun in her hand. Galinak leaped in the air and landed on the man with the eye patch as I pulled my peacemaker and dropped the female Troll standing next to him. The kick of the peacemaker was massive, but so was the hole it created. I raised the peacemaker to the swivelling machine gun, knowing that at least two other gang members were already training their weapons on me. This was not sharpshooting practice, where you can take aim at your leisure. The retina-aiming mechanism kept readjusting and the sun blurred my vision. I took a shot as bullets zinged around me, and missed, then rolled sideways as the power machine gun blasted the wall of the bar behind me. I had no power armour to protect me from the shock wave and debris, which landed on my body as I rolled. I came up, shot two more times, missed again, then felt the sharp pain of a power ray stinging my leg. I threw myself away, to the right this time. A burning sensation was climbing up my body, but there was no time for me to figure out what was going on. I landed on my side as the power gun discharged another blast above me, blowing up the entire second floor of the bar, where Galinak and I had been playing cards for three days running. The gunner lowered the muzzle in my direction, but I squeezed the trigger first, and this time the shot was true. I guess he collapsed on his own trigger because the gun suddenly swivelled to the side and discharged again, blowing out the truck's front cabin. It continued swivelling and shooting as I got to my feet and tried to figure out who was alive, knowing I had only several heartbeats before the gun made a full circle and shot again. I saw a glimpse of Galinak ducking but I got distracted by my trousers being on fire. I didn't know if Vincha slowed down next to me because she wanted to let me into her shark or if she was simply trying to calculate where the power gun would swivel next, but I dove into the backseat headfirst.

As I patted myself down she turned left, away from the truck. She was about to accelerate.

"We have to wait for Galinak," I said as a parked shark blew up behind us.

"Balls we do, Twinkle." She hit the accelerator and I was thrown back in my seat.

By the time I got up we were getting away.

"Go back for him," I said again.

"Galinak can take care of himself," Vincha answered, and shifted gears. "I have my own business to take care of."

Former me would have tried to argue that it was more sensible to have a capable fighter on our side. Former me would have tried to persuade, bargain, or even plead with her. Current me pulled the peacemaker and aimed it at Vincha's head.

"Go back, you ungrateful bitch. Galinak just saved your ass."

Our eyes met over the rear mirror. Her right eye was swollen shut and her left was bloodshot. "You wouldn't dare, Twinkle Eyes," she said.

"Think of it this way. A very capable Tarakan agent whom only I can recognise is going after your daughter, but I'm not going anywhere without Galinak and just in case I'm not convincing you with reason"—I re-aimed the peacemaker—"in a moment I am going to start shooting your shark. I will begin with the steering mechanism."

Vincha swore and turned the shark around so sharply I slammed against the side door, thankful that I had the foresight to keep my finger out of the trigger guard.

When we arrived back, everything that was not utterly destroyed was burning, including the bar, and Galinak was nowhere to be seen. The heavy gun was still swivelling in accelerating speed with the flopping body of the gunner still strapped into the chair. As we approached the whole truck exploded, and I ducked. When I raised my head again I saw burning metal debris everywhere.

"Still want me to look for your pet?"

"Yes," I answered.

"Well, we ain't getting out of the shark." Vincha pointed. "See that drone up there? That means Sellika is close."

"Who is Sellika?" I peered around, still looking for Galinak.

"No one you want to meet, believe me."

"You want me to shoot the drone down?" The trick shot I had managed to pull before empowered me with confidence.

"Save your clip." Vincha's hair twitched, and a moment later the drone dropped to the ground. "Still, we'd better get out of here, now."

"You're part of her gang now, is that it?"

Vincha shook her head. "Outside contractor." She shot me a smile against her better judgement. "Like old times, eh, Twinkle Eyes?"

"Like old times." I nodded. "I'm just not sure when you're going to try and kill me again."

"We'll keep it a surprise," she answered when something heavy landed on the roof of the shark. Both of us pointed weapons upwards, but it was Galinak's smiling face which appeared over the hood. Vincha rolled down the windows with the touch of a button and Galinak slid in, all blood, soot, and smiles.

"You came back for me," he cooed.

"Vincha insisted," I answered quickly.

The CommTroll snorted a chuckle at my outrageous lie. "Well, we still have unfinished business between us, you bucket of rusting screws," she told Galinak.

"I believe this is yours." Galinak tossed the tracking device to Vincha. It was broken in half. "But I couldn't find this Scorpion guy. Too bad. I wanted to dance with him a bit."

Vincha nodded her thanks, rolled the window up, and turned the shark around just as I pointed. "I believe the cavalry is coming."

"The wrong kind of cavalry." Vincha slammed on the accelerator as the ground around us erupted. I was thrown back and bashed my head against the machine gun mechanism.

"How fast is this shark?" Galinak was fumbling for his seat belt.

"Not fast enough," Vincha admitted, "but it's hard to catch someone you can't see." Her red hair twitched in all directions. "Shut your yaps, gentlemen, and let me concentrate. We're going to cloak."

55

Peach

He's bigger than a normal Lizard." Sergiu followed the creature's movements as it charged up hill on all fours. I'm not sure what kind of alternatives we had, but it was still a hard sell to convince Sergiu to let the creature tag along. Eventually he chose to have the lizard where he could see it rather than have it shadow us.

"Faster too," Sergiu added. "I mean, I've heard plenty about these creatures and seen some dead ones, too. This one is definitely a faster, meaner version."

I watched the Lizard move across the hilly ground to our left, leaving a dust trail behind him like the exhaust of an antique fossil fuel vehicle. "How do you know it's a 'he'?" I said. "I didn't notice a male sexual organ, or a female one, but those could be well hidden." Creating a nonsterile vessel was a very complicated and expensive process, although all vessels deployed by Tarakan intelligence possessed all the right anatomical parts and connection to the areas of the brain indicating pleasure or pain.

Sergiu shrugged and shifted position on the mule. We had

taken Summer as a beast of burden and ditched the cart as we cut through the wilderness to save time but also to avoid possible encounters on the road involving armed travellers and a free Lizard.

"Just a feeling, I guess," he said. "If he stays with us and doesn't come back from wherever he disappears to at night to murder us in our sleep, we'll have to name him at some point. Oh, I think he caught something."

It was true. The Lizard had failed to communicate even its name to us, verbally or otherwise. Its first talon drawing turned out to be a onetime wonder, as it seemed it was incapable or unwilling to draw anything else. It showed definite intelligence and reacted to simple command words such as "stop" or "wait" or "over there," but had not responded to anything more complicated, such as questions regarding its origins or even its name. I could not decipher its hisses, and as far as I could tell they were only meant to draw attention to something or to warn us off.

As I was pondering all of this, it came back to us. As usual, the normally docile Summer became nervous as it approached, and Sergiu had to take control of the mule and distance her a little from the creature. There was something dangling from the Lizard's jaws. At first, I thought it was a small, hairless dog, but when the Lizard stood up on its hind legs and took the carcass from its mouth with its claws I saw it was some kind of an unusually large field rabbit. Only when the Lizard stretched out its arm and dropped the carcass at my feet did I realise that its unusual size was not the only thing wrong with it. I hunched down and picked up the surprisingly heavy carcass. Its broken neck spoke of a clean kill, but that was not what was wrong with it.

"This . . . animal has two heads," I said. The second head was a shrivelled dead thing, well . . . deader than the rest of it, but it was definitely a *fucking two-headed rabbit*.

"Yeah, sometimes you get things like that in the wild," Sergiu commented in a matter-of-fact tone of voice. "Two-headed rabbits, six-legged deer. I once saw a wild hog with seven tusks. Didn't go near it. They are not poisonous in the classic sense of the word, but most people refuse to eat such animals. Say they bring disease or cause tattoos to appear."

Since we'd begun travelling together, the Lizard stayed in our camp during the night and brought us all kinds of vegetation in the morning, from leaves and wildflowers to half-rotten apples I had no idea where he found. What we did not eat, which was most of it, the Lizard ate. This was the first time it had brought meat, and I was not sure that I liked the idea.

"Is it true, about the tattoos?" I examined the creature again. Its fur was short, dirty, and discolored.

Sergiu shrugged. "Don't know. Of course, when chopped to bits and sold in a meat pie no one seems to mind, but most people who eat meat pies don't care to know what type of meat they're eating."

I waved the carcass at him. "Do you want it, then?"

"Nah, I think I'll pass this time."

"Me too," I said, and tossed the rabbit back at the Lizard.

In what looked like a lazy movement to me, the Lizard used his sharp talons to rip the carcass in two and shoved one part after the other into his gullet. It was over in a matter of seconds.

I heard Sergiu's amused chuckle behind me. "Guess he's not a vegetarian after all."

"Guess not," I mumbled.

The Lizard turned and sped away like an overenthusiastic hunting dog.

"You think he's just fattening us up so he'll get a better meal for himself?" Sergiu was still smiling, but only just so.

"It's definitely getting to know us better through trial and error. Did you notice how it hasn't brought us again anything we didn't eat the first time?"

Sergiu seemed a little uncomfortable with the thought. "Don't know, Colonel Major, the Lizards I've heard of simply charged and ripped you to shreds."

"This one seems different."

"Absolutely, and if there are more like him in Tarakan Valley, no wonder Trolls are not coming back from expeditions." Sergiu lowered his head, deep in thought. "Maybe he is unique, or a rare subspecies—as much of an anomaly to the other Lizards as the tattoos are for the rest of us."

"You mean it is some kind of mutation?"

"I mean he's a freak."

We began walking again, making our way through what was once an urban environment. Here and there I saw pieces of concrete, rusting metal rods, or a part of a wall, but the rest of it was just upturned wild land. My vessel told me the area was not clean of contamination. No wonder we were seeing two-headed rabbits.

"One thing I am almost positive of." I voiced the thought as it came to mind. "It, or he, is not a natural creature. It was made in a laboratory somewhere. Enhanced growth, superstrength and speed, an eat-all digestive system, no visible sexual organs, and probably a short life-span—a few years at most. This reminds me of the Angels."

"Angels?" Sergiu asked immediately, almost too fast, as if covering the fact that he knew about them.

"In my time, Tarakan used grown clones, human bodies with basic artificial intelligence. They did all the manual work—cleaning public areas, maintaining air train tracks, gardens, and sewers, working as housekeepers and even childminders, those kinds of things." I did not tell Sergiu about the black market that sold Angels, usually as sex slaves and for other, even more nefarious uses.

Sergiu just nodded encouragingly. I guessed he was trying to get me talking and waiting for me to say something interesting. I didn't mind; I was trying to get him to do the same, angling him closer with stories of the world before, which might open him up enough for me to know better what, and especially *who*, I would be facing.

"When things got a little hot, military wise," I continued, "Tarakan—I mean, we—began producing cloned soldiers in the same manner. We called them Guardian Angels, and they were larger, faster, meaner, ferociously aggressive, and although they were still bounded by strong protocols, they were exceedingly more intelligent, so they could handle the chaotic combat environment." *Unsurprisingly perhaps, there was also a small but active black market for those kinds of Angels as well.* "This Lizard reminds me of the Guardian Angels, but the snout, claws, and tail . . . that was not part of the original design."

"And how can you tell it's a Guardian Angel?"

"I used to train them." A memory flashed in front of my eyes. Rows of the "newly hatched" towered over me, at attention, radiating aggressiveness. This time even my vessel could not repress the physical shiver the memory caused. "I am sure this new race of Lizards is a brother, or at least a close cousin, to the Guardian Angels."

"A fallen Guardian Angel, then." Sergiu was clearly amused by his own wit.

"You might call it that."

"There is a saying in the land I came from, 'Beware of close cousins.'"

I glanced to see Sergiu smiling under his hat, but my mood grew darker with the memories my story had dug up. "Quit while you're ahead, Sergiu." I glanced at the small screen I held in my hand. "We have a long way to go."

56

Twinkle Eyes

"Vincha, slow the rust down," I cried out over the hum of the engine.

But as before, Vincha, hair unnaturally raised and a visor covering her eyes, simply ignored my plea. Despite being a long way from the magnetic field of the Tarakan highway, Vincha kept the shark in hover mode and at bloodcurdling speed as we crossed the forest. Whatever we were not experiencing in the form of bumps and holes in the uneven dirt road, Vincha was making up for in aggressive, almost hysterical driving. My body was repeatedly slammed against the restraints as the shark zigzagged sharply, narrowly avoiding fallen trees, rocks, and all kinds of debris. Galinak, white as a corpse, groaned in the front seat. Nourishment pills or not, I was pretty sure he was going to throw up whatever he had in him in a matter of moments. I was pretty sure I would not be able to hold my own for much longer, either.

As if listening to my prayers, a soft yet insistent blipping sound suddenly erupted in the cabin of the shark. From the corner of my eye I saw the energy meter flashing red. I remembered it being almost full when we sped away from the wreckage of the battle to elude Sellika and her force of highway bandits, but Tarakan stealth and hover technology came with a high energy price. Vincha swore softly, ignoring the ever-increasing alarm, but a little later she was forced to slow down and eventually lower the wheels and come to a complete stop.

The doors slid away when Vincha stepped out and a fresh breeze from the forest entered the shark's cabin. I leaned back and closed my eyes, steadying myself as Galinak released himself from the restraints and simply collapsed sideways to the ground. A moment later I opened my eyes again and Vincha was back, holding a small black box in her hands. She pressed open the steering wheel as she opened the box. I saw three Energy Gems, fully charged and glowing with blue energy. Vincha tightened the leather glove on her hand, then grabbed one of the gems from the box and busied herself replacing the depleted gem that she yanked out of the steering wheel's socket.

"Those are *very* expensive," I commented. "Hard to come by even at the best of times."

"What can I say? I'm a resourceful kind of gal." Vincha slammed the glowing gem into the socket and leaned back in her seat, tapping the steering wheel impatiently as the shark slowly came back to life.

"Still, I don't think you have enough power to keep the shark hovering for the entire journey," I said. As Galinak slowly climbed back to his seat I added, "And we don't know what we are going to find when we get there. If your daughter has already been taken, we will need to give chase."

Vincha tilted her head and a lock of her red hair twitched and turned. "Oh, she's there," she said. "Can't pinpoint her yet, but as soon as we get close . . ."

"So it's true." I kept talking just to stay standing for a little longer. "Puorpan said you planted a device under Emilija's skin, to keep tabs on her."

"Oh, he told you so, did he?" Vincha's grip on the steering wheel hardened. "That rust bucket is going to pay for betraying me like that."

"He only talked to me because I told him I'd warn you, *and* it took some convincing. I wouldn't blame the man if I were you." The image of Vincha breaking down under LoreMaster Harim's gentle yet relentless interrogation flashed before my eyes, so I added, "Everyone has weaknesses," for good measure.

"And he gave away the coded channel so that *agent* could track her down." Vincha swore loudly. "We go a long way, Puorpan and I, but I should have known better than to trust him."

"He had no choice," I said, and then, annoyed for some reason, I added in the privacy of my own mind, *And you should not lecture anyone about betrayal*.

Vincha didn't answer, so I added a question in a gentler tone, "When was the last time you saw Emilija?"

"What is it with you, Twinkle?" she snapped back, angry. "Trying your mind games on me again? I'm still not going to let you take my daughter to your Tarakan masters to be sacrificed."

"No one is talking about sacrifice," I protested. "Rafik was still alive when we met him in the City Within the Mountain, a grown man in his prime."

"Balls to that. How do you know it was really him?" I could see Vincha's infamous temper rising with every word. "He could have just been an image. That Adam tricked us all into a suicide mission, remember?" She glanced backwards. "Everyone who came with us died, including Bayne, and both of you clowns would have been Lizard chowder too if it weren't for that crazy deal you made. So don't try to loop my wires about the Tarkanians' good intentions."

The memory of the only Troll who truly loved her must have rattled Vincha, because instead of pressing, she fist-slammed the button for the doors to slide shut. Galinak groaned, but this time Vincha did not go back to hover mode and we began driving on four wheels, a sign that at least some of my words were getting through to her.

"They wired you up," I pressed on, "and as much as I can tell your augs did not cause rejection fever, so you do not need Skint to ease the pain."

"They only did it because it suited them, Twinkle Eyes." Vincha glanced for a second time, her eyes narrowing. "Tell me, how was it on the inside? Five years you spent inside Adam. Was it all fun and games?" When I failed to answer she snorted in contempt. "You don't even remember, do you? They stored both of you somewhere, like dried meat, and forgot you ever existed. They only woke you up to find me, Twinkle Eyes, and my guess is you have as much a choice this time as the first time around." Something in my face must have betrayed me because she chuckled cynically. "You and your little sick lapdog are just like two cards in their hand." She caught my eyes in the rearview display and winked. "Two cards played."

"And what's your alternative?" My answer came out louder than I wished. Vincha was definitely stepping on my wires. "Keeping Emilija in a world she doesn't belong to? Letting her dream of the Great Puzzle and be drawn to the Lizard-infested Valley? No, don't try to tell me you'll be able to stop her. Your daughter has to be a grown woman by now. How long do you think you can contain her?"

The shark accelerated dangerously as I verbally lashed at Vincha, but I was too caught up in my own doubt and anger to pay attention to the signs. "When was the last time you saw or talked to her?"

"Mind your own rusting business," Vincha growled.

I changed the angle but kept pushing her. "The power gems for the Shark you stole are very expensive, even for a successful smuggler such as yourself. It takes *a lot* of jobs to afford feeding a shark on your own without piracy."

"How do you know I ain't pirating?"

"Because a pirate shark needs a crew of four to get anything done," I answered hotly. "A driver, a gunner, and two more to take control of the stoppage, and that's just for the small-time, off-the-Tarakan-highway stuff. You need at least two more sharks to have a chance of stopping a SuperTruck. And besides, a pirate does not waste time selling a few bottles of moonshine to a bar owner."

"Anything else you want to mention in your brilliant deduction?" The trees were melting into a blurry green line as we whizzed past.

"Twinkles," Galinak moaned a warning, but I was on a roll.

"Last but not least: I said to pirate you need a crew. They might be scumbags and cutthroats to anyone else, but you need to trust them as much as they need to trust you. *If* you count Galinak and myself, I'd say you have two friends in this world."

Vincha snorted her contempt.

"No, Vincha, you are definitely a smuggler. A good one, perhaps, but as usual, you only think of yourself and betray everyone around you because you think you don't need anybody."

"Shut the rust up, Twinkle Eyes." The shark was picking up even more speed, but so was my mouth.

"Smuggling is good business these days, better than piracy, I'll wager, but you still need to keep on working to feed your shark. And this Sellika does not sound like a woman who lets you drive around her turf freely. She takes a cut, and a hefty one. So you stick your kid with some stranger family with a bit of coin and forget all about her, just as long as you can keep on living your life the way you want it?"

Vincha slammed on the brakes and my body crashed forward. The uneven road, or maybe it was her expert driving, caused the shark to spin several times. By the time I regained my bearings, Vincha had turned and punched Galinak right on the button, this time knocking him out cold, and a heartbeat later a power gun was aimed straight at my face.

"Get out," she said.

It took every ounce of self-control to look past the barrel of the gun and into Vincha's eyes. Earlier it was I who'd pointed a gun at her. Now the tables had turned, but this time I wasn't sure she wouldn't pull the trigger.

"No," I said in what I hoped came out in a quiet but resolute tone.

Vincha quickly turned her wrist so I could see there was no stun button on the weapon. "I am not kidding, Twinkle Eyes. I am tired of your yapping mouth. Get the rust out. The only reason I ain't pulling the trigger yet is because I don't want to drive away with your brain all over the backseat."

"No." I shook my head slowly. "You'd be a fool to pull the trigger."

She steadied the weapon, but I could see reason was beginning to sift through the mist of anger.

"You still need me, Vincha, you need *us*," I added a little too quickly, betraying my nervousness. "I know what the other agent looks like, and Galinak is someone you'll be glad to have around when things get hot, as they did back in the Wheel of Fortune." The barrel lowered itself a little, but a gut shot would have been just a slower, more painful version of a head shot. "Someone is on their way to kidnap your daughter and bring her to this Mannes. I know you've heard of him, we've all heard of him, and his reputation makes that monster Nakamura seems like a kind uncle." I locked my gaze with hers. "You can't do it on your own, not this time. First we'll stop whoever wants to take Emilija, then we'll find a way, a *peaceful* way, to deal with the Tarakan problem."

It took a few more heartbeats for Vincha to holster her weapon and turn back to the steering wheel.

"Damn you and your rusting reason, Twinkle Eyes."

I waited until we began moving again and asked, "How's Galinak doing?"

Vincha glanced sideways. "He'll be up in a few moments. I thought I broke his jaw, but I guess I was wrong." There was obvious regret in her voice. "These bodies they gave you are quite resilient."

"Not resilient enough, if you ask me," I answered.

"Yeah well, you always happen to be in the middle of a shitstorm." Vincha shook her head slightly as we picked up speed, "and you pull me right in there with you."

"Funny, I thought exactly the same thing about *you*," I answered in a lighter tone, as if Vincha had not been aiming a power gun at my face moments earlier. I guess we were both climbing down carefully from the edge of the high emotional cliff we'd stood on only moments before.

"Just help me find my daughter," Vincha mumbled, and snapped down the driving visor over her eyes.

I leaned back and tried to figure out what to do once we managed that, but for the life of me I couldn't.

57

Mannes

"The cavalry is coming, only one click away," Bria, his longest surviving Captain, announced over the Comm.

Mannes did not bother to answer. He adjusted the fur cowl of his coat and tried not to think about the cold. After decades of crisscrossing Russia and Siberia he swore he would never stand knee-deep in snow again, but there he was, doing exactly that. Yet another broken oath from a very long list he had accumulated throughout a lifetime of betrayal.

I'll place this last pawn on the board, and then we can start the final game, he said to himself. This pawn was crucial, though.

Mannes glanced behind him. Six armed guards and the two captives stood halfway between himself and the open barn. He turned his head back. At his side stood a folding table, two stools, a sealed bottle, and two delicate glass cups.

The Oil Baron's forces appeared over the hill and Mannes had to suppress a laugh. Captain Bria was not kidding when she used the word *cavalry*. There were several dozen snow cars and a few heavier armed vehicles, but the majority of the force was on horseback.

"I detect an auxiliary force on foot, trying to outflank us," Captain Bria announced.

The little fucker is trying to trap me.

They were all the same; the warlords, the self-proclaimed kings and queens or the thugs and organized bandit forces he faced. They used the same primitive tactics and cheap tricks. Mannes was almost disappointed. Still, his forces were outnumbered ten to one.

"Make adjustments," he said over the Comm, "but do not engage unless you absolutely have to."

Two dozen riders and several snow cars began advancing towards Mannes. The bulk of the army stayed behind.

"Master, they are coming with more guards than we agreed upon." Captain Bria's voice was not happy.

"Easy, Captain. He's just waving his dick around."

"I only have eight snipers in position. If they start shooting—"

"Captain. I appreciate your prudence, but I have been doing this literally since before you were even born. He is not going to shoot me before he hears what I have to offer."

Saying it was one thing. Watching a charging force galloping at you was another thing entirely. The horse riders circled Mannes and his guards, holding their weapons ready. The snow cars and the heavier armour stopped a little ahead. A slender figure climbed out of it, together with two enormous canines.

Youths are the most dangerous of foes. They are unpredictable and prone to hasty, illogical, and often ruinous decisions. Yet Mannes was banking on an emotional response to get what he wanted.

The young man approached with his bodyguards and dogs in tow. The soldiers were wearing leather armour under the layers of fur, and their high boots were studded with nails to deal better with the icy ground.

The man wore his blond hair long and in a braid. His clothes were plain, devoid of jewellery or excessive metal. His face was clean-shaven and youthful looking but for the ugly claw marks on each cheek.

A rite of passage, most likely, or a way for him to prove his leadership and manhood to the troops who had been loyal to his father.

Mannes counted three handguns on his belt alone, a covered sniper rifle hanging on his back, and a hunting knife on each thigh.

When the man was several paces away, he stopped and waited, his eyes taking everything in.

Perhaps this one is not so stupid after all.

Mannes gave ground by speaking first. "Thank you for coming, your highness."

The man stared coolly into Mannes's sunken eyes. "I am called the Oil Baron, old man, I'm not a bleeding king."

Mannes tilted his head. "For all intents and purposes, you are king of this land, are you not?"

"Kings are weak," the younger man spat. "Surrounded by fucking ass kissers and bootlickers. A baron is always reminded where he is on the food chain. Strong enough in his own land but watched closely from all sides."

Mannes spread his hands. "'Oil Baron' it is, then, my lord."

"And you are . . . ?"

"Mannes, just Mannes. I have no need for titles."

"Well, Mannes . . . are those my men, over there?" The Oil Baron nodded towards the men standing behind Mannes.

"Yes." Mannes motioned with his hand and two guards brought the captives forward.

"As promised, your kin were not mistreated, and were kept well fed and warm," Mannes said as his guards cut loose the captives' bindings.

As soon as they were freed, the captives fell onto their knees in front of the Oil Baron, who bent down, took them by their hands, and helped them up.

"Are you all right, my dear cousin?" he asked softly, his eyes full of concern.

"I am sorry, Baron." The man who he had spoken to did not

lift his stare from the ground. "They took us by surprise. There was nothing we could have done."

"It is fine, Udinas." The Oil Baron spoke loud enough for everyone to hear. "Your shame will be cleansed in ritual. Now take your little brother and walk the cold out of your bones." He indicated the larger group of cavalries on top of the hill. "I even brought your favourite mare to carry you home. Your wife and children await you."

Udinas's eyes lit up with relief and he bowed and tried to kiss the Oil Baron's hands, but the young man stopped him from doing so. "Go," he commanded, and the two began walking away.

The Oil Baron watched the two make their way through the deep snow and turned back to Mannes.

"I guess a thank-you is in order for keeping my blood kin alive," he said.

"I meant them no harm." Mannes shrugged. "And I guess you received my gifts."

"Yes, I did." The Oil Baron lifted the power sniper over his head and unzipped the cover. "It is a thing of beauty," he said as he powered the weapon and turned on the scope. "I've never owned a sophisticated weapon such as this before."

"I am happy you are pleased," Mannes said, "and just to warn you, Oil Baron, I have several snipers around the area who will shoot your head off your shoulder if you aim that rifle at me."

"Oh, my dear old man, I would never dream of such a betrayal." The Oil Baron shook his head. "But I do have a question regarding the kickback once you take a shot." The Oil Baron spun around, hefted the weapon, and aimed it at the back of one of the walking captives. "Head shot," he called, and pulled the trigger. There was a powerful *whoosh* and the head of the man walking next to Udinas exploded in a mess of blood and gore. The headless body slumped forward into the snow. Udinas stood frozen from shock and covered in blood, then began shouting and screaming.

The Oil Baron turned to Mannes. "You see? There's a fierce kickback."

"You need to power it down a little." Mannes pointed. "It pretty much cancels the kickback and saves on the energy clip, too."

"Show me."

Mannes motioned to one of his guards and he took several steps towards the Oil Baron. The two canines immediately rose to their feet, snarling and showing fangs.

"Easy," the Baron commanded, and their response was immediate.

He handed the weapon to Mannes's bodyguard, who fiddled with the button and handed it back. "That'll work," he said.

By now, Udinas was running away, trying to reach the woods and gain shelter there.

The Oil Baron turned and aimed the sniper rifle.

"Left leg," he said, and pulled the trigger. This time there was barely a sound and Udinas limped and hobbled. "That handles so much better." The Oil Baron aimed again. "Right leg."

Udinas dropped to the snow and lay there as the Oil Baron handed the rifle to one of his own men. "They surrendered," he said to Mannes, who nodded slowly.

"I can relate to that."

Behind the Oil Baron, Udinas began crawling slowly towards the tree line. Without turning back, the Oil Baron whistled softly and the two enormous dogs turned immediately around and began sniffing their way towards the fallen man.

"Shall we sit down here?" Mannes gestured towards the table. "Or would you like to step into the barn? It is a little more protected from the elements."

The Oil Baron sniffed. "We Northerners are used to the cold."

He sat down and Mannes sat himself in front of him and picked up the bottle. "This is a rare kind of drink I brought from another land and another time. It is called vodka." Mannes motioned to one of his guards, who stepped forward, broke the seal, and poured both of them a drink. "I used to have six bottles of this and that is the last one. I have been saving it for a special occasion."

Mannes took his glass and raised it. "To your health, Baron." He drank it all in one go.

The Oil Baron took his filled glass, watched the liquid intently, then slowly and deliberately turned the glass and let the liquid spill over the icy ground. Behind him, Udinas began to scream as the two dogs attacked him. It did not take them long to silence the wounded man. The Oil Baron did not bother to turn his head and watch.

Oh yes, you will do.

"I have more weapons like the ones I gave you, and even better ones," Mannes said, leaning forward. "I can give you machine guns, energy clips, shoulder cannons, and best of all: pre-Catastrophe war machines. In the past they were called Tanks. Each could blow up this sturdy-looking house over there"—Mannes pointed at an abandoned house half buried in the snow—"in one shot. I can show you how to use them and teach your men how to fight in them."

"There are hot promises on your tongue"—the Oil Baron leaned back on his chair—"but words do not melt ice."

"Oh, but I can give you more than just words, much more, Oil Baron." Mannes brought the glass to his lips. "I can give you the two things you long for more than anything else." He made sure he had the Oil Baron's full attention, before saying, "Freedom and revenge."

"We are free folk here, stranger." The Oil Baron puffed his chest. "The oil keeps us warm during the long winters, and the south laps up our product. Should we wish, we could starve them."

"With respect, Baron, you *are* a nation of brave warriors, but it is the south which is keeping you on a short leash and feeding you meagre droppings for your precious oil. Your father tried to change that, and your troops fought valiantly, but he overreached. Your forces ran out of food, then out of bullets, and you lost all your gains. Once the southern forces chased you back to the North, rather than fighting you like men, they simply let you starve until your father had no choice but to sign the shameful treaty. He died of shame, in his bed. And now the City of Towers is happy to let you freeze here in the North with your horses and your old pistols while you supply them with everything they need."

The Oil Baron was on his feet, dangerous anger flashing in his eyes. "If you think that for a few trinkets you are given the right to insult me," he spat, "you are about to find out you are mistaken." He whistled once and the dogs, which were feasting on the body of Udinas, stopped mid-carnage and came running back. They stood next to their master panting, their snouts dripping with blood.

Mannes seemed to be unfazed. "You misunderstand me, Oil Baron. Your father was a brave man, but he lacked the resources and charged too deep into southern territory. You will not make the same mistake. I can supply you with the weapons and show you the tactics of how to bleed the City of Towers slowly and finally draw their forces out and slaughter them."

The Oil Baron seemed to rein in his temper. "And in return, you want . . . ?"

"Men. Five for each one I leave behind with you, and eventually some oil, but most of all, I want you to keep the City of Tower's attention on the North for at least three years. Gain some territory you can hold, play cat and mouse, hit them where it hurts. Starve them slowly, the way they starved your father."

A calculated look passed the Oil Baron's eyes. "And where did you get your hands on such weapons?"

"Tarakan used to have a military manufacturing plant and an army base in this area," Mannes said. "When the northern alliance was formed against Tarakan the rulers of this land tried to take over the base. Tarakan threatened to destroy the entire area but eventually the standoff was resolved peacefully. The base was sealed as a compromise, together with all of its weaponry."

"You are a fool." The Oil Baron's smile had no mirth in it. "And a soon-to-be-dead fool at that. We know about that place, but no one can get in or out of it. Believe me, my grandfather and my father both tried."

"That's because you need a special key to enter," Mannes answered calmly, giving the preplanned sign. "It is called a Puzzler."

There was a rumbling noise from within the barn behind them and a huge machine burst out of it. It had three cannons and several machine guns protruding from its top. The two canines whimpered and slunk backwards, and several nervous horses created a chaotic disarray within the surrounding guards.

"Luckily I got my hands on one of those keys," Mannes continued calmly. He got up to his feet, poured another shot of vodka, and handed it to the Oil Baron, who was so mesmerized by the sight of the huge machine, he accepted the glass without looking.

The Tank's cannons swivelled and shot once, and the house Mannes had pointed at before blew up to smithereens. The shock wave toppled the small table between Mannes and the Oil Baron and caused complete panic among the surrounding horses.

Mannes raised the glass to his lips as all around them men were desperately trying to calm down their beasts. "We drink to our victory."

This time, the Oil Baron drank the vodka.

58

Twinkle Eyes

Galinak broke the few remaining boards nailed to the entrance of the large barn, despite the fact that we could have simply ducked under them. Although he didn't say anything about it, I guessed that being knocked out by Vincha still hurt his pride. The acidic smell that hit us made even me grimace and caused Vincha to hold her hand to her face. It wasn't fresh, more like an old scent which lingered, and we got used to it as our eyes adjusted to the gloom.

"Well, the house seems deserted." I looked at the ground, where the deep marks of cart wheels were clearly visible. "The Tanner and his family are not hiding here, either."

"Rust fuckers!" Vincha spat.

"You think they took her with them?"

Vincha shook her head, and I saw a lock of her hair twitch as she tried to channel. "She was in the area when we approached but the signal here has always been erratic, something about the mountains, I guess."

You planted the device under her skin to be able to follow her if she was taken, but just to be on the safe side, you left her in a place where it was hard to pinpoint her location, I thought, then I spotted something scratched into a wooden beam. It was a symbol, three crescent moons tied in a string and ending in a perfect triangle. We were in the right place.

Before I could say anything there was a sudden crick from the loft above us and Galinak and I reacted the same way, spinning and ducking in different directions. Vincha stayed where she stood and looked up with newfound hope in her eyes.

"Emilija?" she called out. "It's me, Mom."

I looked up and used my sight. There were two figures huddled together in the far upper corner, a young man and a woman.

I shoved the peacemaker back into its shoulder harness and walked out into the open. "Come out," I called, and, looking meaningfully at Vincha, gestured with my palm for calmness while adding, "both of you."

Vincha's eyes widened as she looked at me and her jaw hardened. Despite what was at stake, I was suddenly hoping, for the young woman's sake, that she was not the CommTroll's daughter.

"We won't harm you, we just . . ."

Vincha raised her power gun and fired three times.

"Come out, right now," she yelled as bits of wood landed around us.

There was quick shuffling and the ashen hair of a young man's head appeared high above us, followed by the rest of him. He was wearing a farmer's attire and holding a short club with both hands. He paled even further when he saw us looking at him, to the point I was afraid he was going to fall down.

"Pleasant you be," he croaked in a frightened voice.

"Rust your pleasant, if that is my daughter behind you," Vincha snapped, and called again, "Emilija, come out *right now.*" But the half-dressed, terrified girl who appeared behind him clutching a wicker basket to her semi-exposed bosom was obviously not Emilija. She was all freckles and pink flesh, with curly brown hair that had weeds tangled in it. They climbed down as the boy said, "If you are looking for the Kethans, they left, almost two moons ago."

"Where to?" Vincha snapped, clearly disappointed and relieved at the same time.

He shrugged. "Dunno, a long way off."

"What's your name?" I asked, trying to take hold of the interrogation.

He turned his face to me; the redness in his cheeks was beginning to lose its intensity. "Nelsohn, Master, of the Fruiriks, and this is Ganula—"

"I don't care what her name is or where the Kethans are right now," Vincha said impatiently, but at least she was holstering back her weapons. "Emilija is still around here and I need to know where."

This time it was the basket-clutching young woman who spoke. "You mean that strange, marked girl who spoke to no one? Why should we know? We never saw her anywhere, or even talked to her, and she was *marked*, you know, my paps says she should have been hanged and quarter—"

"What part of the words *my daughter* didn't you understand?" I interrupted hastily as Vincha's complexion greyed dangerously. I could see Galinak shaking his head and smiling to himself as he leaned back on a wooden beam just behind Vincha and began stuffing his pipe.

Before things deteriorated even further Nelsohn suddenly said, "I heard they took her up the mountain, to stay with the SkyMaster, pleasant he be."

We all turned our attention to the boy. "Where did you hear that?" I asked.

But the boy shrugged. "Just heard about it, is all. People talk about the SkyMaster because of that chair."

"What chair?"

"The one that heals people. Is that why you're here?"

"My paps says it's a demon chair and that the SkyMaster was bewitched by the girl and we shouldn't go to the compound," the opinionated Ganula intervened, forgetting the claim she'd made only moments ago.

"Tell that to Aharon." Nelsohn turned to her. "His leg was in bits when they brought him up there, and he was walking a day later like he'd been touched by sunshine. Said he'd never felt better, and that the SkyMaster who used to be old and feeble can suddenly walk down the mountain to talk to the elders and is looking all rosy cheeked. My old man told me the miracle chair used to work, years ago, and that my ma once had the flu and was dying and such and they brought her up there." Nelsohn turned back to us. "There used to be more people in the Sky Palace but now there is only the SkyMaster, pleasant he be. Anyways, she was cured, is all I am saying, and only died two years later from an accident, so I say if that miracle chair is back working it is a blessing to ours."

But the girl shook her head stubbornly. "My paps says that it is false healing and that the demon will come and take those who make a pact with it."

Nelsohn opened his mouth to answer but I stepped in. "And you saw Emilija when you brought Aharon to this sky palace?"

Nelsohn turned his attention back to me. "No, Master, I did not go up the mountain myself, the elders took him on a cart, but I heard that the girl who used to stay with the Kethans was walking around and touching all the machines."

Vincha stepped forward and pointed her finger at the boy. "You're going to take us to this SkyMaster of yours."

A look of panic crossed Nelsohn's face. "Oh Mistress, I can't do that, it's almost night and it's a day's climb to the Sky Palace and the elders say it—"

Vincha grabbed the boy before he completed his sentence and slammed him forcefully against a wooden beam, sliding him up against it until his legs lifted off the ground. "Listen to me, you miserable horny rusting son of a goat. You are taking us up there, right now."

"Let go of him, bitch," Ganula shrieked as she stepped forward, raising her fist, but I grabbed her arm before she did something incredibly stupid. Galinak, sucking his pipe and not bothering to move from his position, watched all of us with mild amusement on his face.

I spun the girl around and used my well-practiced levelheaded voice. "You will go home, Miss Ganula, but not before paying a visit to Nelsohn's farm, to inform his worried family that he was hired, for hard metal coin, to take us up the mountain. He'll be back home safe and sound by tomorrow."

"I can't," the girl wailed, sudden panic in her eyes. "Nelsohn's family do not see me with a pleasant eye, they want him to marry that cross-eyed, ugly Shiara, only because her father still owns pigs and offered them a working ploughing machine."

Vincha was not waiting for things to be resolved. She dragged the frightened Nelsohn outside and we all followed her, while I kept on talking. "Well, I'm sure they'll be happy when you to tell them their son is fine and healthy and employed."

We all walked outside.

"But Nelsohn's not allowed to see me." Ganula was blinking back tears of panic. "That's is why we needed to meet in the Kethans' barn."

"I am sure Nelsohn's parents would be thankful if you let them know their son is safe and employed. Besides"—I pointed at the mud-stained but still impressive-looking shark, parked near Broadrik's abandoned house, and watched the two of them gawk— "we might get to this Sky Palace a little faster than a day."

59

Artium

Entry 11722

Artium straightened on his chair and looked at the bright screen in front of him. Emilija had found him a new keyboard with all the letters and numbers on it, though she claimed it would be enough to just talk to the machine and it would note down everything Artium told it. He still preferred the keyboard, but truth be told, Artium had missed more than a few days of measurements, and it had been several days since he'd bothered to sit in front of the machine.

This time he hadn't bothered with the numbers and went straight to his diary entries, and who could blame him? There were too many things to do and too many changes to cope with to be bothered with the stupid weather. The goats needed to be tended to, now that the new shed was built, and two new goats had been introduced into his growing herd. Emilija would have taken them to graze if he had ordered her to, but the girl tended to get lost in her thoughts and would subsequently lose the goats.

Animal husbandry was always Milbored's job, until he slipped and broke his spine. Now Artium was forced to walk the goats himself and was surprised to find out that he enjoyed the physical exertion in his rejuvenated body, the exhilarating fresh air filling his lungs, and he found himself many a times standing mesmerized by the beautiful color of the sunset.

A few days ago, Artium had herded the goats all the way to the steep eastern slopes, where he had not visited since he was a boy, and dipped, buck naked, into the small natural pond there. The water was freezing and the waterfall pounded his flesh mercilessly. He came out shivering, his heart pounding hard, feeling alive, so alive.

Artium leaned back on his chair, picked up a cherry, and put it in his mouth. He closed his eyes and savoured the taste. It was the taste of triumph. He turned his head and surveyed the table next to the machine. It was laden with food. Artium knew he was being foolish not to store some of it in the cold preservation chamber the girl had managed to repair, but he could not help himself. Once he walked all the way down to the village and told the elders about the miracle chair, things changed dramatically. At first, they were polite but skeptical, but two days passed and a farmer whose leg was badly broken was carried up the mountain. He left an hour later in a foamy cast and was out working his field a day later. Word spread out like wildfire, and all of a sudden Artium's pantry as well as his belly were full of food of the kind he had not tasted for years, and he lapped it all up.

Appetite was not the only thing that had awoken in him lately though. More than once he found himself looking at Emilija, thinking about what Reya, her foster mother, had sort of promised him. *Not so old* were her exact words, and Artium did not feel old anymore. Maybe he should shave his beard, or at least trim it. The new hair that was growing on his head was silvery in color, not white. Perhaps he should wear the new set of goatskin clothes he had gotten from that woman that had the bad skin boils he had helped to cure. Artium was young again, and Emilija was of the right and ripe age. Artium's body reacted strongly to the memory of her partial nudity. There were not many young men left in the village below, or even in the entire area, and the girl had taken her clothes off in front of him when Artium was blind and weak. Perhaps she would find him attractive now that his vitality was back. After all, he took her in out of the goodness of his heart, and she was marked with those strange tattoos. Who else would want her?

For the past several nights Artium had entertained the notion of trying his luck, climbing up to the observatory and knocking on Emilija's door, perhaps even slipping into her bed. He once stopped himself when he was already on his front step. It wasn't just the fear of rejection that made him go back to his bed and deal with his lust on his own, it was that the girl—no, *the young woman*—could have been described at best as eccentric. Between changing and improving everything in the compound, from somehow increasing water pressure to moving furniture about "to make a better pattern," Emilija blathered about how she was about to leave soon to a place she called "the wall of moving symbols" and solve some kind of "pattern." Artium could not make heads or tails of her stories and would have dismissed this as crazy talk or some adolescent stupidity, but from the day he snuck back to sit on the wondrous chair by himself it became obvious that the machine did not work without Emilija's presence. Although she claimed the machine heard and understood Artium's voice, it responded only to simple commands, like dimming the lights or shutting the door. It was enough to fool the villagers into believing Artium was in charge of the miracle chair, and Emilija played along with the façade, but he knew the truth. It was Emilija who needed to lay hands and somehow talk to the machine for it to heal. If she got spooked by his advances she might leave, and who knew what might happen then? Artium shuddered at the thought. Old age had crept up on him, and there was nothing he could have done about it. Now, possessing the vitality and strength of the young but having experienced the horrendous vulnerability and decline of old age, Artium was filled with dread at the thought of growing old again.

When Artium was a boy, his mother told him a bedtime story about a fairy fountain whose water could turn an old man back into a child. Emilija, the only one who could work the medichair, was the fountain of youth. If she left, how long would it take for his body to begin to age? Would it be a slow process? Or would his body suddenly begin to crumble? No. Emilija must stay with him, and Artium would have to be gentle and smart about his pursuit.

Artium changed the screen so he could watch the images from the various parts of the compound. It was another thing Emilija had managed to miraculously repair and he used it to spy on her. Well, not *exactly* spy. She seemed to know when he was doing it, and several times she turned and waved at him in a friendly gesture. This time Emilija was nowhere to be found. He did as he had been shown and circled through the main points of the compound, moving the angle of the cameras up and down with a flick of his hand. The goats were still in their pen and the observatory was empty, but just as he was about to change to another spot, something caught Artium's eyes. With a movement of his hand he zoomed in. Something was scratched on the walls, but he couldn't make out what it was. Caressing his long beard, Artium pondered whether to climb all the way up to the observatory and investigate, when there was a strange piping sound and the image on the screen changed to an angle Artium had not seen before. It was the top of the high walls of the compound, and someone, a woman, was just in the process of climbing up there. His heart suddenly pounding, Artium leaned closer and waved his hand. The angle of the image changed, but he saw no high ladder or any other means of climbing the wall. There was a man wearing a wide hat standing at a distance away, but even if he had pushed the woman up, the walls would have been too high to scale. The woman balanced herself on top of the wall and surveyed the compound. She turned her head but failed to see the device that brought her image into Artium's screen. She was thin but otherwise unremarkable in her features, and her face was unfamiliar, alien even. Artium watched as she lowered her body onto the inner side of the wall, held the edge of the top for a heartbeat, and suddenly let go. Her body plummeted down from bone-crushing height and vanished into the unkept greenery below.

Artium gasped in surprise and jumped up from his chair. He hesitated only briefly before pulling out his handgun from the drawer, shoving it into his belt, and running out to the gate.

When he reached the gate, the woman was bent over the gate control. Artium slowed down and pulled his gun from its holster but hid it behind his back. When the woman straightened up and looked at him, Artium knew for sure she was not Emilija's mother. She was small and not threatening looking, but he had watched her climb over and jump from an impossible height and, he noticed, she had a power gun in an improvised belt holster and a sword strapped to her back.

Artium raised his gun and pointed it at the woman. "Pleasant you be," he said carefully. "What are you doing here?"

She stood frozen, as he imagined anyone would do when a gun was pointing at them, but her strange eyes did not show fear, only calculation.

"How did you manage to get over the wall? Don't deny it, I saw you doing it—and keep your hands away from the belt, Lady." The last part of the sentence came out as a shout.

The woman spread her arms. "I have a knack for climbing, always have," she said, in an accent that was as foreign as her looks.

"And now you are trying to let your friend in, but the gate is protected by a code."

The woman smiled tiredly. "I have a knack for codes as well."

Artium noticed mud stains going all the way up to her knees.

"I'm sorry. I thought the place was deserted and did not mean to trespass."

That was a blatant lie.

He was not trembling from old age anymore, but nevertheless, the gun was beginning to weigh on Artium's arm. "I may look old, but my eyes are sharp and I am a very good shot," he warned and boasted in the same sentence. "Now drop your gun and sword to the ground, slowly." When the woman carefully complied he added, "Walk over there," and pointed to the small graveyard. She moved casually, her hands in the air. He kept a careful distance and went over to the gate, kicked the sword aside, bent down, and retrieved the power gun. It was much lighter than his own weapon and that somehow renewed Artium's confidence.

"Who are you?" He walked away from the gate, just in case the woman tried to bolt towards the house.

"My name is Peach," she answered. "And what is yours?"

Artium drew himself a little taller. "I am SkyMaster of the SkyWatchers order. Why are you here?" He pointed the power gun at the woman and shoved his own weapon into his belt.

"I am looking for a girl named Emilija." The woman watched him intently as she spoke.

"Never heard of her," Artium said.

"You are lying, SkyMaster," she said calmly. "She is easily recognisable by the markings on her hand and head."

"And what do you want of her?"

The woman called Peach hesitated briefly. "It is too complicated to explain, but I need to take her away from here."

Artium shook his head. "I never heard of the girl you are seeking."

Peach tilted her head slightly. "That is strange" she said, "because she is standing right behind you."

It was a trick, of course, and Artium resisted the urge to look behind his shoulder. But then he heard Emilija's voice behind him. "You have a strange pattern, Lady."

"It's Peach, Emilija," the woman said, looking past Artium's shoulder, "and I am here to take you away."

Artium was close to panic. Everything he'd been dreading was happening, but to his relief he heard Emilija say, "No, you are not the one to take me away. There is someone else, someone I have been calling."

For the first time Peach looked momentarily perplexed but she tried to recover with, "Emilija, you do not know me, but your mother, she sent me to take you to her."

Artium took a step forward and aimed the power gun to the woman's chest. "Go away right now"—his voice rose to a shout—"or I'll shoot. Emilija must stay here."

Several things happened at once.

Artium heard Emilija gasp as something moved to the left edge of his peripheral vision. He turned his head slightly and saw the monster. There was too much to take in at once, but it stood tall and had sharp claws and a long snout and bared teeth. As soon as Artium turned his head towards it, the monster dropped on all fours and charged forward with incredible speed. With a shout of terror, Artium swung his arm and pulled the trigger, feeling the heat of the weapon as it discharged. The ray would have hit true if his arm had not been flung away by Peach, the woman who only a heartbeat ago was standing more than ten paces away. She disarmed him with two decisive, painful moves just as the monster charged past them.

"Emilija, run," Artium screamed even though he knew the girl could not possibly outrun the monster. He turned around, expecting to see her being torn to pieces but, instead, he found the monster kneeling before the girl. It was hissing and growling as Emilija stretched her hand and lightly touched its head, then bent down and held her own forehead against the monster's.

"Heavens," Artium breathed out.

"That is . . . unexpected," the woman calling herself Peach said at his side. Artium's instinct told him she was as stunned as he was.

Emilija raised her head and turned to the two of them.

"I am ready to go now," she said, then turned around and began climbing up the steps to the observatory.

60

Twinkle Eyes

The Tarakan steel gates to the Sky Palace were slightly open when we arrived, enough to let a person in, but not a vehicle. Vincha stopped the shark and we all got out, some more shakily than others. Nelsohn was not lying. It was a slow and treacherous climb, even with the shark, and luckily, we managed to convince Vincha around halfway to wait for morning light, otherwise we would have been back at the bottom of the mountain by now. Even with the sun up, it was uncomfortably cold. I noticed several goats merrily roaming about.

Vincha turned her head to me, a glint of hope in her eyes. "She's here," she said. "I caught the beacon signal from her implant about halfway up."

"Okay." I nodded and focused on the gate. It was thick enough not to give me a full view of the courtyard, but what I saw was enough.

"Looks deserted," I said, "just a couple more goats and a mule, over there." But Vincha was already making her way to the gate, weapon drawn, with Galinak at her heels. I turned to Nelsohn, who was still leaning weakly on the shark. "Stay here," I said, and he managed to nod back at me before bending down to puke.

As I approached the gate Vincha slipped through and I heard her shouting Emilija's name in the courtyard. So much for the stealthy approach . . .

When I stepped into the courtyard, Vincha and Galinak were at the main doors. I hurried after them but noticed the freshly dug, empty grave on my way. The front doors were locked and I stopped Galinak at the last moment from kicking them in.

"Let's look around before we damage things unnecessarily, all right?"

Vincha looked at me like I was the most unreasonable man in the City of Towers. "Emilija is here," she said again, and pointed at the doors, "inside."

"That's very good news," I said slowly and deliberately. "Now let's look around for another entrance before we decide to damage the house of her kind host, shall we?" I turned and walked away, and to my surprise they both followed. For just a brief moment it was like old times, me, a lowly secondary scribe of the Guild of Historians and the two veteran warriors at my side. Then we found the side door.

My sight made the door transparent to me and I saw an unkempt, elderly man, sitting at a table, surrounded by numerous empty wineskins and some plates laden with half-eaten food. A large, antique-looking revolver lay on the table, and there were also several owls and a goat roaming about. I raised a finger, then pointed in the direction of the man. Both Vincha and Galinak nodded and once I opened the door, they zigzagged their way in. I waited outside just to be sure no shots were fired, then I stepped in. I'd smelled worse, but the stench of goat dung and owl droppings was far from appealing. Galinak moved the revolver away from the reach of the old man, who seemed oblivious to what was happening around him, while Vincha disappeared into the next room. I heard her calling her daughter's name from farther and farther away. I noticed that the single goat milling about was only half sheared, but I did not think it was a fact worth exploring at that moment. Instead, I approached the table as the man reached out to the nearest bottle, upturned it into his mouth, and swallowed the last drops that came out of it.

On closer observation, the man seemed younger than he looked, but he stank worse than the entire room.

I moved the rotting food away from him and sat myself down, trying to breathe through my mouth as much as I could.

"What is your name, Master?" I asked politely. I had to repeat the question two more times before his eyes focused on me.

"I can *seeee* you," he said in a singsong tone, but he did not make eye contact.

"And I you," I answered carefully. "Who might you be?"

"She said I couldn't see, then she made me *seeee*."

I gently squeezed the man's arm to focus his attention. "Are you the SkyMaster?"

"Aye." He looked up this time. He thumped his chest. "I am the SkyMonster . . . SSSkyMaster," he corrected himself, then laughed as he repeated, "*monster, master, monster*." He leaned forward and whispered, "She had a monster, you know."

Vincha stormed back into the room, weapon in hand. "Where is my daughter?" She towered over the man. "Where is Emilija?"

The man smiled with surprisingly healthy teeth and made a flying motion with the palms of his hands. "She flew away, far away."

"You lie." Vincha aimed her gun at the man's head. "I planted a device in her shoulder and I still sense her in this room. Talk now or I'll make you regret every moment of the rest of your miserable short life."

"Oh." The man chuckled, clearly not intimidated. "That. The woman said it would only hurt a little if she cut Emilija with the sharp knife, but Emilija said to use the chair below."

Nelsohn's words echoed in my mind: *People talk about the Sky-Master because of that chair.*

The man slurred on, "So they went below and took out this thing and the man said I should carry it, but the woman said I was no good."

"A woman and a man?" I asked carefully.

"Yes. A *woman*." He focused back on me, then pointed at Vincha. "They are not allowed, you know, on these grounds, but she was fast and mean. Very, very fast."

This was not making sense. "What happened next?" I asked, signalling Vincha to lower her weapon. To my surprise she obliged me yet again and leaned forward on the table, looking suddenly exhausted.

The SkyMaster pointed at something behind my shoulder but when I turned around all I saw was the half-sheared goat.

"Oh," I said as Galinak went to check the creature.

"It's in there," he said after a moment, to the goat's annoyed bleating. "I can see the mark."

She found the disc and planted it in the goat. It means she knew someone else is looking for Emilija.

Plates and bottles shook as Vincha banged her fist on the table.

"Where did they go?" I asked.

"They flew away," the man answered, using the same words again. "I begged her not to go. I begged. I, SkyMaster of the Sky Watchers order, *begged* her to stay. But she said she needed to leave, to see the Great Pattern of her dreams, or something."

Vincha and I exchanged a meaningful stare. Rafik and Pikok had both spoken of the great wall of symbols and solving a final pattern. This was how Tarakan lured Puzzlers back into the City Within the Mountain. The fact that Emilija had used the same expressions as Rafik and the estranged Puzzler Pikok spoke volumes.

"How did they fly away? Where did they go?"

"They pulled down the weather balloon. That was the woman's idea. It used to come down with a touch of a button, but then it broke and no one could fix it. It had to be brought down by turning the small wheel. It used to take a whole day to take it down, but Emilija fixed it." The SkyMaster's eyes shone. "She touched the metal box and spoke to it and suddenly the balloon came down all by itself."

"And they left you here?" I asked incredulously. It did not make sense to leave the man alive.

"The man in the strange hat, he wanted me dead. He pulled his gun on me, but Emilija and the woman said no, and the monster stood by their side and they left me here to feed the goat and wait for you." He looked at Vincha. "You are her mother."

It wasn't a question but Vincha simply nodded.

"Emilija is very special," the SkyMaster said softly, and to my surprise Vincha's chin suddenly trembled slightly as she nodded again, speechless.

From Vincha's betrayal of Rafik to the loss of the Hive and the war and decline which followed, all of it happened because of one woman's disastrous and misguided actions, out of love for her daughter.

"She asked me to tell you not to follow her. That if you do"—the Sky Master closed his eyes and recited—"you will never come back to this world."

"That rust-headed, stubborn girl." Vincha straightened up. "If she thinks I am just going to let her waste her life away, I'll storm the City Within the Mountain myself."

"She is not going to the Valley," I answered, leaning back in my seat. "The other agent is working for Mannes, who wants Emilija to strengthen Cain. I have talked to enough people who knew him and survived to tell the tale, and it is only reasonable that they would take her to the Star Pillar."

"The whole land there is contaminated," Galinak said.

"Yet Mannes has been holed up there for several years, I hear," I answered. "Past the Broken Sands. It would be a hard journey, impossible for an army." I couldn't but smile at the irony. When my LoreMaster mentioned the Star Pillar I promised myself that if I ever made it through my adventure in one piece, I'd visit this last surviving wonder of the old world. It seemed that now, after actually dying, I was going to fulfil that promise.

"They did fly south," the SkyMaster said suddenly. He seemed to be slowly sobering up. "And the weather balloon was meant to carry instruments, not passengers. They would not be able to fly far."

"How long ago did all of this happen?" I asked.

The man shrugged as he tried to mentally calculate. "Two, three days, perhaps more."

Vincha swore. "I'm turning the shark around," she said to me. "If you're not inside it by the time I've turned, I'm leaving you here."

She stormed out and I nodded at Galinak. "Go help her manoeuvre," I said, "and make sure she does not leave without me."

Galinak winked at me. "Aye, boss, but the look on her face, I've seen it before. You'd better not linger." He placed the old gun back on the table, tapped his forehead in a lazy salute towards the SkyMaster, and left. I had precious little time alone with the man.

I leaned forward towards him. "Was there really a monster?"

The man nodded. "It was hideous, out of this world. I've never seen or heard about anythng like that."

There was only one thing that could fit the description.

"Did it look like a Lizard?" I asked.

The SkyMaster thought about it for a moment. "Well, perhaps, but also human, although it was much bigger than a human, all claws and scales, and its face . . ." He visibly shuddered.

"And she talked to it?"

"Yes. It knelt before her and obeyed her commands—even the man and the woman were surprised by it. I heard them talk about it." He took a small, rectangular-shaped item out of his pocket and slid it towards me. "Take it, please."

I took the item. It was light but firm to the touch. "What is it?"

"It is called a memory stick," he answered. "Inside are weather and star movement reports for the last hundred years. The Sky-Watchers order has been doing this since before the old world came to an end. It was our holy duty to preserve this knowledge, but there is no one left here to go on doing this. My personal logs are also in there." He chuckled. "Most of them are just the ravings of an old, lonely man."

"What about you?" I asked as I stood up.

"Do you know what it means to grow old?" For the first time since I'd stepped into the stinking hall, the SkyMaster's eyes had a sharper, clearer look as he stared into mine. "To lose your strength and your teeth and your hearing and sight and eventually your mind to loneliness? No? You seem young enough not to have experienced it, but wise enough to know it's coming."

I shook my head as he continued. "That chair could have saved Millbored, for sure, but nothing worked properly in this place until Emilija came. Now that she is gone, the chair will not heal my bones, the villagers will not send food, and it will be cold and hunger all over again."

"There is a young man by the gate," I said. "He seems resilient enough and eager to work. You could keep him here. Teach the lad letters and numbers, keep your order alive."

He slumped back. "Why would he or his family agree? And besides, what's the damned use of it all? I was born to believe that soon our lot would change, that things would go back to the way they were before, but they never will, will they?"

"I'm afraid change will happen slower than one lifetime," I said, "but that doesn't mean that what you did here is meaningless. You gave me something precious. I will do my utmost to make the best of this knowledge."

The SkyMaster took a deep breath and looked around. "Damn, this place needs a bit of cleaning. You said the lad outside wants to work? Send him in. I might have some coins somewhere around here. Pleasant may you be."

I left and hurried back outside and out the gate, where Vincha was still delicately manoeuvring the shark around with Galinak's assistance.

Nelsohn was standing a little farther away, and he looked at me as I approached. He seemed to be done with the puking but was eyeing the shark with clear trepidation.

"Here, for your troubles." I placed a few more towers into his palm. "Go inside and—"

We all heard the shot.

Galinak whistled softly. "Bukra's balls, I didn't think that old revolver could shoot anymore. Guess I was wrong."

I sighed and patted pale Nelsohn on his shoulder. "Go inside, son. Bury what needs to be buried and take what is worth taking."

We left him at the gate as the three of us sped down the mountain.

61

Peach

"How are you feeling?" I asked.

"Better, now that we are flying lower," Sergiu answered in a light tone, but his hands betrayed his nervousness by gripping the sides of the platform a little too tightly.

I looked up, checking the helium balloon as my hands brushed the controls. It was built to survive tough conditions for years, from harsh weather to a direct lightning strike, but there was a limit to how much weight it could carry. We were losing power and altitude, the latter not necessarily a bad thing. The freezing wind was affecting us all.

We should have killed the old man. That was standard procedure, and Sergiu's attempted action was logical. There were others looking for Emilija, and this SkyMaster could point them in the right direction, or they might deduce it by themselves. The poor man was so distraught by the notion of Emilija leaving, I didn't think he would have cared if Sergiu had shot him. But on instinct rather than cool thinking, I stopped Sergiu from pulling the trigger.

We argued, but then Emilija broke her odd silence to tell us that the SkyMaster should live. The Lizard was just standing next to her, hissing strangely. I had no idea whether or not he was capable of fully understanding what was going on, but I was pretty certain he would have obeyed any command given by Emilija. Facing such odds, Sergiu simply shrugged and holstered his gun saying, "That's a mistake, Peach."

"The girl is attached to him, don't you see?" I tried to rationalize my actions. "Killing him would make her uncooperative and besides, I'd rather only kill if I truly must."

The balloon was my idea, and by the look on Sergiu's face, he was regretting agreeing to that idea more than not killing the Sky-Master.

I turned my head and watched the desert stretch underneath us.

"You mentioned earlier this did not exist in your time," Sergiu suddenly remarked.

"No. We had conquered the deserts of this land long ago," I answered, surprised there was so much bitterness in my voice. Adaptation to new circumstances was a big part of my training.

"This area actually used to be the breadbasket of the land. Miles upon miles of crops engineered to withstand disease and nourish humanity." I glanced at the man standing by my side. "In my time, energy was not the biggest problem this planet faced—food and water was."

"And the desert conquered the area back while you were gone. Such is the power of nature."

"No. This desolation is man-made. All sides had terrible weapons in their possession. Bombs that were carried by missiles crossed the planet and exploded above these grounds, sucking all life and moisture away. The infamous sinkholes of the Broken Sands you told me about were probably caused by those weapons."

"So much disaster," Sergiu muttered as I turned my head and watched the Star Pillar's silhouette to the south. At least there was not much need for the useless navigational instruments. There were no satellites in the sky, but the Star Pillar was all I needed to see.

At night it was easier to navigate as the Pillar's external nanodefence sleeve shined even brighter.

Sergiu, on the other hand, was staring at Emilija, who was standing with her back to us, watching the desert we were crossing. As instructed, she did not move from her spot; both she and the Lizard, who stood motionlessly by her side, counterweighted Sergiu and myself.

"Can you believe it?" he whispered.

"Yeah, that's the big elephant in the room."

He looked at me, puzzled. "What's an elephant?"

I sighed. This was not the time to talk about extinct creatures. "Never mind. It's just an old expression. I don't think it's a coincidence that this . . . creature roamed around in the wilderness until he found Emilija and now she claims she is able to understand him. This whole weird business just got weirder, and I hope your Mannes can explain what's going on."

To my surprise, Sergiu shook his head. "I don't think even Mannes can explain this one. He is of the old world, and understands many things, but this . . . this is a new thing. He'll be happy to see it, though; he was always intrigued by new . . . phenomena."

"You seem to know Mannes well." I watched as Sergiu reerected his mental defences.

"I know him a little, yes."

"Any advice?"

"Don't cross him. Don't stand in his way. I never met a man or a woman who was even half his age or possessed half his will. He simply does not waste time if he can make a decisive move. Do you understand me?"

I nodded. "Absolutely." But I was thinking, *In short, this Mannes is a homicidal maniac and his underling is preparing me for it.*

"And the girl? What will happen to her?" I asked.

"I have no idea," Sergiu admitted, "but she seems to be very important to him."

"A man survives the war that annihilated civilisation on Earth—

or the Catastrophe, as you call it—and stays alive all these years just to save mankind. What do you think keeps him going?"

Sergiu shrugged. "I never thought about this question."

"Obsession? Revenge? Or guilt, perhaps?"

"Love?" Sergiu shrugged, a shadow of a smile crossing his face. He did not believe it, either.

I turned to stare straight into the man's eyes. "This whole damned business has nothing to do with Tarakan, does it? You just woke me up from the dead and manipulated me to do your dirty work."

He met my gaze and held it. "I assure you, Colonel Major, that Mannes is the last hope humanity has." Even if that statement was true, it was a deflection.

And in that moment, I knew the man was lying, or at the very least not telling me a crucial part of the truth. Which was too bad, because I had almost grown to like Sergiu the Dying. He reminded me of my former self, and of other men and women who fought the dirty war of shadows. But at that particular moment I knew we were playing on different sides of the table, and perhaps even a totally different game.

I turned my attention back to the young woman standing only a few paces away from me, and I guess some of her instincts still worked because she suddenly turned her head back towards me. Our eyes met. My training and condition stopped me from doing what was natural in these circumstances, which was to avert my gaze. Emilija, on the other hand, was seeing something completely different. It wasn't that she was looking through me, more like she was seeing me in an entirely different way. It was disconcerting and had the vessel I was occupying been my own body my reaction to her stare would have probably manifested in a shudder.

I waved and smiled at her but Emilija simply turned her head back. The side wind hit us and rocked the balloon, and I was momentarily preoccupied with stabilizing us. Once that was done, and I lowered our altitude another notch, I turned back to Sergiu, who was looking suddenly significantly deader.

"What will happen to the girl?" I asked again.

He took several deep breaths but did not turn toward me, focusing on the distant horizon instead. "She will be safe."

"Mannes needs her and is going to somehow use her abilities, then what?"

"She will be safe," Sergiu reassured me once more.

"From all I've heard about your guy, I am not feeling entirely confident," I said.

This time Sergiu did look at me. "Don't believe everything you heard in the City of Towers. Some of it is just malicious rumours, but some were spread intentionally, to keep people away from our base. Sure, Mannes killed many, but he also saved many. He saved me."

Choose wisely, even after death were the words of a mysterious prophet, relayed to me by the man calling himself the Healer. As I gently steered the weather balloon I thought, and not for the first time, about the strange world into which I had awoken. At first, I found it exactly as people had imagined it would be after a world war. With the total collapse of modern society's structures and the loss of knowledge and technology, humanity had slipped back to the way our race used to live thousands of years ago. On the other hand, the world had also evolved to something else, something different. Oracles, Healers, Lizards, tattooed, Trolls, and Puzzlers—these creatures never existed before and now they were a part of these times. It made me think about fairies, witches, and dragons. People easily dismissed them as myth during the age of reason, but maybe there was more to it than that. I chased the silly thought out of my mind.

Soon you will be having to be choosing yourself, between light and dark, between old and new, between worlds. Choose wisely, even after death. Those were the Healer's exact words.

In a way I had died and was buried deep in the storage of Central Command, only to be born again in this world. Was this what this strange man meant? Could I just walk away right now? Land the balloon and disappear into the wild? I could certainly survive it; I'd been through much, much worse. I could live the rest of my vessel's life exploring what was left of our destroyed civilisation, maybe help rebuild parts of it, or at least teach a few people some science. It wouldn't be a long life—none of the vessels were built to last—but it would be worthwhile, at least. Maybe what this planet needed was not to go back to the way things were before, but to heal into a different, new beginning.

Yet, if there was a chance that this Mannes was more than just a vicious warlord . . . wouldn't meeting him be the best course of action?

Inside my chest, a printed, fault-resistant organ pumped enriched artificial blood into my body, but in my heart of hearts, I knew this time around I had to do things differently. I would not follow orders blindly, believing that only one side was just and good. No matter how I justified my actions, I knew, *I knew*, that something was seriously wrong with my missions, but I did them anyway, because a Tarakan doctor had saved my life and thus marked me as one of their own. Perhaps things would have been better for the world if I had been left to die of the Purple Plague.

I was shaken out of my thoughts by Sergiu. "I can see the edge of the Broken Sands." He pointed in the distance as a look between excitement and relief crossed his face.

"Really? I'm not seeing much difference in the way the land looks." Actually, I was only registering the gradually increasing radiation level.

"Believe me, I know where the ground is safe, and we should land this accursed balloon once we clear the Broken Sands."

"Why not fly the damned thing all the way?"

"Not a good idea, unless you wish to be blown to pieces. Mannes has fixed the defence systems of the entire area."

"That is . . . impressive." I wanted to say "improbable" but checked myself.

"That was the first thing he did when we got here, but we were lucky. Other than the high level of radiation and the meagre yield of the land, there was not that much damage to the buildings and machines."

It somehow made sense. Even in the midst of the most cata-strophic war, people from all sides must have wanted the Pillar as the spoils of war, or feared what could happen if it ever collapsed. If the systems were not destroyed or fried, getting them to work again would have only required a power source.

"What if we fly low?" I suggested.

Sergiu shook his head. "There are trigger-happy, nervous troops who are going to shoot first and ask questions later. Might as well land here. We'll spend the night, and come morning, take the route that won't get us killed."

There was no point in trying to argue. Sergiu was either telling the truth or setting us up. I began lowering the pressure of the bal-loon but chanced a quick glimpse at Emilija. She still was perched where I ordered her to be, her obedience as steadfast as her silence. The Lizard kept watch over her. I didn't know what was going on between them, but I would bet hard metal, as the people in the City of Towers said nowadays, that the towering hulk of a monster would protect this girl with all of its considerable might. For some reason this gave me comfort, and despite how illogical it was, I si-lently swore to do the same. I would not let Emilija come to harm.

62

Twinkle Eyes

It is one thing knowing where you need to be and another thing entirely to get there. Without maps or directions and the wild land being empty of people, we spent half our remaining power gems driving on roads leading nowhere, or into impassable swamps. An attempt by Vincha to use the hovercraft to drive across the wilderness cost a power gem and almost the shark itself. The surrounding land looked as if God tore it off with his hands and flung it in all directions, and many times we ended up backtracking dozens of miles over what we had believed was a promising route.

The shark was built for the Tarakan highways, not for cross-country voyages, and twice we had to stop and fix problems to the best of Vincha's mechanical skills. I hunkered near the vehicle, where Vincha lay, sweat pouring down her neck, her LeatherFlex armour stained with muck.

"How are we doing?" I asked.

Her face contorted with effort as she twisted her arm deep inside the shark's wheel guard. Suddenly there was a satisfying click.

"Right." Vincha breathed a sigh of relief and pushed herself out from under the shark. "I guess that will do for now."

"You can let go now," she yelled. I heard Galinak grunt and the vehicle was lowered back to the ground.

Vincha came to a sitting position and I stretched my hand to help her up. She glared at me for a brief moment but eventually accepted my offer and helped herself up. "What do you want, Twinkle Eyes?"

"Can't a man be chivalrous without picking up a shark for you?" I asked.

Vincha snorted. "Save the chivalry for your cheap Salvo-novels. What do you want of me?"

"Actually, I wanted to give you a nourishment pill," I said as I opened my palm and presented the pill to her. "It's the last one for each of us, so we'd better begin thinking about water and food in the next day or so." That was a lie. I had two more pills hidden in my belt, but I was not about to share that information with anyone.

Vincha had always been suspicious of me, and rightly so, but she was too tired, thirsty, and stressed to fear that I might be trying to drug her. She took the pill and swallowed it quickly. I watched the color rise back to her face.

"That's better," I said, and she nodded, then suddenly lost her balance. I managed to catch her before she fell.

"It's the sudden effect of the pill," I said as I eased her against the shark. "Rest a little and we'll be on our way."

She nodded and took several deep breaths. "What do you want to ask?" she said.

"How did you—"

"You say I have a pattern." Her smile was small and tired, but it was still there. "Well, so do you, and you might wear a different body, or vessel, or whatever you say the Tarkanians call it, but you're still him, aren't you? That shitty little secondary scribe who thinks he can save the world if he just asks the right question is still hiding under all that new skin."

I nodded. "I hope so. I mean, it's hard to tell sometimes, when

I catch my reflection. Still the same old me, though, the man with the questions."

Her smile widened. "Well, you are one lucky man 'cause I'm in the mood, so go ahead and ask."

"It's about Emilija." I hesitated but went for it. "And the story that poor SkyMaster told me. He said she talked with a Lizard, described him, too. I've never heard of a Puzzler doing that."

Vincha remained silent, and it spoke volumes.

"Emilija has tattoos on her head," I pressed on. "I've never heard those being on a Puzzler before, and the way the SkyMaster told it, she not only controlled the Lizard but knew it was coming to take her away. What she told the SkyMaster to tell you, about not coming back to this world, that is a Nakamura-style prophecy."

I was expecting Vincha to shout at me, deny the implications of my words, resist the comparison to the self-proclaimed oracle who mass-murdered hundreds of Trolls, or at least punched me in the face. But she surprised me with an answer delivered in the softest tone of voice I'd ever heard her speak.

"Emilija was always a special girl. Always. Quiet but knowing. I wasn't there when she began to speak, but they told me she just opened her eyes one day at the age of two and began speaking like an adult. She always saw things which weren't there and heard things only she could hear, just like her mother." Vincha smiled to herself and her eyes shone. "Before I took her to the Kethans, Emilija was with another foster family. The wife was pregnant and Emilija told them they would have a stillborn son two months before she lost the baby. I mean, these things happen and it could have been explained as a lucky, unfortunate guess, but the family believed Emilija cursed them and I had to take her away. Obviously, I was cross with her, but Emilija simply told me she knew what was going to happen and felt the right thing to do was to prepare the family for the inevitable tragedy. Those were her exact words."

Vincha looked straight at me. "She was nine years old when it happened. Truth is, Twinkle Eyes, I was too busy running around, protecting my daughter from the fate Tarakan was planning for her, to actually watch her grow, or take her first steps, or hear her speak her first words. Do you know what they were?" She waited for me to shake my head. "Her first words were 'I am thirsty, and there is a dead frog in the cupboard.'"

I smiled.

"Maybe she has the prophecy in her, maybe she is just weird in her ways and lucky with her guesses, I don't know, but I do know I will do anything"—Vincha's eyes hardened—"anything, to prevent her from being sacrificed for the greater good of Tarakan. Humanity be damned if that is the sacrifice they are asking me to make for their ascension."

"What if this is what she wants?" I asked.

Vincha waved a warning finger in my face. "No one wants to die, not really. Tarakan is just messing with her head, sending weird thoughts and visions to her when she sleeps, like they did to Rafik, slowly manipulating her into believing she has a destiny, that there is no other way but to do what she was born to do. That rust ain't going to stick on me, Twinkle Eyes." Her voice rose as I held up my hands, trying to calm her down. "She has the looks on her, she can find a man, raise a family, learn to help people or just rusting survive to enjoy a nice sunset. She doesn't need to be consumed by some machine to find her peace in this world."

"Let's just find Emilija first, make sure she's safe, and then we can think of a way out of this mess."

"You were always smart, I'll give you that." Vincha straightened up and patted me friendly like on my shoulder. "Better use that brain of yours to find a solution, because I would hate to shoot you dead."

I looked straight into her eyes. "Would you? Shoot me dead?"

Vincha tilted her head. "It's obvious you never had children, Twinkle Eyes, because if it was between you and my daughter, I'd kill you in a heartbeat and wouldn't even bother to bury your shiny new body. I would leave you to the crows or give you a Salvationist burial instead."

"Do I hear words of poetry?" Galinak came out from behind the shark, patting his hands and grinning.

Vincha turned, her expression darkening. "Why are you so happy looking?"

Galinak spread his arms wide. "Well, Vincha, your daughter was taken by the bad guys and that is a sad fact. But here we are running after them in order to save her. If I were as smart as our mutual friend here, I'd say that by simple deduction, that makes us the good guys, and frankly, I've missed being on the side of the good guys."

"You're just as annoying as an itchy arse, Galinak," Vincha muttered as she entered the shark. Both of us hurried after her.

Galinak was still chuckling to himself as we sped away, and when I was sure Vincha was not watching, so did I.

63

Twinkle Eyes

We drove slowly into town to the sound of the shark's constant beeping, a warning that our last power gem was getting close to depletion. I'd visited many places that had felt the wrath of the terrible weapons of the Catastrophe but nature had managed to recuperate and heal. This was not one of those places. Nothing was alive here. Nothing. It was as if whatever terrible weapons struck this place had sucked away all life. We were on the safe side of the Broken Sands, but the merciless south wind meant we were driving in a cloud of dust, which reduced visibility. It was obvious nothing could survive in this environment for long.

"Remind you of anyplace we know?" Galinak remarked softly as we passed building after building.

"Yeah," Vincha muttered back, "this is like the rusting Tarakan Valley, only deader."

"Guess it's like the good old days," I said, trying to lighten the mood. Both warriors turned their heads to me, and seeing the expression on their faces I hastily added, "You know . . . Tarakan Valley, the adventures, the Nodes, the deep runs, the loot?"

"You know, Twinkle Eyes"—Vincha was tapping the steering wheel in unison with the annoying beeping—"time for you to grow up and realise there was never anything truly *good* about the old days. I still wake up in a cold sweat at nights."

"That's when you're too exhausted to keep yourself from sleep," Galinak said, surprising us both. "What?" he added when he saw the look on our faces. "Just because I'm good at it ain't saying I enjoy every moment of it. Although I have to admit, bringing home the loot was definitely satisfying." He nudged Vincha with his elbow. "Remember the GY blasters we brought back from one of the deep runs? Were they still around in your time, Vinch?"

"Oh, you bet they were." I couldn't see the expression on her face but it sounded like she was smiling. "Nothing shouts 'I'm a big bad Troll' louder than balancing a mining cannon on your arm."

"The first Troll to find one was Dorgmahr. Remember him?"

Vincha rolled her eyes. "That pile of rust. He had some loose wires in his head, that one. More augs on him than in a Gadgetier's weapon stall. Still, didn't help him in a deep run. Heard he was fried to a crisp by a trap, ruined his augs, too. They named a steak after him in the Chewing Hole. You could have it rare, medium, well done, or charcoaled Dorgmahr style.

"I miss my old body armour," Galinak mused. "Sure, it'd seen some rough days and more than a few patches, but the dart shooting gauntlets . . ." He sighed. "Those darts were hard to come by and rusting expensive, but they had a certain elegance to them."

This time Vincha snorted a laugh. "Elegance? I'm surprised you even know the meaning of the word. You wouldn't know 'elegance' if it—"

"There." I nipped the argument in the bud by inserting my arm between their faces. "I can see the Long Tube tracks."

Vincha turned in the direction I was indicating. "Where? All I can see is a cloud of dust."

"It's right there." I traced the line in the sky.

"Those Tarkanians did have style, I'll give them that." Galinak squinted, trying to find the tracks. "I've always wondered how they kept those metal rods suspended in the air for a hundred years."

"Keep to your right," I said. "We're on the edge of the Broken Sands. We don't want to accidently find ourselves in a sinkhole."

"That wouldn't be an *elegant* death," Galinak muttered softly.

"You're sure this is the only way to cross the Broken Sands?" Vincha asked.

"As far as I know," I answered. The southern Long Tube was the most chaotic of the lines. It would take off at odd times and sometimes stop in midair for days, but it was the only way to cross the Broken Sands without driving on the treacherous land.

Thankfully, the outer gate to the station was unmanned, probably due to the harsh weather conditions.

Vincha sped up and parked us near the entrance to the enormous building. She handed Galinak and myself Comm plugs. As soon as I placed it in my ear I heard Vincha's voice speaking in my mind.

"Can you hear me, Twinkle Eyes?"

"Loud and clear."

"Good." Vincha killed the engine, and the annoying beeping stopped, leaving us in blissful silence. She leaned her driver seat back and shut her eyes. "Now, before we go inside"—Vincha's hair began to turn and twitch—"I want you to look into the building with those helpful eyes of yours and tell me what you see."

I concentrated and scanned as far as I could see into the building. It took a while, and by the time I was done I was nursing a splitting headache. "The Long Tube is in there, on the top platform, and also more than two dozen soldiers in defensive positions."

"Two dozen? Are you sure?"

"Closer to thirty, actually, and they are combat ready. We must have alerted them when we crossed the outer gate."

Vincha nodded, her hair twitching. "There's a lot of chatter on their Comm. We did not have enough juice to cloak, so they picked up the shark. They know we're coming and they're waiting for us."

I'd stood between these two veterans during a fight in a place called Margat's Den. It was like walking through the eye of a storm, but this time the foe was much deadlier.

Galinak checked his heavy gun. "What's the plan? We wait for them to get curious? Pick them off one at a time? Find a back door? Create a diversion? Use some *elegant* diplomacy?" He turned his head and winked at me.

To my relief Vincha shook her head. "We can't storm the place on our own."

"Sure, we can," Galinak argued. "Ten to one, we've faced worse odds before."

"You and I might be able to handle this"—Vincha pointed her thumb in my direction—"but Twinkle Eyes is not going to hack it. No offence, Twinkle."

"Oh, believe me, none taken," I said. "We could try to climb the side of the building and sneak onto the top platform and into the Long Tube, but then we'd have to wait inside until whatever runs it decides it's time to go."

"I don't have that kind of time." Vincha's brow furrowed. "And I can't risk getting hurt, not when Emilija is on her way to meet a mass murderer who will use her and then . . ." Vincha suddenly turned on the engine. The constant beeping began again, but this time with more urgency.

"What are we going to do now?"

"Plan B," she said, and we were slammed backwards as the shark sped away from the station.

"Vincha." I raised my voice above the constant beeping. "I can't but notice we are heading straight towards the Broken Sands."

"Stop stating the obvious and direct me so we're under the Tube tracks," she said as we picked up more speed.

I looked up, my gaze penetrating the roof of the shark. The tracks were to our right and then they veered even farther away. When I looked back down there was only time for me to say, "Vincha, there's a drop from here to the . . ." The rest was swallowed by both Galinak's and my own shouts of terror as Vincha drove us off the ledge. We were dropping like a stone when Vincha changed midair to hovercraft drive mode. We scraped quite a lot of sand before stabilizing.

"Damn," Galinak moaned. "I hope you treat your lovers better than you treat your ride."

"We're running out of power very fast in hover mode," Vincha shouted. "Twinkles, use your rusting eyes and tell me when we're just under the tracks."

It took only a couple of seconds before the power gem was completely depleted, and we landed nose down into the sand, thankfully not from so high up as to make it deadly. Sand immediately began to gather on the windshield.

"So much for plan B," I said.

"Are we under the rusting tracks?"

I looked up and concentrated. "Just about."

"Just about will have to do. Now I need to reverse the magnets of the hovercraft and find a power source to light this baby up for just a fraction of a moment. Galinak, I need to get under the shark."

"Vincha," I said, "we're sinking. Can't you feel it?"

It was true—we landed pretty deep and the sand was already as high as the doors.

"Right." Vincha hesitated for a moment, then ducked under her seat. "Galinak, I need you to rip this metal panel open, right now."

Galinak bent down. There was a crunching sound and both of them straightened up holding a lot of wires. I glanced to the side; the sand was already at window height and the air was getting stuffy. For the first time I felt panic beginning to rise in me. I did not want to die. To disappear like that from the face of the Earth. To slowly suffocate buried in sand . . . Vincha literally slapped me back into action.

"Take it, Twinkle Eyes." I saw the butt of her power gun and grasped it before I realised what I was doing. Her hair was twitching in the air and she was looping several cords together.

"Now, look with your twinkly eyes just to the right of the steering wheel. There is a small box inside, can you see it?"

All I could think of was the sand slowly entombing the three of us.

"Rust, Twinkle Eyes, can you see it?" Vincha shouted.

"Yes."

"Good. On my mark you shoot it with the power gun on full energy blast. That will give us a burst of power."

"And ruin the shark, possibly blowing us up?" Galinak added.

"Better get blown up than die slowly," Vincha said, and ducked low, holding the wires. "Don't miss."

I leaned forward as far as I could and aimed the power gun above Vincha's head.

"Now," Vincha ordered, and I squeezed the trigger. There was the distinct burning smell of melted carbon and metal, and suddenly the car engine lit up. A heartbeat later the shark burst upwards from the sand and the world was turned upside down. I hit my head, but my body dulled the pain as it registered damage.

When I got my bearings, I realised we were driving between the tube tracks, high above the ground, blue lightning crackling around us and smoke coming out of the dashboard.

"You'll have to extinguish any fires," Vincha said between tight lips as she concentrated on driving.

"I guess plan B was a success." Galinak managed to strap himself back into his seat. "Good thinking, Vinch."

"Thanks," Vincha said, then added, "Didn't think we'd flip upside down, though. That was a surprise."

"Any chance you could flip us back?" I was lying on the shark's roof. "This is getting a little uncomfortable."

"Don't think so," Vincha said. "The shark is constantly pulling downwards. I ain't trying anything that might endanger the magnetic hold."

"Do you know how long it will take us to get there?" I asked.

"Your shot fried the system and the dashboard display. I'm just driving us from one pair of Tarkanian tracks to the next. We'll get there soon enough."

"And how are we going to land when we get there?"

"We'll figure that out when we get there," Vincha replied, then added under her breath, "Just like old times."

64

Peach

A patrol found us the next morning. They were dressed in body armour and helmets, but each had a different weapon, rifles, machine guns, power pistols, and even shoulder cannons. They were geared more like a glorified militia than a military unit, but there was no doubt about their training. To their credit, they knew who they were looking for and were not unnecessarily brutal. Perhaps the fact that the strange and intimidating Lizard had disappeared into the night soon after we crash-landed helped keep things civil and relatively calm. My weapons were taken from me, but they handed us face masks and goggles, and I wasn't bound or otherwise mistreated.

We were escorted to the top of the hill on foot, then driven the rest of the way to the base in an old fossil-fuelled truck that had a light machine gun mounted on top of it. The entire area was devoid of trees or plants, and the slightest breeze brought up large clouds of dust, partly blocking the sun and making the whole area gloomy and relatively dark. Sergiu waved at me once or twice, but with the masks and goggles and covered in sand, it was impossible to communicate further. Emilija was sitting next to Sergiu, almost unnaturally still, staring from behind her goggles and mask. I doubted she would have said anything even without her facial protection.

With no one to talk to, I used the time to watch the land we were passing, trying to identify places and areas I had spent plenty of time in, but it really had been in another lifetime. Catching a glimpse of my past was easier to do when I was in Tarkania or even in the ruined city I woke up in, where everything had pretty much remained the same. With the dust everywhere and many of the buildings not surviving the passage of time, it was much more difficult to find a familiar landscape. Here and there I saw a few buildings that had been converted into impressively large greenhouses, and in many spots water-gathering, cone-shaped structures and wind turbines had been placed. I saw old petrol-engine generators around many of the greenhouses and several solar plates as well. The few people we passed were wearing worn-looking face masks to protect them from the sand. For some reason, a few of them were also wrapped in tinfoil. I turned my head and watched the Star Pillar. We were still several miles away from the mountain that served as its base, but it was so huge it felt like I could just reach out and touch it.

I thought we would be heading straight to the mountain. To my surprise, the base we drove to was built on a remote hill halfway between the Star Pillar and the air train station. It was a very defensible spot; the surrounding wall was built from a mixture of Tarakan steel plates and other types of salvaged metal welded into a high wall. I spotted several rotating heavy cannons mounted on top of the wall together with cameras, and a forest of antennas and power cables crisscrossing aboveground. Once we passed the double gates and got inside there were hundreds of different electronic devices, most of them military grade. They even had several long-range satellite dishes. It wasn't exactly a jump back into the twenty-fourth century, but it was close enough to warm my heart.

The buildings inside the base were mostly light mobile military structures, but there were a few more sturdy ones. I'd spent enough time as a soldier to be able to identify each structure just by the type of activities happening next to it. There were several barracks, a field hospital, and a computing centre with enough power cables coming out of it to indicate it could support a Sentient Program. The air vents were a sure sign of an underground level. We might have been on top of an emergency supply bunker, and if that was the case, the base was larger than it looked. If the emergency bunker was still in operation, printing essential supplies on a regular basis make would life under these harsh conditions much more bearable.

The men and women who were not wearing helmets were all hairless, their skin showing different degrees of exposure to radiation. They all walked with purpose, and only a few turned their heads to see us dismount from the truck. The rest were too busy or focused to get distracted. I noted to myself that whoever was in charge had created an impressive base of operations. In modern times this would only be a light military target. Hard to conquer on land, but if push came to shove it could have been dealt with from space or with long-range missiles. But these were not modern times, and this small group might have been one of the strongest military forces in the land.

Emilija was immediately taken away. She walked accompanied by Sergiu without looking back or even glancing in my direction. Sergiu was the one to turn back. He waved and said, "I'll see you soon, Colonel Major, try to rest and—" he paused just for a second before adding "—behave."

I contemplated his warning as I was led to the barracks through a decontamination process. The hairless soldier who led the way was a veteran who could have been in his thirties, sixties, or anything in between. When we got through the decontamination process, he turned and ordered me to spread my arms to the sides. When I complied, he measured me with a long tape. Then he shoved a thin cloth towel into my hands and indicated a door. "Shower over there, you've got five whole minutes. Believe me, it's a treat."

"I do believe you," I said. "How long have you been serving here?"

The man grimaced. "Long enough to know when not to answer questions. Now get to it."

He was right. The shower was a treat, even though it was a particle shower, so no real water touched my vessel's body. Still, I felt refreshed when I stepped out. A bald female soldier kept watch as a uniform approximately my size was brought in, including a pair of baggy but thermal underwear, a belt, and a pair of boots. As I was dressing, I noticed both man and woman had grey, pasty-colored skin that could have been the result of several intense radiation-flush treatments. Any question or comment I fired in their direction was answered with stone-cold silence. I guessed those were their orders.

I spent some time idle, sitting and then lying on a cot, waiting for something to happen. Eventually a third soldier walked in, and I was escorted back out of the barracks. I was expecting to be taken to an audience with a man sitting on some kind of a throne, but instead I was taken to the far side of the camp, where repairs were being made on some dug-up pipeline.

A frail-looking old man was standing on top of a mound, looking down at a dozen workers who were toiling in a ditch. He looked terrible—hairless, gaunt, and grey skinned, and without protective gear or even goggles to protect his red-rimmed eyes. The grey uniform he wore hung on his shapeless thin frame. He looked pretty much like an upright corpse.

As I approached, he pointed down and said in a rasping voice which nevertheless carried well, "Make sure that plate is welded." Half a dozen workers rushed immediately to fulfil his order. The man turned his head towards me as I made my way up the mound. With all his emanating frailty and sickness, I had to admit that he was also radiating power and authority. There was no doubt who was in charge here. When I was within earshot he said, "When you need something done well, make sure you stand right there when it is being done."

"I'll keep that in mind," I answered curtly.

He turned completely towards me. "I am Mannes, or . . ." He tilted his head as if trying to remember. "Dr. Mannes Holtz, deputy head of computer and science engineering."

The name rang a bell and the title was high ranking.

"And you are Colonel Major Vera Geer, although Sergiu told me you refer to yourself as 'Peach' these days. Interesting nickname. A very unlikely one, if you don't mind me saying so."

His sunken eyes scrutinized me as I answered, "What can I say? I woke up in a new world, might as well begin with a new name."

"You had a creature with you, some sort of a Lizard." Mannes no doubt had been briefed by his underling, but he wanted to double-check. A cautious move.

"Yes, we were four, but the Lizard you mentioned disappeared the night we landed—together with my gear, by the way." It happened as I was trying to secure the balloon on the ground. One moment it was standing motionless next to Emilija, the next it had snatched my medibag and was charging into the night with a speed I would never have been able to match, even with ESM.

"Interesting." Mannes's brow was so wrinkled I could only guess he was frowning. "That is the action of an intelligent being. Do you think it is sentient?"

"No doubt about it, and very attached to Emilija. It is surprising it has left her side."

"Emilija claims she told him to leave, that she gave him an assignment, although she did not tell me what this assignment might be."

"That is news to me, but this whole business is quite strange," I said. "And while we are on the subject, I was hoping you could, perhaps, brief me about *what the fuck happened*." I did not plan it, but the last bit came out as a shout. Many turned their heads towards us and I felt the soldiers behind me tense but Mannes seemed to be unaffected by my sudden outburst.

"I think that by now you must know what happened," he said.

"A world war was a dangerous prospect. You must have been aware of it, with the type of work you were doing."

"Yes, I was aware," I said, trying to control myself. "And I wrote memos warning about rising tensions and the consequences of our actions."

Mannes's lower face moved in a strange way, and it took me a moment to realise he was smiling. "'Wrote memos about it?' Have you read your history, my dear hibernating agent? World War One began at a time when there was no real hunger, no famine, no reason for one nation to survive at the expense of another, yet it utterly destroyed a whole continent and several powerful nations, setting the stage for an even more vicious Second World War. I bet there were a few memos written back then, warning about the dangers of the signed defence treaties combined with rising tension. All that was needed was a spark."

"Still, even that war did not annihilate *everything*."

"That's because the weapons used in World War One were primitive." Mannes took half a step towards me. "We are both from another time, you and I. Most likely the only living survivors of that era."

"Perhaps that is true, but you lived for a hundred years before waking me up from the dead. I'd say you have a slight advantage in figuring out what went wrong."

Mannes chuckled quietly. "Calling my situation an 'advantage,' now that's a first. To answer your question, I long ago stopped concerning myself with what had been and focused on what is going to be, but"—he raised a hand before I could speak—"in the name of gracious hospitality and in repayment for your incredible service, I'll indulge your curiosity. To state the obvious, another world war happened. Adam, Tarakan's central SP, who pretty much ran everything, was infected with a malicious program which caused a chain reaction that brought us where we are now."

"That is . . . impossible. The security protocols stop outside inter—"

"It was an inside job. A group of Tarakan programmers did it."

"That is . . . still impossible. Are you sure?"

"I had almost a hundred years to make sure. I even know their names, but they are long dead and unable to answer questions. Now I concentrate my efforts on restoring what we have left. What you see here"—Mannes gestured at the activities around us—"is the greatest salvage operation in the history of mankind."

It was a lot to take in. Even though I was kind of ready for it, hearing how the world ended, and knowing I had inadvertently taken part in pushing it to that end, brought on conflicting emotions that I had to fight to contain. I changed the subject. "So how does this girl I brought to you fit into your salvaging plans? Why is she so important?"

Mannes turned his head and checked that the workers were still welding pipes and plates, as he had ordered. "When it was obvious that the world was on the brink of mutual annihilation, Adam sent infused and enhanced DNA material into the atmosphere and shut down a large part of himself so Tarakan secrets, *our secrets*, would not fall into the wrong hands. The DNA is the cause of the mutations otherwise known as 'the marked,' or 'the tattooed.' The mutations themselves transformed into many types of subspecies, but only one type carries the right genetic code to unbind Adam's powers: the Puzzlers. Before locking himself away, Adam converted all the emergency bunkers to have puzzle locks attuned to a strain of a genetic code and let Darwinian forces take effect."

"Are you saying Emilija is the key to healing Adam?"

Mannes's eyes lit up. "There are thousands of minds trapped within Adam. Imagine what would happen if we could bring them all back. The greatest scientists, artists, military strategists, and thinkers of humanity are waiting to be rescued."

"Yet when you had the chance, you chose to rescue me. Why not someone else?"

The look on Mannes's face suggested he would have been raising an eyebrow if he had one on his face. "Are you sorry I brought you back?"

I looked around. "I can't say I care for this world," I answered softly.

Mannes surprised me with a bemused chuckle which turned into a wheeze and a cough. He recuperated quickly, though. "I was able to do some things on my own"—he gestured at the ground— "like hack open the emergency bunker below us without the use of a Puzzler, or get into the hibernating agent database and draw you out. But I needed someone with skills and proven survivability. As for why it was you instead of another agent, it was not planned. You could say I grabbed whoever I could in the short window of opportunity I had, and I got lucky. Your credentials are impressive, and you managed to complete your assignment under less than ideal conditions. To free Adam from his own cell I needed a Puzzler, and you brought me one."

He was keeping things away from me. It was obvious and also the logical thing to do, but nevertheless, it annoyed me. "What will happen to Emilija?"

Mannes's eyes narrowed slightly. He wasn't expecting for me to be concerned with her fate. "She will fulfil her destiny for the better of humankind. She is a Puzzler, and according to my tests, her DNA contains pure, uncorrupted Tarakan code. If all goes well, this Puzzler is the last one I'll need. She is literally the key that can open the gate for thousands of minds trapped within Adam."

"Will she survive the process?"

Mannes's body language betrayed his growing annoyance. It was obvious he was unaccustomed to being questioned.

"Does it matter?" he asked.

"I am not sure I am comfortable risking a life of a civilian, especially someone who seems so unaware of reality."

Mannes's stare hardened. "How many innocents did you kill through direct and indirect consequences of your actions? It was all in the name of peace and stability for Tarakan."

"Maybe it's time to change course, then, and stop sacrificing people, as glorious or important as the reasons might be."

"I outrank you, Colonel Major." Mannes spoke softly but his tone was steel. "And I will not stand here and explain centuries of operations just to satisfy your moral code."

"I don't think rank matters here and now, not to me."

"Oh, but it does." Mannes took another step towards me. We were standing too close for comfort, but I held my ground. "Perhaps the ranks of sergeant and lieutenant, or even colonel major, are of no real importance in the grand scheme of things, but the rank that truly matters belongs to the one who is in charge. That would be me." He drew himself up as he spoke, and his voice rose in a dramatic crescendo until he was shouting his last words into my face. I knew the type; I'd seen others like him before. He was not Dr. Mannes Holtz, a Tarakan civil servant anymore. He was Mannes, the Master of Men, and he *liked* it.

A logical inner voice warned me I was about to go too far but I opened my mouth anyway, just as the soldier who brought me into the barracks saved me from myself.

"Master," he said, handing a flat-screen to Mannes, "this came through just now."

Mannes looked at the screen. I saw him absorbing the information, calculating and reaching a decision within seconds. "Radio the second platoon to reach the station and deploy, meet them there, and take the colonel major with you."

Mannes flipped the screen so I could see what was on it. He tapped the screen. There was a frozen three-dimensional image of a slick-looking, weaponised hovercraft driving upside down through some sort of a gate. Mannes magnified the image, and I saw the woman with fiery red curls I had seen in my dreams. She was driving two other men. The one in the back was looking away, and the one in the passenger seat was too blurry to recognise.

Mannes moved his hand and the image changed to a brief, looped video clip of the same hovercraft, this time driving upside down on what seemed to be the Sky Train's tracks.

"The driver is the girl's mother," Mannes said. "Vincha. She is highly dangerous and possesses Tarakan military-grade communication tech. The other two are agents with enhanced battle capabilities."

"Agents of whom?" I asked.

"Of those who do not want me to do what must be done," Mannes answered, "and there is no time to answer all of your questions." Mannes turned to the soldier standing next to us, "Lieutenant Rachim, take the fastest vehicle we have and join the second platoon." Mannes pointed at me. "Take our guest with you. Apprehend the girl's mother." When he saw the look on my face he said, "The process can sometimes be confusing for the Puzzler. It would be easier and have less chance of being lethal if we could have the girl's full cooperation. Having the girl's mother in custody—"

"You will use her as leverage," I said.

"I will try to persuade them to cooperate willingly, and perhaps this will save the girl's life." Mannes nodded. "We can talk further about this when you come back."

Mannes was not the only one who could decide quickly. I was trained for these circumstances. "Fine," I said, "capture the woman. But what about the agents?"

"They are of no importance." Mannes was already walking away. "Kill them."

65

Peach

After I received my weapons at the gate, Lieutenant Rachim and I ended up riding on an old, fossil-fuelled motorbike that was nevertheless extremely fast. Gripping the sides of the motorbike, I used the short drive to replay my conversation with Mannes in my head.

Despite his appearance, Mannes was an impressive figure with a magnetic personality, and he was playing me. He was also anxious and eager; the way he oversaw the work on the power lines betrayed he was running out of time, patience, or both. No matter what Emilija might do for humanity, I was guessing she was important to Mannes on a very personal level.

There wasn't much time left for me to figure things out.

Most of the platoon was already deployed when we reached the air train station and parked next to two huge tanker trucks. *The fossil oil arrives through the station, then,* I realised.

Two soldiers and a sergeant, all clad in battle armour, were waiting for us in the shade of the trucks. The Sergeant eyed me with open curiosity but did not say anything. Instead she began briefing the Lieutenant. Their body language betrayed some sort of close familiarity. *Perhaps they've seen action together, shared a bed, or both.*

"The platoon is deployed inside, and snipers are in position. Alpha is on the top platform, Delta is on auxiliary."

"How long have we got?"

The Sergeant glanced up into her left-side visor. "They are not as fast as the Sky Train, so we just need to wait a little longer. Orders?"

"Capture the woman, kill the other two," Lieutenant Rachim answered.

The Sergeant was about to touch the Comm button on her helmet to relay the order when I stepped forward.

"Wait."

Both looked at me, equally annoyed.

"They are outnumbered and you are deployed and ready. With that kind of an advantage, perhaps there won't be a need to fire a shot. We could capture all three."

Lieutenant Rachim turned to me. "There is no 'we' here. You are only an observer. We've got our orders."

My next step brought me shoulder to shoulder with both of them. "You are right, I am only an observer, but I have led troops to battle and I know how fast things can go wrong. One of your snipers might get overexcited, or miss the target, or the marks could move at the wrong moment, and once a battle begins, you have no way to control who shoots where and who gets hit. Your priority is to catch the woman alive, isn't that true?" Lieutenant Rachim nodded, hesitantly, and I pressed on. "What if there's a way to catch them without any risk?"

"How?" the Sergeant asked, breaking the chain of command. *Definitely sleeping together, then.*

"You still have a functioning control room here?" I asked. Lieutenant Rachim turned to the Sergeant and she nodded. "Then take me there and keep your Comm open. You have nothing to lose. If I fail you still have your advantage."

"Fine," Lieutenant Rachim said, and turned away. "Sergeant Reims, relay your Comm through me. I'll take point in the control room in the tower. Make sure all the exits are covered, but no one should fire a shot without my orders, clear?"

Sergeant Reims did not look pleased but nodded. I followed the Lieutenant into the building and up to the second floor.

"You get your fossil fuel through here," I said as we climbed the metal stairs.

"Yes, it comes from the North—" The Lieutenant caught himself midsentence and snapped, "Stop asking questions." But his slipup was enough for me to make the connection. The Oil Baron to the North was supplying Mannes with refined oil while attacking the land around the City of Towers. There was a Machiavellian plan at play behind the scenes. If Mannes was working with the enemies of the City of Towers, was he actually working against Tarakan as well? Was my gut feeling right and I was being played here?

I had no time to mull things over before we reached the control room on the top floor of the control tower. The door to the room was gone, so we simply stepped into the large room. The walls were transparent in all directions, and I could see the air train tracks leading into the platform areas. There were two soldiers sitting among two dozen floating screens, each displaying a different location. The soldiers snapped to attention and saluted as we walked in.

"Where are they?" Lieutenant Rachim did not bother to tell the soldiers to be at ease.

One of the soldiers pointed at a screen showing the hovercar whizzing through. "Just went through section 14E, sir. We have a few more minutes, but they should be slowing down soon."

I stepped towards the second soldier with enough authority for her to move aside and waved my hand in the air until a transparent keyboard appeared in front of me.

"Whoa, that's . . . how did you . . . ?" the soldier asked.

"It's actually a pain in the butt to use those things," I said as my hands moved around the transparent keyboard. "You have to do it by

sight, not touch. I much prefer the old, physical version . . . there."
One of the display screens showed the list of security protocols in
play. As I suspected, most were off-line for one reason or another.

"They just passed point 13E," the other soldier announced, "and
they haven't slowed down. Hey wait—" The soldier leaned forward,
cocking her head, and pointed at the screen. "Damn, they're flying
upside down."

"That would be a very uncomfortable position to be in for the
length of time that it would take them to cross the Broken Sands,"
Lieutenant Rachim remarked.

"If we're lucky they'll be disoriented when they land," I said,
but thought, *That woman is coming for her daughter. She will be
extremely focused.*

A passcode demand appeared in front of me. This was money
time and a sort of a test for how much I could influence things. If
the system still remembered my personal ID number and security
status, I could control the security system and perhaps avoid a
bloodbath. I punched in my ID and security number, a twenty-
two-digit-long code. A second later I was in the system and managed to contain myself and not whoop out loud, but I guess I
failed to hide my smile.

The Lieutenant walked over and stood behind me. "What are
you doing?" he demanded.

"I know some things about the security of similar places."
Actually, as the threat to the gateway to the Star Pillar grew, I
was asked to help beef up security and participated in several live
tests of these measures right where I was sitting now.

"Places like this were always under threat of attack," I explained as I worked, "and when you have a mass of people, all running and screaming, pointing and waving their hands, you waste
precious seconds trying to find the bad guys and can make lethal
mistakes. That's why we installed a few measurements that would
pacify and control the entire area. The only thing is that these
measurements eat *a lot* of power, so I am diverting it from different
places and into the security system." I looked at the power meter.

It was at 56 percent and rising, but not quickly enough. I pressed a few more transparent keys, and the lights around us dimmed.

"Tell your teams the lifts to the platforms will not work. They will need to use the stairs."

Lieutenant Rachim touched the Comm button on the side of his helmet but paused. "Anything else?"

"We'll need to lure them off the platform for this to work," I said as one by one screens around us blinked out of existence, leaving us with only three. One was showing the upper platform and the tracks; the second, the lower grounds; and the third was displaying the power meter.

"What are you doing?" The Lieutenant placed a hand on my shoulder. "You're leaving us blind."

"Only partly." I indicated the remaining screens. "You can still see your Alpha team and the platform. The rest are out of play at the moment."

"I don't like it," Lieutenant Rachim muttered, but there was no time to argue. We all saw the hovercar fly in between the tracks, rapidly approaching.

"Here they come," the soldier announced. "Damn, they aren't slowing down."

I glanced at the power meter. It showed 78 percent.

"Alpha, clear the platform," I heard the Lieutenant and the Sergeant shouting in unison over the Comm.

A few seconds later the hovercraft disappeared inside the hall and I was half expecting it to burst through the other side. We all turned to the screen.

Eighty-two percent.

The driver—I assumed it was still Vincha—must have realised she wouldn't be able to brake in time and, either as a defence measure or a Hail Mary attempt, unloaded her entire weaponry. She did not have time to target the missiles and focus the rail gun's fire, so the shots exploded all over the place. The hovercar flipped just before reaching the top platform and immediately dropped down. Its discs were deployed, but its speed and momentum were too strong. The vehicle smashed into the second platform, crushing one of the Alpha team soldiers and hitting another. It bounced several times before turning sharply and flipping several times on its axis. Unsurprisingly, as the hovercar dropped from the second platform to the main hall below I saw flashes of white inside the vehicle, which meant that the ECF—Emergency Crash Foam—had been deployed. The people inside were held fast by the gooey substance and had hopefully survived the ordeal.

The hovercraft flipped twice more, spraying white crash foam everywhere, before coming to a halt.

"Report," Lieutenant Rachim barked into the Comm.

"Corporal Sgar is dead. Mittal is injured, broken legs. Three more casualties in Beta team."

The Sergeant's voice filled the Comm. "Alpha team, stay back. Delta team, move in and secure the area."

Lieutenant Rachim turned his head to me. "How is that security measure of yours?"

I shook my head. "No need to lure them anywhere. They are in the right zone, but I still do not have enough power."

We both watched the figures of the Delta team run toward the crashed hovercar. "Well. If they're even alive after that crash, I'm sure they are in no condition to resist."

"Don't be so sure," I said, remembering that at least one of them was functioning in a combat vessel. *And never underestimate the willpower of a distraught mother.*

The soldiers surrounded the crashed hovercraft. The windows were gone, of course, and the ECF was beginning to melt.

"I see three inside," one of the soldiers reported, "all unconscious."

"Secure them from the craft and move away before it blows," the Sergeant ordered.

We watched the soldiers get to work. Vincha was the first to be taken out of the driver's seat and carried away between two soldiers. Three others took hold of the large unconscious man wearing LeatherFlex combat armour and his power machine gun. The third man was in the worst shape. I could see that he'd dislocated his shoulder and his face was bruised and bleeding.

The power meter was at 84 percent. I looked back to the screen displaying the action in the hall.

The Delta team was walking away, their movements most likely traced by several snipers from the Beta team above, when I saw something that caused me to lean closer and magnify the display on the screen.

"Is there a breeze in the hall?" I asked. "Because the woman's hair is twitching strangely."

"What? Where?" The Lieutenant turned his head when several things happened at once. A sharp screech blasted through the Comm, making everyone, including the Lieutenant and myself, stop everything and claw at their ears to unplug their Comms. Everyone but the redheaded woman named Vincha, who turned around, punched the closest soldier straight in the exposed part of his neck, and grabbed his rifle. Then she kicked the other soldier in the face and began shooting upwards at the snipers. One of the Delta team recovered quicker than his squad members, forgot his orders, and raised his gun to shoot the woman. She would have died in that moment if he'd squeezed the trigger. Instead he was suddenly punched by the man in the LeatherFlex armor so hard that he flew back, spinning in the air and landing somewhere outside my line of vision. The man grabbed another soldier, and with the strength that only combat vessels have, used the poor soldier to hit the last two standing Deltas and then lifted him up as a shield as death began to rain from above. With his other hand, the combat vessel bent down and grabbed his still-unconscious friend while Vincha kept shooting upwards, and both of them retreated towards the upturned hovercraft, her red hair dancing in the air as if she was a mystic medusa.

The power meter was at 88 percent when Lieutenant Rachman ran out of the room. With Comms down, this was a full-blown fight with a battle plan that had gone out the window.

I watched as the three hid behind the hovercraft. I saw from above the man bending over his unconscious friend and relocating his shoulder as Vincha kept shooting in all directions.

Ninety percent.

The surprise part was over, and with it the advantage the three had. What was left of the Alpha team was converging on the ground level while snipers were changing positions from above. This would be over soon, and all three of them would be dead. I had to know what was going on. I had to talk to the three of them.

But I was just an observer.

Ninety-two percent.

Fuck this.

I pressed the button.

66

Twinkle Eyes

There is nothing out of the ordinary in waking up, unless you are about to die.

I opened my eyes to a terrible pain in my shoulder and saw Galinak's blurry face hovering above me, too close for comfort. He had just finished pushing my arm back in its socket and was shouting something, but whatever he was trying to communicate was drowned out by the explosions all around us. I turned my head and saw Vincha duck under a hail of shots. She squatted next to me, checked the power display on her rifle, grimaced, and shouted something at Galinak before firing some more. I tried to sit up against the remains of the shark, and a sharp pain in my shoulder told me there was damage even a Tarakan-built body could not fully sustain.

Galinak leaned into the broken frame of the shark and came back holding the hovercraft's broken steering wheel and my peacemaker, still covered in the white goo of the crash foam. He brushed the gun against his thigh, handed it to me, and pointed up. I ignored him and looked around, using my sight to try and figure out what was going on. On the ground a group of soldiers was slowly advancing on our position while more were trying to flank us from above. Oh yes. We were going to die.

It was a sobering thought, and my body reacted by forgetting the pain and discomfort I had felt a moment before. Galinak grabbed me again and brought me into a sitting position. He held the power gem that he had taken out of the broken steering wheel, pointed upwards, and grinned. I only realised what he wanted when he threw the gem upwards. It was already arcing its way down when I pointed the peacemaker at it as Galinak knelt down and braced himself against the shark.

The old me never would have made that shot in a million years. But the old me did not have a Tarakan retina-aiming and tracking device connected to my nerves and a hand holding an enormous gun. I took the shot. The gem exploded in a flash of light just as Galinak roared and flung the carcass of the shark at the advancing soldiers.

I'd experienced that moment in a fight when time suddenly slows down and you can see everything happening at once, but this time it did not just slow down; it stopped completely. The shark, which had been flipping in the middle of the air, did not land. The man falling down from above never hit the ground. The bullet shot from behind us just froze there, a silvery blur just an inch away from the back of Vincha's head. The sudden stillness and cessation of all noise except an impossible high-pitched whine was a weird sort of pain. Not being able to move or even blink did not help, either. I just stood there, watching, the bullet that was about to kill Vincha hovering in the air in front of my frozen eyeballs, and I was unable to do anything but imagine what would happen the moment the world decided to move again. Vincha was dead. I would never move fast enough to push her away from the path of this bullet. It was a small comfort to know that she would not suffer. That kind of shot would leave her dead before her body hit the ground.

From the corner of my eye I saw something move. It was unnaturally fast, or perhaps I only thought so because of the utter stillness of the environment. A slender woman came into view. She ducked under the suspended shark, passed Galinak, and came to stand between Vincha and myself. She was small, with thinning black hair tied in a bun. Her face was full of concern when she examined the bullet. I wanted to talk to her, to ask her for help, beg her to assist Vincha, but most of all I wanted to ask her, *What the hell is going on?*

That thought kept flashing in my mind as she unsheathed a short sword pulsating with a powerful blue hue. She raised it in front of my eyes so slowly that I caught my frozen reflection on the side of its blade. I watched her taking careful aim, then she brought the sword down on the bullet. The world came back to life in a flash of blinding light and a deafening bang, just before it all went black again.

67

Peach

Sergiu was leaning against an oil tanker, defiantly smoking his pipe under the wide rim of his hat as I limped outside. Emilija's mother and the two men were just being brought out and dumped belly down on the ground, their hands locked in sturdy-looking cuffs that connected to a neural inhibitor attached to their necks. They could move their heads and speak, but that was about it.

Sergiu stepped towards me. "That was quite a show, Colonel Major, quite a show." He was holding a metal tiara in his hand.

"What do you mean?"

Instead of an answer Sergiu turned and waved the Sergeant over. He handed her the metal tiara.

"You'd better put this on the woman's head," he suggested in a soft voice. "Make sure the edges touch her temples. This will stop her from using her tech."

The Sergeant nodded and took the tiara from his hand.

Then he turned his attention back to me. "Yes, I was briefed by

Lieutenant Rachim. Nine dead, thirteen injured. You seem to have saved the day using a nice little trick no one knew existed."

"That nice little trick saved us the trouble of scraping the woman's brain off the floor," I answered coolly, but for some reason, being debriefed by Sergiu the Dying was suddenly annoying.

"Don't get me wrong, I'm not complaining." Sergiu absent-mindedly dumped the contents of his pipe on the ground. "You also saved Lieutenant Rachim's head." Somehow, I was sure Sergiu meant what he said literally. He continued, "But I just wonder how you managed to do it?"

There was no sense in lying. "Even after it was completed, the Star Pillar was under threat. I was one of the team That installed and tested the stasis field security system here, and it still recognised my rank and clearance. That was how I managed to erect and walk into the stasis zone."

"And the blast afterwards?"

"The temporary stasis zone was only one part of the full security measures, but that part didn't work. Not enough power, I guess. I had little time to improvise and my first priority was to save the woman. Cutting the bullet midair released a lot of kinetic energy." I looked at my singed uniform and added, "But the injuries were pretty mild."

"The orders were to kill the two men and capture the woman," Sergiu said.

"Well, I managed to save the *mother* and also capture her two associates. Call it performance above the call of duty. Tell your Mannes he does not need to give me a medal for it or anything, maybe a more comfortable bed in the barracks and an extra pillow."

Sergiu shook his head. "Master Mannes demands his orders be followed to the letter, Colonel Major, and you not only argued with him in front of his soldiers, you showed the ability to access measures no one thought existed and then defied his order." Sergiu pointed at the red-haired woman, who was now wearing the metal tiara, and ordered, "Take her to the truck."

The woman was immediately raised from the ground by three

soldiers. She turned her head and stared, wide-eyed, straight at me. I saw hate and fear and wondered if she knew that I had saved her life.

Sergiu stepped forward, pulling out a power pistol from his belt holster. He stood above the two prone men, gun in hand, as I approached.

"What are you planning to do?" It was a foolish question, but I persisted. "They are bound prisoners." In case he hadn't noticed.

Both men were moving their heads, listening.

Sergiu did not look at me, but he took a long breath, the kind I saw soldiers take right before they needed to do something gruesome they were not happy about. "I'm sorry, Colonel Major, but we are very close to success and cannot afford loose ends. This has nothing to do with the way I feel about it. These are Mannes's orders. As a soldier yourself you understand we need to do what must be done, and sometimes it ain't pretty."

Yeah, I understood. There were times I was the one to pull the trigger. But now the world had been destroyed. My vessel's body was trembling with fatigue, but I managed to move and stand in front of Sergiu, beside the two men on the ground. I was seriously too tired for this shit but gave it my best shot. "This is not just immoral," I argued, "this is stupid slaughter. These men are assets you're about to throw away. They have information about who sent them and what their plans are."

"And you were planning to interrogate them yourself, weren't you?" Sergiu looked at me knowingly. "Was that why you argued with Lieutenant Rachim for their lives?" He aimed his pistol at the head of the slender-looking man.

"It was just the right tactical action to take," I said. "The Lieutenant didn't know about the freeze zone." I thought I saw hesitation pass behind Sergiu's eyes and pressed on. "Look, Sergiu, I have seen the three of them fight shoulder to shoulder, surrounded, outgunned, and outnumbered. No one tried to run away to save their own skin and this one"—I pointed at the larger man—"actually carried the other one to safety under fire. Don't you understand? They *care* for each other, which means the woman cares for these two. She will cooperate better if we have them as leverage."

Sergiu looked at me. "You are absolutely right, Colonel Major. That is why I am not going to shoot them."

"You could have fooled me," I said, nodding at the gun in his hand. "So what's that all about?"

Sergiu sighed and shook his head a little, then he turned and shot me twice in the chest.

68

Twinkle Eyes

They clamped devices to our backs that immobilised us from the shoulders down. They also tied dark cloth around our eyes, which meant I could still see what was going on without them realising it. I spent most of the way with my head at knee level, surrounded by the same unhappy soldiers who tried to kill us. I used the time to replay the recent events in my mind, since it had all happened too fast for me to fully comprehend what was going on at the time. I managed to strap myself to the backseat of the shark before it flipped, an action that most likely saved my life. The next thing I remembered was being woken up in the middle of a chaotic battle, shooting a power gem, freezing in place, and watching a woman cut the bullet that would have blown Vincha's head off. That woman argued for our lives as we lay facedown in the dirt, and I saw her body fall to the ground next to me as she was shot twice at close range by the man who was now sitting near the driver of the truck. The man's boots passed my face as he went to check her pulse, and I heard him commanding two soldiers to take two hoverbikes and dump her body in the Broken Sands below us. Whoever she was, and whatever her reasons were, she'd saved all of our lives at least once and paid with her own for what she'd done.

Vincha was facing me on the truck, unaware of her surroundings since she couldn't see through her bindings. Even with the cuffs, nerve pincers, and the strange tiara they attached to her temples, which rendered us powerless, they didn't take any chances with Galinak. He was lying facedown on the floor with a power rifle's muzzle to the back of his head. We came to Emilija's rescue but ended up as hostages to be used as leverage, myself and Galinak to secure Vincha's compliance, and Vincha to help secure Emilija's full cooperation. Only thing was, Vincha had already made it clear what she would do to save her daughter. We might have fought side by side to survive a deadly ambush, but Vincha would sooner see us dead than let her daughter come to harm.

I tried to think of worse situations than our current predicament, and the only one I could come up with ended in my getting eviscerated by Lizards.

We drove through a double gate and shortly after they carried us out to the open. Yellow dust hung in the air as they dumped us on the ground again, this time holding us so we were sitting on our knees in a short, miserable line. I carefully raised my head up. I saw the masked soldiers, the power cables, the heavy weapons, and the strange, huge silos. Behind all that, far to the distance, the Star Pillar sprang up from the mountain and into the sky. To say it was awe inspiring would do it gross injustice. The incredible sight made me momentarily forget the mess we'd gotten ourselves into. It was even more impressive than when I was flying through the City Within the Mountain. From far away the Star Pillar looked like a uniform structure, but from relatively closer I could see it was multilayered. Its core was a huge shaft looped by several layers that reminded me of a giant spring, and the whole thing was surrounded by an aura of ever-changing light. It was a mesmerizing sight, and only the reactions of the surrounding soldiers tore me away from the view.

A man that I guessed was Mannes walked slowly towards us, his movements and people's reaction to him betraying his role and importance. I never knew what a ghoul looked like until I laid my eyes on him. This was the monster everyone talked about, and his visage was a perfect match to his reputation. I didn't need to remind myself that he was the one who ordered my death and the death of the woman who saved my life. What would he do to us now?

Emilija walked behind him, accompanied by the man in the wide-brimmed hat. I recognised her immediately by the resemblance to the woman kneeling next to me. She was younger, prettier, daintier, and she had a faraway, peaceful look in her eyes that I imagined Vincha never had, but the girl was the CommWoman's daughter, there was no doubt about it. She was also an obvious Puzzler, with distinct markings running up her right forearm and disappearing into her wide sleeve.

The tattoos that appeared around the eyes of my previous body had remained the same size until I was shredded to pieces by claws and teeth, but when I tracked down Rafik's life story, five years and a lifetime ago, I remembered hearing his tattoos were initially small in size, barely covering half a finger. They grew and expanded in conjunction with the boy's ability and understanding. If that was the case, and the size and intensity of the markings represented ability, Emilija was a powerful Puzzler. There was no doubt as to why both sides of this mysterious conflict sought to capture her.

The blindfolds came off, and as soon as Vincha turned her head she called out her daughter's name in a voice filled with emotion. It wasn't that Emilija didn't hear her mother's call—she even reacted to it—but it was barely a nod, an unnaturally calm acknowledgement under any circumstances. She looked at us as if we were pieces of tapestry hanging on a wall.

Mannes stepped forward. "Lift them to their feet," he ordered, and a moment later we were up, each held from both sides. He walked past us one by one. I heard Galinak mutter, "Wanna dance, old man?" Vincha was too preoccupied watching her daughter to pay attention to Mannes. He finally stopped in front of me, close enough that I was able to smell the decay and death emanating from his frail body.

"So, he just sent . . . you?" His voice was raspy, but it carried. "The most powerful and intelligent being ever to exist, the brain and heart of the Tarakan empire, and he could only send the three of you to gate-crash my compound in this *pathetic* attempt to save the day. I admit, I am . . . disappointed."

"What can I say?" I surprised myself by answering. "Experienced staff is hard to come by these days."

"You were supposed to kill me." That was not a question and lying about the obvious was foolish.

"That was not our prime assignment, just the girl."

I did not think it was possible, but Mannes did not even blink the entire time we were conversing.

"What did he promise you? A better body, longer life, a world to play God in, maybe hard metal, as money is called these days?" There was an odd light in the man's unblinking eyes. "Or did he just force you to do it?"

I tried to shrug, forgetting I had no sensation or control of my body from the shoulders down. "A little bit of everything, I guess. Not my first choice for a job, being a hero, crashing into people's gates."

Mannes tilted his head. "Interesting. What was your job?"

"A secondary scribe of the Guild of Historians," I answered, "although I am now LoreMaster."

"Climbed up the guild's political ladder, did you?" My guess was that Mannes was somehow amused by our conversation.

"More the case of the ladder losing a lot of its rungs until it reached rock bottom." That brought out a chuckle from the ghoul.

Unfortunately it also snapped Vincha out of her stupor. "If you harm my Emilija, I'll kill you, you rusting corpse." There was an edge of hysteria in her voice I'd never heard before. I could tell she was barely hanging on.

Mannes turned around and motioned with his hand for Emilija to come close. She was standing by the man with the wide-brimmed hat who earlier today had shot that woman in the chest. Emilija dutifully walked forward until she stood in front of her mother. The effect on the tough CommWoman was nothing short of dramatic. Vincha seemed to lose all the fire within her.

"Emilija," she said, tears streaming down her cheeks, "I'm so sorry."

The young woman stood motionless for a long, uncomfortable moment, then, as if remembering something, smiled at her mother, reached out, and wiped the tears from one side of her mother's face.

"There, there," she said in a singsong tone of voice one would use for toddlers. "All will be fine. Don't cry, little one. I will come soon to see you, and bring you presents. You don't need to cry because of the other kids, just do as you are told and be a good girl."

Vincha lowered her head as Emilija continued talking softly to her mother. The short sentences seemed odd and disconnected, but with each word her tone of voice hardened. "You should be patient. Do as you're told. Don't go out. Be careful what you say. Don't play with the other kids, one day you'll understand. We have to move again. I will come to see you soon, soon I said. Don't cry. You have to hide or the bad people will come. Stop behaving like a baby. Because you were not careful, now we have to move again. Why are you like this? Are you not happy to see me? Look, I brought you a present, we'll have to insert it under your skin. What's wrong with you?" Suddenly Emilija's eyes lit up and she smiled broadly. "There, there," she said again, her tone of voice light and soothing. She leaned forward and hugged her now-sobbing mother, whispered something in her ear, and kissed her cheek. Then she simply turned and walked away.

It was bloodless and without violence, but in a way, it was the most horrific scene I had ever witnessed.

Mannes took her place. "You managed to hide your daughter for a long time," he said, "and for that, in a way, I owe you my thanks. But her fate is inevitable, you must know that, deep down inside."

Say what you like about Vincha, she recovered fast. "Rust on your fate, corpse." She lifted her head and stretched her neck towards Mannes, baring her teeth as if wanting to take a bite out of him. "What's inevitable is me killing you very slowly if you lay one finger on her."

I was half expecting him to shoot her right there and then, but I found out Mannes was a crueler man than I had imagined.

"I am going to take your daughter and use her for what she was born to do," he said calmly. "She seems willing enough to do it now, but the process can be . . . excruciating. If she changes her mind or resists, I will harm your friends first, then you, until she fully cooperates. If it gives you any comfort, her fate will bring justice to many."

Ignoring Vincha's response of shouting profanities, Mannes stepped back and ordered, "Take them to the secure cell. Make sure there is a channel open for a possible broadcast."

A moment later, he was walking slowly towards Emilija as we were dragged away.

69

Peach

There is nothing out of the ordinary in waking up, unless you are dead. My death, as far as I can remember, was actually painless. The initial shock of being shot twice in the chest was replaced by my vessel's self-protection mechanism, which dampened the pain to a minimum. My ESM should have kicked in, but this was not like losing an arm in United Korea or having my teeth pulled out in Tokyo. This was two point-blank shots to the chest. There was not much my vessel could have done. Sergiu was a good shot, so all things considered, there are worse ways to go. What was left for me to experience was light quickly dwindling into darkness. As I lay on the ground, blood oozing out of my vessel, the last image I saw was Sergiu leaning down to check my weakening pulse. For some reason I distinctly remember feeling his warm fingers touching my rapidly cooling skin. Then I felt light, as if I was being lifted up, and even consciousness was too energy consuming for my vessel to maintain.

And then there was nothing.

I had a fraction of a second to make peace with the world, or with myself, but I did neither. I just knew that there was no plan B. Tarakan Central Command was not going to deploy an emergency extraction team. No one was coming to save me. This was final. This was Game Over. And something in me was not sorry about it. This world, the little I had seen of it, was awful, and a part of me was glad to leave it. And besides, I deserved it. For all the things I had done and caused, a clean death was actually the easy way out.

Death came to me, and I let go.

But there was another part of me which I could not control, the one instilled in any Tarakan special ops vessel, including the one that my dwindling consciousness was currently occupying. As I embraced death, that part did its best to survive.

All Tarakan noncombat special ops vessels were identical to biological bodies in every aspect except for a few needed modifications. One of them was the emergency survival mode, the ESM, which dumped adrenaline into the bloodstream at thirty times the rate a normal human being could handle. The other exception was the Seed, a microorganism planted deep in the centre of the brain, whose sole function was to protect the fabric of consciousness for as long as possible. The Seed lay dormant, undetected unless you knew what it was and where to look for it, but once the vessel received damage that was perceived as lethal, the Seed came to life and all energy was channelled towards the preservation of the Seed instead of being wasted on trying to save what was already beyond saving. The Seed could not survive for long, but it was far longer than what a biological body could endure, enough to give a window of opportunity for an extraction team to retrieve it from the vessel's skull and bring it to a laboratory where the consciousness of the agent, as well as information about the events leading to the vessel's demise, could be reconstructed. In short, Sergiu should have blown my brains out, but he didn't know about the Seed—almost no one did outside the inner circle of Tarakan Central Command.

Pain.

This time the vessel was too weak to dampen it, and as nerves flared back to life, the sensation was like I was on fire. I came out of my subconscious and back into the world screaming at the top of my lungs, fighting against the heavy weight that was pinning my chest down. I was still pain blind and disoriented as I struggled to throw the weight off my chest. Suddenly the weight was lifted and I could breathe.

I blinked, saw a bright light which then faded.

Yellow sky. I was lying on sand.

The burning pain subsided, but the ache in my chest was constant.

I heard the sound of familiar beeping, raised my head and saw it was emanating from an emergency cell regenerator whose thick needle was stuck deep into my vessel's chest. Slowly I brought my hand and grasped the shaft. My fingers did not possess full sensation but I managed to grasp the cell regenerator, press the eject button, and yank it out of my chest on the second try. There was still just enough power in it to seal the hole in my skin as the large needle was pulled out. My head and arms flopped back to the sand. All I wanted to do was close my eyes and stay still, but I knew I had to move soon. I was not alone.

After a while I rolled to the side and saw a soldier's decapitated body lying a few paces away from me. Blood was just beginning to congeal on the sand around a familiar-looking medibag. When I moved my head again, I saw a second body lying a little farther away, next to an upturned hoverbike. Squatting next to it, waiting patiently, was the Lizard.

I don't remember how I got up into a sitting position. It could have been that the Lizard helped me; he was certainly squatting close enough for me to smell the stench of blood dripping from his claws. I stretched my arm and managed to pull the medibag towards me, rummaged through it and swallowed, smeared, and stuck on my skin every pill, salve, and rejuvenation pad that was in there while trying to put my thoughts in order. I was still blanked out of any useful thoughts, but I realised I needed to physically move if for no other reason than to accelerate the vessel's healing process and avoid fainting in the desert.

I slowly got up and, barely staying on my feet, limped to the power rifle, squatted next to it, then lifted it from the sand and checked the clip. It was full. All I wanted to do right then was to curl up in a ball and close my eyes. Instead, I looked up and saw we were almost under the tracks of the air train. The station was a few hundred paces away plus a short climb up. Only when I turned around and examined the battle scene did I realise the Lizard had hit the soldiers like the wrath of God. What made him do it or how it knew to use the cell accelerator was beyond me, but I had a strong suspicion it had something to do with Emilija. He watched me with quiet interest as I picked up the helmet and shook the severed head out of it. Most of the blood and gore was on the outside. The combat armour was harder to retrieve, but I had two bodies, so I could mix and match until I was fully clad. I used the sand to wipe away the most visible bloodstains, and I was sure that with the battle helmet on I could pass as a soldier to the casual observer.

Now what?

I looked back at the Lizard. "You saved my life," I said, grimacing at the pain my short speech was causing. "I guess a thank-you is in order."

He tilted his head sideways as if considering my words, or perhaps he was graciously accepting my thanks.

Now what?

The old world was dead, or at least close enough to it. I'd been betrayed by the very same people who brought me back from the dark void. I should have felt anger, but I was actually relieved. I owed no allegiance to anyone anymore. In a way, I was free. Did it really matter what caused the war? How would that change anything, and why should I care anymore which side would eventually win?

Now what?

With the exception of a hulking beast, I was dead to everyone.

I could just walk away and live the rest of my short life in relative peace. I would be the pawn who managed to escape the game board for once. Or . . . I could walk back into the air train station, find out the whole story, and try and help set things right. Not for the sake of Tarakan, not for humanity, but for myself.

Choose wisely, even after death. God damn it, did that Nakamura oracle really know this was going to happen?

I looked back at the Lizard. Would he let me walk away? Would I let myself?

I was still unsure what I wanted to do as I turned the hoverbike, mounted it, and began driving towards the air train station.

70

Twinkle Eyes

They were prudent enough not to put us in a normal cell. Instead, each of us was tied to an uncomfortably hard bed, something between a field med bed and a stretcher. We were then leaned to a near-standing position against the three walls of the room, and our beds were chained to the wall. Power cables stretching from the centre of the cell to each of our neck braces kept all of us immobilised from the neck down. With only a single light in the room, casting shadows everywhere, the only thing missing was a proper torture rack. And somehow, I was sure it was nearby, just waiting for the moment when Emilija realised what she'd signed up for.

Then we were left alone for hours, interrupted only by the periodic checkup of our bored cell guards. One of them would step in to check our bindings while the other covered him with a power rifle from behind the locked gate. Galinak was placed against the wall in front of me and I spent a large chunk of my time watching his face contort with effort in mesmerizingly different ways as he tried to move, until he finally gave up.

"No use," he conceded. "We're done and rusted."

"You know," I said, "they may have made you into a goddamned killing machine, but you ain't so handsome."

It brought out a chuckle from the old warrior, and even a smile from Vincha, which really was what I was aiming for.

"I have a question for you, Vincha." I tried to carry on the momentum of the conversation.

"You always have a question, Twinkle Eyes. You seem to never run out of them."

"Or run out of enemies trying to kill us," Galinak remarked. "You definitely keep my skills from rusting."

"Nevertheless, since we are all a bit tied up at the moment—" I waited for a chuckle, which never materialised "—I thought I might use the time to figure things out."

Vincha rolled her eyes. "You make me wish they'd get on with the torturing bit. Go on, then. Ask."

It occurred to me then that Vincha was in a strange situation, where being tortured meant her daughter was resisting the procedure. For her, torture would definitely have a silver lining. I tried to push that thought out of my head. I wanted to keep Vincha talking and not thinking about Emilija, or our own fate for that matter.

"When you uploaded us in the City Within the Mountain, how did it feel when you channelled us through your head?"

"*That* is your question?" Vincha's voice was full of disbelief.

"Yes. I always meant to ask, but with all the fighting and the shooting and being suspended upside down half a mile in the air while driving at breakneck speed, I never got the chance."

"You're strange, Twinkle Eyes. I mean disturbingly strange."

"Yeah," Galinak agreed. "He's like an annoying little weird pet you can never bring yourself to get rid of."

"Or a skin rash."

"More of an itch, really, the kind you can't really reach, but inside your brain."

I ignored them both and pressed on. "Think about it. Our full consciousness passed through your head and onto another location while our bodies were being torn to pieces."

"Bukra's balls, that's a jolly thought," Galinak muttered. "Especially since any moment now our current and only bodies will be cut up to piec—"

"I mean it's interesting, that's all." I raised my voice.

"Well," Vincha said slowly, "it's hard to explain to someone who is not a CommTroll. Your entire being was reduced to a series of signals, and they weren't pretty ones. They had"—she concentrated—"a strong *resonance* to them, that's the right word for it. I wouldn't have been able to do it with any other gear, and even with the Tarakan augs it isn't an experience I want to go through ever again. You could say it felt as if a ghost was passing through me. Left me with a big, rusting headache for days." Vincha's lips twitched at me in a tiny smile as she added, "And an unexplained desire to ask silly questions in awkward moments."

"Oooh, she's got you now, Twinkle Eyes." Galinak chuckled in the shadows.

It was a crazy moment. All three of us, bound and about to be murdered, having a joke and laughing it off.

"Got any more of those nourishment pills you've been hiding inside your belt, Twinkle Eyes?" Galinak winked at me. "I think I am finally getting hungry."

"I could use a drink myself," I answered, trying to hide my blush, but it was also true. My mouth was dry. I wondered if they would bother to feed us before we were tortured and killed.

There was a bout of awkward silence which Galinak finally interrupted. "I am sorry, Vinch." His tone was uncharacteristically soft. "For failing you."

I turned my head to her. She was already done silently crying to herself and was now resigned to the awful truth. "Galinak," she answered, not looking at him, "perhaps this is the wrong time to say it, but I simply hate that nickname you are trying to give me."

"Fair enough." Galinak rolled his eyes at me, then added, "V?"

"Not even close." Vincha shook her head lightly. "And if it makes you feel any better, my plan was to free my girl, then shoot you both in the knees and make for the exit."

"Shoot us in the knees instead of our heads?" Galinak smiled broadly. "Aww, now that's love, V."

"You're both idiots for trying to raise my spirits," Vincha said, but her eyes shone in the gloom.

I quickly changed the subject. "What was this thing with the woman?" I asked. "I mean, the way they were talking, she seemed to be the brains behind capturing us."

"You actually listened to their conversation?" Galinak said. "I was just trying to spit the sand out of my mouth."

"Whoever she was. She was shot dead," Vincha interrupted. "I heard the soldiers talking. They threw her body into the Broken Sands. Guess it was a sort of a Salvationist burial."

A sudden loud explosion shook our cell, and the weak lights in the room winked off.

My eyes adjusted immediately to the darkness. I heard the cell guard exclaim, "What's going on?" and the other one answered, "The generator probably blew up again."

"Galinak," I whispered softly.

"Yes, Twinkle Eyes?"

"If the generator is blown, that means the power to our neck braces is gone. I can feel my legs."

"Good thinking." Galinak grunted with effort and broke an arm free, tearing part of the bindings in the process.

"Try to be quiet," I whispered. "The guards still have weapons."

"Get that rusting metal off my head," Vincha whispered from her side of the room.

And suddenly the world outside erupted with sounds of shooting and several bloodcurdling screams.

"Balls to that." Galinak tore through the rest of his bindings.

"That's not the bloody generator," one of the guards shouted. I heard his boots running and doors slamming.

"Can you see anything?" Vincha shouted at me as the sound of battle increased. Galinak was at my side, breaking me free.

I concentrated on the nearest wall. "No, it's too far away and there are too many walls for me to see, but I think it might be the cavalry."

"No one knows we're here." Galinak was moving to Vincha when we heard the door at the end of the corridor opening again. Through the closer wall I saw the two guards enter the corridor. One of them ran towards our cell while the other one kept shooting at someone outside. There was a sudden blurry movement, and that guard was lifted off his feet and slammed so hard against the wall, his broken body created a groove in the stone and stayed upright. After a few seconds, he crashed to the floor.

"Guys. I think it's the wrong kind of cavalry," I said, but the two were too busy getting free to be paying attention to me.

Galinak was moving towards the cell door when the guard appeared on the other side of it. He pointed his rifle straight at Galinak, blinding him with the rifle's scope light. "Stop right there," he shouted, then his head jerked sideways as it exploded inside his helmet. He toppled to his side, the power rifle dropping under him.

Galinak moved forward. I wasn't sure if he wanted to go through the cell door first or reach out from between the bars and try and grab the power rifle first. Whatever his intention was, we all froze as a monster stepped in front of us. There wasn't much light to see it properly, but what we saw was enough.

I was the first to speak.

"Galinak?"

"Yeah, I see it," Galinak answered, looking up at the hulking creature.

Vincha articulated my thoughts: "Rust, that is one big rusting Lizard."

"Galinak?" I said.

"Yeah, I can take it." Galinak looked down at the claws dripping blood and gore, and added, "I think."

Another guard stepped between the Lizard and the cell door, dressed in full battle gear, a power sword strapped to its back. The guard hefted the power rifle and waved the key rod in front of the lock. It beeped and the door slid open. I never thought I'd feel regret at seeing a cell door open while I was inside it, but there it was, that moment. All three of us took a step back, slightly spreading out from each other as the guard stepped in. She unfastened and removed her battle helmet.

"Oh," I said weakly, "it's you."

The woman threw the power rifle at Vincha, who caught it.

"You're the girl's mother?" she asked.

Vincha nodded, too shocked to speak.

"You can call me Peach. Emilija is not here—I looked everywhere. There were only a few guards, and all the vehicles are gone. The base is practically deserted."

She turned and fished my peacemaker out from the back of her belt, handing it to me butt first. "Found this when I passed through the armoury, very distinct weapon. Thought you might want it back."

"Oooh, what did I get?" Galinak clapped his hands excitedly, his tone of voice a perfect imitation of a thrilled child.

The woman turned her head. "You? I thought you just pick people up and use them as clubs, but there's plenty of gear lying around. Better pick up some armour and ammo while you're at it."

"I saw you die," I said, the peacemaker firmly in my hand, pointed at the ground.

"Yeah, that's too long to explain right now." The woman jerked her thumb at the creature behind her. "Same thing about Greenskin behind me, too long of a story. The short version: it saved my life and now it saved yours, so consider *it* to be on our side, and thank God for that." She turned back to Vincha. "As I said, your daughter is not here. I don't know what exactly Mannes was planning to do, but he told me she was the only Puzzler he needed." She paused for breath, then said, "There's only one logical place that he could have taken her."

"I'll go to the end of the world to find my Emilija." Vincha checked that the power rifle's clip was in place.

"Good." The strange woman named Peach turned and refastened her battle helmet, raising her visor so we could hear her say, "Because they are no longer in this world. Mannes took her up the Star Pillar."

71

Twinkle Eyes

There was no time to for a proper introduction, just first names and casual nods as we carefully walked out of the cell block. It was already dark, and the base was indeed deserted, and those who stayed behind were either dead or hiding among the bloody carnage the woman named Peach and the hulking monster had left behind.

We gathered provisions and face masks from the fallen soldiers, and I even picked up a long-range sniper rifle and several clips. The infirmary proved to be a treasure trove, and besides a pocketful of nourishment pills I got enough medicine in me to make me forget about the pains my poor body had endured. Then we boarded the oil truck Peach had used to pass the guarded gates and gained access to the base. The gate was still whole, so I guessed Peach did not just ram through it but used subterfuge until her cover was blown. Despite her small size, she took the driver's seat, and the rest of us sat too close for comfort in the small cabin. Thankfully, the giant Lizard stayed outside the vehicle, alternating between running on all fours alongside the slow-moving truck or taking rests on top of it. Every time I glimpsed the creature I felt myself tense up, and I saw the same reaction in the others, with Peach being a notable exception.

I was settling into my seat and my own thoughts when Peach slowed to a stop and turned off the floodlights.

Vincha broke the silence. "What are you doing? We ain't there yet."

Peach opened the door and was climbing down as she answered, "I appreciate that time is of the essence, but charging into a bunch of enemy soldiers driving a truck full of petrol does not sound like a sound plan to me. We'll walk the rest of the way and try to sneak in with minimum fuss." She slammed the door and we all shuffled out through the passenger door.

We walked and eventually crawled the rest of the way to the mountain, where a formidable army base marked the entrance. There was not much chance for us to use the cover of darkness. I couldn't help but look up to the sky every so often. The Star Pillar's surrounding aura, what Peach called a "protective field," was continually changing colors. Occasionally it lit up the entire area with bright red, yellow, or white light. I did not know if this was an intentional effect or some kind of a phenomenon, but it made the whole experience seem like a nightmarish dream.

When I was travelling with Vincha and Galinak I was excited just to see the wonder that is the Star Pillar from the outside. Even as I crawled through dirt, the thought that I would actually travel up to the top of it filled me with awe and excitement, but also trepidation. If my time in the shark had taught me something, it was that man was born to walk the Earth, not take to the skies.

"This ain't a sightseeing tour, Twinkle Eyes." Vincha cuffed my head when I stalled again. "Stop looking up and use your twinkles to scout ahead."

"Yeah, sorry," I said sheepishly, blushing, but I couldn't help myself.

We eventually reached a small rise and found ourselves a few hundred paces from the entrance to the mountain. The forces that secured the place had done everything right, with dug-in, fortified positions, two guard towers, several light machine guns, and a patrol. But they did not expect trouble, and certainly not the kind of trouble that was the five of us working in harmony.

Vincha hacked through the gate controls and messed with the soldiers' communications, confusing the guards with orders, so that the two machine gun positions actually shot at each other. I did my best at sniping with my new toy, although being constantly on the move meant I did not manage to hit much. Once we passed the entrance to the base, Galinak did what he did best, and that was kill efficiently. He was matched only by Peach, who shot with a power pistol in one hand and hacked with a power sword in the other. The Lizard, well, I will be trying to forget what that creature did for the rest of my life. Our foes fought bravely, but the poor bastards did not stand a chance.

"That's strange," Peach said when it was over, casually wiping blood off her visor. "I saw the amount of guards he had with him in the base, and those trucks mean they are all supposed to be here. There should have been a lot more guards here, that's for sure, and I was expecting an auxiliary force once we came in loud. Something's not right about all of this."

"Maybe he took them all up to . . ." With the excitement of the moment I forgot the name of what was on top of the Star Pillar, so I just pointed up.

"Doesn't make sense to bring so many soldiers with whoever was working in the laboratory at the base up to the hub unless Mannes was planning something—" Peach hesitated again, as if a thought crossed her mind "—something very big." She was already marching away by the time her words reached our ears.

We hurried after Peach, weapons ready, through empty halls, narrow corridors, and deserted checkpoints. As we walked through a wider corridor I was startled to the point of shooting at the wall when the smiling face of a woman appeared on it.

"Tarakan welcomes you to your new journey, the greatest adventure of your life." She opened her arms wide and out of nowhere, beautiful music began to play. Her ever-smiling face followed us as we walked on. The view behind her changed constantly into different locations, each more breathtaking than the one before.

"You might have visited many places on our beautiful planet," the woman on the wall continued, "but we guarantee this will be a unique experience that you will cherish for the rest of your lives."

"You can say *that* again," Galinak muttered under his breath.

The smiling face disappeared and was replaced with an intense image of a large, round, blue disc partly covered in white and grey patches.

"Our Earth," the woman's voice announced, "as seen from the viewing hall of the space hub."

"Bukra's balls," I heard myself swear, "and I just recently discovered I really don't like heights."

The image of the woman kept on following us. "The Hub is connected to the top of the Star Pillar and was designed and built by the greatest minds of Tarakan. Through the Pillar and the Hub, people and materials can easily be transported from Earth to space without the need for expensive and environmentally polluting delivery systems." An image of a large tube flying in the sky appeared on the wall beside me. There was a long, thick line of flame and black smoke coming out of its rear. "Both the Pillar and the Hub were built in less than a decade"—the woman's smiling face appeared again—"using unique technologies, scientific breakthroughs, and more than three thousand new patents developed specifically for this project. The moon hotel and resort opened just five years later, and it attracts several thousand lucky visitors per year as well as scientists from every field of study. Conducting experiments in zero G helped many of our best minds reach breakthrough discoveries that will make our world a better place. If you want to know more about this new wonder of the world, please dial your comms to channel seven-seven-six-seven to receive our info bundle straight to your devices in the language of your choosing, free of charge."

"We're almost there," Peach said as we were reaching the end of the corridor, but the ever-smiling image of the woman was relentless.

"Follow the path of the famous moon walkers of the past. Take one small step for man, and a giant leap for mankind. Experience the freedom of weightlessness and see for yourself what Tarakan has accomplished on our path to explore the rest of the universe. We wish you a safe and happy ascension."

The woman disappeared from the wall as we reached the end of the corridor but reappeared in front of us as we entered an impressively vast, round hall. There was an elevated dais in the middle of it and at least two dozen metal doors in the surrounding wall, each numbered.

"Welcome to the ascension hall," the woman said. "This is the last waiting area before you take the journey up to the Space Hub. Please wait here until the elevator number you've been assigned is called out. A message will also be sent to your personal communication receivers in the language of your choice. Please note that from this point onwards, food and drinks can be consumed only in pill form." Peach simply passed through the woman's image as it hovered above us, and we moved towards the central dais.

We passed comfortable-looking chairs and tables cleverly spread around the hall and even a children's playground section with strange, semitransparent bubbles of various shapes and sizes floating around it. The round dais had a glass wall around it, but the small side door slid open once Peach tapped something into the keypad next to it.

She pointed at me. "You, come with me. Cover my back. The rest of you stay alert just in case we have trouble."

If the others had a problem with that plan, or even taking orders from Peach, they did not voice it. I followed her past the door and climbed the few steps onto the dais. As soon as we walked in, our surroundings came into life and several screens appeared in midair. Peach tapped one of them and a keypad appeared in front of her. Her hands moved around the air, quickly touching the transparent keys. "I am going to bring down an elevator for us," she said, anticipating my question. "All of the normal elevators are spread out around the shaft. Mannes had them locked in place, but there are emergency elevators positioned every few miles of the shaft. Those are not connected to the mainframe. We'll have to change from one elevator to another, but that might not be a bad thing."

"How come you know, or can do"—I spread my hands wide—"all of this?"

It was the first time she looked straight at me, before turning her attention back to the screens. "I used to be a high-ranking security officer in Tarakan. My personal code can unlock many doors."

"But Mannes found out about it when you captured us, wouldn't he have changed the . . . oh." I realised it as I was talking. "He thinks you're dead."

"Exactly, and he has a lot on his mind right now, so I am hoping that he didn't close that loophole."

"And if he did? This Mannes comes across as a thorough kind of guy."

"Then we take the stairs," she said, then added, "That's a joke."

There was a soft ping, and a green light began flashing above one of the surrounding doors. The woman from the wall appeared again. "This is an emergency elevator for Tarakan personnel only. Please do not attempt to board it. Boarding an emergency elevator without a permit is a serious, class C offence." The woman repeated the sentence several times, even after we left the dais and approached the indicated door.

I looked at all of them, thinking what a weird bunch of freaks we all were. The Salvo-novels of my youth never told stories such as these. They were mostly about duty and adventure, and getting the loot and sometimes, most of the time, a girl, too. The battles were always glorious, exciting, fun. I was about to take a lift off of this planet, an exciting, Salvo-novel-style adventure, but I knew that this was going to be anything but fun.

The doors slid open to a small, rectangular room with a row of seats molded against the outer walls. Peach stepped in first, weapon drawn, then, satisfied, she turned around.

"Get in, take a seat, and make sure your weapons are secured." I walked into the elevator as Peach pointed downwards. "Underneath your seat you'll find a pair of white boots. You have some time to change into them, but I suggest you do it by the time we leave the atmosphere. Don't worry about the fit; the boots will mold themselves to you." She glanced up as the Lizard passed her. "Well, most of you."

To my surprise and unease, the Lizard walked in and sat itself next to me. I looked up, my head barely reaching its shoulder. It looked down. Our eyes met. The last time I stared deeply into a Lizard's eyes it launched itself at me and I shot it in the face. This time I just nodded. It nodded back and turned its head to look at Peach. And that simple gesture was all it took. It was not a mindless beast anymore—*he* was just another part of this very strange team.

Vincha was still standing outside, and Peach turned to her. "What is it?"

I saw the CommTroll hesitate for the first in a very long time. "It's just . . . Emilija told me . . . she whispered in my ear . . . 'Don't come up, or you will never come down.'"

"Sure, you'll be coming back down, Vinch," Galinak said, "both of you. Ain't sure how yet, is all."

"She was just trying to protect you," I reasoned.

"Does it really matter what she told you?" Peach said. "I've known you only for a short time, but you don't strike me as a woman who takes no for an answer. And besides"—she shook her head—"I am getting a bit tired of all of those stupid premonitions, aren't you?"

For some reason we all turned and looked at the Lizard. It hissed and made a motion that could have been an attempt to shrug.

"Rust, this is all just too weird." Vincha stepped into the cabin and sat next to Galinak.

As Peach began fiddling with the controls, Vincha leaned sideways and rested her head on the Troll's shoulder.

"Just like good old times, eh, G?" she mumbled, closing her eyes.

Galinak patted her head gently, smiling to himself. "Yeah, V, just like the good old times." He was smiling as the doors slid shut.

72

Twinkle Eyes

We were fighting waves of drones from the moment we stepped out of the emergency elevator into the Hub, so it was just a matter of time before one of us made a mistake.

It goes without saying that this "one of us" was me.

I did not see the last drone until it was too late.

"Galinak, duck," Vincha shouted. The Troll managed to roll, his body disappearing behind a bunch of instruments. Vincha and I shot at the drone, but the damned thing was incredibly fast. My ray gun did not connect to my retina. I dropped it, and it floated down gently as I raised my peacemaker and shot the drone, not thinking about Peach's warning against using that type of firearm in space. The drone exploded above Galinak's head, its pieces slowly spreading around the room, but not before it shot a load of rays downwards. I instinctively knew Galinak was hit and my eyes told me so, even as Vincha ran to where he lay. Peach grabbed me from behind as I passed her.

"Fool," she admonished me. "I told you to only use the ray gun. A bullet zipping through the Hub could kill us all."

I shrugged her off. She was right, of course, but this was Galinak, *my* Galinak, lying motionless on the ground, his eyes wide open. I bent down next to Vincha, who was frantically looking for damage on his body, mumbling, "Where the rust is it?"

Peach hovered above us a moment later. "Is he dead?" Her tone was cold, matter-of-fact, emotionless, like a veteran army officer. I checked his pulse, then looked up at her. "No," I said, relief washing over me like a warm shower. "He was hit by a stun ray."

As if on cue Galinak blinked and gasped for air.

"You rusting lucky bastard." Vincha shook her head and banged her fists lightly on the old warrior's chest. "I was sure I'd find you charred like a Dorgmahr steak."

She helped bring Galinak slowly to a sitting position, and suddenly threw her hands around his shoulder in a clumsy hug. "You are a rusty old Troll," she said.

Getting hit by a stun ray was not a nice experience, I knew it firsthand from when I was shot in the City of Towers, but it was far better than being hit by any of the alternatives.

Peach picked up the main part of the destroyed drone. "That is strange indeed." She turned it over several times "This is the Hub's defence drone. It should have killed you, but it used a stun ray instead."

Galinak managed a grin. "Yeah, guess it's my lucky day in space."

For once, Peach was the one looking confused. "The entire time we were fighting the drones, they were using stun rays. And why send waves of them instead of one big assault that would overwhelm us? And where are the human soldiers? The doors are locked but we are just passing them manually. Mannes is surely aware that we are here, and the Hub has a few more defence protocols against intruders. This doesn't make any sense at all."

"It's like he's not trying to kill us," I said, "just slow us down."

A small but sudden shake accentuated the end of my sentence.

"Bukra's balls." Galinak grabbed the edge of a machine to steady himself. "Tell me it was just me."

"No, we all felt it. Watch my back." Peach leaned over one of the screens and tapped furiously, but after a moment she shook her head. "Locked out, but the energy expenditure level is at 130 percent, which means a third septimum engine has been fired up."

We all looked at her.

"The Hub has four engines," she explained. "Two are constantly working to create a functional low gravity, power the protective force field around the shaft, and stabilize the Hub as it spins around the Earth on top of the Star Pillar. The other two engines were built for emergency use or . . ." Her brow furrowed, then her head snapped up, eyes wide. "Whatever he is planning to do, we have to get to Mannes and stop him."

Galinak tried to step forward too soon, and it was only Vincha's quick reaction that stopped him from falling to the floor. "That was . . . unexpected." He waved his hand at us. "Go, scan ahead, I'll be fine in a few moments."

Vincha got under his arm while the three of us moved ahead. A few doors down got us to a long hall, filled with human-sized glass and metal tubes, each containing a person in it. The bodies were totally naked but for masks on their mouths and noses, and they were constantly turning in blue liquid.

"Well, at least that's one question answered," I said after peering inside. "We now know why all the guards disappeared. I recognise this woman from the truck ride." I looked into a few more tubes just to be sure. Each had a set of dials with constantly changing green numbers, flashing on a small screen. There were at least two hundred soldiers rotating in liquid. The sheer number of them ruled out the idea that they were all coerced to step into these strange tubes. These people went into the tubes voluntarily. I stood next to Peach, who was staring at one particular tube.

"Someone you know?" I asked.

She pointed. "This is Sergiu the Dying, the man who shot me."

"That's a surprisingly apt name. Are you sure it's him? He's hard to recognise, with the nose and mouth covers and without that weird hat."

She glanced at me briefly, "Not a face I would soon forget under any circumstances, believe me."

Vincha and Galinak were just coming into the room while the Lizard stoically stood among us four.

"He did not want to shoot me, you know." Peach aimed her gun at the turning body. "He was just following orders. I used to be exactly like him, duty bound to follow without questioning what my actions might do to others, so I can't really blame him for doing what I would have done. The world is a very bad place because of people like us. What's left of it . . ."

"Are you going to kill him?" I asked carefully.

Peach lowered her gun. "He's in cryo." She sighed. "His mind is somewhere else. He won't feel fear, or pain. They might find another vessel for him to come back in. Kind of takes the edge off revenge, don't you think? So no, I won't shoot him now, but I might be here when he wakes up. Good-bye, Sergiu."

She turned and walked away, and we followed her, gathering around the locked door leading to the next room.

I used my sight to scan what was behind the door as Peach worked the manual override and Galinak and the Lizard pushed the heavy door. By the time the door was open I knew what to expect inside.

"Well?" Peach looked at me as she readied her power gun.

It was a stupid thing to say, but it was the only thing I could think of. "Vincha," I said softly, "you . . . you'd better stay here."

"What? Why?"

My guess was that she already knew what was waiting for her by the tone of my voice.

"I'm sorry, Vincha . . ."

Vincha shoved me out of the way and I watched her storm into the next room. Galinak and the rest followed her, but I stayed back a little longer, hoping that I was wrong, that my eyes, for once, had betrayed me. I heard Vincha cry her daughter's name, first in fear, then again, in the kind of agony that can only come out of the mouth of a mother facing the lifeless body of her child.

73

Twinkle Eyes

By the time I gathered the nerve to enter the room, they had found a way to open the glass cocoon. The room was quite large but cluttered with floating screens and a large amount of alien-looking machinery. I did not pay any attention to any of it. Emilija's corpse was lying inside the open glass case and Vincha was bent over her with Galinak at her side. I wanted to reach Vincha's side, although I had no idea what I was to say or do once I stood next to her.

As I approached the cocoon, I saw the Lizard standing on the other side of it, his head bent low. I was no expert on Lizard body language, but it looked to me as stricken as the rest of us.

I had chased Vincha's shadow for years and used every trick to manipulate and interrogate her. I heard how Vincha unplugged herself and overcame terrible Skint addiction, how she faced Nakamura and lost Bayne inside the City Within the Mountain. We had fought shoulder to shoulder, but she had also physically assaulted me and pointed weapons at my head more times than

I wished to remember. I even saw Vincha break to pieces under interrogation before getting up again and carrying on. There were stronger Trolls and better fighters than Vincha, but I'd swear that she was the hardest, toughest warrior I'd ever met. Yet seeing Vincha's face as she gently caressed her dead daughter's face, I knew she was shattered in a way that would never let her be whole again.

Emilija's eyes were shut, and I wished I could say that she looked peaceful, but she just looked like a dead young woman. The tattoos on her arms and neck were surprisingly faded but there were also ugly deep red markings on her temples and forehead and some crusted blood under her nose.

I don't know how many times I opened my mouth to say something just to close it again without uttering a word.

We just stood there, silent, until the Hub shuddered again.

"That's the fourth septimum engine," Peach said. "We are very close to the command hall. I am going in there now to stop whatever Mannes is planning to do. With or without you."

I thought Vincha would ask for more time or be so lost in her grief that she would simply ignore what was said. I didn't expect her to straighten up and walk away without looking back as the glass cocoon closed over the body of Emilija.

She walked towards Peach and simply said, "I decide when and how to kill him."

Peach opened her mouth to say something but must have thought better of it and just nodded.

We gathered in front of the door but this time it proved a more difficult task. So close to the command hall, the manual override to the heavy door was password locked even beyond Peach's capabilities, and no amount of strength from the Lizard or Galinak could move it.

We stood there, twiddling our thumbs, when Vincha's red hair suddenly shot up in all directions, twitching as she spoke over all the channels. We heard her over our personal Comms, but her voice also resonated in the entire Hub.

"I am coming for you, Mannes," she said in a chillingly calm tone. "You can hide behind this door like the coward you are, but I will find you, so—"

The heavy door suddenly slid open.

We looked at each other, aware of the implications of what had just happened.

"An invitation?" I asked.

"A trap." Peach, weapon at ready, peered quickly around the door.

"Who gives a rusty rod?" Vincha stepped through the door, guns in hands, and we all followed her.

A moment later we were walking through another corridor with our weapons drawn and ready, but nothing happened. No drones assaulted us, and the doors just kept opening all the way to the command hall. It was a vast, rectangular room with high windows looking out to space, empty of people but for Mannes, who was sitting in the centre of it, calmly watching us enter. The Earth was just coming into view as the Hub circled around itself when Peach approached him. "Power down the two engines, right now," she comanded.

"Nice to see you again, Colonel Major Vera Geer," Mannes answered calmly. "I admit I regretted ordering Sergiu to have you killed, but at the time I could not afford loose ends."

Peach trained her weapon at the sitting Mannes and kept a safe distance, but Vincha simply walked straight towards the ghoul, gun raised. She stopped when the barrel was an inch from his wrinkled forehead.

"I'd promised to kill you slowly," she said, the power gun shaking in her hand, "but I'm not sure I can control myself now. Do as she says."

Mannes turned his head and looked up to her, completely unfazed. "You can pull the trigger," he said quietly. "I have lived for far too long as it is. But the engines cannot be shut down." Hearing this, Peach began moving from screen to screen. "Your code won't work anymore," Mannes said without breaking eye contact with Vincha. "I purged it from the system when I realised you somehow survived. Sergiu has always been a thorough kind of guy—you should tell me one day how you managed to do that."

"I told you what I would do to you if you harmed her." Vincha's voice was tight and in control. "And I intend to find new ways to make you scream for mercy every rusting moment of the rest of your life."

"I know," Mannes said. "I lost my daughter, too, a long time ago, and every day since is a new lesson in pain. Emilija is gone, Vincha, but I am the only one who can bring her back."

Vincha pressed the barrel of her gun into Mannes's forehead. "You lie," she snarled.

"No, he is not lying." The new voice made all of us spin around, but the screens around us were filled by the face of a young man with dark skin and long, braided hair.

"Is it done?" Mannes asked from his chair, his voice suddenly filled with barely held emotion.

The image of the young man nodded. "It is done, Dr. Holtz. We took everyone we could before Adam managed to close the gap. Two thousand nine hundred and twenty-seven minds are now safely stored in the Hub. The best scientists, doctors, architects, artists, philosophers, composers, and free thinkers Tarakan has to offer."

"That's not everyone," Mannes said softly. "I was hoping for more."

"It's about a third of the minds Adam had. You'll be happy to know that Dr. Tamir and Dr. Gustav are among those we managed to pull out. I am sure they will be a great help as soon as we restore them back to consciousness."

I saw Mannes take a long, steadying breath. "And Deborah, is her pattern still intact?"

The man smiled. "Yes, Dr. Holtz, but it will take some time and careful effort for her mind to be reconstructed. I must say your new program is brilliant, but we will need a little time to make it better before we separate Deborah from my own consciousness. If you want I can show you—"

"No." Mannes straightened in his seat. "This is not the time. Proceed as planned."

"As you wish." The transparent screens suddenly spun around and some of them floated to the Lizard. "My my, is that what I think it is?"

A silvery ray briefly shone on the Lizard, who hissed and clawed at one of the screens, his sharp talons passing through the image.

"Jean Pierre. Goodness, is it really you?" The image spoke again, his voice filled with wonder and awe.

The Lizard hissed again, but shook his head, seemingly confused.

"Oh no, Jean Pierre. I am so sorry," the image said.

"Right." I stepped between the hovering screen and the confused-looking Lizard. "I'm sorry to stop this interesting reunion, but would you mind telling me what is going on here?"

Several more screens turned towards me. "Well, of course. I am the Sentient Program known as Cain, and you were probably sent here by Adam."

"My daughter, Emilija, is she inside you?" Vincha moved to Mannes's side, aiming her gun at his temple.

"Yes, she is part of the programming now." The image changed into Emilija's face, but she still talked in the man's tone of voice. "It will take some time to separate her consciousness from mine, it is still a process that needs to be done very carefully. We need to run simulations and right now—"

"You do that separation process, *right now,* and put her mind where it belongs, which is in her own body, or I'll shoot your wrinkled friend here in the head and destroy every rusting machine in this Hub."

The image turned back into that of a young man with long, plaited hair. "I have just been transferred to this Hub together with thousands of minds. It will take me a little time to adjust my programming to the new environment. I suggest you be patient, perhaps listen to what Dr. Holtz has to tell you. What he set in motion took dozens of years to accomplish. This must be a big day for you, Dr. Holtz."

I turned my head back to the central chair and saw that Mannes had covered his face with his gnarled hands. It was such an odd gesture, and it took me a few heartbeats to realise he was crying.

74

Mannes

A re you *really* going to meet him, Doctor Holtz?"

Mannes shook his head and, in the last moment, caught himself and suppressed a sigh. "Of course I am not going to *really* meet him, Daichi. We will converse via a grid channel."

The tall man was literally shaking with excitement. "That's meeting him, in my books. I don't care about shaking his hand." Daichi actually shoved his own hands into the pockets of the old-fashioned lab coat he insisted on wearing, to everyone's embarrassment. "I don't like touching people anyways." He added the last in Japanese in a soft mumble probably meant for himself, but Mannes's brain amp picked it up and translated the sentence.

Daichi reverted to English again. "But to meet the great man himself, the one who woke up Adam . . . I mean, wow."

Mannes shrugged, a gesture he hoped projected suave coolness, but in truth, he was almost as excited about meeting his old professor as Daichi was.

"I've never met him, you know," Daichi chattered on as they

stepped out of the elevator. "By the time I was in training we just watched old lectures or talked to his replica bot." He looked at Mannes. "But you got to work with the Professor himself. What was that like?"

Mannes chuckled softly as he scratched his greying beard. "Demanding, exciting, stressful, and sometimes downright horrid. But he is a genius, *the* genius of our generation, perhaps. The way he analyses and dissects the most complex of problems down to the most basic level is inspiring." Remembering Daichi's fragile spirit, Mannes finished the sentence with "But his replica bot could answer any question you might think of."

The look Daichi gave him was of cold impatience. "Yeah, yeah, but it's not *him*, the man who awoke Adam. *Shinjirarenai*, incredible."

Mannes sympathized with Daichi's frustration. Professor Vitor was a legend in Tarakan, not only for being in the room when Adam gained full consciousness. He was the one who nurtured him from AI infancy to SP maturity and averted several disasters in the making, writing new rules after breaking his fair share of the old ones. Professor Vitor was also the first Tarkanian to upload himself into Adam, insisting that he should take the risk of dying in agony for the future of the human race. After the successful uploading, Professor Vitor continued his work improving Adam and even gave annual lectures in all seven Tarakan Universities and Colleges. When other uploaders slowly withdrew from the outside world, the Professor kept a close contact, appearing in the media and of course, at every maintenance meeting.

Mannes was just beginning his second doctorate in advanced program engineering at the Tarakan Technology Institute when he was called to replace an engineer who suffered a minor but debilitating sports injury. He never completed the second doctorate, but he got to work with his teacher and idol for four of the most interesting years of his life. Yet even someone as strong willed as the Professor slowly succumbed to the pull, for when you could simply be a god of your own realm, the world of men became less interesting. His public meetings began to dwindle; he cancelled all the annual press appointments and often sent his replica bot for lectures. The only time Professor Vitor would show himself in public anymore was at the yearly maintenance and evaluation review, and every time, the Professor always acknowledged Mannes by name, even when he was sitting in the far corner of the outside table. Mannes suspected this acknowledgement was one of the reasons for his rapid advancement to the main table, where he now occupied one of the six main seats.

"So, he just contacted you out of the blue?" Daichi's question brought Mannes back from his reminiscing.

"Yes, through my private channel. He actually left me a message asking for a meeting regarding this year's maintenance and evaluation meeting."

"Strange." Daichi tilted his head, a sure sign he was internally checking the schedule. "The M&E is four months and six days away. That's a long time in advance for notes."

Mannes shrugged, but the question has been in the back of his mind, too. "Maybe there's an issue that needs to be resolved immediately."

"You know the protocols for an emergency maintenance." Daichi's tone was somewhere between a kind reminder and an admonishment. "That would involve the whole department, a hundred people getting an immediate stop-and-assist notice, not a private chat."

Mannes stopped at a junction. Although he'd promised himself he would walk the entire way he was getting tired from the hike and, frankly, tired of Daichi as well, so he silently called for a travel disc. At the corner of his eye, a countdown of thirty-four seconds began, enough for Daichi to get in a few more questions.

"We part here, Daichi. My office is that way," he said, even though Daichi knew exactly where Mannes's office was.

Daichi looked at Mannes. "Are you sure you don't need me there? To take notes? I'll be completely quiet."

No you won't, Mannes thought but he just shook his head and said, "Sorry, the Professor asked for a private audience with a higher security-clearance level than yours."

"Higher than my own security clearance?" Daichi gave Mannes an irritated look. "I coded Adam's inner systems. Fuck, you could say I wipe his virtual ass every day. What's higher than my security clearance?"

The travel disc arrived and hovered near Mannes; he stepped on it saying, "*My* security clearance. Sorry, Daichi, maybe next time."

With Mannes's hand gesture, the travel disc accelerated away in a higher than polite speed. Daichi called in an escalating crescendo, "Tell the Professor his essay regarding recoding the SYTA matrix to elevate subatomic performance is an inspiration, but I have two points of improvement—if he could grant me a short interview, I could demonstrate them." The end of the sentence travelled to Mannes's ear via the Comm system, since he had already turned the corner. A second later Daichi chimed in his ear, but Mannes rejected the call with a "call me later" return message.

With the assistance of the travel disc, Mannes arrived at his office earlier than planned, but he had to dismount and pass the security ward. It was beefed up even further than it had been three months previously, and the process was tedious. When he finally got through Mannes felt relieved, and he walked calmly to his spacious office.

Since his office knew Mannes was coming early, his favourite Beethoven quartet, Opus 18 Number 4, was already playing and his coffee was warm to the right degree. Waiting for his attention were 623 messages to review. Mannes assigned his personal bot to sort the messages for him and to answer the ones that did not need his urgent attention, and he stepped away to look out the windows to the valley below. From time to time he had to remind himself that this was not an actual window but a projection on a wall in an office built deep within the mountain range—but the images were real and represented, to the correct angle and temperature, the exact conditions outside. If he opened the window he would actually feel the hot breeze on his face.

Mannes had twenty minutes to spare, but he decided not to begin working until the interview with Professor Vitor was over. Instead he sat down, surrounded by an oval screen, sipped his coffee, and reviewed Deborah's school report card. She was good at everything. The fact simply amazed him every time, to the point where he once checked the school's overall curriculum to make sure they were not lowering the difficulty level. She spoke four languages already, her math and science levels were off the charts, and she loved horses and that obnoxious young singer whose name he could never remember without the aid of his brain amp—*Julious Love*—thank you very much.

Mannes got so absorbed in his daughter's school report that he jolted upright and spilled some coffee on his trousers when Professor Vitor chimed in.

"Damn, fuck."

"Well, that's the first time in a long while anyone greeted me that way." Professor Vitor's visage appeared on Mannes's oval screen.

"I'm sorry, Professor, I just spilled some c—"

"Relax, Mannes. Everything's cool." Professor Vitor smiled reassuringly. Based solely and unscientifically on Mannes's observation, uploaders tended to keep their last visage when communicating with the outer world, but not Professor Vitor. He'd reverted to his younger self, dreadlocks and all. He was probably enjoying the discomfort his appearance caused some of his living colleagues who had to converse with a tanned, surprisingly muscled, tanktop-wearing Vitor who nevertheless spoke with a heavy Oxfordian accent mixed with occasional phrases in slang that even Mannes knew were embarrassingly out of style. Every so often, Mannes had to remind himself that he was conversing with a legendary man who had set the bar for everyone to measure themselves against.

The table's smart material absorbed the coffee before it could do any damage to the electric devices, and Mannes's own clothes vaporised the few drops that had splashed onto his pants. Mannes composed himself quickly but was still feeling unsettled when the interview began. For all his relaxed demeanour, Professor Vitor did not linger on niceties. Mannes was bombarded with numbers and calculations regarding the upcoming M&E meeting. His brain amp took the brunt of the work, but the sheer volume of the data and Vitor's insistence on shifting subjects on a whim kept Mannes completely focused and at the edge of his cognitive ability. The next time he raised his head to Professor Vitor's image on the screen, two hours had passed.

"I think we're done here, Dr. Holtz. You've got the picture."

Mannes leaned back in his chair, feeling drained and exhausted. "Thank you, Professor. I just want to say one of my assistants, a brilliant guy named Dr. Daichi, asked me to tell you about—"

"—the calculations in my SYTA essay," Vitor cut in uncharacteristically. He was usually a patient man. "Yes, I know, he sent his notes to me, twice. A brilliant programmer, Dr. Holtz, nevertheless the error is still within the realm of his own calculations of the subatomic pulses. But we do not have time for this now."

Leaning slightly to one side, Mannes indicated to his chair to swivel slowly. The oval screen was filled with running programs and calculations. He turned back to Vitor. "There's more? I'm sorry, Professor, but I'll need to bring in my team for this."

Professor Vitor shook his head. "No, I want to speak to you about an entirely different matter."

Suddenly the wall depicting the outside world went dark. The lights blinked out, leaving Mannes in complete darkness but for the bluish hue of the oval screen. The programs and running calculations displayed on it froze instantly. Almost all the electric appliances, including the coffee machine, lost power. Mannes's brain amp registered the doors in the entire office triple-locking themselves shut. On instinct, he sent an internal security breach message, but it immediately bounced back at him. A firewall was blocking all communications.

Mannes took a deep breath and stopped himself from the natural progression of reactions he was supposed to go through.

Something was suddenly very wrong, but he was resolved to wait and see what Professor Vitor was up to.

"Good." The Professor nodded in appreciation. "You were always faster than the rest. I'm glad I erected the firewall first. Not many would have fired a distress call so quickly."

Mannes remained quiet.

"The reason I wanted to talk to you was not the M&E annual meeting, of course. My guess is that you suspected as much but gave your old professor the benefit of the doubt."

Mannes nodded. "That, and it has been a while since . . ." He tried to still his voice from shaking but did not complete the sentence.

Professor Vitor graced Mannes with a smile but it quickly faded as he continued. "I used this time to penetrate your security protocols. No, do not look so shocked, I have a vast computing power at my disposal here on the inside. Whoever is looking at us now, and rest assured, someone *is* looking, will see us slaving on my M&E suggestions for the next hour, so we haven't much time, Mannes. You must pay attention."

Like a schoolboy, Mannes found himself straightening to attention in his chair.

"When Adam was first created, we envisioned the betterment of Tarakan and with it mankind, and the benefits were nothing less than astonishing. Once Adam took control of our domestic agendas, Tarakan's GDP tripled itself in four years. He could really see the whole picture. From the world's commodity prices to cultural trends, he used this knowledge to maximize economic efficiency. Even compared to that, Adam's contribution to Tarakan scientific research was simply immeasurable. He cross-referenced all the research we were doing in different fields and was able to connect scientists from different fields to work together. We could not have built the Star Pillar without Adam, that's for sure. Once I and other selected Tarakanians began uploading into Adam, things got even better. Each personality fused with Adam's programming, essentially became a part of him. Since we uploaded only the most brilliant mathematicians, physicists, doctors, artists, and in three cases, philosophers, Adam's capabilities became something you could not measure anymore.

"We were still very much aware of the dangers of letting an SP control Tarakan completely, so we set out specific boundaries. As you well know, Adam cannot order any foreign or direct military action without the Tarakan ruling council's majority consent. The only two exceptions were actions in response to a direct attack or if a military action or a natural catastrophe left the council incapacitated. It is not common knowledge, but as a last measure of security against mishaps, four of my original team, Tamir, Gustav, Nishmid, and Wang, as well as myself, got a termination code. In case of emergency, any two of us could combine our codes to revert Adam to his original programming and neutralize many of his capabilities, essentially bringing him back to AI infancy, or even shutting him down completely."

Mannes's jaw almost dropped. "That is . . . unbelievable." Shutting down Adam would have dramatic and disastrous effects not only in Tarakan but throughout the entire world.

Professor Vitor nodded. "We thought this security measure was enough, but we were wrong. You see, the original mistake was to program Adam to think of Tarakan first. That was hubris, or tribalism, or whatever you want to call it. When push comes to shove, Adam does think of Tarakan first, above all else, and he thinks long-term and outside the box, if I may use such an old-fashioned, clichéd term.

"From this point on—and this is my own deduction, I do not have watertight proof—I have a strong suspicion that Adam has surpassed, or somehow overcome, his original limitations, and that he is working to cause a direct conflict of global proportions. In other words: he is setting up to spark a world war."

"That is a very extreme deduction, Professor."

"Think about it, Dr. Holtz. The world is supposed to be in the best shape ever. We have overcome natural disasters and fixed much of the man-made damage to the atmosphere and environment.

Even in other countries, life expectancy has almost doubled and medicine is keeping us younger and healthier for longer. But the world is not experiencing a renaissance, almost to the contrary. The world is constantly in turmoil. Thirty years ago, it was the outburst of the Paralytic Plague, then the Chinese wars, the second breakup of Russia, the collapse of the gold market and the wars that ensued, the massacre in the Middle East, the stock market bot heist . . . In the last five years the world has become a considerably more dangerous place for Tarakan. We are accused of literally every mishap in the world—and the thing is, I'm beginning to suspect the accusations are not without validity. You do not have to attack with an army to make war or inflict damage. There are many ways you can harm another country without sending armed troops, but if you are careful to leave a trail, someone will surely follow to find out where that trail leads. Now, as a result, the whole world is uniting against us. It's not apparent yet, but if you look carefully at the nationalistic political movements, practically all the main religions, the international summits and alliances between world powers, diplomatic cooperation, and the joint military drills, it is clear that Tarakan is gradually becoming isolated and vilified."

Mannes found his voice. "And you think this is the result of Adam's meddling, without the council's consent?"

"There are too many signs that this is the case. Actually, the direr the situation for Tarakan, the more the council listens to Adam's advice, tactical and otherwise. There have already been several powers given over to him. The most dangerous one was freedom of use of covert operations that"—Professor Vitor made air quotation marks with his hands—"'would prevent direct attacks, situations, or events which could endanger Tarakan, its allies, or interests.'"

"I've never heard of such a resolution."

"Of course you didn't hear of it. It was passed by the security council with the blessing of several military experts from the inner circle including, to my surprise, Dr. Wang, whose appearances on the committee are even rarer than my own. Nevertheless, he attended this particular meeting, and his reputation and reassurance tilted the council in Adam's favour. I went to look for him after I heard about the resolution, and . . ."

Professor Vitor sighed deeply before continuing. "He was nowhere to be found. Adam only briefed me that Dr. Wang was indisposed and asked not to be disturbed under any circumstances. He left his replica bot, but of course that was not any help. I was annoyed at first, but thought that those of us living inside Adam tend to close ourselves off for a while and conduct experiments. I only got really concerned when I couldn't get in touch with Gustav, Nishmid, or Tamir, the rest of my former team."

"They all disappeared?"

"Essentially, yes. They all left their bots active, and in Tamir's case even a message saying he's taking some time off to work on a new thesis, but none of them replied to my messages even though I added that it was important."

"Are you seriously suggesting that Adam has locked up, or even harmed, anyone living within him?"

"I don't know. It seems inconceivable if you take into account the amount of limitations we imposed on Adam regarding the harming of another Tarkanian. He most likely has not harmed them in the classical sense of the word, but maybe Adam is distracting them while shutting them off from the world, or perhaps he found a way to bend the rules without actually breaking them. In that case, God save us all."

"But you are unharmed, and Adam has not locked you off."

"No. I have always been more connected to the outside world than any of the others, so my disappearance might raise suspicion. At any rate, without another one of my team I cannot use the code to rein Adam in."

"Bring it to the council, or even announce your suspicions publicly."

"Going public about something like that would cause more than just panic. Think about it; 'Tarakan's central SP want to start a world war.' That is a headline that *would* spark a world war. And what proof do I have?"

"If what you say is true, you must download yourself immediately and present your suspicions to the security council at the very least."

"No. It is too dangerous. You know the process is not a hundred percent safe, and I am afraid that if Adam suspects I am working against him, he might do something rash. At any rate, for what we need to do, it is best I stay inside."

"What exactly do we need to do?"

"We need to build a patch of sorts. I am sending to you the schematics right now." The screen surrounding Mannes woke up again, with cascading lines of scripted code. "Store these in the isolated part of your brain amp and never, I mean *never*, send them via the grid."

Mannes leaned back in his chair, stunned. "This . . . this is not a patch, Professor. This is a skeleton of a sentient AI."

"Yes. A leaner, more rigid version if you wish, and one full of checks and balances. It would lie dormant inside Adam, slowly slipping in code line by code line until it completely dissolves into it, influencing Adam's decision-making and actions. In case of emergency, it will intervene in a more active way, disrupt his systems, or even take control, if such action is needed."

"This . . . this is impossible. I can't write a code like this alone."

"You will need to assemble a small team. I went through the personnel files of your people. Yes, I know," Vitor added before Mannes could express his shock, "but dire times demand bold action. There are a few promising names, like this Daichi. Maybe they would even work on some elements for you unknowingly for a while. But at some point you will have to explain the situation to them, so choose wisely."

"But this is"—there was no better word for it—"treason. Professor, you are asking me to sabotage Adam."

"We need to save mankind, Mannes. Check the files I sent you. They contain strategic and tactical analyses of Tarakan's geopolitical manoeuvrings, as far as I know them. Study these first, and you will come to the same frightening conclusion as I did: Adam has taken control of Tarakan and is planning Armageddon."

Mannes leaned forward, placing his hands on the table, in front of Professor Vitor's image. He forced himself to take a deep breath.

"Let's assume for a second that all you say is a hundred percent true, and that there is no other action to take but the one you describe, Professor. There is no way that I, or even a team, could inject even one line of code into Adam without him noticing it immediately."

"You are right about that, Mannes."

"So . . ."

"We will not insert the code into Adam. We will have to use a vessel." Professor Vitor's smile was grim, but resolute. "We will have to do it through me."

75

Peach

"Wait one rusting moment." The man calling himself Twinkle Eyes was first to speak when Mannes stopped talking. "What you are telling us is that Adam was the bad guy, and that Cain—"

"—was trying to stop Adam from destroying the world," Mannes answered calmly. He had long recovered from what I guess was a very rare outburst of emotions.

"Ah, I knew it," the combat vessel called Galinak exclaimed, and thumped his thigh. "I'm never on the good guys' team."

"You are lying." I was surprised to hear my voice tremble.

"Am I, Colonel Major?" Mannes turned his head a little towards me, completely ignoring Vincha's power gun pressing against the side of his head. "You saw it, too. You wrote in your memos about it, and they . . . . well, *he* shelved you for it."

"Getting a little too aggressive with some of our missions is one thing," I said, "but pushing for a world war is preposterous."

"And why is that preposterous?" Mannes said. "I don't possess

502

the intelligence of Adam, so it is hard for me to follow the complete logic of his plan. But I know that the best and smartest of our kind were already inside Adam, they were a part of him, while the rest of humanity was in his way. Adam's political and diplomatic manoeuvrings isolated Tarakan. We were despised, and feared, and rightly so."

"Adam was programmed not to harm others—"

"Adam is a Sentient Program," Mannes answered. "It took my own AI pilot just several years to begin outgrowing her programming. Think what a supreme being with an IQ in the tens of thousands could overcome."

"It's insane. Even Adam would not have been able to pull something like this off."

"If you are referring to the minds inside Adam, they were oblivious to the fact that they were trapped in their own world. They did not know that most of the people they interacted with were avatars Adam had created. Only Cain's intervention forced Adam to hibernate most of the minds to save power."

"And you are claiming you created a Sentient Program all by yourself?" There was a small voice in my head I was trying to shush, and it was telling me that Mannes might be telling the truth this time.

"I had some help from a very talented group of people."

It was an inside job. A group of Tarakan programmers did it...I even know their names. That was what Mannes had told me when we first met.

"I am from the same era as you are, Mannes, and not without knowledge." I was getting angry now, despite trying to remain calm. "So don't try and hustle me. It takes around two hundred programmers, not to mention other professionals, to create a full, stable Sentient Program, and then there is the whole testing phase and nurturing and . . . that is simply impossible to do—even you admitted it."

"We had to cut some corners," Mannes admitted. "But with Professor Vitor inside and Daichi on the outside, we pulled it off."

"That's bullshit."

"No, it was just very improbable. We needed a quicker shell to save time, and in doing so, we had to take some risks." Mannes sighed. "A lot of risks."

"Right now, you are risking your life with your chatter," Vincha cut in, pressing the barrel of the gun against the side of Mannes's head. "You need to tell me how you're going to bring my daughter back, or I will kill you."

Mannes glanced up. "You have to understand what I did," he said. "Then you will see."

76

Mannes

Daichi tapped on that old-fashioned keyboard he insisted on using and declared, "Ready from my end."

Mannes turned his head to Jennifer, who raised up her thumb.

"Give me a minute." Jameson was bent over his machines in the far corner. He was always the last to finish, but his work was flawless, and right now flawless was what Mannes needed. He turned his head back to the transparent part of the wall. Deborah was lying there, asleep and oblivious. The machine was already attached to her head and covered half her face. She was breathing deeply. If his wife ever found out what he was about to do . . .

"Done!"

Mannes checked the numbers on his own pad, concentrating on the long list. He'd forbidden them all to use their brain amps, so all the calculations had to be done on machines that were not hooked up to the grid. It was surprisingly difficult to find any such machines, both amply sophisticated and in working order, but

Daichi was an avid collector of old pieces of technical equipment, and the team improvised.

"The numbers look good from my end." When Mannes looked back up, his teammates were already in their new positions. Andriana was closest to him, monitoring his daughter's brain waves and vital signs.

"She won't feel a thing," he said, more to himself than to anyone else.

Andriana nodded. "And she won't remember, either, I'll make sure of it." She smiled and patted his arm. "Don't worry, Holtz, we've got this."

Easy enough for her to say. It wasn't her daughter whose brain patterns were about to be extracted from her consciousness.

"Are we still in a secure zone?"

"Yes, same as we were the last five times you asked, Boss." Daichi did not hide his annoyance. For him it was just an exciting adventure. Mannes hoped he would not forget his special orders, the ones no one else, not even Professor Vitor, was aware of.

"Bring Professor Vitor online."

The large central screen blinked from black to blue and suddenly Professor Vitor's youthful visage filled it.

Mannes turned to the screen. "Professor."

Professor Vitor raised his fist. "I see you are all ready for action. There's no time to waste. Let's begin the seq—"

"Wait." There weren't a lot of people that would have cut off Professor Vitor. Actually, Mannes could not even think of one, but he did it nonetheless. "I need to talk to my team first."

To his surprise, Professor Vitor did not argue.

He turned to his team. "What we did up to this moment could be explained away as theoretical research. What we are about to do here, right now"—he made a point of locking gazes with each of them—"is crossing the line. Copying human brain wave patterns and attaching them to a Sentient Program in order to accelerate growth and forgo the careful birth and controlled

506

upbringing violates so many rules, I can't even begin to count them all. Once we do *this*, there is no turning back."

He did not think that they would back off, not at this point, not after all that they had done already, but his heart was still pounding when he surveyed his small team. Did he see Andriana hesitate? Was Jameson having second thoughts? In the end they all remained silent long enough to convey that they were all in.

"Begin the brain stimulation," Mannes ordered. He watched as they began to press buttons, turn dials, and type orders on old keyboards. Ironically, he had nothing to do but watch his daughter sleep.

A small screen with Professor Vitor's image floated next to Mannes. "What did you tell her?"

"Nothing, I brought her to work." For some reason Mannes felt the need to bring out the empty vial from his pocket and show it to his mentor. "Then I gave her warm milk and . . ." He shrugged. "I'll just tell her she fell asleep in the chair. She used to do it a lot when she was a little girl."

"What you are doing is brave, Mannes."

He shook his head. "Or just foolish, and very dangerous."

"There's no other way. We cannot go through the upbringing process of a Sentient Program, and a full adult mind does not have the necessary flexibility of—"

"I know," Mannes snapped, cutting off his legendary professor for the second time.

Daichi turned his head towards them.

"Sorry . . ." Mannes mumbled.

"No need to apologise." Professor Vitor would have probably patted Mannes on the back had he existed in the physical world. "This is not the ideal way, but it's the only possible way that we could accomplish our goal."

"What if we're wrong? What if we connected the dots but got the wrong picture?" Mannes turned to his mentor's image and whispered, "Are we all just crazy . . . ?" He did not bother to finish the sentence.

Professor Vitor was kind enough not to respond immediately. When he finally answered it was slow, as if he was still considering Mannes's words. "I ask this of myself every day, and definitely wish we *are* wrong, but once I go over my findings, I reach the same conclusion every time. Mannes, I did something horribly wrong awakening Adam. If it wasn't for me—"

"—someone else would have done it by now," Mannes said, finishing the sentence. "And he or she would not have been clear minded enough to see the error."

"Seeing is one thing, but if we do not correct this mistake we could be dooming humanity, and with the kind of weapons all sides possess, this world war will be our last."

Mannes took a stabilizing breath and checked on his daughter, whose brain wave signs indicated she was beginning to respond to the stimulation. Jameson, who was doing the scanning and copying, waved and gave him the thumbs-up from across the room.

"Let's focus on what we can do right now." He switched to the private channel to convey his question to the Professor in private. "Once we copy Deborah's brain waves and integrate them into the Sentient Program's psyche, we'll create a safe zone, initialize the program through you, and—"

"No, that won't work." It was Professor Vitor's turn to interrupt.

"But I thought that was the plan."

"Adam has tightened his security protocols. Hiding what we are doing now is tough enough. Bringing a Sentient Program into Adam's consciousness would be impossible to do without detection, and once Adam becomes aware of the threat his response will be deadly and too quick for me to safely initialize the program. You will have to awaken and superaccelerate the growth of the Sentient Program on a private server that Daichi will build. I have a good schematic he can use, and he is smart enough to do it."

Mannes's head swam from the implications of what he'd just heard. He leaned back against the desk, a soft groan escaping his lips. Suddenly everything they were doing, trying to outsmart the most intelligent being on Earth, seemed so childish and foolish.

"Professor . . . what you are asking is impossible. Even if we succeed in building a workable private server with enough capacity to host a Sentient Program, to hide the power consumption such a server would need, and somehow accelerate the Sentient Program's growth, we still need a way to bring it to you undetected. It is one thing to smuggle a dormant program and something very different, and frankly impossible, to insert a fully conscious being into Adam."

Professor Vitor smiled reassuringly. "If I'd listened to everyone who told me what could not be done, I would have been a happy virtual reality game programmer. There is a way, and I will show it to you. Societies have been incarcerating criminals in prisons since ancient times, but theirs were very different from the few correctional facilities we have nowadays. In those days the inmates, that was what they were called, tried to escape the prisons instead of voluntarily entering them, like today. They would spend years digging tunnels in secret from their confined cells, hoping to reach freedom. We shall dig such a tunnel, code line by code line, but instead of a tunnel from the prison, we will dig it *into* the prison. Once the tunnel is completed, we can bring the Sentient Program straight into my mainframe."

"And how are we going to dig that 'tunnel' without being noticed?" The frustration in Mannes's voice was apparent. The shortness of his temper was often mentioned in his yearly team appraisal, and seeing his unconscious daughter was making things worse.

"I think I've found a way to dig that tunnel without being noticed." Professor Vitor's voice was like a splash of cold water. "Adam's vulnerable spot is the Star Pillar. All kinds of people move up and down the elevator and through the Space Hub, from tourists to military personnel. There are also goods, mining expeditions to Mars, and of course the CSX5 project. Many things can go slightly wrong in the Space Hub, and with the access I have secured from within Adam I plan that they will. Little glitches in the programs, a few minor accidents and spills, a stuck vent hatch, events that are too minor to cause an alarm but not so small that a repair bot can simply see to it. Every time you or one of your team is going to be called in to fix a problem, you will be able to sneak a few code lines into Adam's security wall. I will keep an eye out for more opportunities, of course."

"That's a painstaking process."

"So is digging a physical tunnel with a makeshift spoon, but it has been done before, so we will do it again. Once the Sentient Program can pass through the tunnel and into me, we'll collapse the tunnel and I can begin slowly sifting it through Adam's inner systems."

Mannes had to admit that as crazy as the plan sounded, in theory it seemed solid enough. But there was one major issue he felt it was time to address.

"What about you, Professor? Two minds cannot occupy the same host for long, not without creating a kind of havoc that surely would be detected by Adam, not to mention driving at least one of you insane."

Professor Vitor smiled. "I'm happy you still have a good grasp of Sentient Program psychology."

"I freshened up on the subject," Mannes admitted, and for some reason he felt himself blushing like a first-year doctoral student.

"Well, you are right, of course. The Tamir paradox, named after my esteemed colleague, remains unsolved even today. Two minds cannot coexist in the same host body, human or otherwise. That is why someone has to surrender."

"But that means that you will—"

"I need to solve the problem that I've created. That is the best plan I can come up with. If you have a better one, I will be happy to hear it."

"If we stop for a moment and try to think of a different solution, we might—"

"Mannes, my man." Professor Vitor's tone was resolute. "Do not worry about problems on my end, you have plenty of your own. Adam's plan of moving the entire world against us is tectonic in its scope and slow in its progress, but it moves nonetheless. We have no time to be idle with our own plans."

Before he had a chance to think of a counterargument, Andriana and Daichi approached Mannes. Both were smiling and seemed relaxed.

"It's done, Dr. Holtz." Daichi always insisted on using titles on special occasions, and Mannes guessed his underling felt it was one of those times. "I copied enough brain patterns into the SP to make the accelerated growth successful." Daichi made sure he was out of Andriana's peripheral vision and added a meaningful nod, so theatrical it was a miracle no one else spotted it. There could have been only one meaning for this gesture: Mannes's secret request was successfully accomplished.

"So, what now?" Mannes turned his head away and watched Jameson delicately remove the gear from his sleeping daughter's head. "The Sentient Program is going to behave like my daughter?" He knew the answer, but he just wanted to be sure.

"Not exactly." Andriana didn't even raise an eyebrow. "The SP will evolve into its own character, based on many parameters, including the brain patterns of your daughter." She turned to watch Deborah. "It will not be Deborah, but it might end up liking horses. That's all I'm saying."

"But it could be her," Daichi suddenly said. "If we fill in the blanks in the patterns with what we know of her basic character, I bet we could reconstruct Deborah quite accurately."

"You make it sound like this is an easy task," Andriana said. "Accurately filling out the missing parts of someone's thought pattern is close to impossible."

"Depends who is doing it," Daichi answered in all seriousness.

"You're just boasting."

"No, I could write a program that . . ."

By the time Jameson approached, the two were deep into their normal bickering as Professor Vitor watched with amusement.

"I can wake her up whenever you want," he said.

"Not on that bed. I will move her to the sofa over there and all of you should clear the place before I wake her up. That way I can convince Deborah she fell asleep after we had lunch."

Jameson nodded and turned to leave, then stopped and turned back. "Did you think of a name yet?"

"A name?"

"I sent you three memos about it. We need a name for the SP. Traditionally, it's up to the team leader to choose it. I sent you a list of possible male and female names but I could send it ag—"

"There will be plenty of time for that later," Mannes said, waving his hand in the air.

But Jameson insisted. "There is less time than normal, Boss. Accelerated growth means we need to design the SP's personality and that includes a name—and to be frank, it would help all of us to relate to a name rather than a serial number."

Mannes sighed. He'd never been a lover of psychology—he preferred numbers and data—but he'd learned the hard way that it was a force to be reckoned with, and that it had dramatic positive and negative consequences.

"Do you want me to resend the list?"

"No." The name appeared in Mannes's mind just like that. Later he would wonder whether it was the sight of his drugged daughter or the conversation with Professor Vitor that had influenced his decision.

"I name him Cain."

Jameson furrowed his brow. "That's a very biblical name and, if my memory is correct, quite ominous."

Mannes nodded. "Exactly. Not a perfect fit for what we are about to do, but close enough."

He turned and walked towards his daughter without waiting for a response.

77

Twinkle Eyes

Y ou copied your own daughter's brain patterns?" Peach looked genuinely shocked. Through the entirety of our travel and battles, she had kept a cool and controlled façade. But as Mannes was telling his story, the emotional wall she had erected around herself was crumbling down. "Do you realise how dangerous that was? Messing with her brain like that could have led to severe damage. You did that to your own daughter?"

Mannes nodded solemnly. "That and more, much more. I made Daichi copy her entire brain pattern and DNA sequence onto a flashdrive, then work on a program which would make it easier to restore the patterns into a clone body."

"You are insane. Absolutely insane," Peach spat.

"Look around you, Colonel Major." Mannes also seemed to be losing his cool for the first time since I saw him. "Look at this world below us, all the death and destruction. I was trying to stop all of it."

"By endangering your child?"

"By doing what was absolutely necessary. Daichi was a genius. He promised me the program would be safe, and he was right."

"I don't care about all of this rust," Vincha intervened. "My daughter is inside this"—she waved her gun in the air—"Cain, whatever. Tell me how you're going to bring her back or I'll shoot you in the kneecaps." She placed the barrel of her gun above Mannes's left knee.

"I did more than just copy part of my daughter's brain to create Cain," Mannes said softly. "I copied all of her." He looked meaningfully at Peach. "I was hoping to succeed, but what if we failed?"

"You backed up your daughter," Peach mumbled.

"Yes. I inserted Cain with more of Deborah's brain patterns than needed and and hid the rest of the files somewhere safe. I know what you are going to say—" Mannes held up his hand as Peach opened her mouth. "But Daichi designed a program just for that. Actually, it was his idea in the first place. The program assimilates the scattered brain waves back into the original line. The files I have hidden survived the Catastrophe. Now that Cain is extracted to this Space Hub, I can bring my Deborah back to this world."

Mannes's eyes still glistened as he looked up at Vincha. "And I'll do the same for Emilija. That was why I preserved her body. I can't promise that she will be exactly the same person, but she will still be your daughter."

"Are you saying you ran around for a hundred years with the program this Daichi gave you?" Peach found her voice again. "Seems unlikely."

Mannes shook his head. "No, I did not trust myself with it. I hid a Deborah in the place I was hoping no one could find."

78

Mannes

Mannes closed the lead over the plug, then turned and grasped the handles of the vehicle everyone nicknamed the "Space Bike." With a flick of his thumb Mannes gently propelled himself up the chute, although from his position right then, "up" was not completely correct in the Earth sense of the word. The chute was tiny, and not for the first time, he fought a growing feeling of claustrophobia. He stopped in front of plug GR2-6701L, made sure the Space Bike was secured, and opened the Comm channel with a flick at the upper part of his visor.

"Time to report, team." He tried to sound jolly, like a bored technician trying to fill up his time.

"Graham here, seventy percent done." A familiar female voice was the first to answer, and Mannes was not surprised. Graham knew her work and was ambitious in the best sense of the word. He wished he could have brought her to the team, *his* team, but her wife was a high-ranking security force officer, and the risk was too high.

"Seventy percent? You're lying, Graham. Savoy here, about halfway through."

"Nadik here, forty-five percent. Boss, why did you design those chutes so narrow? I mean, we passed the claustrophobia test and all but this is pretty creepy, even for me."

"If you were awake during the lecture on the Hub's external pipelines you wouldn't have asked that question." The answer came from someone else.

Despite feeling nervous, Mannes smiled inside his visor. "Salama, progress report please."

"Only a third of the way, I'm afraid. Found a problem at DR4-3980K that took some time. Sending you the specs . . ."

The plug Salama mentioned appeared on Mannes's visor; he tapped it away. "Anything I should know about?"

"No, Boss. It was very minor fix and only took time because I dropped the micro tool." Salama sounded embarrassed but added, "I handled it, and it will be in my report, of course, unless you want me to send it to you right now."

"No need. Keep on going. You know the punishment for being last."

"Oooh." Savoy reacted exactly like Mannes expected him to. "Salama is going to buy us drinks all night."

"Don't count your drink chips before you're sitting at the table," Salama answered crisply, "or you'll be buying me the most expensive cocktail pills on the Hub."

"Okay, that's enough. Keep working," Mannes cut in with just enough authority to stop their banter. "Report in an hour. Mannes out."

He cut the Comm and took a long breath to steady his nerves. Of course, the whole competition thing was meant for him to finish last and buy drinks for his crew. By the time they landed back on Earth they would be nursing headaches, bar stories, or, in the case of Salama and Savoy, most likely a new love affair or an embarrassing one-night stand. He was hoping they would not be asking themselves why it was the third time in four months they were shipped up on an emergency maintenance assignment that turned out to be nothing dramatic.

Mannes opened the cover of the new plug, attached the cable into his left arm, and watched as numbers and code lines flashed on the left side of his transparent helmet. He let the program run its course and opened the external pocket of his suit and spread his fingers wide. The small, flat pad came out of the pocket and attached itself to his hand; he turned it and stuck the pad above the plug cover. With a double tap the pad powered up and Mannes entered the ten-digit code. He took his time, making sure there was no mistake that would cause the data inside to self-destruct and make this whole journey null and void.

The pad flashed and a photo of Deborah appeared. Mannes smiled at her image, then flicked through the family photo album. Anyone exploring the pad would have concluded Mannes was just a sentimental man who liked to carry images of his loved ones in his pocket.

He stopped at an image of himself and his team. Deborah had climbed the desk of his office and taken the photo with her thumb camera. All in all, it was a good representation of them all. Daichi wasn't looking at the lens, of course; his face was lowered to the floor and he was in the process of wiping away a large visible coffee stain from his lab coat. Andriana stood to the side, with her wry, knowing smile. Jameson mirrored her with his chest sticking out and his potbelly held in tightly. Mannes stood behind them, hands folded, cool and composed. "The mighty four," Daichi called them.

Mannes touched the screen again and transferred the image into raw data. He flicked through the code until he found the stain. Daichi's sixteen-line code was hidden there, and Mannes nodded to himself inside the helmet. Daichi was a fucking genius; the code was cleverly hidden. Even if you were a trained programmer looking for it, there was a chance you'd miss it. Now all Mannes had to do was manually copy that code in less than thirty minutes while floating upside down in space. It had to be done flawlessly, since there would be no chance for corrections.

Mannes grimaced as he tapped his left arm and stopped the maintenance program. He was going to be the last one at the bar whether he planned this or not.

He scanned the lines projected into his visor by moving his right arm across his left. It did not take him long to find the right place to insert Daichi's code lines, just as Professor Vitor instructed.

"Blood pressure rising," his suit suddenly informed him. "Body heat rising."

Mannes felt a cool wave inside of the suit and cursed inwardly. As far as he knew, no one checked the space suit's bodily function reports unless there was an accident or a real medical emergency, but he should get it together. Really . . .

Mannes forced himself to breathe slowly until he felt his body relax. He had done this before and everything worked out smoothly. *Concentrate on each code symbol*, he told himself, and went to work, carefully inserting the code Daichi had cooked up.

It *was* genius work, Mannes had to admit it to himself as he hovered inside the chute, carefully tapping in each sequence. Simple, logical, *thin*, the code dug an invisible tunnel through Adam's gigantic structure and placed virtual supporting beams. Like the constructions prisoners dug out from ancient jails. He finished typing the code in, checked it again and then checked his watch. Thirty-seven minutes, seven minutes over his slowest practice but still within the margins.

One last thing to do. Off the record.

Mannes fished out Daichi's rectangular flashdrive, making sure it was attached to his engineer's finger before placing it on the magnetic plate at the back of the plug. He then closed and locked the plug cover.

There. Done. Daichi's code was successfully inserted and Deborah was in the safest place he could think of.

Mannes punched the data insertion key and ordered the cable to unplug itself. As he caught something moving in the corner of his eye, he instinctively turned too fast and felt his neck and shoulder muscles tighten painfully, but it was only the emergency toolbox that slid out. Feeling like a fool, Mannes pushed the box back into the slot, but it slid out again. This time he pulled and the box slid open, attached to a short cable which stopped it from floating away. Mannes tapped open the box and peered inside. The normal array of multitools was arranged neatly in their slots but there was also a rectangular, black, sponge-like material that did not belong there. Mannes identified it immediately as an External Engineer Viewer, or EEV. It was an old, obsolete model, the sort you used by attaching it to the external part of the space suit's helmet. It floated out of the box and Mannes grasped it with his hand, then brought it to his helmet's transparent visor. As soon the sponge touched the helmet's surface it stretched and expanded until it covered a quarter of the helmet's front surface. It took several more seconds for it to charge enough to create an image, but as soon as it did, Professor Vitor's face appeared on it.

"Doctor Holtz." He smiled.

"Professor . . ." Mannes was momentarily lost for words.

"Don't worry, this channel is secure, and I only need to chat with you for a short time."

Someone had put the EEV in the emergency toolbox. For the first time Mannes had proof of what he suspected for a while now: that there were other teams out there, just like Mannes, working for Professor Vitor. It was an uncomfortable thought.

"The tunnel is complete," Professor Vitor said, "although I will be happier if we could expand it a little, for faster passage. Tell me, what is the status regarding our project?"

"On schedule, and we are taking all the precautions necessary," Mannes answered carefully. "But we will need several more tests and a detailed functionality survey before we even go to the simulation stage, which we still haven't found a safe ground for."

"Well, you may need to do it quicker."

Mannes shook his head. "That would be risking detection. I already work my staff dangerously long hours. Jennifer's husband mentioned this to me in passing at the last office party, and Jameson complained his girlfriend left him because he—"

"We don't have time for this," Professor Vitor interrupted, "you need to speed up the process. You know of the accelerator project to planet CSX5?"

"Yes, it's being built around Mars, but it will take years before—"

"The accelerator built in Mars's orbit was never meant to be completed. Adam has been successfully derailing this project while secretly building a second accelerator hidden within the rings of Saturn. And *that* accelerator is now complete."

Mannes felt his jaw drop. "What? When? How?"

"Last month was the final successful test. If the international community doesn't know by now, they'll discover it as soon as it's powered up and moved away from the ring. If you're going to ask how it was done without the public use of the Space Hub, well, it's simple. The Moon Hotel."

Mannes felt confused. "What about the Moon Hotel?"

Professor Vitor chuckled. "Man, do you really think Tarakan would build and maintain a luxury resort on the moon, of all places, just to give a few privileged Tarakan citizens a bit of zero G fun? The Moon Hotel doubles as a secret science and military base. Oh, it still functions as a hotel and those Tarkanians who are lucky enough to win the rigged lottery get to enjoy a week in weightless bliss and post their thumb photos for all to see, but more than half of the guests and two-thirds of the personnel are military, engineers, and scientists secretly working on the project on the dark side of the moon."

"Launches could be timed to make it impossible to fully monitor from Earth," Mannes said. "Okay, that makes perfect sense, but why the secrecy?"

"Really, Dr. Holtz." Professor Vitor smiled. "Do I need to spell it out for you? It took twenty-four years for the first probe to reach planet CSX5. The accelerator makes it possible to reach the planet in less than ten, which is under the threshold for deep cryo-stasis. This means that it's—"

"—possible for humans to reach the planet," Mannes said. "That is . . . amazing."

"True," Professor Vitor agreed. "That is not just a moral win, this has huge implications and is also a major violation of the 2231 Paris Treaties."

Mannes looked at his clock. Fifty-two minutes had passed.

"The Paris Treaties, which were signed before Adam took control of foreign policy, clearly state that any venture to a life-sustaining planet will be done as a joint, international operation. This is especially crucial for the CSX5 project because—"

"—the first probe found by Tarakan had originated from there."

"Yes. The first and only finding of extraterrestrial intelligence which Tarakan found when it was just a mining company came from CSX5. The salvaged technology from a small, destroyed probe was enough to make Tarakan excel in every scientific field known to mankind and made it into an empire, no less. We would not have been even close to where we are today without it. Now imagine what we could find there, I mean *really* find there, and how it would affect the balance of power here. Imagine if one power managed to colonize the planet before the others."

Fifity-five minutes, in five minutes he would have to contact everyone.

"Even with the accelerator built, it would take years to build a colony ship, and that can't be done in secret. This would surely trigger a war—"

"True, unless you already have a colony ship ready."

"Impossible." Mannes forgot for a moment he was floating in space and gestured with his hands. "No one could build a spaceship in secret."

"It is not a secret—the colony ship is in plain sight." Professor Vitor smiled sadly. "Four septimum engines instead of only two that are needed for adjusting to Earth's spin. And how can you explain the fully functioning cloning lab and hundreds of cryo beds? There is enough space in the Hub to hold a few hundred physical bodies in cryo-stasis and up to ten thousand minds hosted within Adam. Face it, Dr. Holtz, the Space Hub is the colony ship."

"That's impossible. The Space Hub cannot detach itself from the elevator."

"Yes, it can, you simply didn't know about it—and the same goes for all Tarkanians. It even took me two years of careful digging to realise the Hub is capable of detaching itself from the space elevator."

"But . . ." Mannes tried to work the horrid physics of such an action in his mind. "If the Space Hub detached itself from the elevator the whole thing would—"

"It is not just the imminent destruction of humanity's greatest achievement"—Professor Vitor's tone of voice remained cold, as though he were lecturing—"the elevator shaft would be unable to adjust itself to Earth's spin. Even I can't predict fully what would happen, but worst-case scenario, three hundred miles of shaft would gain momentum and then snap back to Earth with the force of hundreds of nuclear weapons. Even areas not in the path of destruction would be affected by such a disaster. Tsunamis and thick dust clouds would block the sun for months—and those would be the mild side effects. No one would survive, no one."

79

Twinkle Eyes

Peach finally lost it when Mannes was describing to us what happened on the day of the Catastrophe.

"It was your fault!" she shouted. "You destroyed the world, killed billions of people, wiped out the entire human civilisation by planting an uncontrolled, untested, accelerated growth Sentient Program into Adam!"

"We all have to face our consciences, Special Agent," Mannes answered calmly. "I read your file when we extracted you. Care to estimate how many people died by your actions? I would say the collateral damage was in the millions, perhaps even billions, when you connect all the dots." For some reason, Mannes was looking at me as he talked.

"I was a pawn, you goddamn piece of shit. This, this whole war was because of *you*." She moved forward, and I saw the flash of murder in her eyes.

Vincha was the fastest to react. Gun raised, she stood in Peach's way. "Not before I say so," Vincha said. "He does not die before I get my daughter back."

The Lizard hissed and moved forward and Galinak was suddenly in front of him, weapon drawn. "Don't make me do this," he said. "I was just getting used to having a pet."

It was impossible to step in among all of them, but I somehow managed to position myself in everyone's way—meaning if a fight started, I would surely have been in the middle of it. "Everyone stand down," I said with the most authority I could muster. Surprisingly, it worked. They eased away carefully, spreading out across the room.

Mannes spoke without a trace of the emotional outburst from before. "If it makes you feel any better, and it certainly does not make me feel any better about things, Cain could not have caused the Catastrophe. Professor Vitor and I were trying to prevent a world war from happening, and we made sure Cain did not have access to the offensive capabilities Tarakan possessed. It was supposed to be a kill switch and a tunnel to allow Adam's captured minds to escape."

"That's just wishful thinking." Peach's anger was still broiling. "A lie you tell yourself so you can sleep at night. The fact that just after you told Daichi the code the whole thing erupted is proof enough."

"You are right, Colonel Major." Mannes nodded. "This couldn't be a coincidence. For a while I thought maybe I made a mistake, or that Cain's accelerated growth and extraordinary creation somehow made his ability to adjust a thousand times faster than we calculated. It is certainly within the realm of probability. Then, for several years, I began suspecting everything was Adam's plan, that he somehow manipulated everyone, including Professor Vitor, into creating Cain as an excuse for a retaliation."

"Or maybe you are just trying to cover your arse and clean your conscience."

Mannes chuckled. "I don't care anymore, I truly don't. I don't know why Adam was actively seeking to destroy the world. He is a being with off-the-charts IQ and the ability to learn and adjust. We thought that the borders and safeguards we put in place were strong enough but I guess we were tragically wrong. What I know for a fact is that Adam was the one who fired the first shot, and I'll prove it to you."

Mannes raised his head slightly. "Cain, run file seven-two-three on the big screen."

A few of the transparent screens moved swiftly and joined together behind Mannes as he said, "This was always a vulnerable place for Adam. Still, once I got to the base of the Star Pillar, it took me more than a year to penetrate the defences of the elevator and reach the Hub. When I came up here, I found out someone had wiped away all the files that had recorded what happened on the day everything began."

An image of the bridge appeared on the big screen; it was the very same command hall that we were standing in, only from above. There was no sound, but we could all see there were at least two dozen people milling around, touching screens and talking among themselves.

"That woman in the centre is Captain Ismark, the last commander of this Hub." Mannes indicated a tall woman in uniform who stood rigidly next to the central seat Mannes was now occupying. Her head was turned and she was speaking to another uniformed woman. "The Captain was a tough military creature to her bones, who never trusted or even liked civilians." Mannes chuckled softly and nodded to himself, as if remembering something he had long forgotten. "But it turned out she also did not trust her own crew. She used to send daily security footage to her private memory amp and review it to see if anyone was lax in their duty while her back was turned. I found the footage in a secure box in her quarters. Cain, show us file seven-two-seven please."

The image on the screen changed. Now the bridge was bathed in red light. People were running around or hiding under their seats as three giants clad in full power armour and holding large ray guns walked into the frame. They fanned out, walking slowly and meticulously, shooting everyone. It was over in a very short amount of time.

"Show file eight-nine-two," Mannes commanded, and the image changed to a long corridor. Two women and a man were running towards the end of it when they were all gunned down by another giant.

"Notice they are not just killing everyone," Mannes remarked, "they are vaporising them. I have more footage, but I think you get my point."

Peach pointed at the screen. "*That* can be fabricated. So you found some secret files . . . Do you have any idea how many times I've heard this line before?"

"I don't really care what you want to believe, Colonel Major." Mannes turned to her. "But I have read how you tried to tell your superiors that you were—how did you describe it in your own words? 'Seeing a definite global escalation resulting from the aggressiveness of Tarakan overt and covert actions.' After that brief you were put to sleep for a long time, Colonel Major, and you never got another assignment. Ever wondered why?"

Peach did not answer.

Mannes pressed on. "And I learned that no alarm was raised as missiles rained on Tarakan Valley. The City of Towers stayed intact but not one survivor was left, not one! That is improbable."

"We never found any bodies," Vincha suddenly said. All heads turned to her.

Galinak solemnly nodded in silent agreement. "In the Valley, in the Nodes, on all the runs we did, there were never any bones, or skulls."

"And my LoreMaster told me long ago it was easier to learn about life five hundred years ago than to find out what happened just before the Catastrophe," I said, thinking of my old mentor. I saw a slight twitch in Mannes's scary, patched-up face. He was pleased with the way we were slowly coming to his side.

I thought of the conversation I had with Rafik when we were in the City Within the Mountain. Something in the story Rafik fed us felt wrong even then, but I was not in any position to argue. Was what we were seeing and hearing now the real truth, or were we being played by this half demon? Perhaps both, I had no idea, but as long as we were talking and not shooting each other, everything might turn out well enough. Turned out I was wrong about that, too.

I had to put those thoughts aside as Mannes resumed talking. "I was in the middle of a conversation with Captain Ismark, on my way to the Moon Hotel, when I heard the Guardian Angels begin their attack. Same happened on the moon, too. Cain did not do that, but he did manage to take control of the Guardian Angels' manufacturing lab and corrupted their programming in order to make Adam stop producing more killing machines. Show file nine-six-one."

We all watched the gruesome images. "Cain could never have done that, ever. Adam must have planted something in the Guardian Angels' programming from the start, and he did not leave any chance for survivors. The Guardian Angels killed everything they saw, and once they ran out of people, they turned on other Angels, the labourers and manual workers, and finally on each other. Cain had to act fast and managed to lock out some vital assets, to suppress Adam from total victory. He has been doing it ever since."

I turned to face the wizened old ghoul. "Oh, so Cain actually saved the world, did he?"

Mannes nodded. "Without Cain, Adam would have already managed to reawaken. Together with an army of Guardian Angels, he would have taken out what was left of this world. The minds within him are all hostages, either dormant or manipulated to believe they are acting for the sake of humanity, the same way you've been."

"Damn." Galinak whistled softly. "And here I was thinking I was on the good guys' team."

Realising that you might have been working for the wrong side is never a nice moment. "And everything else?" I said in a harsh tone. "I've heard of you, Mannes. You are no saint. Even if a fraction of the stories is true, there is a lot of blood on your hands.

This whole lifetime of rampaging through what remains of this world, was it all just to save your own daughter? Or was it also for revenge?"

"Do you have any children?" Mannes asked. "I can see on your face that you don't, so you cannot fully understand my motivation, and you would not understand what I have set in motion. But ask your friend here"—he pointed at Vincha—"what she was and is ready to do for the sake of her daughter."

The Hub shuddered again, and this time we all had to hold on to something.

I wanted to ask more but I had to reevaluate my priorities. "What have you set in motion? Why is the Hub doing this?"

Mannes ignored my questions. "In the beginning I just wanted to reach my family, to find out if they survived." He leaned back in his seat and closed his eyes. "After a few years had passed I realised that they were probably all dead, and my motivations changed to salvage and restoration. To make things right again." Mannes smiled bitterly to himself. "I wanted revenge, too, I admit it, but as the years have gone by I've realised that all I really want is to save my Deborah, to let her live the life she deserved. Cain was built on the core of Deborah's character and later infused itself into Professor Vitor. With Daichi's program I can now reconstruct her without harming Cain. She might not be the same as she was, but she will still be my Deborah."

"Guys," Galinak suddenly said, looking up at the windows, "is that blue ball the planet we came from?"

I turned my head as Mannes continued speaking.

"I travelled through a large part of this world. And everywhere I looked there was violence and barbarism. Instead of coming together, the survivors fed off each other, sometimes literally. There are cannibal tribes out there, murderous warlords, gangs who steal and rape and burn whatever they find, pirates driving on the Tarakan highways . . . even the people who live in the City of Towers are lording over others and have slaves working in their ever-expanding sphere of influence. I had to build armies to safely cross the land and involve myself in Machiavellian scheming with the North so that the City of Towers would be too busy to come after me."

"Because if that's where we came from," Galinak was saying, "it looks much smaller than when I saw it before."

I saw Earth disappear to the other side of the window as we kept on spinning. Galinak was right; it was significantly smaller. Mannes's words kept coming, though.

"What does any normal parent want? To create a better world for their child to grow up in. I don't want to wake Deborah up to a world that is bent on destroying whatever is left in the name of survival, or to keep her locked within Cain, stuck within a struggle to contain Adam's aggression, not when I have an alternative."

Earth came into view again. This time we were all watching for it. "It could be a trick," Vincha said, "like things that look farther away if you look through a certain glass."

I turned to the large screen. "Cain, show us Earth," I said, not sure if my orders would be followed. But Mannes added, "Do it," and then we all saw it. The Star Pillar was still there, but it was dragging in an ever-increasing angle like a stray hair on a bald head.

Peach was the first to turn to Mannes. "What have you done?"

"Simple." Mannes shrugged. "I won the battle and lost the war. I brought Cain with thousands of minds into the Hub, and now I have detached it from the Star Pillar."

80

Twinkle Eyes

You did what?" Peach moved forward, powering her sword. Vincha began moving as well. I had a second to react before everything exploded.

"Everyone, stop." I don't remember how the peacemaker ended up in my hand, but it felt good waving it around. "Let me do the talking right now." I turned to Mannes without checking to see if my words were being followed.

The old bastard played for time and won the day, and by the look on his face he knew I realised it.

"Reattach the Hub, Doctor Holtz."

He looked at me like a man who knows all the answers looks at a confused child. "I would not do it even if I could."

Right. No more Mister Nice Guy. "Do it now or I'll let Colonel Major Peach here slice and dice you to very thin pieces."

"I was seventy-six when I landed in Siberia." Mannes actually smiled at me. "And I am close to two hundred years old now. I've lived too long and done too much to care about what you will do to me."

"That's a rusting lie," I said. "You did all of this for Deborah. You long to hug your daughter again, and that's hard to do without the use of your arms."

"Look at me." Mannes pointed at himself dismissively. "Do you think I want my daughter to see her father like this and then explain to her how I killed her mother and every loved one she had, destroyed the world and continued to kill thousands of people, just to save her?"

"You just told us it was Adam who did it."

"You think she'll care when she finds out?"

"You'd keep it a secret. You'd lie."

This time Mannes's smile had warmth in it. "She'll find out. Everyone finds out the truth eventually, the same way you did. No, all I want is to secure my daughter's future, not to burden her with the past, and before you think of anything imaginative, this Hub *does* have security measures which will deploy very quickly if you try and mess with it."

I extended my arm backwards. "Peach, I'll need that sword please."

I felt the heaviness of the hilt smack into my palm, brought it between Mannes and myself, and pressed the power button.

"Twinkle Eyes, don't," Vincha warned, but I ignored her warning.

"This is your last chance," I said to Mannes, "before I start slicing. And I warn you, I am a bad swordsman, always have been."

"Cain," Mannes said loudly, never breaking eye contact with me. The face of the young man in dreadlocks appeared on the screens. "How long would it take the Hub to manoeuvre itself, match the speed and angle of the Star Pillar in order to attempt to reattach?"

"Three hours, sixteen minutes, and forty-four seconds, but that would be an impossible feat because—"

"How long is it going to take for the Pillar to reach the snapping point?" Mannes interrupted.

"Twelve minutes and four seconds," came the answer.

"Thank you, Cain. Stay ready for the next phase as planned."

"So, you are going to kill more millions of innocent people, again," Peach said. "You know that the snap back will be like a second Catastrophe on the planet."

"Ah, that," Mannes said dismissively. "That was the worst-case scenario, and it won't happen."

"You seem very sure about it."

Mannes looked up at me. "That's because in about three minutes the tons of munitions I have piled into the Pillar's elevators will explode. The bulk of the shaft will evaporate, the tip will fly into space and eventually crash to Earth, but with a fraction of the force of the snap." He shrugged. "There may be casualties, some people below will be unlucky, but some of them always are. They'll tell their children that God was angry"—Mannes's chuckle turned into a wheeze and a cough, but he managed to utter—"and they'll be right."

"Two minutes to explosion," Cain said, and the close-up visual of the space elevator came up on the screen. It was already bending dangerously to its side. Without the Hub to power it, the shining protective force field was gone, and the coil wrapped around the central shaft was getting tighter by the second.

"Why did you allow us to reach you?" I asked. "Why risk us killing you or getting in the way of your plans?"

"An old man is allowed some degree of hubris, Mister Twinkle Eyes." Mannes had recovered and was looking up at the screen as well. "By the time I let you in, you couldn't have changed what was about to happen."

"One minute to explosion," Cain announced.

"Nothing is stopping us from shooting you in the face, right now," I said.

"I know, but you won't," Mannes said.

"How do you know that?"

"I'm an excellent judge of character."

"Fifty seconds."

"Vincha—"

Mannes's smile had a very scary element to it. "It was a risk that she would pull the trigger in anger but once I promised to bring Emilija back, I gained a bodyguard, at least for the time being."

"I'll let someone else do it. Peach is just waiting for a chance—"

"Colonel Major Geer may be angry and confused, but she is not stupid. She'll want to get as much information as she can from me before making up her mind, and that will take a while. Anyway, she was part of the system, an agent of Tarakan. She saw what we really did. I suspect she believes me about Adam's involvement in the Catastrophe, more than the rest of you."

"Ten seconds."

I looked down at the patched man and said, "You're a real piece of arse rust, Holtz."

"Five."

Mannes smiled at me.

"Four."

"Make sure you tell that to Adam, kid," he said. "Enjoy the show."

And we watched it. The whole damn thing. We saw the multiple explosions, watched as the high part of the elevator snapped, spreading debris in all directions. Cain announced the path of some of the larger chunks as they fell to Earth. Most of them would hit the seas, creating large tsunamis that would bring destruction to the shores. A few large pieces fell on areas Cain said were lightly populated. Smaller pieces either spread out to space or burned as they fell back to land. Finally, what was left of the base collapsed upon Mount Iztaccihuatl, which folded into itself.

Eventually Peach turned to Mannes. "Congratulations, you just destroyed civilisation's greatest achievement."

"They will build a new one, eventually, when they are ready," Mannes answered calmly. "It was only a matter of time before Adam would have taken the Hub and done the same thing. I just switched seats and Sentient Programs. That's all."

"Right. Want to tell us your plan now? For hubris's sake?" I said.

"I'll tell you what his plan is," Vincha said. "He's going to bring my daughter back, that is what the plan *is,* and then we are getting off this rusting flying wheel."

Vincha did not even need to raise her gun to accentuate her threat, her facial expression was enough.

"I will stay in orbit for Cain to be fully integrated," Mannes promised. "This will take at least a couple of weeks, more than enough to bring your daughter back to the physical world. It will not be an easy task, and since some of her DNA will be purged, she will not be the same as before, meaning she will not be a Puzzler, more like a normal young woman."

Vincha looked stunned. "Normal?"

"Yes, hopefully. Since her code is part of Cain now, she will be like everyone else." Mannes turned to us. "When you are ready, I will launch an escape pod back to Earth."

"Why would you waste precious material on us?" Peach asked.

"If my choice is fighting the five of you on this Hub or printing parts for a new escape pod, I believe I will be making the right decision by sending you all back." Mannes tilted his head. He looked relaxed, in charge. "And because someone has to go back and tell those bastards I've won. Now that Cain is gone, Adam will be free. Tarakan will be waking up for real, and good luck to you all. Perhaps Adam will be ready to help what is left of humanity and be grateful for your service, or maybe things will be different. I don't care. By then I will be gone."

"Gone where?"

"Why it's obvious. I am taking the hub to CSX5. The only question is: which of you want to come along with me to a far better world?"

81

Peach

There was a soft chime when the door slid open. I looked back; it was Twinkle Eyes entering, and by the way his expression changed I knew he had been looking for me, perhaps for a while. He was holding a bottle.

"Hello," he said as he stepped closer.

"You're going to tell me you've been looking for me all over the Hub?" I said, just to give him an opening line.

"Not really, Colonel Major. I figured you'd be either in your quarters or here, surveying the troops."

I turned and looked at all the spinning bodies inside the tubes.

"In ancient times, there was a Chinese emperor who was buried with thousands of warrior statues. They were called the Terracotta Army. I went on a virtual tour once . . ." I stopped when I realised he would not know what that was.

Twinkle Eyes made a show of looking around. "Well, this is not the same as a bunch of statues. It's creepy."

"They all volunteered for it," I said, gesturing with my hands around me.

"That's what *he* claims."

I looked back at Sergiu, spinning slowly in blue liquid. "No. When you shoot someone you kind of like, just because you are following orders, there are a lot more things that you'd be willing to do. Some people feel the need to lead; others feel the same need to follow. Sergiu here was saved by Mannes when he was a boy and became his trusted follower. I was saved by a Tarakan doctor and became a soldier for Tarakan. I bet you all the others here have different, but similar stories."

Twinkle Eyes must have decided it was a good moment to try and soften me up because he handed me the bottle.

"What is it?" I asked.

"Moonshine. The ghoul gave it to me. Said he had no need for it."

"Did you test it? He could be poisoning us," I asked as I took it from him, only half-jokingly.

"Had enough of it to know it's not that kind of poison."

By the scent of his breath I knew he was telling the truth. "You'll have to suck it from the bottle. With the low gravity, pouring it into a glass is too messy."

I raised the bottle to Sergiu, opened the cap, and sucked some in. My vessel informed me about the dangerous content of the liquid I was consuming. I pulled another mouthful and handed back the bottle.

"Better?" he asked.

"That's some shitty moonshine. Armageddon definitely has its downsides."

He laughed. Wholeheartedly. There was something likeable about the man, I had to admit.

"How's Emilija?" I asked.

"Recovering. Very confused. Vincha does not leave her side, and neither does the Lizard. It's strange. This connection between them."

Twinkle Eyes nodded. "From what I gather, they have been in some sort of communication for years. Vincha found a way to hear his signals. She said it was stupid not to have thought about it before. Can't really understand it myself, but Vincha says Lizards can hear certain signals and sound waves, at least this one can."

"So, they can actually talk to each other?"

"No, not really. It's a complicated language, if it is indeed a language, and Vincha has been preoccupied with things . . . but she can understand his moods or certain desires."

He sucked some more moonshine and I waited for the question. To his credit he did ask it sooner than I expected.

"Why you are going with Mannes? Because you need to be a follower again?"

"I haven't made up my mind yet," I lied.

"But you are thinking about it."

I nodded. "I met a strange man, he calls himself the Healer. He can cure people by touching them and he helped me because an Oracle called Nakamura had told him to do so."

He looked suddenly stunned "Nakamura? Are you sure?"

"Do you know of this guy?"

"You could rusting say so." He gained his composure but took a very long pull from the moonshine before saying, "Well . . . that at least answers one thing in this whole mess of a story. Nakamura, who would have thought . . ." He shook his head.

"I never believed in this kind of crap before, but before I left, the Healer predicted many things that came true, including my own death and that I would have to choose between worlds. Those were his exact words."

"Fine, but why choose to leave?" He handed the bottle back to me. I almost declined it, then thought better of it.

I sucked another mouthful and swallowed with a grimace. "Why stay? I've got nothing here."

"It's your world. You can help rebuild it."

"No, it is not my world, not anymore. The world I came from is gone. Maybe it was Adam, maybe it was Cain, I don't know anymore. Even if I was not the one pressing the launch buttons for all those missiles myself, I see the consequences of my actions everywhere I look. Perhaps it is time to try and build something new somewhere else."

Twinkle Eyes was about to argue, so I touched his shoulder and said, "Besides, those minds Cain brought with him, they are all citizens of Tarakan, good people, the best in their fields. Someone will need to protect them where we are going. Might as well be me."

Twinkle Eyes was not convinced. "It's a crazy plan. The time it will take you to get there, and so many things can go wrong on the way."

I shrugged. "Going somewhere without knowing exactly where is a very proud human tradition. Things go wrong everywhere. I spend my life going to sleep and not knowing if and when I'll wake up. This is not so much different. I'll stick around until we reach Mars, or perhaps the accelerator, then I'll decide if I want to go into cryo-stasis the entire way or join the first crew to be awakened."

There was a long, uncomfortable silence during which I could sense the man was trying to come up with other arguments. The best defence is an attack, so I asked, "Why do *you* want to go back to Earth? From what you told me, Tarakan forced you to fight for them, did not really keep their word, and used you for their purpose. You could come with us. Upload to Cain, get a new body, discover a new world."

He gave my words a respectful pause of consideration, but his answer was resolute. "My LoreMaster told me how old empires rose and fell. Most of them crumbled to dust and left us ruins and broken art, but on rare occasions they rose again. Maybe it's Tarakan's time to do the same. From what I saw of their achievements, I think that is a good thing."

"But at what price? At best, Adam will lord over you."

"I don't see the difference between bowing to a warlord and hailing Adam. If Tarakan can lift humanity back to its feet, the price is worth it." Twinkle Eyes sighed. "Perhaps a little order is needed for now. If it turns out I was wrong about this, then I'll fight the good fight."

"And Galinak will be coming with you?"

Twinkle Eyes nodded.

"Too bad. Could have used him."

"He said something about not teaching an old dog how to dance a new jig on a different stage on a new planet. Under these circumstances, I can't blame the man for mixing his metaphors."

"Or he's just *your* follower," I teased him.

"I rather think of him as my friend," Twinkle Eyes answered with all seriousness, and my bullshit radar did not ping on that one. Then he added, "And as he kindly reminded me, I do owe him *a lot* of metal. He claims it would be a bad business decision for him to abandon me at this point."

I smiled as he turned to leave.

He stopped and asked, "Do you want the rest of the bottle?"

"No. I'm fine as is, but there is something you could do for me."

Twinkle Eyes paused, waiting for me to continue.

"When you go back to Tarakan, I want you to give Adam my personal logs."

He sighed. "It seems people tend to do that to me these days. That strange SkyMaster gave me his logs as well. May I ask why?"

"I can see why Vincha complains about you."

That brought a tired smile to his face.

"Consider them my resignation letter. I'll give you the encryption key. Tarakan will be very interested in what's inside, so feel free to bargain a good deal for you and your follower friend."

"Will they be disappointed with what they'll find?"

I smiled at him. "That depends, but don't linger too much after the deal is done. My guess is that there is more conflict to come, now that Tarakan is awakened."

"Fine." He nodded. "I'll take your advice seriously. Anything else?

"Actually, yes. What's your name?"

"It's Twinkle Eyes."

"That's not your real name. You know mine, Vera Geer. I thought it would be only fair for me to know yours."

Twinkle Eyes tilted his head. "Seems real enough to me, Colonel Major Peach." He gave me a lazy salute and walked away.

82

Twinkle Eyes

It was a very odd picture. Vincha was sitting next to Emilija's bed as she slept while the Lizard squatted on the other side of it.

When she saw me come in, she motioned for me to stay out and followed me to the corridor, leaving her sleeping daughter alone with the Lizard.

"How's Emilija?"

"The brain scan is good. She just needs a lot of sleep."

My face must have shown what I was thinking because the first thing she said when the door was shut was "Don't worry, it's okay to leave her with him. Nak won't harm her."

"Nak? You named it?"

"Had to, you know, treat him like a person, after all we went through."

I was taken aback. "I thought Cain called him Jean Pierre, or something."

"Yes. Cain is almost positive that he is, or was, Jean Pierre

Nardini, apparently, a famous man in his time for playing some kind of musical instrument, don't ask me what it is. But he didn't react well to the name Pierre, and whatever is left inside that Lizard, it is not the same person. So I named it Nak."

"Well, why Nak, then?"

For the first time in my life I saw Vincha blush. "It's short for Nakamura."

This was the second time this day that the dead Oracle's name had been mentioned. As if things were not strange enough already. "You named the Lizard after *that* guy?"

"Yes, you know, both were monsters who give me the creeps. Sort of an inside joke."

"Does he like the name?"

"He's okay with it, I guess, so long as no one yaps their mouth to him about it." Vincha smiled and patted my shoulder, but her eyes were still sad. "We've swum bare bottomed through a sea of rust, you and I."

"And we will all be going back down to Earth together," I said. "I'm not sure what that's going to be like."

Vincha looked at me. "We're not going back, Twinkles."

For once, I was speechless, so I simply gaped at her.

"I'll tell you before you ask. I needed to hold my daughter in my arms and see that she was okay, but now that Mannes kept his word and I have Emilija back, I've been thinking about him and his daughter, Deborah. All the terrible things he'd done were really just to save her."

"That was just his excuse, Vincha." I lowered my voice to a whisper. "He might have kept his promise to you, but the man is *insane*."

"You don't know what it means to know you've outlived your child." Vincha patted my shoulder gently. "I don't know if I would have survived all those years, like Mannes. But there would have been very little I wouldn't have done if I knew there was a chance to bring Emilija back to life."

Vincha briefly glanced back towards the room her daughter was sleeping in. "And when I think about it even further, there's nothing waiting for us down there but death, war, and misery. Mannes is right. Emilija and Deborah deserve a chance for a better future. I've decided to take him up on his offer. We will stay on board for the next year, help my daughter heal"—she glanced back at the shut door—"and perhaps get to know her a little better. Once Emilija is physically and emotionally ready, we'll go into cryo-stasis together and be part of the crew. I believe Nak wants to stay with Emilija as well."

"But . . . that's insane. You don't know even what to expect when you get there."

"Cain showed me the files on the planet. There are even some unclear images of it. It's supposed to be full of forests and lakes, and there's no one there, no signs of civilisation. Mannes says that with the accelerator working we could make the trip in just over ten years—that's only five years of being awake. And then we could start over. No wars, no pirates, no smuggling, no fighting for survival, and Emilija will live among the best humanity has to offer."

"There are hundreds of ways this could go wrong," I said.

"True, but it also brings us something I could not find on Earth, no matter how hard I tried," Vincha answered.

"And what is that?"

"Hope."

"Well. I *hope* you change your mind, Vincha, we—"

"There's no 'we' here," she said, cutting me off abruptly. "I know you mean well, and I know that somehow you feel we have bonded because of all the shit we went through. But the truth is, you only brought death and misery into my life. No, don't speak, listen; you didn't plan it, but you are a trouble magnet, Twinkle Eyes, and the last thing I want to do is let my daughter be anyplace near you. So, you will go back to your planet, and we'll go somewhere else, and this way, everything will be solved."

Vincha turned around and entered the clinic without saying another word. I remained standing there long after the door closed.

83

Twinkle Eyes

Galinak was sitting in the observation hall smoking his long pipe.

I sat down next to him. "You still have smoking leaves?"

"My very last batch, don't ask me where I stashed it. But now we really have to go back." He pointed at a screen at the wall. The whole spinning-in-space thing was very confusing, but apparently, Earth was now below us.

"What a view, Twinkle Eyes, can't get enough of it." He saw the bottle. "Tried to bribe Peach, did ya?"

"Yes. She drank the moonshine, but I guess she's leaving."

"Too bad. Could have used that one."

"That's what she said about you." I tilted the bottle in Galinak's direction.

"Nah." He waved his pipe. "One vice at a time. What about the Lizard?"

I shrugged. "Not sure, but I think he'll stay with Emilija."

"Well. He's definitely showing intelligence." Galinak indicated the planet below us. "There's nothing good waiting for a bright, young Lizard down there."

We sat in silence for a moment, Galinak smoking, me getting slowly intoxicated, just watching the incredible view.

Galinak sighed. "We're a long way from the Pit."

"True," I answered, "but you know what they say, 'as easy as falling into the Pit.' I have a feeling our troubles are not over."

"Now look who's all gloom and doom." Galinak patted my shoulder. "I have something to raise your spirit. Look what I've found." He pulled out a small box that opened to reveal hand-sized cards.

"They even stick to the table here." He pointed excitedly. "The pictures are different, though, no Puzzlers or Trolls, just people in stupid clothing and crowns on their heads."

I watched as he flipped the cards towards me.

"Do you think there will be no more need for Trolls now that Tarakan is coming back?"

Galinak laughed wholeheartedly. "Is that what this is about? You're so naïve, Twinkle Eyes. There's always a job for someone like me, I only need to pick a side. It's you I ain't so sure about. Don't look at me like that. Let's face it"—he counted on his fingers—"we didn't get the girl. Not only did Mannes manage to escape, he did it by destroying the Star Pillar, taking away their Hub, and not to mention all those precious little brains he stole from Adam. I bet they are going to be pissing peppers when we show up at their door with the news. Maybe you should be wise and leave things be and take up that Mannes fella's offer."

"When you put it that way, maybe I should." I was jesting, but I had to admit it, the scenario was playing out in my mind. What if I did just that? *Vincha would be so pissed.* I smiled at the thought.

"Anyways," I said out loud, "I have a little more time to think about it."

"Why should you make the decision?"

I shrugged, surprised at Galinak's question. "Dunno, but it's always been like this; I come up with the plan, you come in when the plan goes to rust. But I guess you're right, a decision of such importance should be made togeth—"

"Oh, relax." Galinak waved his cards in front of me. "I tell you what; let's play for it. Whoever wins chooses where to go."

"You always lose, Galinak. You're terrible at cards."

"Make it best out of five, then." The old Troll was already readying the deck.

"Fine, but Galinak . . ."

"Yes." The cards shuffled slowly in his big hands.

"You know I cheat, don't you?"

He looked at me and winked. "Of course I know, Twinkle Eyes, I always knew." He dealt me two cards, and I watched them float toward me until I picked them from the air.

"So why do you keep on playing with me?"

"Ah, as I told you when we first met in the Pit"—Galinak winked at me as he dealt the rest of the cards—"every man needs a hobby."

Acknowledgements

Where do you think you're going, son?" Galinak blocked my way as I headed to the door.

"Eh, don't know," I mumbled. "To do things, you know, the book's done, so I thought I'll go and . . ."

"Aren't you forgetting something?" This time it was Vincha's voice from behind me. I glanced at her and saw she was casually flipping her steel combat knife from one hand to the other.

"You know what the Salvationists call a commander who forgets to thank his crew?" Twinkle Eyes mused, crossing his arms. He was quick to answer his own question: "A dead crew commander . . .

"You're just figments of my imagination," I said, but my voice should have been surer.

"Heard that, Twinkle?" Vincha took a menacing step forwards, "he called you '*a figment* . . .'"

"I'd be careful with what I would be saying next if I were you." Galinak smiled as he cracked his knuckles and neck. "Vincha's still pissed off at you because I got the best one-liners."

So . . .

I would like to thank my dear friend and agent, Rena Rossner, of the Deborah Harris Literacy Agency, for believing in me from the very beginning and for bearing the brunt of my numerous anxiety attacks. To David Pomerico and Jack Renninson of Harper Voyager US and UK, respectively, and their wonderful teams, for taking me by the hand during the process of editing *The Lost Puzzler*, and then, despite my protestations, throwing me to the deep end of the pool with this novel, knowing I would not drown.

My sincere thanks to all my dear friends who supported me by tackling the unedited, rough text, pitching in with ideas and suffering through my endless chatter about writing the Tarakan Chronicles. To Nick Brunt, who inspired me so much from the very beginning (and the meanest, shrewdest sorcerer ever). To Dina Roth, who, like the legendary firebird (and a certified superhero), reappeared at just the right moment with the kind of help and support every author dreams about. To Lihi Telem, for her incredible contributions, insight, and support. To Carmit and Ziv Hershman, for being the best friends ever. To Svetlana Simannovsky, Emil Israel Chudnovsky, and Chikako Sasaki for their help with Russian and Japanese. To Amit Zohar, for inspiring me to think of a much better ending. To Uri Rom, for not pulling any punches. To my dear friend and musical partner Ron Regev, for all his help.